Another State

This Other England Series, Episode 2

by

George Barr

This novel is a work of fiction. Any names, organisations and events are used in a fictitious manner. Any resemblance to actual persons, living or dead, or actual events is purely coincidental.

First published in 2020.

First edition
Copyright © George Barr 2020

The rights of George Barr to be identified as the
author of this work have been asserted by him in accordance with the Copyright, Designs and Patents Act 1988

All rights reserved. No part of this publication may be reproduced, stored in or introduced into a retrieval system, or transmitted, in any form, or by any means (electronic, mechanical, photocopying, recording or otherwise) without the prior written permission of the author or publisher. Any person who does any unauthorised act in relation to this publication may be liable to criminal prosecution and civil claims for damages.

This book is sold subject to the condition that it will not, by way of trade or otherwise, be lent, re-sold, hired out, or otherwise circulated without the authors or publishers prior consent in any form of binding or cover other than that in which it is published and without a similar condition including this condition being imposed on the subsequent purchaser.

Tomorrow, and tomorrow, and tomorrow,
Creeps in this petty pace from day to day,
To the last syllable of recorded time,
And all our yesterdays have lighted fools
The way to a dusty death…
Macbeth, Act 5 Scene 5, William Shakespeare

PROLOGUE

Estonia, the near future.

In the distance, artillery rounds were still screaming onto their targets. At speed, the column of armoured personnel carriers entered a village, wheels whipping up muddy slush. Two of the leading vehicles slewed off to the side and screeched to a halt. A handful of troops rapidly disembarked from the back of each and took up position in doorways by shop fronts.

From the front of the lead vehicle an officer stepped out. He stood in the street with a nonchalance that belied the potential danger of the situation and took out a hipflask, as he watched more of the column pass. On discovering it nearly empty he discarded it into the snow. On cue, another flask duly appeared from his left. The Captain took a draw on it, and then returned it to its owner. Lieutenant Paul Dolman snapped the cap shut.

'It's as good as anywhere,' Dolman said.

'We shouldn't be running,' Captain Trant stated with disgust.

They watched more vehicles pass with some demoralized soldiers atop. This was now the appearance of the British contingent of the NATO 'tripwire' in Estonia, on its rapid retreat to safety.

Their Airborne Support Company had been airlifted in to back up the beleaguered Brigade; specifically for its anti-tank platoon. Only two nights ago they'd been high above the North Sea, walking around checking equipment in the belly of the US transport aircraft, hearing just the steady hum of its engines. They could only imagine the freezing hell they were about to descend into below. Since then, with the heavy fighting they'd lost two-thirds of their company; including their commander. As the remaining senior officer, Captain Trant had assumed command of what was left, and they'd taken whatever transport they could find. In the retreat, they'd been further whittled down in rear-guard actions.

One of the last of the retreating vehicles stopped. It too had a group of cold, damp, dirt-covered soldiers sitting in a huddle atop; tired, dejected, unshaven. Some were coughing, faces ashen, already displaying the first symptoms of the virus.

A young officer got out of the passenger side. 'Why have you pulled off?' he asked. 'Is there a problem?' It was a well-educated voice. 'Oh, I'm sorry Sir!' The man, a Second Lieutenant, instantly stood to attention and saluted as soon as he saw Trant's rank insignia.

'Don't salute me here, Lieutenant,' Trant told him. 'The enemy might be short on ammo,' he added with a sardonic grin.

'Apologies, I didn't know-

'No worries. Now get on your way. We're going to buy you boys a bit more time.'

The officer looked anxiously at the two before him. 'On rear-guard, just yourselves?' he asked incredulously. 'Sir with respect you must be...'

'Mad? Yes, we quite probably are,' Trant replied.

'I could help, of course, but my men are through.'

'And of no use to me now, Lieutenant, so don't worry yourself!' Trant smiled cruelly at the young officer's sudden look of relief. 'Now go on, get going! You need to get them to the airport, if that's cut off then make for the coast. I've heard that a Marine landing ship is still risking the journey in.'

'What about the port at Tallinn?' the perturbed young officer asked.

'Forget it,' Dolman replied. 'It was bombed to buggery days ago, mate.'

The nervous officer glanced back at his peer, resenting his casual arrogance despite the situation, as well as his estuary English. He then glanced queasily at the scattering of men in the vicinity; rough, laconic types who held their weapons with cocky casualness. Two of them were dexterously setting up a 7.62 Machine Gun on a tripod, supervised by a tall, sandy-browed Lance Corporal. Two other troops hefted the base and barrel of an anti-tank system from the back of another vehicle. The young officer locked eyes uncomfortably with another who wore his helmet at a rakish tilt, weapon held barrel skywards in one hand, his dark eyes at once mocking and vaguely menacing.

He returned his attention to the Captain for confirmation. Captain Trant nodded at him to leave, surveying him coldly with blue eyes. Without further bidding or saluting, the young officer dizzily turned and jumped back into the passenger seat of his idling vehicle.

'Well, he could at least have wished us the best of luck!' Dolman quipped as the door slammed.

One of the more spirited troops atop the vehicle shouted to the men in the street. 'Ruddy airborne, bunch of head cases the lot of you!' The vehicle sped off, wheels spinning up muddy slush.

More vehicles passed, further attracting the attention of locals, standing in doorways or leaning out of windows. Some shouted and jeered, and a few objects began to get thrown at the vehicles. Any troops clinging to their hulls had to raise their arms and duck down.

Once the last of the column had passed them by and disappeared through the village, the sound of church bells ringing could be heard, along with the sonorous chiming bells of a clock. The place looked old and grey but it sounded like a Swiss toy town; an image enhanced by its being decked out with Christmas decorations. The inhabitants, however, were clearly unimpressed by the NATO retreat.

Sergeant-Major Halshaw turned up. Tall, heavy-set, grizzled and intimidating, Mick Halshaw was the one senior NCO left.

'All set-up, Boss,' he said. 'We've got a good field of fire, and our anti-tank is deployed down a side street, so maybe they won't be able to take it out too fast this time.'

'Good,' Trant replied. 'We're going to borrow Ritchie's section to take a quick look round. Things are getting a bit ugly with the locals. Take over here for a minute.'

'Roger that, boss. Any trouble, just shout. I'll have the lads cover you with a jimpy,' the Warrant Officer said, referring to one of the two General Purpose Machine Guns now set up on tripods.

Trant turned and signaled to Dolman and several others to follow him. Two drones were launched, flying up the street ahead of them. These were controlled by a kneeling soldier looking down at a display showing the aerial footage being transmitted back from the drones.

'Change levers to auto,' Trant told his team.

With their rifles held muzzle-down, the two officers walked casually up the centre of the street, several troopers on each opposite pavement, slightly ahead and behind, moving tactically and rapidly scanning every doorway and window to their front.

Standing beside the drone operator, Sergeant-Major Halshaw watched them move down the street. He shook his head and grinned at his commander's reckless audacity, before turning to raise his binoculars and scan the snowy wasteland that his rear-guard team was now aiming out at.

As Trant's group continued up the street, the ringing of the church bells became louder to them. The inhabitants began to retreat back into their homes. A large, scruffy brown dog with wolf-like looks ran out from a doorway, barking and snarling.

Without hesitation, Dolman turned and dropped it with a burst of automatic fire, and carried on. The distraught owner, an old man, followed his pet out of the doorway too late. He knelt by its body and cradled its head, looking up at the passing troops in tearful disbelief.

Dolman's firing had made most of the other inhabitants run for their homes, and the few who remained in the street hastened indoors as the sound of shelling got closer, and the ground began to shake. Undeterred, the soldiers carried on. In front of them now there was only an old hunched woman in drab brown clothes, her head covered by a black shawl, hurrying across the street to her home. They could hear a baby crying from one of the open windows before it was slammed shut.

The sound of a voice behind made them turn.

'Hey, bro! Tovarich, eh? Russkiy? Nyet? Ameerika? Briti?' The young man was tall, fair-haired and unshaven, and wore a heavy dark coat over a collarless white shirt.

They waited to see what he wanted. 'You British, yes? I get it right, eh? You bastards kill his dog. Why you do that?'

'Who're you?' Trant asked.

'I his family.'

'Really?' Dolman asked, finger moving over his trigger. 'We've recently been encountering lots of young men just like you, and they've been trying to kill us.'

'Go fuck yourselves,' the young man spat defiantly.

Dolman moved forward and smashed the butt of his rifle into the young man's jaw. He dropped to the ground in a howl of pain. Dolman kicked him in the back for good measure.

They turned and continued to walk up the street, without glancing back. A square with a town hall at the far end of it was coming into view.

'Psst!'

The noise to his left made Trant look around. In the shop door, an old man in a heavy black winter coat and black peaked hat waved them towards him.

'Briti yes? The Russkies, they here already. You best leave now, or there is trouble for you.'

'Where are they?' Trant asked impatiently.

'Everywhere. Nowhere.'

Trant grabbed him by the lapels of his jacket. 'Tell me, old man! Where? How many?'

'They wear no uniform. You hurt Kristof, but he not one of them. You arseholes, they out to get *you*! If you stay here, they bring fire down on us all again. You leave, now!'

Trant pushed the old man roughly back into the wall and he slumped down, starting to bleed from a cut he had somehow sustained to the paper-thin skin on his head. Trant left him where he was.

'You cowards, they get you,' the old man shouted back at them feebly. 'You lose war, just bring destruction and disease to us. You no good for us…'

'Probably not,' Trant replied as they continued.

'Perhaps he was right, about an insurgent force?' Dolman suggested.

'In which case, we're about to find out pretty soon,' Trant replied.

A few seconds later another artillery salvo landed, but this time far closer, and began hitting the outskirts of the village. They ducked down.

'There's an observation post somewhere nearby,' Trant shouted. 'Chances are it's somewhere high.'

'Church tower?' Dolman shouted back.

'Too noisy, indefensible, and not directly visible from here. Seems like they've just spotted us, which is what's drawing the fire in. The bracketing shots mean they've not pre-ranged this place, but they'll soon be landing close-by nevertheless.'

'Then they're close. Town hall ahead, maybe?'

'My thoughts exactly', Trant replied. He spoke into his PRR (Personal Role Radio) transmitter to the soldier controlling the drones. 'Silcott? You see the OP?'

'*Town hall, top floor, boss,*' came the reply on his radio headset.

Trant turned again to Dolman. 'Okay, Paul, contact Mick, tell him to direct sustained fire into the top floor windows.' Trant took out his mobile and accessed a map of the village as Dolman spoke into his headset to Halshaw's machine gun team. A minute later, Trant shouted to him, 'Take half the section down this side street and you'll emerge here, on their blind side. Enter here. I'll carry on and draw their fire. Go!'

Whilst Dolman's team set off to work their way through the side streets in an attempt to approach the town hall entrance unnoticed, Trant waited for two minutes. Once Dolman's team was in position, Trant's team moved into the square in front of the town hall as sustained fire hit the upper floor windows.

Dolman's team took a side door and surprised a gunman waiting in the lobby. As he turned Dolman dropped him. The assault troops cautiously checked the rest of the lobby, and then advanced fast up the stairs.

Whilst listening to Dolman's progress on his headset, Trant heard shells landing closer. 'Go!' he shouted to his team, and he led them across the square at a sprint, supported by a fire team laying down fire at the top floor windows. Automatic fire was returned from three of the windows, bullets ricocheting off of the stones around their feet. Near the entrance one of them fell, hit in the arm, and skidded to a halt. His comrade returned and pulled him to cover as he fired his rifle with one hand.

Meanwhile, Dolman's team was on the top floor landing, racing towards the source of the firing. Dolman himself kicked the door open and one of the troopers threw a grenade into the room. After the explosion Dolman ran in to clear it, spraying the room and dispatching its three injured occupants with automatic fire.

'Clear!' Dolman shouted. 'Evans, Mitchell, check the bodies, Clayton, with me!' The dead men all wore dark civilian clothes or worn camouflage uniforms without insignia, similar to those they'd encountered in the forests back nearer the front line. These were supposedly Estonian nationalists sympathetic to Russia but were almost certainly Russian airborne or special forces troops.

By now, Trant and the others had made it to the lobby. They made a rapid search of the ground floor rooms before being re-joined by Dolman and his team. Outside the shelling was getting more intense.

'Halshaw has reported an enemy motorized unit on its way,' Trant told Dolman. 'We need to make tracks, and fast!'

As they ran back down the street they were forced to dive to the ground, as a barrage of multiple launch missiles hit the town square behind them.

'Looks like they'd D-F'd their own position when they knew we were onto them!' Dolman shouted to Trant.

'No shit, Sherlock!' Trant replied.

Before Dolman had a chance to reply, there was an explosion down the street they were headed, followed by the sound of 7.62 machine gun firing; the men of the rear guard were already engaging an enemy advancing towards the town. All of a sudden a Russian armoured personnel carrier which had broken through was driving towards them up the street, firing main armament and its coaxial machine gun. Again, Trant's team hit the ground or found cover in doorways as shells and machine-gun bullets whipped past them, hitting masonry around them and gouging up ice from the road.

Another explosion made the Russian vehicle suddenly lose control and lurch to a stop, side-on, black smoke billowing from its engine compartment. Sergeant-Major Halshaw's anti-tank team had done its job!

Trant's group gingerly got up from their respective positions and ran towards the burning vehicle. They ushered as prisoners the three choking survivors from the back of the burning vehicle, who slumped down into the snow, unable to even raise their hands for coughing.

'That's it, boss,' Sergeant-Major Halshaw said to Trant.

'It was a recce unit, for sure,' Trant replied. 'This lot haven't even bothered to remove their insignia.'

'You think they'll attack in force?' Halshaw asked.

Dolman answered. 'More likely they'll hammer this town into the ground.'

Already they could hear the distant sound of ground attack helicopters thudding in.

'Right,' Trant answered, 'no point hanging about any longer, time to make a move.'

'Pity, I was just beginning to like this place,' Dolman replied.

'Yeah,' Trant said. 'I guess the old man was right. We've just signed its death warrant.'

1

Bristol, England. Seven years later.

Jonathan Barnes awoke to the sound of gunfire. He jumped out of bed, ready with the pistol he kept under his pillow; an acquired habit which he saw no reason to dispense with. Slowly, he began to realise where he was and walked from the bedroom into the main living area.

The television was on, and Julie was sitting with her breakfast, watching it. He looked at her as she sat in one of his T-shirts, cradling a mug of coffee, and thought himself a lucky man to have been given a second chance. She was a petite light-brunette with a figure that often attracted attention, but of all the possibilities available to her she'd chosen him, a very average ex-University intellectual, albeit with now above average fitness. But he was bespectacled, middle-aged, and probably a few pounds underweight. At least he was still dark-haired, although there wasn't much left of it. No, he still couldn't figure it.

She changed channel to the news. He knew she hated it, but she accepted the need to know what was going on, and where. More conflict, but somewhere else this time. Before, it had always been somewhere else; never here. As far as extensive civil disorder went, Britain had always seemed to get away with it before, smugly immune, a triumph of the West. With his former military background, Professor Jonathan Barnes was probably one of the few of those remaining alive who knew for certain that Britain itself was, at least in part, responsible for losing its own stability and security.

A gust of wind pushed against the window. The autumn gales which had recently battered the UK presaged an indeterminate winter. It could continue on in the same manner, mostly wet and mild due to the prevailing Trade Winds. Or, it could freeze again, as the once-warming currents of the Gulf Stream had been desalinated by the ever melting polar icecaps, and temporary disruption to the jet stream brought down air from the North East. Jonathan mused at the irony. It wasn't the only thing visiting from the direction of Russia these days. After the debacle in Estonia, which had tested NATO to breaking point, Russian influence in a Britain once reduced to anarchy had never entirely gone away, despite the presence of American forces.

He looked out across the city. He still found the view to be breath-taking. They were fifteen stories up in what had once been an office block, the tables and chairs now piled up in a corner as useful stock to burn when the need arose. However, King had arranged for engineers to connect a secondary generator, to beat the rolling power-cuts imposed by the military council. For the past three years, Jonathan and Julie had lived there in relative comfort, with enough power to cook, and the constant low hum of air-conditioning to keep the expanse of that wing of the fifteenth floor warm. Above them on the roof was a store of clean water, and the old service engineer's rooftop office had been converted to a greenhouse. It supplied them with a small selection of fresh produce to supplement their stock of canned food. They just needed to remember to draw across the black-out blinds before turning any lights on.

After the destruction of the Morton Down research facility, he had expected King to retreat to some underground bunker in the countryside, not to a major city. When questioned on the matter, King's logic had been simple. Underground out in the countryside they could easily be caught like rats in a trap; especially if there was a security leak or a spy in the camp. Cities, on the other hand, tended to suck up armies like sponges and spit them out. With the superior technology that the Americans had brought to bear, helicopters and drones now searched the countryside for heat signatures and any other signs of life. These would soon attract a patrol or maybe a cruise missile. Such technology was useless in a city that was still home to several hundred thousand civilians, and full of rival gangs armed to the teeth.

Furthermore, the Americans hadn't even yet taken all of London, and whilst they were focused on the capital, Bristol was relatively safe; at least for the time being. King was right to come here, he thought; it was literally like hiding in a crowd.

He watched whilst two stealth fighter jets flew in formation between buildings several blocks away and knew it was just a standard patrol. The American's weren't about to bomb a British city, however much they might want to.

He poured himself a coffee from the glass Cafetiere and sat down next to Julie to watch the news. It was a news discussion programme on British Broadcasting. The old corporation had turned into a mouthpiece for the government, known to the resistance as simply 'The Regime'. There was a constant diet of dramas and sitcoms depicting perfect people conforming to life under the regime as if it were normal, and the only other broadcasts were the official news programmes and interviews. There was little else; and certainly very little from 'before'.

They knew that if they tuned to different satellite channels they might get a truer picture, but the propaganda of the military council had its uses. First and foremost was in 'knowing one's enemy'. Once one accepted that most of what they said was a pack of lies intended to weaken the resistance and encourage conformity, one could, through a process of elimination, infer the truth that they were attempting to cover up. As a former researcher and interviewer for British broadcasting, Julie was very sensitive to what was being pumped out on the terrestrial channels now; and was superbly qualified to read between the lines. She even sometimes briefed King at some of the meetings of the regional command, an event Jonathan periodically attended.

In the programme presently on the monitor, supposedly set in a peaceful Westminster by the Thames (impossible, as they well knew), a fair, bouffant-haired young male interviewer spoke to two senior military officers and the Defence Secretary, Selwyn Barton-Smith. One of the officers was British, Brigadier Jack Trelawney, and one was an American two-star General, Major-General Wesley Easton. They were discussing the investigations of some years back in a supposedly candid way. However, their conclusions belied their true intent.

In his early fifties, short and sleek, Brigadier Trelawney, or 'Mad Jack' as he was known by the press and in military circles, wore a neat, well-fitting khaki-green dress uniform with Sam Browne belt and strap. His receding and greying side-parted hairstyle was cut in an anachronistic way, and was neatly oiled; but not quite well enough to keep in check an unruly bit of fringe that lolled over his temple. It somehow gave him a slightly seedy look. He would periodically brush the errant fringe back to the side, and in doing so had over the years created a finger-shaped bald patch at the front of his parting.

'It's quite clear now,' the Brigadier continued in an authoritative and sanctimonious tone, 'that those investigations did no good whatsoever, none at all. They just served to decrease public confidence in our Armed Forces, which were at the time facing the tremendously difficult task of attempting to keep law and order. And we must remember that this occurred straight *after* the Baltic War, and at the start of the outbreak. Our forces were seriously depleted in numbers due to those events, and stretched to breaking point.'

'So would you say,' the bland, shallow young interviewer prompted, 'that in fact the enquiries actually made matters *worse?*'

Brigadier Trelawney flicked his errant fringe back again and answered in a reasonable if rather patronising manner. There was after all nothing challenging in this interview; rather, it was set up as a vehicle to enable him to make his points, unhindered by awkward questions. 'Well, of course, Martin, it's all very well to be wise after the event. I'm sure that the people concerned, the civil rights activists, the government, and even our own boards of inquiry all thought that they were doing the right thing at the time. But let's be clear about one thing, those were not ordinary times, and the men on the ground faced extraordinary pressures. I know only too well, as it was my forces that faced a board of inquiry for my quite lawful intervention in this city during the early riots. And, again in hindsight, we can see now where that led. We can only be thankful that we had our American allies on hand to come to our aid when they did.'

'Quite so,' agreed the interviewer.

'And we must remember,' Trelawney continued, 'that looting didn't just imply the ransacking of shops, but also peoples' homes. Lives were taken, as well as possessions. Bearing all of that in mind, and with the knowledge in hindsight that our security forces were on the edge of losing control entirely, we surely have to re-assess what *actually* constituted a reasonable response that was inappropriate to the situation. Once we'd seen a political change, the officers on the ground under my command could be exonerated, and rightly so.'

'Mad Jack's a war criminal!' Julie screamed at the television.

'Indeed,' said the interviewer as he unknowingly agreed with Julie, 'which brings me on to my next question. This is to you, General Wesley Easton. Do you think that you have finally achieved stabilisation in the United Kingdom?'

The picture switched to the American Major-General with a greying buzz-cut, sitting in his neatly pressed digital camouflage uniform of grey, green, and beige. His frame was a once-athletic one, now given a few extra pounds, and a full, sanguine face which had suddenly assumed an intense, pensive look.

'Overall, the answer is a cautious yes,' General Easton replied. 'Our forces have made a big difference in the last six to nine months, particularly since the surge. However, I would need to qualify this, as experience in conducting stabilisation operations in other theatres of operation over the years has taught us that an early withdrawal generally leads to a resurgence of activity.'

'And we're looking at more rioting, looting, that sort of thing?' the interviewer prompted with mock concern.

'What we saw a few years ago was more than just that. Disparate armed groups targeted your police and security forces, all of which were failing to cope, given their weakened state due to the effects of another viral outbreak. It's impossible to say how dangerous the insurgent factions were to society, but my government judged that they had formed a significant threat to the civilian population, which became their prey at a desperate time. We simply couldn't stand by and watch a valued ally descend into civil war and anarchy.'

'Thank you, General. And now I want to turn to the Defence Secretary, Selwyn Barton-Smith. Selwyn, what does the emergency cabinet plan for next; and when would you feel confident to take back control from the American military council?'

Barton-Smith wore a traditional dark suit and a stripy tie that attempted to appear ex-military, but only achieved school-boyish. He was an unprepossessing man with close-set eyes, and an insincere smile in a pock-marked, peanut-shaped face held aloft by a skinny neck. Atop this was a receding comb-over of thinning, mousey-red hair. 'Well, to be honest, General Easton is quite right in his assessment. As long as criminal groups still inhabit the cities, rioting, looting, and terrorizing people, then we still need to retain an American presence to back up the efforts of our own brave security forces. I cannot praise the soldiers of both our nations enough.'

'So', the interviewer summed up, 'it would seem that our American cousins must remain here for the duration?'

'And a good thing too!' Barton-Smith scoffed. 'The outrageous behaviour of some sections of our society needs to be discouraged. It's clearly a result of the liberal attitudes of the last few decades, whereby we saw a general breakdown in law and order. And let me remind you, it occurred *even* before the outbreak of the virus. It's quite certain that the political elements that led to this situation have been discredited as - and I don't use this word lightly - traitorous.'

The interviewer didn't even raise an eyebrow, he was clearly in full agreement and then asked what should have been a critical question in such a lacklustre manner that it came across as merely obligatory. 'And finally, Selwyn, there is a concern that we live in a state whereby we have one political party in control, supported by a foreign military power, and that we have lost democracy in this country.'

'Well, all I can say to that is that *we* are the party of stability, and we are just emerging from a time of extraordinary national crisis. I am in full agreement with the Prime Minister, who is of the opinion that to dissolve the emergency cabinet and return to democratic elections is, at the very least, premature. All I can say to those in a hurry to get things back to normal is to look at how far we've come in the last three years since we declared a state of emergency. We no longer have to provide stable food supplies at the centres around the United Kingdom, and the people in the safe havens are now moving back into the cities. We have re-established reliable energy supplies. And we even have flourishing international businesses investing in us again-

Julie switched the television off. 'I'm sorry, I can't stand any more of it; I want to keep my breakfast down!'

'I don't blame you, darling,' Jonathan replied. 'That was pretty appalling rubbish, wasn't it, with only the pretence of counter-argument.' He knew just how much it hurt her to see what British broadcasting had descended to.

'The lies are nothing new,' she continued. 'But they've totally airbrushed *us* out of history. The UK Resistance is just depicted as a bunch of looters.'

'I know,' he sighed. 'They're not even urging us to give up the struggle anymore. They're acting as if they're victorious and everything is back to normal.'

'So, that's it? And what do people really know? They're all in their own little bubbles, fed the news that's tailored for them.'

'Eight hundred years of democracy, and we've ended up as a one-party military state,' he rued sadly.

'It'll be our future for a long time if we're not careful. We have to continue to fight it.' She was irked, indignant, and angry.

Whilst they were not positive emotions, Jonathan knew that they might just help to keep her alive. 'Of course,' he continued, 'what they put out isn't the truth. We know we'd still end up with a smart bomb down the chimney if they ever located us here. *That's* the truth. It's still a fight for survival.' He looked at her and suddenly felt worn and anxious. It was all too much for first thing in the morning. 'Did you get anything from the papers online?'

'Not much more than we know already. Oh, more on that Replenishment Scheme, an offer to women of child-bearing age and the right background-

'WASP, of course,' Jonathan interrupted.

'Of course,' she replied, 'to give up work, in return for marriage to a member of the government or security forces, and have lots of children. It's disgusting!'

Jonathan sighed. 'It's their way of re-building the population, but with people in their own image. What else?'

'Not much. They're now trashing postmodern discourse, moral relativism, and other so-called liberal values. Plus, binary gender differences are back. Oh yes, and by order of the style council, the miniskirt has made a comeback! Apparently, that's also one in the eye for feminism'.

'Oh good, I wondered when that'd make a return. Want to go shopping?' he smiled.

'Oh shut up, you male chauvinist pig!' she joked and threw a pillow at him.

2

US Military Airbase Fairfield, Gloustershire, England.

The four-wheeled military transport vehicle pulled up to the main gate, and the driver lowered his window to show a pass. The guard was somewhat bewildered by being assailed by a sudden barrage of German techno music, but at Sergeant the driver outranked him. He also wore Airborne flashes, so the guard wasn't about to argue. A barrier was raised and the vehicle moved forward to stop at the second checkpoint.

It was only then that two more poker-faced guards in body armour dared to venture out of their bombproof guardhouse. They too seemed somewhat bemused by the music, although it was suddenly cut for their benefit. They asked the two occupants to get out, take their sunglasses off, and show their passes. Metal detectors were then passed over their bodies.

The guards continued to look dutifully suspicious at the two newcomers. One was a dark-haired Hispanic Sergeant from the 355th Airborne, and the other was one of those cold, laconic Brit special forces-looking types in black combats, offset by light brown hair, buzz-cut to a slightly grown-out grade one. He was taller than his driver, fairer, and with athletic, well-chiselled, and slightly disdainful good looks. Even to a hard nut from the Bronx and a tough Southerner from Tennessee, he exuded an outward calm yet an implicit menace. He glanced at them with his light blue eyes, a look that made them feel almost invisible; as if they were so insignificant that he was actually looking *through* them. If they wanted to they could make this guy's life difficult for an hour or so. However, they knew that if they did so, they might end up spending the coming winter upcountry in some damned Brit forest on hard rations, getting cold, wet, tired, and frequently shot at. They thought better of it.

Captain Paul Dolman replaced his sunglasses, and casually glanced around, whilst his driver answered more of their questions and waited whilst the vehicle was searched. It was good to feel the sun on his face after so many weeks of rain and to swap his faded, torn camouflage for a dry uniform. Weeks spent in the field leading his counter-insurgent group on the latest operation had degraded him physically; and he looked forward to a few days of superior US airbase rations, and maybe a decent gym to work-out in. He noticed through the wire a couple of female air personnel walk past and both salute a senior officer, and realised that there was something else he could do with.

As they continued their drive over the expanse of the airbase, his driver, Sergeant Steve Rodriguez, commented on the security.

'At least those guys looked as if they knew what they were about, eh Captain? I sure feel a bit safer after seeing all that.'

'Don't be,' Dolman replied. 'Even with our airpower, an attack in force could still do a place as big as this bad damage. I've learned to never underestimate the insurgent. Even the liberal-left ones can give the appearance of naïve decency, but they have a cunning native intelligence. A casual glance at the last hundred years of conflict against them shows how effective they can be. They spin their lies and twist and turn any truth you might say, undermine any society they belong to. They're a natural enemy.'

'Whoa, and I was hoping for decent night's sleep here, Captain!' Rodriguez replied.

'We'll be able to rest one day, Sergeant, when our work is done. Hopefully, that'll be soon. I'm damned tired of all of this.'

'Really?'

Dolman looked at him. 'I suppose if we *are* the side that speaks the truth and stands up for decency and old fashioned, God-fearing morality…then, honest answer - no!'

'Gee, Cap'n, you sure crack me up sometimes!' Steve Rodriguez smiled.

3

Jonathan Barnes was the last to make it to the large meeting room, next to what had once been a Managing Director's office. With the lifts out of commission, he'd used the stairs as usual. They could have used meeting rooms on floors down below or even in the basement, but King said that height would give them a better chance in the case of detection. His heart still thumping from the ascent, he wondered quite why it *had* to be the very top floor. However, he was really more concerned by just how out of shape he was.

He walked across a plush open-plan office that had at one time accommodated top executives and their staff. Now all that remained were a few dust-covered desks and dead computer screens, and a few large pots containing nothing but dried out earth; their plants long ago rotted away to nothing. There were still dust-encased cups on desks, old calendars, and the occasional grimy jacket on the back of a chair. There was no other sign of what might have become of any of these people. Maybe the top ones would have had enough money to get out, he thought cynically. It was almost certainly too bad for the rest.

He approached the door guard, who was armed with an automatic rifle, and who knocked on the door for him. Jonathan entered.

'Professor Barnes, good of you to make it,' King said in his soft Irish lilt.

'Sorry about being slightly late,' Jonathan apologised in a perfunctory and rather insincere manner.

King smiled ironically. A big man with tousled light brown hair, he had an open, friendly face which was usually covered with a few days worth of growth. 'It's alright,' he replied amicably. 'I'm just getting the sketch from the field commanders.'

Jonathan hadn't rushed up for this reason and listened inattentively to the men around the table as they tiredly recited their reports to King. With any electronic communications liable to interception and rapid decoding by the latest quantum computer programs, they'd resorted to old methods. Around the table were some commanders, but in many cases just their proxies. These were mostly their lieutenants or even just unit runners. The written memo had even made a come-back, sometimes secreted in various dead-letter boxes around the city.

After polishing his glasses, Jonathan looked at the faces around the table. They weren't ostensibly very different to those he'd seen in any meeting of military officers, prior to his leaving the Army for good at Morton Down. However, there were subtle differences. There was a more multi-ethnic mix, and like King few bothered to shave on a daily basis, or to make any attempt at military-grade haircuts. It was more than that though. All looked slightly hunted. Nevertheless, each one still had a certain spirit, at once indomitable but also with another dimension; humour. Quite often at these meetings, there was a laugh or a joke. He knew this showed another dimension, repressed in the right-wing regime that was being propped up by the Americans. There, only fear, mistrust, and paranoia reigned supreme. These men were free to be expressive, spontaneous. He knew that this probably accounted for how they were still achieving their victories and running rings around the enemy, despite the weight of firepower the Americans could bring to bear on behalf of the Regime.

Once they had finished, King began. 'Thank you all, gentlemen. Okay, well, there is another reason I've called this meeting here today,' King stated, 'and also, why I specifically called Professor Barnes to attend. I think he may be able to help us. We value his brains.'

'Okay?' Jonathan replied uncertainly, despite the flattery.

'A situation has emerged, possibly an opportunity,' King stated. 'We've been collating various pieces of intelligence from different sources, including from our friends in the east, and what we have seen has led us to conclude that there is a potential weakness in the coalition.'

Jonathan almost winced at the suggestion of Russians and Chinese involvement.

King continued. 'Now that the virus has burnt itself out – I am correct in saying that, aren't I Jonathan?'

'Yes,' Jonathan replied, glad that he was able to talk on his old specialisation after so long, 'it would appear that, after three years, the virus is a victim of its own success. This time it took people down too fast, before they could infect too many others.'

'Well, that's something at least, thanks Jonathan,' King said to him before continuing. 'Anyway, now they've regained some control, we believe that the British government is growing weary of the continued American presence. Plus, Washington appears to be growing impatient at the lack of progress made by the combined forces in quelling the insurgency. Apparently, since the wars, the viruses, and the financial crisis, Capitol Hill is asking to reduce military spending on foreign operations.

'Now, I've always said, this is a long-distance run not a sprint. We're playing the long game here, boys. We know that we only have to wait the Americans out, and maybe only for a change of administration next month. However, we have reason to believe we have the chance to kill two birds with one stone, to score a victory which could help go a long way towards splitting the alliance.'

There was interest around the table as people began to take more notice, but some also looked concerned. This wouldn't have been the first time that the Brigade Commander had suggested an audacious plan that would 'win the war by Christmas', but just result in thinning their ranks out further.

'Are you suggesting that we try to affect a coalition with any of the Islamic groups?' one of the officers across the table asked. He was a short British man of Jewish origin, Marcus Samuels. He had dark eyes and dark centre-parted hair, and he usually had a five O-clock shadow before mid-morning.

'No, nothing like that, Marcus,' King replied. 'You know I'm against that. And I'm not suggesting we invites in any more of them with snow on their boots, either! Something tells me that one day, we're going to have as much trouble getting them to leave as the U-K government does with the Uncle Sam!'

There were a few laughs around the table. Jonathan almost sighed with relief and reached for one of the flasks of coffee. He poured the steaming black liquid into one of the posh cups left by the former managing director. He took a sip, then a bite of a crumbly home-made biscuit.

'No,' King continued. 'We have it on good authority that a certain senior field officer wants to come across to our side, a Lieutenant-Colonel by the name of Trant.'

Jonathan coughed, indeed almost choked.

King looked at him with a knowing smile. 'Are you alright there, Professor? Well, I remember you mentioned on your de-brief two years ago that the two of you had been acquainted.'

Jonathan instantly felt put on the spot. He glanced at the alert, expectant looks from around the table. 'Yes, briefly. The man was a deluded fool,' he replied dismissively. 'He seemed fiercely loyal, too. I can't imagine what might have brought about such a change of heart.'

'Really?' King answered incredulously. 'Professor, you had also held the rank of Lieutenant-Colonel, hadn't you?'

'A substantive rank, yes, and I was under duress. My path in the military was purely accidental, due to the direction of my research. It just evolved that way.'

'I think there was a little bit more to it than that, wasn't there, Professor? We've had intel, from the East. Would you believe it, they had the files of every single British serviceman and woman who had ever served! Blame it on the hackers I suppose. Anyways, it seems you were at a research facility in Riga during the war, conducting, shall we say, *experiments*.'

Jonathan Barnes looked hunted.

'Don't worry, Professor, we all have history, and we ask no questions. We aren't punitive, either. Maybe one day, when life's back to normal, we'll have the luxury of being able to judge each other; but not when life's so short. However, you may agree, this does make you a bit of a liability. I had to stick my neck out for you with senior command in the first place. Maybe just keep that in mind with what I've got to say next.'

Jonathan remained very quiet. He felt vaguely ill and could feel a cold sweat on his forehead.

King consulted his notes. 'So, Lieutenant-Colonel Trant. Present whereabouts, a garrison in Wales. They conduct patrols from there and have effectively dominated the whole area for months. From that position, they can get across the bridges, which the American hold, and on into Bristol. So, indeed, his garrison is yet another possible threat to us. But it seems that Colonel Trant has become disillusioned with their cause. I take it from your response, Professor, that you would have no idea as to why that would be?'

'None. Are you sure it's not a trap?'

'Professor, these days one can be sure of nothing. But we don't go in blind. Our eastern friends have also told us that the regime has been alerted to Colonel Trant's change of heart.'

'Well, I've given you my opinion, Commander,' Jonathan replied conclusively.

'Yes, that you have,' King replied. 'But... I think you might be able to be of more help than that.'

Jonathan had to resist slumping back into his chair, as he guessed what was coming next. He felt his energy draining away at the idea.

King continued. 'We want to send a team down there to make contact with the Colonel, and try to extract him. That is, before they do.'

'Where do I come into all of this?' Jonathan asked, as neutrally as he could manage.

'He knows you, trusts you.'

'He thinks I'm dead,' Jonathan stated emphatically.

'Dead men don't lie, Professor,' King replied, somewhat cryptically.

'Surely the regime will extract him by air? They're likely to get to him long before we do.'

'Maybe, but we've got to take that risk. This man's too important. He saved a battalion in Estonia, got himself a medal. If he comes over to us then he's a high-profile defector. He'll give us more legitimacy, and further weaken the American resolve in Washington.'

Jonathan regained his confidence as he saw the flaw in the plan. 'In all honesty, the US government must look on us as just another failed nation. I don't think this'll make the slightest bit of difference. We've got to win politically. This group is just one of many insurgent factions, and is carrying on the bloodshed all the time we resist.'

King listened as patiently as he could before answering. 'Three years ago, we'd almost beaten them. They were finished.'

'Yes,' Jonathan agreed, 'but then the Americans stepped in. Now the Russians are here, and they've got the Chinese behind them. It's got just too convoluted. You can't take on three super-powers and win. They're going to carve this country up.'

King was pensively quiet for a second. 'I accept what you're saying, Professor. But I want to try it my way first. You've been living very well on us for the last three years, and this is the first thing we've really asked of you. So, are you with us?'

'I'll have to be,' Jonathan replied reluctantly.

'Good. Professor, I'm not interested in fighting the Americans unless I have to. I have nothing against them, and they've often been sympathetic to the Irish cause. But the type of British government in place at the moment is the vilest of regimes presently in the whole of Europe, and that's saying something.'

'Then you have to convince the Americans of that.'

'At the moment, they're blind to it.'

'They weren't in World War Two.'

'Ay, you've a point there, to be sure,' King admitted. 'But they took their time coming round to that opinion though, didn't they?'

'Yeah', Jonathan replied. 'But, to the here-and-now. If I go, you'll take care of my wife?'

'Goes without saying,' King replied.

Jonathan swallowed nervously. 'So, what's the plan, and when do I leave?'

4

'So, he was your company commander in Estonia?' the senior American officer, Major-General Wesley D. Easton, asked Dolman.

On the large LCD screen on the wall of the meeting room was a montage of photos of Lieutenant-Colonel Trant, Distinguished Conduct Order, from his days at Sandhurst, through to various airborne exercises, a few in tropical and desert regions; and finally a publicity shot after Estonia, when he'd been presented with the medal.

'Yes Sir, that's right,' Dolman answered. He was fast getting bored by this questioning.

General Easton glanced at his greying and tiredly lugubrious intelligence officer, Major Charles Schreiber, and then to his African-American ADC, Captain Melanie Cartwright, who surveyed Dolman with no more than professional politeness. The General looked back at Dolman.

'Okay son, I'll get to the point,' the General said. 'We need to be sure that you're the right man for the job.'

'Job, Sir?' Dolman asked. Sitting upright with effort, both hands relaxed flat on the table, he could hardly hide his fatigue.

'Mission. We've agreed it with your present commander.'

'A mission? Concerning Colonel Trant?' Dolman asked with tired confusion.

'Correct.'

'He's a British officer, of course,' Dolman stated. 'No longer attached to your Air Mobile.'

'Yes,' Major Schreiber came in, 'he's in charge of an infantry battalion, presently in a stronghold in Wales. It's in a commanding position, which they have to be these days.'

'Without a doubt, Sir,' Dolman replied, before sipping some black coffee.

'Problem is, it'd be difficult for us to gain entry if something went wrong,' Schreiber added.

'Could it?' Dolman tried to affect interest.

'Potentially,' Schreiber replied tersely.

'May I ask how?'

'We have intelligence.'

'Yes?'

'We are all under observation,' Schreiber stated.

'Naturally,' Dolman said with barely disguised indignation.

'Son,' General Easton came in with a more relaxed tone, 'I'm told that there are AI algorithms which tell us what a man is thinking now, and what he's liable to be thinking ten years down the line. Colonel Trant has recently registered above the noise floor. He's on our radar, and we want to know why.'

'Okay, Sir,' Dolman said as patiently as he could. 'And what, these programs have predicted that Colonel Trant is somehow going to betray us? With respect, I can assure you that I've never worked for a more dedicated, loyal officer, one who is duty-bound to the cause.'

'You know what, Captain?' General Easton replied with a grin, 'the programs told us you'd say that!'

Dolman wasn't in the slightest bit amused by what he regarded as high-tech chicanery mixed with psycho-babble.

The General continued. 'An order was sent to Colonel Trant instructing him to report here. He sent back some bullshit communiqué, telling us that he was presently indisposed due to enemy action. Well, I can tell you for sure that's a damned lie, son. We've had no reports of any significant insurgent activity in that sector for months. That guy was too damn efficient for his own good! All that's nearby now is a safe-haven full of damned hippies and lazy punks smoking dope, all getting fed courtesy of Uncle Sam!'

'If I might ask, why me Sir? Why not someone from your own team here?'

General Easton sat back. 'Ask away, son, we need you to be fully clued-up. Chuck?' he turned to his intelligence officer Major Schreiber.

'Captain, you are the best placed to relieve Colonel Trant of his command,' Schreiber stated, attempting to win Dolman over with praise. 'We had to find a Brit with some status who'd worked with him, and quite simply… there aren't that many of you left.'

'I see. But why do you think he'll trust me and do as I suggest?'

'We're aware that he was your commander in Estonia,' Major Schreiber continued. 'We also know that he was possibly responsible for the needless destruction of a town during the retreat, albeit indirectly.'

Dolman's jaw tightened.

'Don't worry son,' said the General soothingly, 'these things happen in war, no one's out to prosecute you now. What got him his medal probably helped at least two companies of men to make it to the beaches. But the Estonians were our allies.'

Schreiber waited a second or two to ensure the General had finished. 'However, Captain, it's not necessary for Colonel Trant to know that. We believe he needs to feel…a little chastened.'

'Really, Sir?' Dolman asked.

Schreiber paused a second, clearly unused to being openly doubted. 'Our psyops evaluation of him indicates a man with enormous self-possession and confidence. These may be great traits in a senior officer, but not in the absence of any self-questioning, any negative feedback. He's an alpha male in charge of his own kingdom up there, in his own Valhalla.'

'And damn it,' General Easton interjected, 'he's one obstinate son-of-a-bitch! We only wanted to run him through a battery of goddam tests. Now he's facing being relieved of his command.'

Dolman glanced down at his hands to mask his annoyance at their casual insults, aimed at a man he respected behind his back.

'Look,' the General continued wearily with as much patience and understanding as he could muster. 'We know you think highly of him. However, there are a few things which you probably ought to know about your Colonel. Mel?'

For a second unprepared, Captain Cartwright blinked with mild anxiety before clicking on her laptop to project photos of Morton Down – before, and then after, the airstrike. Then pictures appeared, labelled 'Colonel Jonathan Barnes', 'Major Duncan Roberts' and 'Captain Edward Barrett'. The pictures were all also annotated as 'Missing, presumed dead'.

Dolman attempted to hide his surprise, now sitting with his fingers on his chin in classic critical pose. He had, however, flushed slightly.

Major Schreiber picked up the narrative again. 'You might recognise your cousin, Captain Edward Barrett? We believe he perished when the Morton Down Research facility was compromised, along with Colonel Jonathan Barnes, a senior research scientist whom he'd escorted down from the Bristol Area headquarters three years ago.'

'Ed died at Morton Down?' Dolman asked with a note of surprise. 'I was told he'd been killed in an ambush in Bristol, during the evacuation of the area headquarters.'

'That was the official line, son,' the General said. 'We wanted to keep a lid on the whole damned thing. The destruction of Morton Down effectively ended British research into the virus. However, your cousin had tried to hold the facility. 355th Airborne couldn't get there in time and the place was over-run. Seems some goddam son-of-a-bitch gave them the correct code-word in order to avoid our airstrike. By the time we'd realized and burned the place, the insurgents had made it out with hell knows what.'

'And,' Major Schreiber came in, 'we analyzed audio recordings taken at the end. It seems that Captain Barrett knew that the base had been compromised, and actually ordered the airstrike down onto his own position, before it was rescinded by someone unknown.'

'Your cousin was a goddam hero, son!' the General stated. 'But there's one more thing you need to know.'

'Yes,' Schreiber continued. 'Colonel Trant's last call to the base forbade any idea of retreat. It seems that the base commander, Major Roberts, had seriously over-extended his meagre forces right to the wire, and that your cousin knew it. With our 355th Airborne stuck five clicks away, it would have made better tactical sense to attempt a breakout, and get at least some of those scientists out.'

'Instead,' General Easton continued, 'Trant ordered them to fight to the last round, like the ruddy Fuhrer at Berlin; boys and old men, and we were left with diddly squat! Once the facility had been compromised the whole thing had to be leveled, and our research into the virus went back to square one, zilch.'

'We think' Schreiber added, 'that Major Roberts was deploying police guys, security guards, and even boy cadets at the end. They were up against an organized insurgent unit with a back-bone of ex-military and private security operators.'

'Deserters and traitors,' the General muttered with disgust.

'Did they get any other chemical or biological materials?' Dolman asked.

'Well, if they did and they tried to use it, they'd know what the response would be,' the General growled darkly.

'We've seen no evidence of the use of such weapons anytime in the last three years,' Schreiber affirmed.

'Point is,' the General continued, 'Trant essentially gave your cousin and that whole damn base a death sentence, plus anyone who subsequently contracted the bug. It was over-optimistic incompetence. Both the Brit commanders involved, Roberts and Trant, were culpable.'

Dolman could see what they were trying to do. 'In his defence, Sir, Colonel Trant may not have fully appreciated the seriousness of the situation. And his attitude is informed by the airborne ethos, no retreat.'

'Bullshit! Your Colonel made a bad call. This wasn't the time for the sort of heroics he displayed in Estonia; too much else was at stake. Get with the program here will you, son!' the General said in a tone of mock despair.

Dolman reluctantly conceded the point and nodded in acquiescence. 'Okay, Sir, I do see that, of course.'

'Sure,' the General said. 'It's good to see loyalty, and I'm not asking you to disrespect the man. But what I'm trying to do is help you to steel yourself to take the initiative when you go meet with him up there. I want *you* to have the upper hand, not him. And let me tell you that although that guy made a bad call back then, he's still on track for a top job. We've just got to just make sure he's still on-side with us as well. We've seen too many turn-coats. So, are you with us?'

'Absolutely, Sir.'

'Good,' Easton replied but looked at him dubiously.

'So,' continued Major Schreiber, 'my intelligence team will brief you more fully as to the details, but essentially the plan is to take the usual weekly supplies convoy up.'

'Why not a helicopter?' Dolman asked.

'We've learned from experience not to risk senior officers by that means of transport anymore,' Schreiber explained. We've long suspected there to be Russian special forces incursions in Scotland and the North of England, and we've had several choppers taken out by what we suspect to be Russian supplied ground-to-air systems.'

'But keep that under your hat, son,' the General cautioned.

'And you think there could be a risk up there?' Dolman asked.

Major Schreiber replied. 'Our field intel reports suggest that some insurgent forces have been supported and trained by Russian Spetznaz units for longer than we ever suspected.'

'It'd be unusual if they weren't involved,' the General added. 'We've all played the same game. We were in their backyard years ago.'

Dolman nodded. 'I've been aware of them for some time, Sir. We captured a few Russian irregulars a month ago, they appeared to be the usual airborne or special forces types. We didn't get much out of them, so sent them back down the line for questioning, and heard nothing more about it.'

'They'd be part of it,' Schreiber stated. 'We've all known for years about their cyber warfare and the agitprop on social media, but this is a direct incursion onto U-K soil, a huge step up from the usual spooks.'

'A riskier policy, as well,' Dolman added.

'Anyway, suffice it to say that the addition of anti-aircraft missiles is a game-changer for us, too,' Schreiber stated.

'And are convoys any safer?' Dolman asked.

'Marginally. You'll be joining a regular supply convoy of four eight-rads. Those vehicles can take a moderately heavy IED blast to the chassis. They're driven up by 32nd Brigade Support and Sustainment Battalion. Only the lead vehicle is manned, the rest are autonomous – driverless, in Ex-L-F mode…that's expedient leader-follower. It's from our Automated Ground Supply Program, and has significantly reduced casualties in logistics outfits.'

'So, they only have to take out the lead vehicle,' Dolman stated and sniffed. 'Any known anti-tank in that sector?'

The General looked at him, impressed by his threat awareness and the fact that he seemed to be more engaged than he had been five minutes ago.

Major Schreiber answered. 'Not seen on this route, Captain. We consulted with the Area Security and Force Protection officer for Sustainment Command; he says it's been event-free for months. As we said, Colonel Trant's patrols have been pretty effective. Anyway, these vehicles aren't used in any offensive role. The most they've ever seen are pot-shots. Since we established the safe havens and food drops no one's starving now, so they leave our supply columns alone. Seems they're not so keen to risk their necks for Army rations anymore!'

Dolman smiled. 'I'm really not surprised, though they're still better than British rations! Anyway, it looks sound. I assume we'll return with the same convoy?'

'Spot on, Captain,' Schreiber replied. 'The Logistics Lieutenant in charge will be instructed to delay his return journey until you've – um – *convinced* the Colonel to also make the return trip!'

'Fair enough. What other support do I have?'

'The usual. Satellite tracking, fast air flying high, ground assault copters minutes away, drones, and so on. And we've got quick response and casevac teams on standby twenty-four-seven.'

'Are you with us, son?' General Easton asked again.

Dolman nodded assent. 'Yes Sir.'

'Okay Chuck,' Easton said to Schreiber, 'get him fully clued-up.'

5

It was impossible to get Julie to shift on this one, especially after she'd spoken to King. As far as he was concerned everyone was equal in his command, irrespective of their gender.

This wasn't helped by the others assigned by King for this mission. Commandant Marcus Samuels, the Jewish team leader, had indicated how women had served beside men in units of the Israeli Defence Forces. Marcus' lieutenant, Akam, was equally unhelpful. As a Kurd, he had recited how women had fought against Islamic State in Syria. They were thus all unsympathetic to Jonathan Barnes' argument, which they'd jokingly labelled as being hopelessly sexist and anachronistic, and how on earth could Jonathan really still call himself a liberal? King conceded that he could understand where Jonathan was coming from in trying to protect a loved one, but that he didn't have the resources under his command to show preferential treatment for every couple, gay or straight.

So, Julie was part of the team. The night before they left, Jonathan had only just kept his temper as she had gloated over the victory, seemingly indifferent to his anxieties. She only seemed interested in her own victory of equality; to be considered as good as any man. Being privately honest with himself, it was not the first time he'd had reason to question modern liberal wisdom and female emancipation, before scolding himself for the thought. However, whilst this operation wasn't envisaged to involve anything too physically gruelling or dangerous, he knew full well that everything out there was dangerous and unpredictable.

Jonathan had to remind himself that Julie had actually once been a field operative; it was the only reason he had met her at all, as a member of Sean King's brigade. She had been a section medic and signaller and was also a fair shot with a long-range rifle. Such skills meant that she fitted well as an integral part of any team for a mission of this nature. King simply couldn't object, and Jonathan had no counter-arguments; at least none that weren't either selfish or chauvinistic.

So, she had duly joined them in the pre-mission briefing and prep, and the drawing of arms and equipment. Each was issued with a military-issue pack, rugged clothing with inbuilt thermal cloaking, and military-style boots. They all had photographs taken wearing military issue jackets.

'What's this for?' Jonathan asked.

'Need to know, Jonathan,' Marcus told him. 'The less any of you know, the less you'll be able to give away in case of capture. It's about plausible deniability and all that tosh.'

That evening eight of them set out in a large four-by-four that would only take them as far as the city limits, whereafter they'd have to break through the cordon on foot. Marcus was the leader and Jonathan his second in command. Moustachioed Akam, heavy-set and middle-aged, was usually Marcus' second but was happy to step aside for Jonathan and just act as the fire team commander.

There was young Riordan, King's nephew, a slight and rather pale young man with red hair, and the team's demolitions expert. Carrying the medium machine gun, their only method of fire support, was Keith, a local from the Bristol militia. Keith was an Afro-Caribbean ex-soldier with a local Bristol accent. Then there was Conrad, another older ex-military man, six foot three with short-cropped grey hair, who had worked on the private security business in the Middle East. Finally, there was Steve, athletic and shaven-headed, who had run his own martial arts gym in Bristol after studying in the Far East.

The weather was foul, with another high wind and near-horizontal rain. Marcus shouted to them that this would work in their favour, but having dismounted from a warm vehicle into weather that left them soaked to the skin within minutes, no one was too impressed. However, as they reached the city limits and rested on an embankment, it was clear that Marcus was quite correct in his estimation. In front of them was part of the string of bright lights and security cameras surrounding the city. As these devices swayed on their makeshift mountings, the team could see that they were very unlikely to cope with this level of movement and the obscuring rain. The digital signals emitted from the cameras would almost certainly be subject to intermittent cut out. Furthermore, none of the small patrol drones or even larger helicopters would be up in such weather. Satellites might detect them if they happened to be scanning that particular area, but that was usually of little use without some prior human intelligence tie-up.

The only technology they would have to worry about was low-level heat detection, ground vibration sensors or maybe treading on a pressure pad. The passive infrared and active infra-red beam sensors would be going wild in this. Assuming they weren't unlucky and bump into a wandering patrol, they should make it through the perimeter with ease.

'We're lucky that the Americans objected to the regime's use of landmines,' Marcus told the group. 'At least if we hit the pressure-sensitive pads or cut a beam we stand a fighting chance.'

'I didn't know that was the case?' Jonathan asked.

'Yeah,' Akam said, 'just one of the bones of contention between them and the regime. I've known trigger-happy Americans and some nervous ones. But they still like to *think* they've got the moral high ground. They're more religious than you Brits are nowadays.'

Jonathan Barnes disliked the insinuation that lack of religious belief inferred a loosening of morals, but he wasn't about to get into such an argument here. However, he was beginning to perceive some evidence of the rift between the two nations that King wanted to exploit. Colonel Trant was a man of principle and may have even retained some religious beliefs. This contrasted with the nature of the UK regime, which had seen fit to abandon even the pretence of such in order to win. Their moral compass had broken long ago.

An hour later and they were through the cordon. They continued, well past the area of most patrols, and headed out in a direction to locate their transport, another four-by-four. The plan was to drive north to avoid the Severn crossings and to just skirt Gloucester as they headed into Wales.

'How are you doing?' Barnes shouted at Julie above the wind and rain, behind a cupped hand to her hood.

'Fine,' she replied defiantly and glanced around at him challengingly.

'Good,' he replied. 'You know it's still not too late if you-

'Don't even go there!' she replied dangerously.

'Okay, I was just saying because, well, I've already got a blister,' he replied.

'So, you go back then!'

'I assure you, darling, I'd love to.'

6

'So what's his story, Chuck?' Major-General Easton asked.

Major Schreiber avoided even glancing at Captain Cartwright, sitting across the table from him. The General had shown little interest in Dolman's biography and psych-evaluation when Schreiber had presented it, two days before their briefing of Captain Dolman. Then he had just wanted to know the salient points, no detail.

As well as being impatient with some detail, General Easton could certainly be obstinate at times. Despite a keen intelligence and good education, Harvard then WestPoint, it was no longer wise to be seen to be too intellectual. He now had a well-developed impatience for what he regarded to be trivia. Charles Schreiber wasn't sure as to whether or not this was truly disingenuous, a clever affectation; the political Wes Easton, or the real Wes Easton. In all probability, the General himself no longer knew.

'Mel,' General Easton instructed his ADC, 'pull up Captain Dolman's dossier will you?'

'Will do, Sir,' she replied.

The dossier appeared on the screen, with his photo on the top left side. For a second Schreiber caught himself thinking how easily Dolman's file could also soon read 'Missing, presumed dead', along with those of the Morton Down group they'd viewed earlier. Officers didn't seem to last long in the field nowadays.

Schreiber began. 'Dolman, Paul, Captain, age thirty seven. After college, he passed airborne selection and was then assigned as a platoon commander to Support Company in their Second Battalion. A few quiet tours, then one hot one in the Sahel fighting alongside the French Foreign Legion, before the Baltic War. There he was involved in one of the most bitterly fought actions, as his company, eventually taken over by the then Captain Trant, was placed in support of an Estonian infantry battalion. They took the brunt of a Russian armoured spearhead.

By the end of the action, Trant's company numbered thirty-five not killed or wounded. It had effectively been wiped out, and by the end of the war, only half that number made it back to the UK, those who hadn't immediately succumbed to the virus. Dolman himself was incapacitated for a couple of weeks with the virus, and was then re-assigned to the then Lieutenant-Colonel Jack Trelawney's battalion and promoted to Captain, a year before the London riots.'

'Mad Jack,' the General growled. 'I met the bastard just three days ago for that broadcast. He was too smooth by far.'

'Yes Sir,' Schreiber agreed.

'They're all too damned polite, even Dolman. They've got impeachable manners,' he said the last two words with a vintage Hollywood English accent, 'but they're killers underneath. So, who gave the order to fire on the rioters?'

'That's never been established, Sir. It could have been the Captain, or his commanding officer, Brigadier

Trelawney. However, remember that in some nearby areas black flags were purportedly being flown'.

'Yeah Chuck,' the General countered, 'so were a heap of others, the Union Jack, the Cross of Saint George, even the Dixie flag for Chrissakes! Means nothing. We know how mixed-up things got here.'

'But these certainly weren't normal London riots as compared with anything hitherto, Sir. Dolman's unit faced Molotov cocktails, and the sound of shots had been reported, prior to their opening fire.'

'Okay, so the guy may be cleaner than we thought. What's his psychological profile say about him? Is he a sociopath, or some goddam Nazi?'

'If he's either then he's been relatively clever at hiding such things; he majored in Economics at college, but only got awarded a pass degree, no honours. Apparently, one of his final essays was about the economic effects of immigration on housing and business. His argument went along the lines that, at the turn of the century, politicians in successive governments on both sides of the house had increased immigration, whilst failing to build enough social housing, thus massively increasing its the value.'

'For years real estate was the only goddamn stock worth anything!' Easton smiled wryly.

'Indeed,' Schreiber concurred. 'Dolman's argument also was that the effect of immigration on business was simple in that it reduced wages. The natural conclusion to this was, he wrote, Brexit.'

'No wonder this guy came out with a low grade!' Easton chuckled. 'The academics must have hated him.'

'Quite probably,' Schreiber said, 'but he made it clear that his argument wasn't with the immigrants themselves, but those who profited from them. He also wrote that they'd stifled dissention by labeling any disagreement as politically incorrect. Bottom line, Dolman's anti-Left, not blanket racist.'

'Hmm, it sort of figures, looking at his driver and a few others from the 355th he's borrowed.'

'He's stated that he doesn't care what a man looks like if he puts his life on the line for his country,' Schreiber said.

Easton raised his eyebrows, impressed.

'Otherwise,' Schreiber continued, 'Dolman did try to temper his hypothesis with a few counter-arguments, such as the fact that the effect of immigration on wages helped stave inflation off for so long.'

'Whatever, Chuck,' Easton said with a dismissive wave, now getting bored of the academic talk. 'Bring me more up to date. This guy's seen a lot of combat. What were the effects on him?'

'Well, to be sure, no signs of post-traumatic after the last war, as far as battle stress went it seems it was like water off a duck's back. He dabbled briefly with the British Patriots after the Baltic, but he seemed to grow bored with them. Almost certainly a Right-wing populist though.'

'No shit. Well, Chuck, not an entirely unusual character to find in the military. Still, different to his cousin. Chalk and cheese, you could say,' the General stated. 'Ed Barrett's dossier showed he was politically neutral, but also a shrink's case-book; a walking head-case even before Trant sent him to Morton Down. Is Dolman straight or gay?'

'He's straight, but only able to sustain a string of casual relationships after a failed marriage. At college he neatly fitted the 'incel' profile, probably because of his views, and his membership of the officer training corps. Those things wouldn't have gone down well with staff or students.'

'And if you can't get laid at college, Chuck, you can't get laid!' Easton quipped with an ironic smile.

Major Schreiber chuckled and then continued. 'It seems his cousin, Captain Barrett, was a moderating factor in Dolman's life, though. He looked up to Barrett as an elder without question, probably followed him into the service. We dug up an old e-mail chain between them, shortly after they'd both returned from the Baltic War. Seems Dolman was coy about his political affiliations, sensed Barrett was more moderate. After the London riots, all communication stopped.'

'So, what's Dolman done since?' Easton asked.

'He's now equivalent to an 18-A Captain.'

'Huh, another snake-eater!' the General joked.

Schreiber smiled. 'The unit he commands is an anti-insurgent company which operates outside of the normal chain of command, sort of like an *ad hoc* Ranger unit, bulked up with some of our team. It evolved during the emergency period, effective in long-range reconnaissance patrolling, and became successful in shoot-and-scoot ops. In addition to proving very elusive and successful, it eventually achieved a certain level of notoriety. Operating with minimal technology, apart from first-rate intelligence and communications, it turned up in places when and where it was least expected, hitting supply lines or the outfits themselves.

'Several insurgent groups have been closed down completely, whereas our special force units or drone strikes often just focus on taking out a unit commander, who is only to be replaced by another within hours. Dolman's unit may disappear for days, playing a long waiting game, before surrounding their quarry and closing in.

'Although he gained a certain notoriety from the London riots, it's been phased by his more recent exploits. As a result, several commanders of different insurgent factions have put a price on his head.'

'Couldn't this be a liability, Chuck?' General Easton asked.

'Possibly so, Sir, but not in the Wales sector; there he's a relative unknown. The London rioting is old news, there's been much worse since.'

'Good. We don't want another high-value hostage in their hands if things go wrong.'

'Of course, but its Colonel Trant I'm more concerned about from that perspective, Sir.'

'Well, either we proceed with plan A and send Dolman up there, or we can send in a team from here.'

'Not to be advised, Sir. Despite the official line, the Brits are getting uptight about spans of control. Some of their senior officers would look askance at a Battalion Commander being relieved by an American team.'

'So, do we still have our insurance?'

'Yes Sir, and ready to fly when the order is given.'

7

Not long before midnight, they reached their first safe-house, where they'd rest up for the remainder of the night and then continue on their way in another four-by-four. To foil any satellite tracking they'd abandoned their transport in a roadside copse and walked the last four miles in driving wind and rain. They approached the large farmhouse cautiously, and within seconds a guard unit sheltering in a lean-to by a nearby barn challenged them. Once they'd given their password they were welcome in by a rotund team commander named Neil.

'Make yourselves at home,' he told them in the hall. 'There's hot water upstairs for any that needs it, and dry clothes. Once you've dried yourselves off come down, Ian's had a lamb hotpot been going these past two hours, enough to feed an Army. Meat's so tender it falls off the bone. We weren't sure when you'd be here.'

'Thanks, Neil,' Marcus replied, 'much appreciated.'

'There's also hot cocoa in there,' Neil said, as Julie pushed past him. 'Ian will serve...' he trailed-off, addressing the others. He looked back towards the kitchen, where Julie was slumped against the kitchen counter, already tearing into a large chunk of home-made bread. It was washed down with a mug of hot cocoa, handed to her by the cook, Ian. She acknowledged silently with a nod.

'I think she's hungry,' Jonathan explained by way of an apology.

'Aye, it's a rough night out there indeed,' Neil replied sympathetically, waterproofs still dripping. 'I've got a thick roll-neck sweater on but I think I needed more.'

'It's not so bad when you're on the move,' Marcus stated, 'but when on foot we started to feel it as we lost energy.'

'I'll be sure to pack you off with a good breakfast, but hopefully, you'll have no cause to abandon the land cruiser we've got out the back.'

Jonathan went in to the kitchen see Julie. 'Are you alright, darling?'

She glanced at him and nodded her head. It had clearly been a harder trek than she'd imagined. 'Sugar crash,' was all she said.

'Hopefully, we won't be doing too much more of that, now we've got wheels again,' Jonathan replied.

She nodded. 'I used to be good at this. Problem is I haven't had the opportunity to keep my fitness up for a few years.'

'It'll come back,' Jonathan replied reassuringly. 'I was feeling it out there,' he said as he took a grateful swig of the hot cocoa. 'We all were. Come on, let's sit down and eat.'

They made for the kitchen table and were soon joined by the others, who had merely removed their wet outer garments.

8

The atmosphere at the large kitchen table of the safe house was convivial. Neil was a welcoming host, a hail-fellow-well-met extrovert, larger than life in some ways. He certainly enjoyed his food, and if the privations of the first few years after the viral outbreak had seen him lose weight, then he'd certainly piled it on again since. He dominated the conversation, mainly because he possessed the ability to talk between mouthfuls, and even with one. The others were simply too tired and hungry to want to do much more than listen patiently.

With the dramatic accompaniment of the gusting wind outside, which made objects outside clatter and loosened the occasional roof tile, he expounded on his ideas as to the future.

'Aye, it'll be a lot better now that the virus has died down. We're looking at a new age of opportunity.'

'I'd hoped for that, once,' Jonathan stated.

Julie put her dessert spoon down and yawned loudly, only just remembering to cover her mouth politely. 'Excuse me, but I'm going to have to go to bed.' She got up and gave her husband a peck on the cheek. 'Goodnight darling,' she said.

'Yes, I'll be up shortly,' Jonathan replied.

Once she'd left the kitchen and began to make her way upstairs, Neil continued his monologue.

'You know, there really are a lot worse things than being invaded by the Americans.'

'If you're the right country,' Jonathan countered.

'Oh for sure, for sure,' he admitted. 'But look at Germany or Japan after the Second World War.'

'Or look at the Middle East,' Jonathan replied. 'Remember, World War Two essentially made America into the leading power, though arguably it had been on course to be ascendant from the turn of the twentieth century. But it made some bad calls after that.'

Neil frowned. 'But, if I might say – present company accepted of course – they can be a pretty fractious lot in the Middle East, don't you think? They didn't see the trends, fought at every turn.'

'Not all,' Jonathan countered again.

'No, not all. And that's my point. The ones that went with the flow ended up better off. Those that fought to continue to be disruptive and tyrannical did end up worse off, though.'

'Sorry, but what's your point?' Jonathan asked.

'My point, Jonathan, is that you have to choose your side.'

'I think we have, haven't we?' Jonathan frowned.

'Yes. And we're presently on a collision course with the Americans, a super-power still.'

At this Marcus came in. 'That's because they stepped in to support what they regarded as the legitimate government in power at the time. As Brigade

Commander King recently reminded us, that government was on the edge of capitulation. A few more weeks and it would have been *us* the Americans were talking with, not the regime.'

'Aye', Neil said ruefully, 'more's the pity.'

'It might not always be the case,' Marcus continued.

'Just how's that?' Neil replied doubtfully, biting a loose bit of nail on his thumb.

Akam looked at Marcus reprovingly. 'Need to know,' he reminded his leader.

'Yeah, Akam's right,' Marcus told Neil. 'We can't compromise our assignment.'

'But, it's more than the usual shoot-and-scoot, I take it. Suffice it to say, something big?'

Several in the team looked at their host blankly, but none of them replied. Riordan was still on his main course, soaking up the gravy with bread. Keith put his dessert spoon down and shoved his bowl away thanklessly, wiping his mouth with the back of his hand and surreptitiously burping. Conrad and Steve were still finishing their desserts.

'Ah mean,' Neil continued, 'more than the usual pissy little operation. Well, I mean, it's all gone on for too long, too long. Too much killing.'

They watched him as he got up, handed out shot glasses, and passed around a bottle of brandy. Jonathan, Akam, and Keith refused. Neil poured himself three shots in succession, quickly necking each of them.

'So, don't you worry yourselves,' he continued. 'I know, standard operating procedure and all that, of course I do. All I want to know is – and this is a rhetorical question – how on Earth do you think you'll really change things?'

'Rhetorical questions need no answers,' Marcus stated with a polite smile. 'I must say, I never did much see the point of them!'

'Or rhetorical questions can have rhetorical answers,' Jonathan stated with a half-smile.

'Yeah, maybe you're right.' Marcus said with a glint in his eye. 'Okay then, Neil. Let me quote the boss man again. This is a long-distance run, not a sprint.'

'Right, right, we know that,' Neil replied impatiently, and downed yet another shot of brandy, his fifth.

Marcus surveyed him disapprovingly. 'Just to be sure we're on the same page though. If its quick victories you're wanting, then you're playing in the wrong game.'

Neil looked at him without focus. 'Sure, but can you get to the point?' he asked, beginning to slur.

'Okay,' Marcus said. 'We've identified cracks in the special relationship. The Americans like to be seen to be backing the right side, not corrupt or tyrannical regimes.'

'No, true, true,' Neil agreed. He was getting drowsy and shook himself awake. 'So...?'

'So, we need to prove we have the moral high ground, and also the authority.'

'Authority...?' Neil asked, as with his vision, his concentration seemed to have lost focus and then drifted back. 'Authority? Yes, yes I see. And this relates to your mission, no? Ah, right, I know...its need to know. Mum's the word and all!' he touched the side of his nose, grinned stupidly, and then swallowed another brandy.

'Um, maybe you've had enough?' Marcus suggested.

'Don't YOU tell me I've had enough!' Neil objected angrily.

'I'm sorry,' Marcus apologised.

Neil rested his forehead head onto his crossed arms before him. 'No, no, no. It's me who should be sorry. I've got it wrong. All wrong. Of *course* the regime's bad. Wrong, wrong...just wrong. The Americans don't know. But they will,' he lifted his head and pointed a fat finger at Marcus. 'You'll make them see, won't you?' He belched.

'If we're successful, then maybe we can.'

Neil's head crashed back down onto his arms. 'It was the virus. It changed everything. All those people, gone. Sometimes, it feels so… lonely.'

Keith was getting twitchy. 'Mate, I don't like this.'

'What?' Jonathan asked.

'Nah, something's wrong here. With him,' Keith nodded towards Neil nervously.

Neil lifted his head, and looked at them with bleary eyes. 'He's right. Go. Get out. Get the fuck out! The lot of you!'

'What?' Marcus asked with concern.

'Get away, now!'

'Why,' Jonathan asked, 'what's the matter?'

'Fuck it mate, can't you see?' Keith said. 'He's fucking betrayed us!'

Marcus got up. 'Jonathan, go and get Julie. We're getting out of here. Riordan, go and find our transport. Akam, Keith, cover the exits.'

As Jonathan ran upstairs, Marcus shook Neil. 'What's coming? What's on the way?'

Neil groaned. 'Black ops', he murmured.

'Just what the fuck? Why? Why'd you do it? Mate, why?'

'Ughh…,' Neil groaned. '…just, lost faith.'

'How long have we got?'

'They're close by…was going to give once you were asleep.'

'A hit squad?'

'No, they wanted you alive, for interrogation.'

'You piece of shit!' Marcus said. He wanted to pistol-whip him and raised his handgun as if to do so. Neil glanced up and squirmed, raising his hand.

'No, please!'

'How were they going to get us out?' Marcus asked.

'Extraction was to have been a chopper, but they didn't want to risk it in this weather so...'

'So?'

'Where're the others?' Neil looked around, suddenly concerned.

'Looking for the transport,' Marcus replied. 'Neil? Neil? What else is coming?'

9

Julie had been fast asleep when Jonathan reached her; he hadn't been sure which bedroom it was.

'Come on darling, you have to get up!' he said, shaking her awake.

'Why? No! I'm so tired!'

'It's a trap, this place is a trap. Come on!'

Luckily she'd fallen asleep in her clothes and just had to pull her hiking boots on. However, they were wet and her feet were swollen and blistered. She squealed in pain as she rammed her feet in, and Jonathan tied up her laces. With watery eyes, she grabbed her pack and her assault rifle, which she'd had beside her in bed.

*

'It's here!' Riordan had whispered back at Keith as he had gone to check the vehicle. He ran over to it.

'No, wait,' Keith cautioned. He looked about to see if anyone was around, and only saw Conrad, down onto one knee and scanning to their rear. Riordan opened the drivers-side door and got in.

'Great, the key is already in, ready to go. Go and tell the others, I'll get it started.'

'Whoa! Hold on a minute there, bro!' Keith said,

*

The explosion went off as just Jonathan and Julie were making their way down the stairs. 'Shit what was that?' she cried, as the whole house seemed to shake and windows shattered. Very soon after, there was a sound of automatic gunfire close-by.

*

Keith had been blown back into a dry-stone wall by the force of the exploding vehicle and slumped to the ground. There was nothing recognisable left of young Riordan, in the remains of the now-burning vehicle.

Stunned, Conrad picked himself and his weapon off of the ground, saw the vehicle on fire, and a lifeless Keith nearby. As he got up he was hit by several rounds and was dead before he hit the ground.

*

Realising what had probably happened, Akam and Steve instinctively dived to the ground. It was still dark and windy, and rain lashed down. They watched as shadowy figures rushed to the courtyard behind the kitchen. Cautiously Akam got up and followed them. Something was on fire, illuminating the surrounding farm buildings and barn. 'Steve, go back and cover the entrance,' he whispered.

He carefully glanced around the corner to see the four-by-four burning fiercely, despite the rain falling onto it. He heard shouted orders being given from what appeared to be Neil's team.

'…yeah, they've just got here and are entering from the field on the south side. They need to know that the compound is secure. Use flashlights and open the gate, they need to see we're friendlies.'

'Right, this is a fuck-up,' said another.

'Tell me about it mate, now go!'

Akam cautiously edged around the side of the building in the darkness. Very soon he heard American voices speaking into a communicator.

'...Roger that, three pax down, insurgent vehicle destroyed. Five pax unaccounted for in house...Alpha team to enter and engage, over.'

Akam realised he had seconds to potentially save his comrades, and flicked off his safety catch. He moved out of cover and fired one burst into the two men in front. He dived back into cover when he realised he was being engaged from another position, as silenced bullets took chunks out of the corner wall. Instead of waiting there to die, he ran back to the front door.

*

As Jonathan and Julie arrived at the kitchen entrance, they were met by Marcus. His face was bloody and his left arm a mess of lacerations, but he physically stopped them from entering. Jonathan glanced past him to see a very pale Neil lying on the floor, twitching in death throes, as blood gushed out of open wounds.

As they heard what remained of the kitchen door being kicked in, Marcus pushed them down the narrow hall as said softly but urgently, 'Grenade!'

After the grenade had exploded in the kitchen, they ran into Akam. 'Front seems clear, boss, but gotta be quick!' he said.

'Okay move, I'll cover,' Marcus said, flicking off the hall light.

Akam turned and took the lead and ran down the walled garden path and out into the lane, followed by Jonathan, Julie, and Marcus, with Steve covering from a kneeled position at the gate. He saw some figures approaching from his left, threw an enhanced thunder-flash to dazzle any night-sights, and then opened fire. He was hit in the mouth by a return burst.

In the lane, they heard the sound of approaching vehicles and saw headlights approaching from around the bend through the hedges. Jonathan looked to his left and found a gap in the hedge next to them. 'You lot', he shouted, 'this way.'

Without argument they all followed him, climbing up a bank and pushing desperately through a narrow gap in the hedge. It caught on their clothes and tore at their faces and hands. But they were up and out of the lane and into a muddy field that ran up a hill. Heavy rain was still beating down as they attempted to run up it, the ground sucking their boots in. Behind them, in the lane, the vehicles had stopped with a screech of brakes. The team headed for a gate that would take them through another hedge. Ahead, further up the hill, was a forest. Their running was still impeded by the glutinous mud, and they hoped against hope that they wouldn't be located by night vision.

When they had finally reached the treeline they clambered over a barbed-wire fence, Julie squealing as she cut her hand. Akam lowered the fence for her but her jeans then became snagged. He lifted her off and threw her over.

'Sorry, no time to stop and appreciate the view!' Akam quipped as he stepped over.

'Thanks,' she replied, getting up with Jonathan's help.

They carried on running through the forest, occasionally getting caught on unseen twigs or stumbling over fallen branches. Only when they were well clear of the farmhouse did they go to ground and evaluate what had just happened, on the edge of another field. Between them, they only had their weapons and three packs.

'Where's Steve?' Jonathan asked as he caught his breath. 'Is this it?'

'I saw Steve fall, hit whilst covering us,' Marcus said, gulping down air into his lungs. 'Look…we can't do anything about it now. Now, get your shit together, hoods up or hats on, and I want a SITREP, folks,' he continued between pants. 'Usual routine; ammo, injuries, and details of the last contact. Julie?'

'No ammo used,' Julie replied breathlessly, 'cut hand.' She couldn't just then have uttered more if there had been a gun held to her head.

'Okay, treat it, then I want you to check comms – no, belay that order – we don't need comms just yet, it could compromise our position.' Marcus told her. 'Okay, Jonathan?'

'No ammo used, no injuries,' he replied tiredly.

'Fine. Akam?'

'Ammo good, only one clip gone, eight left,' Akam reported, 'No injuries. We lost Riordan, Conrad, and Keith to a booby-trapped vehicle.'

'Details?' Marcus asked.

'Huh, that's it, no more,' Akam said defensively. 'All I know is that the four-by-four was rigged, we lost three guys and one more in the contact that ensued.'

'Okay, I realise that,' Marcus said calmly. 'You used one clip of ammo, I take it that means you got into a contact outside of the house?'

'Yeah, that's right,' Akam now recalled. 'I engaged two personnel. I overheard a radio transmission, they appeared to be American.'

'Okay, piecing that all together, it appears that we were betrayed back there by Neil. He's dead. It also appears that he may have saved what's left of us with his last-minute change of heart. That black ops team was caught unawares, it hadn't gone to plan. The plan was to lift us whilst we were asleep. That and the weather are the only reasons we are still alive or not in captivity. Now I suggest we need to carry on and find shelter. A-S-A-P.'

'And the mission continues?' Jonathan asked.

Marcus considered it for a second. 'Yes. There is no reason to believe that the next safe-house has been similarly compromised, Neil was kept out of the loop there, as he was about our mission. The safe houses are chosen randomly. We just landed on a snake rather than a ladder.'

'And what about your injuries, Marcus?' Julie asked.

'I'm alright. Treat me when we find shelter.'

10

When the explosion occurred and the shooting had started, Ian, the cook, had awoken from his nap in a nearby out-house. As he rubbed his eyes and reached for his glasses he knew that things hadn't gone to plan, and stayed low until all the noise had died down. He knew better than to go outside with all the black ops boys doing their thing. He was concerned for Neil, but not enough to risk his own life. Instead, he just dressed, cleaned his teeth, and tried to tame his light-brown thatch with water and gel.

Six weeks earlier Neil had turned Ian, but only after he was sure that Ian felt the same way. In Ian's case, it hadn't been so much disillusionment with the cause due to ideological reasons, nor Neil's particular sympathy for the Americans. Ian was born resentful; he had always had a problem with authority, but largely in a passive-aggressive way. It was therefore not apparent to most, and he generally came across as affable and educated, albeit from a humble background, and had once had a job he described as 'something in computers'.

He had never sought a leadership position, eschewed any ideas of promotion to management, and preferred to stay technical. When he was honest with himself he admitted that he probably wasn't a people-person. His problem was that many managers were, and he'd hated their glib adherence to the company line, enthusiastically spouting all of the mindless exhortations. He also hated their shallow estimation of him, which was almost always superficial, and never once got to the real Ian; whoever he was. Sometimes even he wasn't sure, and for that reason, he was damned certain that they actually had no idea. But they pretended to. And the character that they created for him, good, affable, conformist, co-operative and pliable Ian, was one that suited them. As long as he didn't break out of the mold that they'd created for him, everything would be fine. He'd continue doing what he loved, playing around with computers, and they'd continue to pay him, occasionally stressing him out with impossible deadlines or tasks (for few of the systems he operated worked very well; in most cases, the managers had gone cheap on them or had rushed the developers…usually both).

When the virus had hit and the rebellion began, he'd at first been very fearful. Everything had broken down, and fast. Supply chains were disrupted within days, and he wondered if he'd starve to death before ever catching the virus. With food and fuel rationed, continuing to go into the office became impossible. Only those who could work from home stood a chance of keeping things going, and only for a bit longer, as cyber-attacks from Russia hit the infrastructure. He was glad that this meant he'd be less likely to catch the virus. Luckily he'd been working at home when a woman from HR had thoughtlessly turned up to the office, despite their having been warned to stay away if they exhibited any of the symptoms. Her Army husband had just returned from Estonia. There she was, coughing and sneezing before her perturbed manager finally had the guts to ask her to go home; but by then it was too late for a lot of them. It had ripped through three departments in as many weeks.

A few weeks later Ian knew it was all falling apart, and that dwindling food supplies meant that he'd have to do something, and fast if he was to survive. Official advice on the news channels was to stay at home and await help. However, it was clear to Ian that none would come, and he was down to his last few tins of food. It was also clear that the official line was rubbish, and that the government itself was breaking down. To some extent this surprised him little, given his natural cynicism regarding authority. An avid player of post-apocalyptic computer games, he knew he needed others to help him to survive, the most armed the better. That was when he went online, to search out any unofficial sources of organisation which he guessed would have naturally evolved.

Despite his predilection for violent computer games, he came from a liberal-left nature and discounted many of the websites as being too extreme. He abhorred their ready calls to violence. There seemed to be a plethora of groups, ranging from those forming enclaves of people promoting self-help and food production to the milder form of survivalist types, through to those clearly on the extremes of both right and Left-wing politics. Some were heavily religious. Others were clearly quite crazy, such as motorcycle gangs who offered food in return for petrol and guns. Almost all seemed to be suggesting radical ways to replace what had crumbled.

Eventually, Ian stumbled upon the UK Resistance Party. Whilst militaristic in nature, it had one of the slickest looking and best-constructed websites. It advertised food, shelter, and security in exchange for skills and loyalty. Ian was resigned to the fact that with the clear breakdown in law and order, some ability of a group to provide security would be necessary; he couldn't do it alone for very long. As it resonated with his survivalist computer games the idea was starting to make good sense. At first glance, it appeared that only those with military skills would gain admittance, but then he found that there was a communications unit within the organisation, which sought anyone left who had IT skills, irrespective of their background.

The next challenge was in locating the group. This involved a riddle, in order to evade whatever security forces there were left. Part of it appeared to involve innate military knowledge. The other part was a location, but only a county was given, and a cryptic clue. If this could be solved then Ian stood a chance. With the aid of the internet and stretching his limited military knowledge, it took him a couple of days, and by then his food supplies had dwindled to a critically low level. With only a quarter of a tank of petrol left, he set off on his way. This proved to be a slight problem, as many of the major roads now had concrete roadblocks and military checkpoints. The authorities were trying to contain the virus by keeping people where they were. Ian wasted valuable fuel following convoluted routes on country roads. Eventually, the clue led him off-road, and his car laboured over rutted farm tracks, before finally running out of fuel. With a pack containing what meagre provisions he had left, he started out on foot; making for what he thought would be the location. He knew that this would be the end if he didn't make it. Although it was a sunny April afternoon, the nights could still be bitterly cold, and he wasn't equipped with sufficient warm gear.

Within a few hours of walking, he'd lost most of his remaining energy, and as the sun disappeared below the horizon he was getting colder than he'd ever been before. By his reckoning, however, he was there. A deserted copse up a very slight rise, in the middle of rural nowhere; empty, alone, amongst ploughed fields. He would die here, he thought to himself as he shivered. This was the end.

Suddenly he saw a point of red light on his chest. Two more followed. Within seconds he was facing a man wearing a military contamination-proof suit and respirator. In fact, so uniform and professional did they look that he was sure he'd been captured by the Army, having walked into a trap. He dropped his pack and put his hands up, just as he'd seen prisoners of war do in the films.

'Who are you? Give us your name, address, occupation?'

He replied.

'Okay check it out,' the first soldier said to his companion.

There was a tense second whilst they consulted using a mobile information device.

'Are you alone?' his interrogator asked aggressively.

'Yes.'

'Do you know who we are?'

'Yes, you're the UK Resistance Party.'

'How did you find out about us?'

'Your website,' Ian replied.

'Any military experience?'

'Not really?'

'What do you mean, 'not really'? Yes or no, do you have any military experience?'

'No.'

'So why'd you fucking lie to us? We need you to tell the truth at all times, it's the difference between life and death.'

'I'm cold, and I'm hungry,' Ian replied, now too weak to care if they shot him there and then.

'Not good enough. What else do you do?'

'I work with computers. I want to join your communications cell.'

'If you're any good, you might. If not you'll be running errands, or learning to kill. You got a problem with that?'

'No,' he replied, too weak to care.

'Once you're in, there's no leaving. If you're a spy we'll shoot you. If you betray us, we'll shoot you. Turn around now and you're free to go, but we'll be gone. We never return to the same location twice. Still want in?'

'Yes,' Ian stated, as sure of this as he'd ever been of anything.

'Any I-D?'

'Yes, here's my passport. I've also got my driving licence.'

'Good.'

'He's clean, checks out,' said the man with the device.

'How did you get here?' the interrogator asked.

'Car, which ran out of petrol. Then I walked.'

'How far?'

'I don't know, maybe five or six miles.'

'Good.' The man handed Ian a flask of hot coffee and a home-made pasty. 'When you've finished we'll carry on. It's about ten miles. Do you think you can make it?'

Ian sat down, wondering if he could get up again. 'Yes,' he answered, and ate hungrily.

'Disappointing haul this time,' he heard one of the men comment to another.

*

A few months later and he'd been integrated into the group as an IT and Communications expert. They'd also found that he was an able cook. Being of a slight build and having spent most of his adult working life doing little more than sitting in an office, they judged that he was not suited to the rigours of combat operations. In the early days with them, he very rarely got out into the field and spent most of his time at their underground headquarters.

As time went on and casualties to both combat and the virus mounted, he couldn't avoid it. He attended a few night ambushes, operating communications gear and hearing a cacophony of explosions and shooting in the background. On one occasion some firing seemed to crack overhead. On another, the ambush went horribly wrong, and he and his team had to run for their lives, pursued by an armoured car and a couple of four-by-four's, and then soldiers on foot with dogs. Being light he was fleet of foot and was one of only three to survive.

But as the campaign against the authorities wore on, the units he supported were confidently conducting raids on road checkpoints and Police stations in the open daylight, manned by increasingly thinned-out units of demoralised men.

Seeing the slaughter in the clear light of day and up close turned Ian's stomach. There was no mercy for those who didn't surrender immediately. If the insurgents had sustained casualties in an assault, there were likely to be reprisals; in some cases, whole guard posts were executed after surrendering too tardily. Although too afraid to object, Ian saw no need for it. He was never asked to participate, and most of the unit commanders regarded him as a queasy weakling. When the executions began he would always walk away. One day they caught a middle-aged Policeman amongst a group of soldiers at a concrete bunker, and he begged for his life, catching Ian's eye. Ian just turned and walked away, tears streaming down his face. The moment the shot came was the moment that he lost faith in the UK Resistance Party.

He wanted to walk away but knew he was in it up to his neck. As a communications expert, he knew too much. He knew most of the commanders, the locations, and the codes. It was very unlikely by then that they would have let him leave with his life.

Later, he was at the battle of Morton Down, monitoring enemy communications. Again, he didn't participate in the actual combat but heard what was going on as it happened. He was shocked by the losses to his side, and placated somewhat by the fact that two of the more murderous assault teams he had worked alongside had been completely wiped out in the tunnels underneath the facility. Formerly a very rational man, dismissive of religion and superstition, he began to believe that some law of retribution had been their judge, jury, and executioner. Ian would not hitherto have given such an idea any credence. Now, he was even becoming more spiritual.

Three years on, after the American occupation, movement for insurgent groups became much more difficult. Tactics began to mirror those that the Taliban had employed during the war in Afghanistan in the early two-thousands, and the opportunity arose for Ian to join a field unit which specialised in manning safe houses for units on the move. He volunteered on the basis of his having good communications and IT skills, and also his ability to cook. With the superior American surveillance teams now rendering electronic communications generally unviable, it was Ian's ability to cook which swung it.

He was assigned to Commander Neil Porlock's unit, and for a few months, he was almost content. Neil was instinctive enough to see, however, that Ian's heart wasn't in it. Although there were no more executions, and no real sign of combat apart from the abundance of weapons being bandied about the place, the damage had been done to Ian's spirit. He was frequently depressed, sometimes short-tempered, and sometimes tearful. He slept badly, and when he did sleep he had nightmares.

When Neil had a quiet word with him – ostensibly about his attitude – he was able to suggest that there was another way. What Neil said had made sense to Ian. It was clear that Neil sympathised with the Americans rather than the British regime, but also that continuing to fight was futile and wasteful. Ian certainly didn't have the stomach for it, and whilst he still harboured a plan to just disappear from the farmhouse,

Neil's plan made much more sense. With the American patrols, drones, air-cover, and satellites, hiding out in the middle of nowhere without a cover story would be more difficult. It made sense to go with the prevailing tide.

When Neil told him of a meeting with an American contact at a pre-arranged location, Ian was more hopeful than he had been for many years. The American, who in civilian clothes looked like some sort of CIA operative, had made it clear that in return for co-operation a new life beckoned, away in the United States. There would be no penalty for his time served in the resistance, and his help in ending the bloody conflict would be rewarded. The way it was put to Ian by the American was that, in years to come, the mental scars of this time would for him be akin to that of the people who had lived through the bad times in Europe during the 1930s and 1940s. It would never go. But that time would heal it. There would eventually be no recriminations for whatever had been done, people would be living in a new period, and re-building society.

Ian was fully on-board by the time that he and Neil left the American. And, a few weeks later when the news of Marcus's mission came through, Ian knew this would be an end to years of misery.

*

There was a knock on his door. With trepidation, he went to see who it was and looked out of the side window. There were three Americans in combat gear. He opened the door.

'Is your name Ian Simmonds?' one of the Americans asked.

'Yes, I am,' Ian replied unsurely.

'You need to come with us.'

'Why?'

'Don't ask questions,' the man said coldly. 'You need to move, now.'

11

It was 'hurry up and wait', as ever. Following breakfast, Dolman had turned up at the supply depot over an hour before with his field pack and assault rifle, and was told he could wait around and chat to the team as they prepared the convoy. The team would be small, which he was ambivalent about. Unable to hide in a crowd, he would be more prominent as an outsider. However, there were less unknown variables in the form of possibly stupid or immature personalities to compromise the mission. He was confident that he could easily dominate four others, especially logistics types.

First of all, kneeling on the top of the large, dark-green lead vehicle, cleaning the front windows, was Specialist Michael Kowalski, the driver, lean and grizzled-looking.

'Hey, Mike, have you seen, we got ourselves a new Second Lieutenant?' shouted Specialist Gabriela Martinez, the Ex-LF vehicle supervisor, over the noise of an engine being tested in one of the vehicles behind.

'Really?' The reply was disinterested.

'Yeah, the S-Four told Sergeant Kelly last night, he'll be riding with us too.'

'Huh, right,' Kowalski replied tersely.

Dolman figured that, as the only female in the team, Martinez was probably out of place. It was clear to him that she was more garrulous than her male counterparts, and probably craved conversation. When she turned and walked towards him, he fast turned his attention elsewhere. She was short and probably more heavily set than the type of women he went for generally, lumpy in her shapeless combats and clumpy boots. He had already noticed slight dark hair-growth on her upper lip. However, she had attractive eyes.

'Hey, Captain, you can put your kit on board now, Sir.' This was Corporal Phil Gresham, the crew commander. With short-cropped sandy hair and average size and features, he was the average technical soldier. He hailed from Staten Island, New York City.

'Thank you,' Dolman replied.

'We'll be heading off soon, Sir,' Gresham added. 'Ned –that is Specialist Plaskett– is just completing the last checks, and just needs to top-up coolant in vehicle four.'

'That's okay. I take it Ned's going to be on top cover?'

'Correct, Sir, he's the gunner.'

'And you've got a new Lieutenant along for the ride?'

'That's so, Sir.'

'I assume he'll be taking command of the convoy?'

'Sir, that is correct.'

With his kit, Dolman entered the rear doors of the eight-wheeled vehicle. The inside was already lit up, the interior walls and ceiling painted in a glossy off-white.

Being larger than the British versions of that type of vehicle, there was more floor space between the rows of seats along each side of the compartment. At the end was a seat with a control panel and keyboard, presumably Specialist Martinez's position as autonomous vehicle supervisor.

'Hi,' said a voice behind him. He turned to see a lean, bespectacled figure with squashed combat cap in the same grey-green-beige digital camouflage as his wrinkled uniform, atop short-cropped blond hair. 'I'm Second Lieutenant Will Courtney, 32nd Brigade Support and Sustainment Battalion. I'm overseeing this convoy,' he was too smiley, in a self-effacing way. 'Good to have you aboard. I'd like to say we don't take many passengers, but to be honest we've started to feel like a taxi service of late!'

Big round glasses made his eyes look large, and Dolman immediately felt like the top dog, compared to this Sergeant-Major's nightmare. 'I'll try not to be too much bother,' he said. 'And you'll certainly get your tip at the end of the journey!'

'Tip? Oh, yeah, I get it. Taxi, tip, right? Okay yeah, Huh!' Courtney brayed nasally as he got the joke. Dolman thought he was probably a good home-spun Wyoming farm boy.

Once Courtney had finished shaking, he continued. 'We'll be heading off soon then, Sir. Will you be comfortable in here?'

'I should think so.'

'Airborne guy, huh? No travel queasiness then.'

'It doesn't always follow, but, no.'

'Really? Gee, I thought all you guys were made of steel, with iron constitutions. I would have liked to have been a paratrooper, failed the first week, huh! Physical.'

'It's not for everyone,' Dolman stated as sympathetically as he could. Had he failed, he'd have gone back to try again.

'No, I guess it wasn't me,' the Lieutenant replied ruefully. 'Anyway, I always take a travel pill each morning, especially before getting in one of these tin cans. We usually travel battened-down, even top cover inside at times. It can get pretty rough in here, like being at sea.'

'Really?'

'Um, yeah, especially on some of those mountain passes. It's like the Hindu Kush or Yemen.'

'You were in those places?'

'Er, no, but I heard about them from a Master-Sergeant one night over chow,' he admitted sheepishly.

'Right,' Dolman eyed him with scorn.

'Well, anyway, I guess I'll go and take a look-see how the team is doing.' He smiled again and walked off to irritate Corporal Gresham with pointless questions.

As Dolman sat and checked his kit, he was joined by Specialist Gabriela Martinez. She sat down in front of him at her position at the control terminal and loosened her helmet strap.

She glanced at him uncertainly. 'You met our new Lieutenant?' she asked.

'Yes,' he replied neutrally.

'Hm, I think he's got a learning curve ahead of him,' she stated.

'I agree,' he replied. She glanced at him, clearly wanting more from him, but he wasn't about to play politics with this team. He just wanted to get in as fast as possible, and out with Trant.

12

That morning they found themselves in a deserted sheep shed. Despite sharing her sleeping bag with Jonathan, Julie was shivering. All of their clothes were still soaked through from the night before, and they'd awoken to a clear, bright, and very fresh morning.

Akam had taken the last guard shift of the night, and he walked in. 'How's Marcus?' he asked.

'He's still asleep,' Jonathan replied. 'Julie's patch-up job last night was okay, stopped the bleeding, but he really needs to be in an infirmary. I think he should step out at the next safe-house.'

'Hmm, trust me, he won't,' Akam replied. 'I've worked with him for too long. He's a known bullet magnet. I've seen him carry on in worse a state than this.'

'We've still a way to go, and without transport just now. Looking at the map we've got to make thirty-six miles. We won't do that by tonight, not with patrols, dogs, drones, and such like. And now the weather's good they have all forms of aircraft up, plus satellite.'

'True, that's if we were making for the safe-house that we were headed for, and we had the wheels,' Akam stated.

'You mean there's another?'

'King knows that we always need a plan-B. If that vehicle had broken down or we'd met with a patrol and dispersed, then we'd have needed somewhere else to go.'

Jonathan glanced at his wife, who was already looking more cheerful. 'How far?'

'Just two or three miles,' Akam smiled. 'But –

'Let's go!' Julie said.

'But,' Akam continued, 'we'll have to wait until there's more movement out there. Although this is farmland, there's little going on just now.'

'But we're still too close to the other safe-house,' Jonathan said. 'The patrols will be all over this area soon, with drones and dogs, surely?'

'Trust me, it's riskier to move just now. We need cloud cover or else their aerial and sat assets will be all over us.'

'Any other ideas? We can't just sit here,' Jonathan said.

'Hmm, well, maybe there is one. They're looking for four of us, armed and with back-packs.'

'Okay?'

'We set off in intervals, staggered. Leave the packs and the assault rifles, take side-arms only, and what we can stuff in our pockets. When we get to the next safe-house we pick up new weapons and equipment, and maybe get a new team member if there's anyone with operational experience.'

'Will this work?'

'It's tried and tested. It leaves us severely out-gunned if we do meet a patrol, but it means we stand a chance of getting through. We would just register as locals, farm workers going about their daily rounds.'

'Fine, I like it,' Jonathan said. 'What's our order of march?'

'I suggest Marcus goes first, and then you and Julie go out together. You'll just look like a farming couple out to feed the animals. Grab a bucket from around the side. Take one of the maps and I'll give you a grid reference. I'll follow on later.'

13

'Okay Gabs, ready to go?' Gresham asked her from the rear doors.

'Yep,' she replied, 'all systems A-Okay.'

'Good. Keep 'em lined up as usual, nut-to-butt.'

'Wilco,' she replied.

Specialist Plaskett nudged past them to climb up into his position in the rotating gun platform, just past Gabriela's control terminal.

'All okay Ned?' Gresham asked.

'Fine Corp,' the tall, lanky Plaskett replied in a thick Louisiana drawl.

'Okay, it'll be the same routine as usual. Once we get into the hills I want you down below, you hear that? I ain't gonna give you no more Purple Heart citations!'

Plaskett gave a casual half-salute. 'Why thank you, Corp, I wasn't planning on getting my head blown off neither.'

Dolman looked at the Corporal. 'I thought this route was quiet, Corporal?'

'Well, Sir, it just depends on how you define quiet.'

'Pot-shots at most, I was told,' Dolman replied.

'Ah well, there's the official news, then there's the truth. Let's just say it can get a bit kinetic out there. We've had to call in fast air twice in at least three months.'

Corporal Gresham turned to leave a distinctly unimpressed Dolman, to take up his position as navigator and co-driver in the front next to Specialist Kowalski, the driver. Second Lieutenant Courtney climbed in and secured the back door. He took his place, strapping-in and putting his helmet on. Dolman noticed that he also now wore body armour over his chest. The gauche young Lieutenant gave a toothy grin to the others, but then noticed something about their guest. 'Huh, you may want to put your helmet on, Captain, it gives extra protection in case of roll-over.'

'Are you anticipating such an event, Lieutenant?' Dolman asked mildly.

'Hopefully not, Sir, but we go through the drills and…well, let's just say it's a good precaution.'

'Fine,' Dolman replied, reaching down for the US pattern helmet he'd just been issued, with its green and sand coloured digital camouflage cover and in-built earphones.

The engine started, and within a few minutes, they were on the move.

On Gabriela Martinez's bank of LCD screens, Dolman could see a driver's view of the airfield in front of them, and on another the train of vehicles moving remotely and silently behind them, in tandem. It was as if they were connected by an invisible coupling, and it was so accurate that he barely ever saw any sign of the two behind the first autonomous vehicle. Martinez was staring intently at one screen, which showed a variety of measurements and statistics relating to each vehicle, such as fuel, oil and coolant levels, or tire pressures, as well as engine management information.

Courtney whistled through his teeth and threw Dolman a pair of goggles, which Dolman placed over his helmet as Courtney pointed to the hatches above. He tapped the side of his helmet and indicated to Dolman that he had a personal role communicator at the side, and demonstrated by pulling his down over his mouth. He watched as Courtney undid the hatch above him, and stood on his seat to raise himself chest-height out. Dolman followed suite himself. A second later he was looking out over the airfield, feeling the fresh morning air against his face, mixed with the smell of oil and diesel fumes from one of the top exhausts.

The tinny sound of Courtney's voice through the communicator registered in his earphones. '*Cool, isn't it?*'

Dolman nodded in agreement as he lowered his goggles over his eyes. He was glad to be out of the confines of the vehicle for a while, and appreciate a rare sight of the bright autumn sunshine. In front, he could see Specialist Plaskett in his gun turret, testing the rotational movement. Behind, the autonomous vehicles dutifully followed. It was an uncanny sight, knowing that each driving compartment was empty as if driven by ghosts.

As they reached the main entrance and drew to a stop, Lieutenant Courtney piped-up again. '*Once we're through the gate I suggest we get below, Sir.*'

Corporal Gresham spoke to the guard and the barriers were lifted. Lieutenant Courtney lowered himself back down into the main compartment, and Dolman followed suite. As they sat back down Martinez didn't even give them a glance.

'We'll be making for the bridges as usual,' Courtney stated. 'We have better control of them than Gloucester. The M4 is still good once we're over, then we head north. But we never take the same route twice.'

'I see,' Dolman replied, feigning ignorance as to their plan. 'What's our E-T-A, if I might ask?'

'About sixteen-hundred hours. All the checkpoints and usual delays have been factored in. This team makes the run once a month.'

'Sir?' It was Martinez. 'Diagnostics indicators show there's a problem with the engine compression on vehicle three.'

'Oh golly,' Lieutenant Courtney said. 'Okay, okay, I guess we'd better pull over and call up a mobile repair team.' He turned to Dolman apologetically. 'Oh well, they say fail early, eh?'

Dolman didn't share his apathetic humour.

14

'Sir?' Major Schreiber caught Major-General Easton in the corridor as he was leaving the Officers Mess after breakfast. 'There's been a development on the Wales border.'

'Go ahead,' Wes Easton replied, wiping his uniform free of any toast crumbs as he walked.

'There was a contact at point three-one-four, Captain Mason sent a casualty report. Quick Response and Medical Emergency Response teams were dispatched.'

'That's the safe-house that had the turn-coats, awaiting an insurgent ops team, right?' the General asked.

'Correct Sir, the A-team suffered several casualties, one dead, three wounded. Three insurgent bodies have been recovered, and one was captured alive. The rest got away.'

'Goddamit! How did that happen?'

'The turncoats wired their escape vehicle. Something went wrong, and one of the insurgents triggered it early. The plan had been to lift them whilst they rested. The bad weather meant that we couldn't use drones or air support to locate them. We're looking for them now.'

'A clusterfuck, in other words. So, what was this insurgent team doing, and where was it headed?'

'Into Wales, Sir.'

'Hmm, we don't need trouble there just now, Chuck.'

'My thoughts exactly, Sir.'

'And so what of the turn-coats?'

'One died in the contact. The other one is being choppered-back with the prisoner.'

'Anything from the preliminary de-brief?'

'Not much. They were a team of eight from the so-called UK Resistance Party, well-armed and equipped."

'Okay. Any more detail?'

'Yes. The turn-coat said that the composition of the party seemed odd. There was one female, part of a husband and wife team. She could have been a fighter, but looked exhausted, went to bed early. Her husband didn't look like a fighter at all, more the academic type, balding, glasses. Not a known player.'

'A female, eh? Any names elicited?'

'Yes, she was called Julie. She called him Jonathan.' The Major waited for the penny to drop.

'The group that calls itself the UK Resistance Party was the one that took out Morton Down, wasn't it? Goddam it, Chuck, Get a fighter patrol up to escort that chopper in!'

15

It was decided that the third autonomous vehicle would be taken out of the convoy, as the diagnostics and repairs would have taken too long. Already they were behind schedule. On good roads, the vehicles were able to reach near to motorway speeds for heavy goods vehicles, but the roads from Fairfield airbase were B-class for many miles. It took an hour to reach an open highway, and another to the bridge over into Wales. At the checkpoint before the crossing there were delays. Questions were asked: Why did the paperwork state that they were in a four-vehicle convoy when there were only three?

Lieutenant Courtney was of no help in this situation whatsoever. He immediately clashed with the guards, pulling rank, using referent power in the shape of his unit commander back at Fairfield, and threatening them with transfer to a less convivial posting up north. All of this was delivered unconvincingly and with just enough assertiveness to be annoying. Leaning against the hull of the command vehicle a few meters away, arms crossed, Dolman looked on with mild irritation as he watched large dark-grey storm-clouds moving in up the Bristol Channel from the south-west.

Corporal Gresham stepped in to save the day. 'Corporal', he spoke neutrally to his opposite number, 'please call through to this number, to a Staff Sergeant Bill Valence at Fairfield. He'll confirm that our shipment is short one autonomous, its power pack failed as we were already en route, and we didn't have time to collect new documentation.'

'Well Corporal', the guard replied, still irked from his Lieutenant's grilling, 'this is all highly irregular. But I'll make the call for you.'

'Thank you', Gresham replied, without even glancing at his Lieutenant.

Within minutes they were cleared to go. Lieutenant Courtney avoided eye contact with the others as he made his way back to the command vehicle. Up in the gun turret, Ned Plaskett glared down at him, then gave a thumbs down sign to Gresham as he walked back from the checkpoint. Corporal Gresham raised his eyebrows back at Ned and shook his head despairingly. Watching the show by his door as he chewed gum, Mike Kowalski spat it out and sniggered cynically.

'Corporal, I think we've got to get moving now,' Courtney said, trying to regain his authority with the team.

'Why gee shit, Lieutenant!' Gresham replied, his patience finally giving.

'Alright Corporal, you'd damn well better start showing a ranking officer a bit more respect, or you'll be on a charge faster than you can say 'glass-house'!' Courtney replied angrily.

'Sorry, Sir, it was on accident. I'll try to be more respectful next time.'

'Yeah, well, you make sure you are. Rest assured I'll have your stripes for that,' Courtney said and climbed into the back of the vehicle, irked.

Dolman afforded himself a brief grin, unfolded his arms, and followed Courtney.

As they proceeded across the bridge, Dolman opened the hatch above his seat and looked out. The storm clouds were as bad as they'd looked earlier, now heading in from the mouth of the Bristol Channel.

'Going to be a wild night!' It was Courtney's voice crackling through Dolman's ear-pieces. He glanced behind to see the Lieutenant grinning at him from the other hatch, with his ballistic eye-shield on. He certainly didn't waste any time mulling over the incident at the bridge checkpoint. Dolman was vaguely impressed; maybe the man was more mature than he gave him credit for. Or, more worryingly, he was an unstable mood-swinger. 'Yep, wild and woolly,' Dolman replied into his intercom.

'Hah! I like that. Like one of the sheep up in them thar hills! Wild and woolly', Courtney chortled into his mike.

'Maybe,' Dolman replied tersely, and settled on mood swinger, as he lowered himself back down into the crew compartment, slamming down the hatch overhead.

Courtney seemed to want to remain up top to admire the view. Dolman noticed Martinez glance back at him briefly with a look of concern, before returning her attention to the multi-screened console. It was clear that the whole team was rapidly losing faith in their quirky goofball of a new commander. In peacetime, such a man would be a nuisance but probably little more. In a combat zone, he might well be a distinct liability. Any hint of incompetence that might lead to getting them all killed was bound to cause consternation. Dolman knew that his own Captain's rank now held more sway with the crew, whoever's army he was in. Martinez was clearly now viewing him as more than just a passenger.

*

As they continued on the M4 towards Cardiff they were hit by a deluge of rain. Like a scorched stoat, Ned Plaskett slid down from his gun position and closed his hatch, with rivulets of water pouring in around him.

'Batten down the hatches and prepare to dive!' Lieutenant Courtney quipped, in a poor mock-English accent. He was amusing himself an no one else.

Dolman glanced at him with disdain.

Courtney looked at him with a stupid smile. 'Captain Bligh? No? Mutiny on the Bounty?'

'I don't think he commanded a submarine, Lieutenant,' Dolman replied drily.

'No, huh, I'm mixing my narratives there for sure, but no apologies. Yo-ho-ho!'

Dolman was itching to tell him to shut the heck up, maybe less pleasantly. The man seemed way too excitable by far.

Courtney continued. 'I told you this was like being at sea. Wait till we get to the hills!'

'Yeah, whatever,' Dolman replied dismissively.

16

Five miles from the farmhouse where the team had been betrayed, armoured drones sped over the Welsh hills at break-neck speed to the area where satellite imagery had spotted people on foot. These devices were designed to stay low so that they could evade radar and used lasers to precisely measure their height from ground and other obstacles. As well as light weaponry, they were fitted with infra-red scanning technology, able to pick up on body heat. Very soon they were at the location identified by satellite and located a man and a woman walking down a lane towards a house. Very soon a larger drone was circling the farmhouse, a surveillance version. Within twenty minutes a helicopter full of black-clad troops landed in a field nearby and surrounded the farmhouse.

Just as assault teams were about to enter via the back and front entrances, the front door opened. Safety catches were released. A large man in a scruffy white wool roll-neck sweater stood before them looking dumbfounded. He was about to take his large Golden Retriever for a walk. He was joined a few seconds later by his wife, wearing an apron and with an oven glove on her hand. The placid dog gave out one perfunctory bark.

They heard one of the Americans talking into his personal role radio: 'Okay as you were, as you were, belay my last. Someone's jacked-up here!'

17

In addition to his fear, Ian had disliked his helicopter ride intently. What was more, he privately questioned just why he was in the same compartment as a prisoner, who was sitting on one of the opposite seats to him, head bleeding and hands bound with a tie-wrap. The man looked recalcitrant, defiant. An American soldier opposite kept the rifle on his knees pointed at him.

'We'll get you for this, mate! There'll be no hiding. You're a fucking traitor.' Keith said to Ian.

'Keep quiet!' his guard said.

'Hah! Don't worry, I will! From now on, you won't get a thing out of me!' Keith turned to look at another guard, an Afro-American. 'Hey, bro, what're you doing here with this lot?'

'Keep quiet!' the guard opposite barked.

The black American soldier looked at Keith. 'Man, I'm just doing my job.'

Keith scoffed with disgust.

Ian looked at Keith, and felt perturbed and just a little ashamed. He was, after all, part of the betrayal.

Once they'd landed they were separated for interrogation; only in Ian's case it was labelled 'debrief'.

18

In a small hamlet comprising just a deserted hairdressers shop and a vehicle repair business in an old garage, the team waited in a small attic room above the workshop. It comprised four beds, a chest of drawers and there was a stove on the corner.

They had taken an old white van from the last safe-house to this, their next intended rendezvous; the place that they should have arrived at from the compromised safe-house of the night before.

A medic had seen to Marcus, and he lay on one of four old beds. His good arm rested over his eyes to shield them from the daylight, his other was beside him, bandaged up.

Akam and Julie were sitting on their beds, cleaning their weapons, as one of the safe-house guards ascended the creaky old stairs to the attic room. 'Time to relieve your mate,' he said to Akam.

'Sure, no probs, just getting this back together,' he replied, as he re-assembled his new assault rifle, a British Army personal weapon.

'Hope that'll do?' the guard asked.

'Yep, it'll have to do. It's seen better days.'

'Sorry mate, it was the best we could manage. We've got plenty of these, but they wouldn't fit the bill,' he said as he handed Akam his own Russian-made assault rifle to inspect.

'It looks like it's hardly been fired,' Akam replied, impressed.

'It probably hasn't, it's from a new batch we took delivery of some weeks ago.'

'Did it come with any other goodies?' Akam asked.

'If it's anti-tank or anti-aircraft you're after, well, that's already out there in the field. They're training us up on that. If you ask me, the Russkies are cagey about letting those things out of their sight.'

Akam handed the assault rifle back, and with a few clicks of his weapon he'd put it back together and stood up, ready to relieve Jonathan from his stint on guard duty. 'Russians, eh? They say how long they'd be training you up for?'

'Nope. They're here for as long-as. I reckon they're also acting as observers.'

'Yeah, could be,' Akam replied. 'Cheers mate,' he said, as the guard handed him a box of 5.56mm ammunition before Akam descended the stairs.

The guard then looked at Marcus. 'How's he then?' he asked Julie. 'Do you think he'll really be good to go?'

'He's fine', replied Marcus, who hadn't been asleep. 'And yes, he'll be good to go, thank you.' Talking about himself in the third person sarcastically, he lifted his arm away from his eyes and glanced blearily at the clock sitting atop the old Victorian fireplace opposite. 'God, is that really the time?'

'It's over an hour to nightfall yet,' Julie stated.

'Yes, but I've got to prepare, pack. You lot have done all that and cleaned your weapons. I'm in shit state.'

'It's all done,' Julie said soothingly.

'Pardon?'

'Whilst you were asleep. It's been a long, boring day up here with nothing much else to do.'

'My kit's ready?'

'Yes. Jonathan is just on his way up, he was hoping to discuss the route with you,' she stated.

'Oh, right. Thanks,' Marcus said gratefully.

'No worries,' she replied.

'You got enough sleep?' he asked.

'Some. I couldn't sleep long. Too anxious I suppose. I'll have plenty of time to sleep in the back of the vehicle.'

'Regret coming?'

'Not for a second,' Julie replied honestly. 'I couldn't let Jonathan go alone.'

'You know he's not alone, he's with us.'

'Yes, but not being funny; look at us. Half our team are down, and you're in no fit state to soldier,' Julie replied.

'This could easily get worse,' Marcus stated grimly. 'There are at least three strong men down there who could join us. You could stand down for one of them, wait back here.'

'With half the American Army looking for us in this area? And, no, I wouldn't leave Jonathan.'

'Okay,' Marcus conceded, 'but don't say I didn't give you the option.'

Jonathan ascended the wooden attic steps from the workshop, clutching a British Army rifle without enthusiasm. His clothes had taken on a slightly oily odour. He smiled at Julie.

'You okay?' she asked.

'Yes darling, fine thanks.'

'Are you hungry?' she asked.

'Yeah, a bit.'

'There's still soup and biscuits left on the stove, in the pan under the muslin. I prepared some sandwiches for the journey.'

'Marvellous, thanks darling.' He turned to Marcus. 'Ah, good to see you awake. Are you ready to discuss the plan?'

'Yep.'

Julie interrupted. 'If you'll excuse me, I'm just going to powder my nose.'

'Okay darling,' Jonathan replied. 'I tried to give the facilities a bit of a clean.'

'Don't worry; it is what it is; a greasy-balled mechanics loo, seat left up and oily grime everywhere. Oh, and there's just a tiny bit of cracked dirty soap.'

'I'll call room service,' Marcus joked. 'Put in a complaint to the manager!'

With a tilt of her head, Julie gave him a sarcastic smile before she descended the steps.

Jonathan waited until she was gone. 'I'll tell you, I'm a bit skeptical. Have you seen what's down in the garage?'

'Yes. It's quite a monster, isn't it?'

'A bit. Apparently, they picked it up from an over-run Army checkpoint a while back. So that, and a load of old uniforms, and you think we'll actually make it through? What about documentation, passes, authorisation chits, and such-like?'

'Done. What do you think those photos were for? We've all been placed onto the system, Army numbers the lot, with the help of a clever Russian hacker. They're all over the M-O-D systems, after some botched upgrade performed by an outsourced contractor.' Marcus said smiling, as he propped himself against the wall with a pillow at the end of his bed.

'Hmm, I'm still nervous about it.'

'Sorry, mate, I don't see your problem?'

'Hmm, call it natural inbuilt skepticism,' Jonathan replied, as he sat down on the bed opposite.

Marcus ran his hands through his thick dark hair. 'Okay, look at it like this. No one but the military has the fuel to drive any distance nowadays. Even in agricultural areas like this, it's rationed. As soon we go any distance at all, I-STAR assets and drones will be all over us. Even if we were to avoid them, we'd just have to be unlucky with a random vehicle checkpoint somewhere. So, you were a Colonel, weren't you? Well, I was a Flight Sergeant in the RAF. We know the military, Jonathan. There's a guy downstairs, Stan, who spent nine years in REME as a vehicle mechanic, he's coming along with us to make up numbers. Once we get there Akam will have to hole-up a while, out of sight. And if you want Julie with us, well, she'll have to blag it. She just needs to tie her hair up.'

Jonathan sucked through his teeth at the thought of Julie actually agreeing to wear a British Army uniform and appear in the slightest bit military.

'I know, it's a long shot,' Marcus continued.

'If we're rumbled they're likely to shoot us out of hand.'

'They've been doing a pretty good job attempting that as it is. That black ops team last night was definitely a shoot-first-ask-questions-later mob.'

'Hmm, maybe you're right,' Jonathan admitted. 'You know, it's so audacious, so damned stupid... it just might work.'

'I don't know why we've never tried it before,' Marcus said, encouraged by Jonathan's agreement.

'Just the fact that we *haven't* gives it a better chance,' Jonathan stated.

'Eh? Oh, yeah, right.'

'And it'll take us all the way in, maybe?'

'Theoretically,' Marcus replied.

'I do prefer the tried and tested.'

'Don't we all. It makes us predictable though.'

19

Despite the high winds and heavy rainfall, the column made up some time on the M4 towards Cardiff. The weight of the vehicles gave them reasonably good momentum, and the quality of the motorway was still reasonably good, patched up by the US Corps of Engineers. Most, if not all of the sparse traffic on it was military, and to any casual onlooker – if indeed there were any out in such weather – the vehicles appeared to be just another armoured supply convoy, headlights on against the rain and the subdued light.

For the occupants of the vehicle, there was little else to do but sit and endure the ride. They could see from some of Martinez's screens the view from the front, and of course, the vehicles following on behind. Paul Dolman sat as patiently as he could and stretched his legs out before him as far as he could. Across from him and slightly to his right was Ned Plaskett, temporarily redundant. Theoretically, Ned should have provided Martinez a break on the consoles, but she seemed reluctant to let him take over.

Now Ned rested with his legs apart and his hands thrust deep in his pockets, showing no signs of emotion as he avoided eye contact with Dolman. Dolman figured the man didn't have a lot going on inside his head, or simply didn't like mixing with officers. Across from Ned, now sitting on the same row of seats as Dolman, was Will Courtney, snoozing. He had dispensed with helmet and the peak of his squashy cap was shielding his eyes. Dolman noticed Ned's eyelids begin to droop to closure, and he thought he too should try for some rest. He slumped down in his seat, crossed his hands, and closed his eyes for a few seconds. He opened them again to look up with irritation at the light above his head.

'We can switch to red light if you like,' Martinez said to him. 'We do if we have a night op, but we're not due to stop for another half hour, and you guys were looking at maps earlier.'

'Yeah, red light please,' Dolman affirmed.

Martinez flicked a switch and they were suddenly bathed in red light. Dolman sat back again and closed his eyes.

'You are a Captain, aren't you?' Martinez asked.

'Yes,' Dolman replied without opening his eyes, trying to sound interested.

'Right,' Martinez said.

'In the British Army,' he qualified his statement, glancing at her.

'Yeah, of course,' she replied and looked with disdain at Lieutenant Courtney, who was now snoring lightly. She looked back at Dolman for a second too long, before returning her attention to her consoles.

Nothing more needed to be said, he knew his estimation of her from earlier was correct.

'Fifteen miles to the fuel depot,' it was Corporal Gresham's voice from the driving compartment.

'Roger that,' she replied.

20

As night fell they readied themselves to leave. In the garage downstairs the last of the supplies and ammunition had been loaded into the six-wheeled AFV (Armoured Fighting Vehicle). Julie was the last to have changed. Marcus, who was in the uniform of a British Army Lieutenant, stood with Stan and Akam, who also wore similar, with the rank slips of a Corporal and Lance-Corporal respectively. Tall and fair, Stan was nicknamed either 'Big Stan' or sometimes 'Afghan Stan', due to his having been on a training tour there.

As Julie descended from the upstairs bedroom into the garage they were amazed at the transformation. In her Army uniform and with her hair tied up in a bun just beneath her beret, she looked neat, professional, if a bit severe.

Stan made the first comment. 'You know, you looked utterly convincing until you gave that self-conscious smile of yours! Remember, these are confident extraverts, a bit cut off from their own inner life. Just act officious, authoritarian, and a bit numb. And definitely, quit that smiling!'

At that, she attempted to pull a serious face but was soon giggling.

'Okay, stand easy men!' Jonathan Barnes said as he entered in an officer's uniform. 'And, look here, I want to see no more of this levity.'

'I hate you!' Julie told him jokily. 'Just look at me. I feel so… butch!'

Jonathan smiled. 'Now, let's be clear about one thing, there'll be more respect for senior officers around here.'

She frowned. 'Hmm. Well, you've got another thing coming. Like a ton of crockery thrown at a thousand miles an hour! I mean, look at this stuff.'

'I don't know what you're complaining about,' said Stan. 'Mine's got a bullet hole in just below the left pocket. I think whoever wore it before went and died in it!'

'Man, that's bad karma!' said Akam. 'Couldn't you have found another jacket?'

'Not one that fitted me, no,' replied Stan ruefully.

'Yeah, and I look like a sack of shit for a Lieutenant,' Marcus stated. 'Still, you look okay, Jonathan. Hey, but only a Captain? Bit of a come-down, eh?'

'And a tad ironic,' Jonathan Barnes replied grimly.

'Eh?'

'Oh, it's nothing. I just think that perhaps my uniform has bad karma, too.'

'Right,' Marcus said, a little impatient to leave. 'Well, it makes sense for you to hold the rank; you know the territory, so to speak.'

'Unfortunately, yes,' Jonathan replied. 'But my experience is down-level. And we have no idea as to a lot of the tech and passwords. Who has the most recent military experience here?'

'Stan here, he came over to us two years ago,' Marcus stated.

'That not nearly good enough,' Jonathan replied. 'Regime forces have become intimately integrated with the American military in that time. Lots of British equipment has been replaced, it's sourced from American stocks now, as our manufacturers and supply chains got closed down long ago. As a unit, we are looking more than a bit anachronistic. Do we have any American gear?'

'Good point,' Marcus replied, 'but don't worry about that, all of our belt kits are American G-I issue, plus a few of our weapons. But you're right, with our economy up the spout, the British Army is supplied and pay-rolled by Uncle Sam these days. And, to answer your point about tech and passwords, that's all in order. We have some ruggedized pads and comms stuff, but most of it is dumb and just for show, none of it is hooked-up. What'll get us by the checkpoints and maybe into the base hasn't been activated yet. But I assure you, we have someone who can get us in.'

'Hmm, alright,' Jonathan replied uncertainly. 'Who?'

'Me,' a voice behind him said. Jonathan turned to see a short, lean but athletic fellow with a grade one haircut and an intense, amused stare. He looked haughty, arrogantly over-confident, and also wore a British Army uniform. 'My name is Pavel. This is all you need to know.'

Jonathan turned to Marcus. 'Marcus, I think I need to know a lot more! Russian?'

'Yes, he's part of our team. He carries the rank of Lieutenant.'

'Russian special forces?'

'Err…yeah, I believe he's from a Russian airborne Special Purpose Detachment.'

'And?'

'And, his team have the intel and skills we need to get about.'

'Team?'

'He's agreed to split his group down. There's only him, and three others.'

'Fyodor, Nickolai, and Pyotr,' Pavel interrupted. 'There's room, your vehicle carries eight, plus two crew. To be authentic you'll need someone on top-cover most of the time. Fyodor, we call him 'Bear', he good with your Gatling gun, has studied spec well! Fifty cal, even! And our Nickolai, our 'Professor', he re-programmed the AI auto-control function on it and stocked up on triple the ammo. You got a good weapons system there, matey.'

Jonathan looked around, to see three other Eastern-European characters in British camouflage uniforms loading packs, communications kit, and a long box into the back.

Pavel continued. 'And, as a –what you say- sweetener for yourselves? I bring you one man-portable air-defence, with multi-spectral optical seeker, U-V and infrared-

'What?' Jonathan asked Marcus, in a tone of incredulous outrage. 'I didn't agree to this. Why didn't you tell me before, Marcus?'

'I assure you, Jonathan, it was sprung on me at the last minute, once the head-shed knew of our losses. But to be frank, we could do the fire-power.'

'Do we? Do we really?' Jonathan asked rhetorically and looked at his wife, who looked spaced out and a little scared. 'And just *what* are these men going to be doing up there with *that* gear, starting World War Three?'

'Jonathan...Professor...' Marcus began angrily, muted through clenched teeth. 'Remember what King said.'

Jonathan was stalled and looked at Marcus, outrage quickly evaporating. 'Alright then,' he conceded. 'I suppose at the end of the day, I don't have much say in all this.'

'No, Professor, I do not think you have *any* say,' Pavel stated. 'You have, as they say, no leg to stand on!'

Jonathan glanced back at him to catch a dangerous glare before the Russian officer turned to see to his team.

'Okay team,' Marcus shouted, 'we leave in ten. Take your positions. Jonathan, Stan will drive, you take the first spell in the passenger seat. Julie, you can sit near the front if you like.'

Julie haughtily ignored him and walked to the rear of the vehicle. Jonathan glanced at Marcus with contempt and went to comfort her before the journey.

Technicians performed final checks on the engine and tire pressures. One gave Marcus a thumbs-up. 'Thanks, guys', he said, as Akam and Stan walked up.

'Akam,' Marcus said to him in a low voice. 'Keep an eye on them.'

'Who, boss?'

Marcus shook his head in despair as he picked up his American assault rifle and kit. 'All of them!'

21

There was a knock on Major-General Easton's door, and Major Charles Schreiber was shown in. Easton cleared his throat to get his clerical Sergeant's attention. 'Sergeant, can you call Captain Cartwright over, I want her in on this.'

'Yes Sir,' the Sergeant answered.

General Easton looked at his Intelligence officer 'So what's the situation, Chuck?'

'We haven't got much from the prisoner,' Major Schreiber replied. 'But the turncoat said that he and the others were from the Bristol faction of the UK Resistance Party.'

'Bristol's a no-go zone politically, we know that,' Easton stated. What else, what were they after?'

'The team was briefed on a need-to-know basis. All we elicited was that their target was a high-value asset in South Wales.'

'Are they after the Research Facility in Cardiff, as they were with Morton Down? We haven't established yet just *why* an assault was made on that facility, have we? They certainly seem to have had it in for nerds.'

'Maybe, but it appears not in this case. A team of eight wouldn't pose much of a threat. This wasn't an assassination operation either, nor even surveillance.'

'Chuck, you're not giving me much here,' Easton said.

'That's because they've been pretty damn careful here, Sir.'

'Okay, so what of the turn-coat?'

'Well, he positively identified several members of the team, and we are running them through the database now. Plus, we have positive identification of Lieutenant-Colonel Jonathan Barnes.'

'So, the bastard did survive, and went over to the other side!'

'So it appears sir,' Schreiber replied.

'Any ideas as to why?' Easton asked.

'Left-wing sympathies, probably from University onwards,' Schreiber answered

'Hmm, no surprises there,' Easton said cynically. 'So, just how the hell did he end up in the military in the first place?'

'Well, Sir, it was hard to get many educated men who *weren't* somewhat Left-wing, even amongst the technocrats. I assure you, he didn't stand out as being very exceptional in those regards.'

'But, he turned in the end,' Easton said with disgust. 'My hunch is that with that guy Barnes they're going to infiltrate the Cardiff Research Facility. Everything points to that, don't you think?'

Schreiber looked doubtful. 'Hmm, maybe Sir.'

'Well, until you've got something more conclusive, that's the narrative I'm going with. Double down on security on that facility. Divert our Q-R-F assets down there.'

'Yes Sir,' Schreiber replied reluctantly.

22

After re-fuelling, the American supply column took a route north, towards the hills and valleys of South Wales, and Trant's bastion. All of the delays had added up and extended their journey time by nearly three hours.

At one checkpoint they were stopped by a nervy British officer, a young Second Lieutenant. Corporal Gresham and Lieutenant Courtney dismounted from the vehicle and began to negotiate with the young officer, who was covered-off by a few cold, wet, tired, and rather surly looking soldiers.

Dolman walked up and took over from Courtney, and addressed the young British officer. 'What seems to be the matter, Lieutenant?'

'I'm sorry, you are?' he replied.

Dolman hesitated.

'Your name, rank, unit!' the Lieutenant snapped.

'Relax Lieutenant,' Dolman said as he reached into his combat jacket inner pocket to produce his ID and show it to the anxious younger officer.

'Oh, I'm sorry Sir. This just seemed quite irregular,' he explained.

'Really? In this day and age?' Dolman smiled, replacing his pass.

'Well, maybe not,' the young officer continued, as the penny slowly dropped that the officer before him might well be some sort of irregular black ops type. He began to afford him a bit more respect. 'Anyway, I'm sure you won't want to be troubled any further, Sir. May I just ask where you're headed?'

'You can certainly ask, Lieutenant,' Dolman replied, glancing at Courtney. 'But this is clearly just a routine supply column headed north.'

'Yes, of course, Sir. I didn't mean to be intrusive. It's just that we've had some trouble in recent hours.'

'Oh yes? What's been happening?'

'Sporadic reports of a few contacts with hostiles, and communications seem to be down with the supply depot five miles up the road.'

'Have you reported this?'

'Yes, of course, Sir, it's being investigated, but things are slowed down by this weather. To be honest it's like the bad times again, just when we thought we'd regained control-

'Alright Lieutenant, let's not jump to conclusions and head down into a defeatist rabbit hole, eh?' Dolman mildly chided.

'Sorry Sir,' the young officer replied ruefully.

'It could be anything, faulty comms, someone slacking, who knows?'

'Right, yes of course.' The young officer was clearly degrading due to the weather conditions, as well as the possible danger.

'Okay, stick with it. We'll be passing that area ourselves, so anything out of the ordinary and we'll report it back down the line.'

'Thank you, Sir,' the Lieutenant said, and saluted as Dolman and the others turned back to the vehicle.

Once inside and their vehicle resuming its journey, Dolman thought to be more candid with Lieutenant Courtney. 'We are skirting that area and supply depot eighteen, right?'

'Yeah, yeah that's right,' Courtney replied uncertainly as he shook the rainwater from his cap.

Dolman glanced at him with irritation, unimpressed at his vagueness.

Courtney continued defensively. 'Well to be honest Captain, that's a British base, and we don't often have cause to stop there.'

Dolman glanced at Martinez, who was frowning. 'Sorry Sir,' she said to Courtney, 'I know you're new, but I have to correct you. It's depot eighteen, we stop there every trip.'

Courtney was irked but tried to hide it. 'Oh, right, is that the concrete bunker set-up? Yeah, yeah, of course, thank you, Specialist Martinez. Darn it, why, all these names confuse me,' he said, then looked back at Dolman. 'Sorry Captain, it's been a long day.'

Dolman repressed his anger. 'Okay, Lieutenant. I'll let you catch up on your mission plan. So, it seems we're due to make a stop at depot eighteen. Now, despite what I said to that checkpoint commander, it's likely that the depot has indeed been compromised. It could still be hot.'

'Oh, oh, I see!' Courtney swallowed hard as he realised, and glanced at the others nervously. 'Well, um, maybe we want to give it a wide berth, eh Captain?'

'Much as I would like to do so, we're the nearest unit in the area.'

'Oh whoa! Whoa! This isn't a combat unit, Captain. Why, what if it's insurgents up there, maybe supported by Russki anti-tank? No. No way. I'm sorry, Captain, I will not countenance this. It's way beyond our remit to get involved.'

Dolman felt his patience wearing thin. 'If the depot has been compromised by insurgents, then it's likely to have been shoot-and-scoot. They won't hang around with the amount of firepower our side can bring to bear.'

'Hey, you said it yourself, or that Lieutenant out there did...this weather's causing chaos. Fast air, drones, Q-R-F, all delayed. I'm not risking my team up there and that's final. I have jurisdiction here.'

Dolman thought for a second. 'Fair enough, Lieutenant. But I request that you contact H-Q for advice forthwith. At the very least we need to ensure that they're aware of the situation.' Dolman looked down.

Courtney considered it for a second. 'Okay, good call. Um, Martinez, do as Captain Dolman asks, will you?'

Five minutes later, a reply came through. Courtney reddened with anger as the message contradicted his decision.

'...at the present, you are the nearest unit in area and are tasked to offer assistance as necessary....'

Without second bidding Martinez picked up her assault rifle and checked the magazine as Ned Plaskett eagerly climbed up into his cupola with a gleeful smirk on his face.

Courtney looked around him, dazed. He then glared for a second at Dolman. 'Damn it, with respect Captain, I would like it to go on record that this is not what I deem to be a good idea. It's putting my crew's lives at risk.'

'Point taken, Lieutenant, but to be honest your team doesn't seem all that unhappy at the prospect of doing a bit of real soldiering,' Dolman replied, in as magnanimous a tone as he could muster.

As the vehicle swayed as it rounded a corner, Courtney remained silent and glowered sullenly like a frustrated teenage boy.

23

It had started to rain again, and the wind was getting up. In the armoured vehicle, Fyodor, nick-named 'the Bear', had spent little time manning the gun position on top cover, and instead took a place sitting down with the others. On the seats, which ran along the sides of the vehicle, the Russians had gravitated to the back. Julie eventually deigned to sit closer to them, as it afforded a partial view through to the driving compartment, to try to offset her increasing feelings of travel sickness. She now wished she'd accepted Marcus' offer to sit in the front with Stan. When Fyodor gave up on top cover he sat down next to her, roughly brushing the rainwater from his uniform without any consideration for her, including from his short, dark curly hair, which he shook like a wet dog. He was large and muscular, with blunt features and what was probably a permanent five o'clock shadow. He looked to her like a convict.

The other side of her, by the entrance to the driving compartment, was Akam. Marcus sat opposite him, with a spare seat between him and Pavel. This was occupied by packs loaded on top of one another. The other two Russians sat by the rear door. Pyotr was leaner and fair, his hair trimmed to grade two or three. Next to him was Nickolai, 'the professor', the technical and communications specialist, who looked to Julie like an 'overfed skinny guy'; dark-haired and slightly chubby. Although he wasn't actually wearing glasses, she thought they wouldn't look out of place; whereas on the rough Fyodor they'd be completely incongruous. With some irritation, she decided that Fyodor was definitely from peasant stock, and quite uncouth.

The rutted, twisting country roads didn't make for a comfortable journey, and she began to feel more nauseous. She looked at the 'situational display unit' which gave a view from external cameras. It was placed at the rear left of the compartment, and whilst looking at it she inadvertently caught the eyes of several of the Russians. They seemed indifferent, tough, and professional. She quickly turned her head back to the driving compartment, to see a hedgerow moving from left to right, illuminated by headlights as they took another corner. This was through windscreens with wipers working hard to keep them cleared of driving rain.

'Hey? Hey girlie, you want to swap seats?'

She looked around. It was the Russian team leader, Pavel, who was addressing her.

'Pyotr will swap with you,' Pavel continued. 'You look out front, not get sick.' He grinned at her mockingly.

She looked at where his offer would place her. 'No, no thank you,' she said, and instantly regretted it, as the vehicle lurched around another corner and found yet another pot-hole.

'Don't be stupid!' he chided humorously. 'Pyotr swap with you. He trained paratrooper like us, it no matter to him, eh Pyotr?'

Pyotr looked at her with bored disdain as he placed his assault rifle onto its butt, ready to get up and move seats.

Another lurch of the vehicle in the other direction convinced her. She twisted the clip of her four-strap safety harness to release it, and got up, passing Pyotr awkwardly and falling on him as the vehicle started to climb a steep hill.

Soon she was in her new seat and strapped in by the time it had cleared the crest and begun its steep descent down the other side. The motion of this vehicle was rather like being at sea. A minute later the men passed a pack of travel pills back to her.

'They from your commander,' Pavel said. 'He said they act fast.'

She took one out of the foil and swallowed it dry. A few minutes later, with that and the better view, she was feeling a little less queasy. The uncouth bear Fyodor glanced at her with a dismissive, superior look. She felt challenged and irritated, but glad to be no longer sitting next to him and having to vie for space against his meaty arms, and smell his sweat. Their officer, Pavel, was far smaller and seemed to keep himself to himself. He seemed by nature more respectful of personal space.

In front, through a rain-washed windscreen, she saw more evidence of where they were, as white road signs in both English and Welsh were briefly illuminated. Then more of the incessant hedgerows and trees, interrupted by the occasional roadside stone dwelling or farm building. However, so far, there had been no Army checkpoints. So far, so good.

24

Dolman took control, and as the depot was under British jurisdiction he had insisted that they do it his way. He asked Lieutenant Courtney if he could borrow Corporal Gresham and Specialist Martinez as part of a dismounted team. He wanted to keep Ned Plaskett on top cover for fire support. Courtney was visibly peeved.

'You're asking me to risk half my team on this? Uh-uh. No.'

Used to democratic decision making in his teams, Dolman affected to understand the American Lieutenant's concerns. 'So, what's your plan, Lieutenant?' he asked mildly.

'We take the rigs in. Use fire support from this one'.

'I take it you've never seen the effect of anti-tank on an armoured vehicle when used in anger?'

'Er, no, I was too young to see action in Estonia, was still in the training depot…but – well – it makes no difference,' he spluttered. 'I mean, what if you're seen?'

'There's less likelihood of that with three people on foot, than three ruddy great lumbering A-F-V's turning up! I'll take point. I just want someone to cover my back.'

Courtney winced. Dolman's logic was unassailable. 'Well, alright then. But what if you need extraction?'

'I'm sure you'll do fine if it should come to it. We don't know the situation at the depot, but if it has been compromised and that Lieutenant knew about it, then it happened hours ago. I don't expect to encounter much resistance.'

'Okay. So how close do we get?'

Dolman got up and walked over to Martinez's console, and Courtney followed.

'Can you highlight the area around the depot?' Dolman asked her. She tapped in the coordinates, and a map appeared on the screen. She increased the magnification of the area.

'So,' Dolman pointed to the screen with a pencil, 'we'll approach up the hill to within five-hundred meters. We'll be driving up a tree-lined lane, and in this weather, it'd take an elephant to hear us. I want you to take up position here, by this farm gate. Plaskett's main armament will be firing indirect, on my mark. You won't pick up our P-R-R, so hear me on I-T-N smartphone.'

'Fine,' Courtney said simply. He seemed a bit bored and dejected, like a small boy being left out of a game of war.

Five minutes later, they'd taken up position, and sat in red light. After Dolman had briefed Gresham and Martinez, they checked their weapons and comms, and then put on their combat equipment.

Ned Plaskett had been watching, clearly a little envious of his colleagues having been chosen over him. He put his helmet on and a waterproof cape, and got ready to take up his position.

As he secured the straps on his combat gloves, Dolman looked at the two he'd selected. Both looked a little nervous, but this was the best he had. He rated Plaskett as a hot-head and Courtney as a physically and mentally clumsy liability. Gresham and Martinez were quietly professional and probably had reasonable drills and skills. However, Gresham seemed unable to stop yawning, and Martinez was inhaling deeply through her nostrils, making a good effort to stop herself from hyperventilating, whilst attempting to mask her fear with the moue of a more aggressive appearance.

'We'll be okay,' Dolman assured them, patting Gresham on the shoulder. 'I'll be taking point. I just want you to cover my back.'

'Sure, Captain,' Gresham replied, stifling another yawn. Martinez handed him a glucose sweet, which he gratefully accepted.

Very soon, they were just pulling chinstraps tight on helmets and ensuring ammo pouches were secure, ready for the off.

'Okay, make ready,' Dolman said.

'Lock and load,' Courtney interpreted.

Rifle bolts were pulled, chambering rounds and safety catches double-checked.

'Lights,' Dolman commanded, and Courtney temporarily switched the compartment lights off.

Dolman, sitting at the back, got up and opened the rear door. Instantly, rain assailed his face. He jumped down into rutted mud beside the road and moved forward, followed by Gresham and Martinez.

They walked in double file up the lane; Dolman in front, Gresham the other side, and Martinez at the rear, in line with Dolman. The lane was bordered by dry-stone walls, and they were almost bent double as they pushed forward up the incline, lashed by wind and rain.

Dolman spoke into his personal-role radio. 'Keep to a spacing of no more than two meters or we'll lose one another.'

The lane climbed halfway up the hill, and they reached the entrance to the depot. One of the gates was half off its mounting, the other swung open freely in the wind. The toughened windows of the guard post looked ominously dark and deserted. As they got closer there were clear signs of a fire-fight having taken place, with bullet-marked walls and doors. The door was half-open, being pushed by the wind against something. Dolman pushed hard on it, the resistance offered was that of a dead soldier's body. He used a red-filter flashlight and established these men had probably been killed by a grenade blast, before having been riddled by automatic fire for good measure.

Gresham followed him in whilst Martinez remained outside, down on one knee and scanning into the darkness through her rifle night-sight.

Dolman picked up a bullet case. 'Seven-point-six-two, A-K rounds, these men have been killed by Russian weapons,' he surmised.

'Do you think Russians did it?' Gresham asked.

'Maybe, maybe not,' Dolman replied. 'But it certainly means that their ordnance has reached this far south.'

Dolman stepped back out into the rain and with a hand signal indicated for them to continue on up the road, up a slight slope towards a domed concrete structure, half-illuminated by two security lights placed high up metal poles, which were being buffeted by the wind. Their white light picked up rain being pushed almost horizontally through their beams, their fittings whistling in the wind. The lanyard on a nearby flag pole clattered against it with a hollow, metallic sound.

They arrived at some steps which led down to a small bunker lined with metal guard rails. Covered by the other two, Dolman descended the steps to try the steel door, but it was locked.

He shook his head and ascended halfway up, and motioned to the other two to get down low. He took out his auto-enhanced night vision binoculars to look at the entrance to the complex.

'Several bodies, more signs of a forced entrance,' he said into his PRR to the other two. 'This needs to be passed back, it's a sign that the insurgency has taken to attacking well-manned outposts again, and also again has the strength to compromise them. I want to take a closer look, out.'

He opened up his Smartphone to communicate the situation to Courtney. 'This is Delta 33 Alpha. Definite signs of forced entry,' Dolman spoke quietly.

'Sitrep to be passed back to Hotel Golf Alpha zero-one, over.'

'Roger that Delta 33 Alpha, any signs of hostiles? Over,' Courtney's voice squawked.

'No, out.' Dolman replied, and climbed the steps to pass by Gresham and Martinez.

'Cover us,' he said to Martinez. 'With me,' he said to Corporal Gresham.

They moved cautiously towards the entrance. As they drew closer to another blockhouse, Dolman noticed three parked vehicles; two trucks and a four-by-four. They were being loaded up by paramilitaries with slung assault rifles on their backs, with a guard walking around, scanning out into the driving rain. Dolman and Gresham froze, and then Gresham followed Dolman in slowly dropping down onto one knee.

'We'll need to extract,' Dolman said quietly. 'I've seen three to four, and estimate there to be twice that number, given the size of the vehicles.'

One of the trucks suddenly started up and switched its headlights on. Dolman indicated to Gresham to move to behind the blockhouse beside them, and quickly followed, hoping that Martinez behind would have the sense to similarly find cover.

'Martinez, hostile vehicle approaching!' he just had time to say into his PRR.

The truck passed without stopping. Dolman moved to where he could see the insurgents again. He spoke into his Smartphone.

'This is Delta 33 Alpha. Insurgent vehicle leaving the compound. Do not engage unless necessary. Repeat, no NOT engage. What's your sitrep? Over.'

No reply. A minute later there was the sound of heavy automatic fire some distance away. Dolman glanced at the men loading the last truck, startled and looking towards the sound of the firing. A commander with a pistol rushed out and shouted at them to secure the back of the truck and leave immediately. He then ran to the four-by-four and got in.

Just as it started its engine, Dolman heard the rumble of another vehicle approaching from the lane behind. He guessed what was happening before he even looked back, and saw Courtney's approaching 8-wheeled AFV. The four-by-four at the compound started up and gunned its engine before screeching towards them down the road, it's only means of escape from the base and directly towards the oncoming personnel carrier. It was an ill-matched contest. The main armament on Courtney's vehicle opened up, and shells ripped through the windscreen of the approaching vehicle. One shell caught some ordnance inside and the rear exploded, erupting into a fireball before it collided with the front of Courtney's vehicle. The large AFV crushed and ran over what remained of it, with a bump.

When the AFV stopped, Dolman heard Plaskett issue a Southerners' whoop of joy as he opened up on the truck by the compound, the engine of which had been failing to start. The effect was just as dramatic, and the entire loading bay was engulfed in an explosion. All that was left was the burning chassis of the truck.

Plaskett seemed to be high on adrenaline, and continued firing into the depot loading bay, his aim slightly wild. The Fifty calibre rounds began to tear chunks out of the concrete of the building, exposing parts of the steel re-enforcement rods of the structure.

'Cut! Cut your fire, Plaskett, damn it!' Dolman shouted into the Smartphone.

Plaskett stopped and whooped again. 'Jeez! My, I ain't never seen such a thing as what ah just done there! Why, they didn't stand no chance. Reckon ah's due a Bronze Star at least!'

As Dolman looked up at him with annoyance, rounds ricocheted around Plaskett's cupola and off of his armour-plated gun shield.

'Oh my!' he shouted as he fell back down into the crew compartment.

'More like a Purple Heart, mate,' Dolman said, as he turned to locate the source of the fire. The familiar star-shaped burst from an American-made M-class assault rifle opened up from the entrance of the main building.

Dolman was surprised to find Lieutenant Courtney by his side.

'Hiya!' Courtney said. 'What d'ya reckon, I'll take the left flank, Gresham stays here to draw his fire and you take the right? And, when Plaskett finds his nuts again, he lays down fire support?'

Dolman couldn't disagree. 'Fine.'

'How many pax are we up against?' Courtney asked

'I reckon there're no more than two or three still in that building. Let's go.' He looked round to see Martinez join them, limping slightly.

'You okay?' Dolman asked.

'Yeah, Captain, just twisted my ankle jumping down those steps when the truck passed.'

'Okay, you stay here, cover us off,' he commanded. Martinez nodded in assent, clearly hurt, stressed, tired, cold; and now not as keen to play. She wiped rainwater out of her eyes.

'Gresham, with me,' Dolman said.

Martinez awkwardly lay down on the tarmac by the pavement, and aimed her rifle at the source of the fire, as the others moved forward.

Dolman and Gresham moved carefully along the front of the main building, which was a huge, solid, window-less concrete dome. They had lost sight of Courtney. In this area, the base consisted of several bunkers and block-houses, some close to others, and ones maybe containing explosive ordnance sited further away. He and Gresham moved towards the door. Dolman took out a grenade, removed the pin and lobbed it into the entrance. They ducked back down just before it exploded.

Inside one insurgent lay dead, and another was moaning in what appeared to be Russian. Dolman finished him off as Courtney and Gresham rushed past him and the bodies of British soldiers killed earlier.

The depot was little more than a large warehouse, a supply complex manned mainly by Logistics soldiers. Under the concrete dome was line upon line of high shelves containing all varieties of food, equipment, and spare parts to service the needs of the British military in Wales. Whilst bright lighting hung from high in the ceiling above, at floor level it seemed dim, the corridors formed by high shelves leaving some areas in near-darkness.

Without any bidding, Courtney disappeared off, down one aisle alone. Dolman looked at Gresham. 'One is just as good as another,' he said. They ran into the nearest aisle.

They slowed down and eventually stopped to listen. This was now a game of nerve, of hunter and hunted. Furthermore, they'd have to be careful to avoid a 'blue-on-blue', should they meet Courtney.

The shelves formed distinct and very straight corridors, intersected by others at junctions. The view down the aisles would have been clear if it wasn't for a small number of dark-green Army fork-lift trucks, left parked up. There were also stacks of boxes on pallets that had been lifted down from shelves. All of this made the warehouse a great place for ambushes.

Dolman rounded a corner, covered by Gresham, and saw an insurgent just three meters in front of him, looking down another aisle.

'Drop your weapon!' Dolman ordered.

The man turned, and as he lifted his weapon to fire Dolman dropped him with a burst of automatic fire.

In an aisle to their left, there was another burst of automatic fire, and another insurgent dropped, this time from a height. He had climbed up one of the shelves and would almost certainly have shot Gresham, standing behind Dolman. Courtney walked over his body. 'Hmm, nailed him just in time I think.'

Gresham was visibly shaken. 'Huh! Thanks, Sir. He'd have had me for sure.'

'Don't mention it,' Courtney said with disinterest.

'Okay,' Dolman said, 'enough cat-and-mouse. I suggest we can't clear this entire compound by ourselves, and nor should we even try, it'll need a reaction force up here. Let's get the sitrep in and get on our way.'

'Sure, agreed,' Courtney said. 'I've had enough excitement for one night.'

'Our E-T-A has gone to rats, though,' Dolman stated with irritation. 'We won't make Trant's base until the late evening now.'

'C'est la vie,' Courtney said.

*

They got back to the AFV to find a very relieved Martinez, shivering, her uniform now soaked through by the incessant rain.

'Come on, we're outta here,' Courtney told her. 'Get your stuff in the back.'

Gresham helped her up and she put her arm around his shoulder as she limped back to the armoured vehicle.

Dolman looked at Courtney. 'That was pretty good shooting back there, Lieutenant.'

'Aw, shucks, cheers Cap'n,' Courtney said with an irritatingly facetious tone of self-effacement.

25

As they neared the vicinity of the base, Pavel instructed them to stop and let his team out, along with Akam.

'We have travelled far enough as British soldiers, now we fight again as Russians,' he told them, as he removed his British Army camouflage jacket. The others did the same, pulling dark, non-descript military-style clothing out of their packs. After swapping jackets, they blackened their faces with camouflage cream and prepared their weapons.

When they were ready, Pavel looked at his fellow travellers. 'Farewell, for now, my friends. Let's hope our mission is successful. We will rendezvous with you when you have your quarry. And remember, always be prepared to use plan-B.'

Jonathan stepped through from the driving compartment to watch them go, as Julie hunched her shoulders and carefully made her way through the crowd towards him from the back seat.

Pavel surveyed Jonathan with a mocking glare. 'One war over, another goes on. We are friends now, eh? Well, some of us, at least.'

Jonathan winced. 'I hope so.'

'There may be investigations one day, Professor. My people do not forget.'

Jonathan swallowed. Holding onto him, Julie looked up at him perplexed. 'What's he talking about?'

Pavel continued. 'My country, it suffer as much as this one did. You insist it flu epidemic. We know better. Bio-weapon made to look like flu. Genius. And we thought we were masters of, what you say, fake news, and insurrection. In Estonia, you not know who your enemies were. So you release killer bug and call it flu.'

'Jonathan?' Julie asked.

Jonathan looked ill.

'But first, you test it on Russian prisoners.'

'Jonathan, is this true?' Julie asked with rising agitation, letting go of him and sitting down.

Jonathan looked at her, then Pavel. 'Yes, and no. Yes, I led the teams in the development of this. We all develop these things, even your side, Pavel.'

'And you used one in a war,' Pavel stated, accusingly. 'Only, it went wrong.'

'Yes, it went wrong,' Jonathan admitted.

'You have a lot of death on your hands, Professor.'

'I didn't give the order to release it.'

'Okay, but you test it on Russian prisoners.'

'I was testing a vaccine, on men from the field who were already infected.'

Pavel went silent.

Marcus looked up at Jonathan with surprise. 'So you weren't actually testing and distributing it?'

'I was flown out as part of a medical team to investigate cases of the outbreak. Everything was done on a need-to-know basis, and even I wasn't aware of the release of the virus, although I suspected from the symptoms being exhibited. It was all too coincidental. Back in Britain, I had also suspected something was up. Just before I left for Estonia, part of my research facility had been made temporarily off-limits. I heard from a security man on the main gate that a team under armed guard had entered my area. They'd left in a convoy of armoured vehicles with police outriders. I assure you, that virus was released well before I arrived in theatre.'

They all looked at him, even some of the Russians who barely understood any English. Julie remained seated by Marcus, in a state of numb shock.

Pavel broke the silence. 'Our records – um – *your* records, say that only two of our men survived your tests.'

'Yes, they were older men and were liable to survive anyway. I couldn't save the others. I didn't in fact save anyone, the vaccine was useless.'

'Vaccine? Not real virus?'

'No, not the real virus!' Jonathan said with wearied exasperation. 'They knew that worked well enough already. Well, they knew it killed people. They thought it only killed certain *types* of people.'

'They? You! You, Professor. *You* knew. But you were wrong. It killed *anyone*.'

'Yes, I was wrong,' Jonathan replied. 'But, don't you see? I'm not a murderer! I helped create it, yes. But I certainly didn't deploy it.' He looked at them. 'Don't you believe me? Julie? I'm not a mass murderer!'

She looked up at him with disgust. 'I'd known that you'd worked there, but I didn't know you worked on *that*. You could have done anything, gone back to University to lecture; anything.'

'I had no choice, I was the leading man in my field; it was where my research had led me. And, I saw the risks of being defenceless. I saw the Baltic War coming, but never thought we'd actually use that vile thing unilaterally.'

She looked down, desolate.

'I don't know,' Marcus said, 'but this explains a lot. To be honest, after finding you at Morton Down and getting the intelligence that we did, we'd all rather thought the worst of you. All I can say in your defence is that you don't come across as the war criminal type, though I suppose they do talk about the banality of evil.'

Pavel made to open the door. 'It is now like, as you say, the fog of war. I will say I am honest and now don't know what is truth. You may not be criminal, but you definitely involved. Be careful, my friend. If you innocent, get yourself evidence, and good lawyer!'

At that he jumped out into the rain and darkness, followed by the other three men in his team. Before disembarking, chubby Nickolai caught Julie's eye and gave her a half-smile. She had a sudden irrational urge to tell him to be careful.

26

Corporal Gresham had taken over driving from Mike Kowalski, and Ned had finally given an exhausted Gabriela Martinez a break from the consoles. She slept, covered by a blanket, beside a dozing Paul Dolman and a snoring Will Courtney.

As they neared the base Ned Plaskett threw an unopened energy bar at Gabriela Martinez to wake her up. After the combat, she had been close to hypothermia in her damp uniform. Her camouflage jacket presently hung on a hook over a heater. The energy bar hadn't done the trick and was followed by a pack of biscuits hitting her cheek.

'Uh?' she awoke wearily. 'Say, what time is it?'

'It's nearly eight,' he said. 'You gonna wake the brass, or shall I?'

Martinez kicked on her Lieutenant's boot and leaned over to give Dolman a gentle nudge. He lifted the peak of his soft cap from his eyes and squinted in the light, as Courtney convulsed back into consciousness.

'Nearly there?' Dolman asked.

'Yes Sir,' she replied and yawned.

'Feel better?' he asked.

'Somewhat,' she replied tersely. She was privately disappointed at how much her first real combat experience had taken out of her.

'It gets easier, the more you do it. You did well tonight,' he reassured her.

'Yeah, well, it wasn't exactly Special Forces stuff, was it?'

'That's not your job, but you were getting there, your drills and skills were good, as I thought they would be. When your tour here is over you'll have a fine story to tell your grandkids.'

She smiled. 'Yeah, I guess it's not every day I have to dodge exploding jeeps!'

'Nor suppress effective enemy fire,' he added.

'It were sure a bit of a buzz, eh,' Ned added enthusiastically.

Courtney woke up and listened with an affected, humorous frown. 'Well, I do declare Captain, you went and turned my unit into your very own black ops team. In and out with no casualties, save for Gabriela's ankle.'

Dolman smiled.

27

After the deserted roads, hills, and remote farms, the insurgent team found themselves travelling through the valleys of South Wales. Most of the roads stuck to the valley floors, and they passed through town after town, all of which were very quiet. They encountered five Army checkpoints along the way, and casually showed their passes to various bored guards, none of whom wanted to spend too long standing out in the wind and rain, checking up on yet another passing military vehicle. As they passed the sixth, their confidence was growing.

'I don't know why we never tried pulling this one before,' Marcus said with a grin on his face, kneeling behind Jonathan and Stan in the driving compartment.

'Probably because travelling in an Army vehicle was a risky venture until recently. That is, for the Army!' Jonathan stated. 'So, what's the plan when we arrive?'

Marcus glanced back at him. 'Working from right to left, our main objective is to make contact with Trant.'

'Can we get him out, in this?'

Marcus shook his head. 'Almost definitely not. We'll need a good story just to extract *ourselves*.'

'So, what's the point of it all?' Stan asked.

Marcus answered. 'We're trying to turn him. If successful, he could come of his own accord, and be very useful for our side.'

Jonathan continued to explain to Stan. 'It's about trying to weaken the legitimacy of the regime, in the eyes of the Americans. With the U-S election coming up very soon, this could be critical if a Democrat gets into the Whitehouse. They won't want to be seen to be propping-up another Right wing dictatorship. We could easily see an American withdrawal within the first two years of the next administration.'

'Assuming it *is* the Democrats who get in,' Marcus added.

'True,' Jonathan admitted, 'but they presently hold Congress, and they're limiting the ability of the President to increase the size of their forces here. We're unlikely to see any more major troop surges. If anything, they want to stabilize things and bug-out as fast as possible. Should we manage to discredit our present government and win a few victories, it'll be *us* they'll be talking to, not the regime.'

'Nicely put, Jonathan,' Marcus said.

'I think I get it,' Stan said. 'So this guy Trant, he's important?'

'He's a Lieutenant-Colonel,' Marcus said. 'Maybe not that high a rank, but he's also decorated, and respectable. Intelligence that we have on him indicates that he's disenchanted with the policies of the regime, as well as the excesses of some of the politicians.'

'Is that from the Russians, again?' Jonathan asked with a grin.

Marcus just smiled in reply. 'Anyhow, we're approaching the base soon. It's been a long journey, but I want everybody to switch-on. Once we're on the inside I want you to start acting and thinking like soldiers. We'll probably get split up, according to our ranks. Jonathan, you're to make contact with the Colonel at the earliest opportunity. Our rendezvous time to leave is eighteen-hundred hours tomorrow, objective achieved or not. We're all on mobiles, so keep alert to any text messages.'

From the last town they'd driven through, they began to climb the hill towards Trant's base. Within a few minutes, they were up on high, mainly open hills; with the lights of distant towns and villages in the distance below. They passed dark enclosures of coniferous trees.

'This is it, we're near the Afan Forest,' Marcus stated. Even in the dark, they could make out tall wind turbines, and the tops of pine trees.

'Okay, yes,' Marcus said, 'just here, on the left, that's the road to the base.'

Stan turned the wheel just in time, and the heavy vehicle lurched onto a side road. This was the riskiest part; at least the part of the operation that was predictably risky. As they approached the main gates they were instructed to stop by a soldier with his rifle at the ready. Another guard with a rifle approached.

'What's the matter with you, don't you know to cut your main lights?'

'Aw, sorry mate, forgot,' Stan replied.

'S-O-P, another second and we could have opened fire.'

'Yeah, alright mate, it's been a long night,' Stan said with just enough convincing irritation.

'Yes, and not just for you,' the guard retorted irascibly. He looked at Stan's pass. 'Okay, park up over there and come into the office to get your vehicle pass.'

Jonathan thought fast as they parked. 'They look to be on some sort of alert,' he whispered to Stan and Marcus.

'You reckon it's about us?' Marcus asked.

'No. I think something else is going on' Jonathan replied. 'This could work to our advantage.'

They all got out and entered the guard office. Jonathan was saluted by the soldier manning the desk. 'Sir!' he said.

'Okay, stand easy,' Jonathan instructed commandingly as he returned the salute.

'May I see your passes please?' the soldier on the desk asked respectfully.

'Of course,' Jonathan replied. They all produced their identification. The guard typed their names into a log and then checked his system.

'May I ask the purpose of your visit, Sir?' he asked.

'I'm here to see Lieutenant-Colonel Trant,' Jonathan stated honestly.

'Okay, so you're not here for tomorrow then, Sir?'

'Sorry?'

'No, my mistake, Sir,' the guard corrected himself. 'There's a lot going on tonight. So, how long do you expect to be here?'

As little time as possible, Jonathan thought. 'Oh, less than twenty-four hours,' he replied.

Jonathan noticed a wooden sign in place, indicating that the security status of the complex was up to 'Bikini Amber'. He glanced at the soldier on the desk as he scrutinized his screen.

'So what's the situation out there, Corporal?' he asked in an attempt to distract the man.

'We had a supply depot compromised a few hours ago, Sir. Looks like things are ramping up again.'

'Lord, I hope not,' Jonathan replied. 'With the Americans here, the insurgents should surely be tracked down and destroyed?'

'Yeah, you'd think so wouldn't you? But they seem to be using this bad weather to their advantage.'

'Yes, it does rather seem as if our techy stuff isn't always to be relied upon,' Jonathan stated cheekily.

'Apparently not,' the soldier replied. 'Right, there you go Sir, all good. Corporal?' he addressed Stan. 'There's your vehicle pass,' he handed him the slip of coloured paper. 'Make your way through to the car park by building five. One of my guys will ride with you and escort you to your respective quarters.'

As Marcus had predicted, they'd all be split up by rank and trade. As they made their way back to their armoured vehicle with a guard carrying a rifle, Jonathan glanced at Marcus, who was silently pursing his lips as if to say 'phew!'

Jonathan glanced over at Julie. She had ignored him for over an hour now. He was now certain that one night apart wasn't going to worry her in the slightest; even in the middle of the hornets' nest!

Back in their vehicle, the guard took his place upfront with Stan, whilst the others sat in the passenger compartment behind. As Stan started the vehicle Jonathan took out his notebook, scribbled something, tore the page out and handed it to Marcus. Marcus in turn showed it to Julie.

It read: *'Something's definitely going on tomorrow. It could complicate things, or it could work to our advantage. Be ready.'*

Marcus nodded at Jonathan, as he scrunched the paper up and put it in his mouth to chew.

In the front, Stan made small talk with the guard.

'A lot going on, I heard?' Stan asked casually.

'Yeah, been freaking mental tonight, mate! Bloody typical, the night before a guard-of-honour parade,' the soldier replied in disgust.

'Yeah, that's a bummer. What's it about, mate?' Stan asked.

'Don't know, all we was told was to look all spick-and-span and to be on our best behaviour. Reckon it's some bigwig turning up from the head-shed.'

'How's that?' Stan asked.

'Dunno,' the soldier replied, 'stands to reason though. Tell you what, we thought you lot was more of them black ops, till that Prof of yours walked in!'

Stan was quiet for a second but picked up on the likely coincidence. 'Oh yeah, right,' he chuckled, and said under his breath, 'Sir is a bit of geek alright.'

'But you want brains at the top, right?' the guard replied. 'Tell you what, though, you should have seen some of the ally kit the black ops guys was carrying. I could do with some of that. Reckon I might get fit and have a crack at selection and all. Anyway, yeah, just turn left here, mate, pull into any marked bay.'

Once Stan had parked up and they'd dismounted, the guard walked with them to the reception area.

He addressed Jonathan. 'There's an officers mess, Sir, and an all-ranks bar. But I'll expect you want to be shown to your accommodation first?'

Jonathan looked at Marcus, then back at the guard. 'Yes, thank you.'

'The bar and common rest area is part of the main M-T hangar, should you need to give any orders before bedtime?'

'Yes, whereabouts?' Jonathan asked.

'That entrance on the right of the roller doors.'

'Thank you.'

Another man approached from behind them. 'Good evening,' he said in a voice tinged with officiousness.

They turned to see a Sergeant with a light moustache and greying hair, neat as a pin in a crisp camouflage uniform and wearing a khaki beret. The sergeant came briefly to attention and gave a textbook salute to Jonathan and Marcus. Marcus returned it with alacrity, whilst Jonathan's salute was somewhat more tardy and casual.

'Sarn't,' Jonathan said to him by way of a greeting.

'Sir! May I ask your business here?'

'Yes, we're here to see Colonel Trant.'

'Fine, Sir. Lieutenant-Colonel Trant has retired for the night.'

'Of course, no matter, we didn't expect to see him straight away. Do you know when he might be available tomorrow?'

'Well, he'll no doubt be out at seven for his early morning constitutional,' he chortled. 'After that, goodness knows, his published schedule is all at sea, what with this surprise visit tomorrow and all. But I expect you'd know all about that, Sir?'

'Yes of course,' Jonathan lied. 'Anyway, we're rather tired after a long journey, would you mind showing us to our quarters.'

'Yes, of course, Sir, follow me.' The Sergeant turned to the guard and continued unnecessarily, indicating Stan and Julie. 'You, make sure they're properly billeted.'

'Yes Sergeant,' the guard replied with a trace of irony.

The guard directed Julie and Stan towards their respective blocks, whilst the Sergeant escorted Jonathan and Marcus to the officers' quarters. These were two-storey blocks not far from those for other ranks. An armed guard stood on the door. Once inside they were greeted at reception by a young female soldier and given room key-cards.

'Thank you, Sergeant,' Jonathan said. The Sergeant saluted and left.

Up in his room, Jonathan deposited his kit onto his bed. To him, Army accommodation always looked and smelled the same. He pulled the cord on the slightly anachronistic curtains. His room seemed like any good hotel room, but with highly polished wood furnishings. It was quiet, save for the low hum of air conditioning, and it felt overly warm.

He heard a knock on his door was joined by Marcus.

'What now, Sir?' Marcus asked, aware that they might be being observed or listened to.

'Hmm, once I've had a team debrief, I think I'll go for a run. Care to join me?' Jonathan sounded to himself like someone playing a dashing British pilot from an old black and white World War Two movie.

'Yes, fine,' Marcus replied with an amused frown, 'old man!'

28

Corporal Gresham came through on Ned's speaker. *'Approaching the main gate now.'*

They slowed down and then came to a stop, waved down by two guards in waterproof jackets.

Inside the vehicle they watched Ned's screens as they found a marked bay by the gatehouse, illuminated, where the vehicle waited whilst soldiers checked it over.

Once they'd all signed in at the main guard-house, they carried on through to the main compound.

Unknowingly the convoy drove past the insurgent vehicle and reached a large building, and a high steel roller door opened before them. A soldier waved them through.

'Yeah, all good,' the soldier said. 'Carry on in.'

Once all three vehicles were inside the hangar and parked up, Ned closed his consoles down as Martinez began to put her combat jacket on. It was still damp. 'Ee-yeu!' she exclaimed. She then grabbed her equipment, opened the rear doors, and jumped out, followed by Dolman, Courtney, and Ned Plaskett.

Corporal Gresham and Mike Kowalski were already out from the driving compartment and ambling around on the shiny green-painted floor of this motor-transport pool area. The size of this warehouse dwarfed the previous one, made even larger by the absence of as much racking, and the yellow-white glow of the ceiling lights was more efficient at ground level.

'Well, we're here,' Lieutenant Courtney said to Dolman, pointlessly.

'We're here,' Dolman replied flatly, as he watched a soldier approach. It was a Sergeant, short, squat, and greying, with a light-brown moustache.

'My, you lot are later than normal,' he stated. 'And with only three vehicles, did you encounter trouble?'

'Yeah,' Courtney replied, 'breakdown, but way back at Fairfield. Also, you might have heard on the net, one of your bases down the way was compromised.'

'Tell me about it,' the Sergeant said, 'we've been stood-to all evening, got patrols out and all. Nothing like this has happened for a few years, not since you boys arrived on the scene. Anyway,' he looked at Martinez, 'you lot look in need of a hot shower, scoff and a bed.'

'Yeah, that sounds good, Sergeant,' Courtney replied.

'Stand-to at four, followed by roll-call!' the Sergeant joked.

'Sure hope you're kidding?' Courtney smiled. 'Say, where can I get a cola around here? I'm hellishly thirsty.'

'Yes, well you guys supply them, thought you'd have had some in the back! Anyway, see that door over there? That goes over to our lounge area, bar, and canteen. There's a vending machine just in the corridor outside.'

'Hmm, you guys got any Brit coins? I'm out.' Courtney said, turning to the others in his team.

Dolman reached into his jacket pocket for his wallet, whilst the others headed towards shower blocks and rest areas.

'There you go, Lieutenant.'

'Thanks, old man,' Courtney, still the joker, replied in mock-British accent before he walked off.

Dolman turned to the Sergeant. 'Sergeant, I'm Captain Paul Dolman, I'm here to see Colonel Trant.'

The Sergeant hadn't initially recognised Dolman as a British officer in his American combat jacket, but then came to attention and saluted once he did. 'Sir! The Colonel is just getting some rest now. He's not rested since we heard about depot eighteen. No doubt he'll be up at seven for his early morning constitutional.'

'Ha! No changes there,' Dolman replied.

'You're acquainted then, Sir?'

'I served with him in Estonia.'

'Oh, right. Well, as I said, he'll be ready to see you by about O-nine-hundred hours I should think, Sir.'

'Fine. Were you aware of any update on depot eighteen?'

'Q-R-F turned up, found the place in a bit of a mess, no survivors. Like the bad old days.'

'Yes,' Dolman replied. 'Well, we can't let them get ahead again.'

'Don't you worry, Sir, the Colonel will be all over them. He'll have more patrols out first thing.'

'I know he will.'

The Sergeant glanced to his left. 'Oh, stand by your beds, looks like the duty officer is coming, young Mister Enderby. Also Major Fuller, our Intelligence Officer.'

Dolman watched as the two officers walked over, one a short young Lieutenant, good looking with thick dark hair beneath his beret, and with him a taller officer with grey hair, possibly grown to as long as regulations might allow, and whose face somehow resembled that of an elderly simian.

The Sergeant saluted crisply and the two officers returned it. Major Fuller surveyed Dolman with suspicion. The Sergeant introduced him. 'Major Fuller, Sir! This is Captain Dolman, came in with the American re-supply convoy.'

'Yes, thank you, Sergeant. I already know who he is,' Fuller stated, then turned to Dolman. 'Well, Captain, this is a surprise. I've read about some of your recent exploits up north. What gives us the honour of your presence?'

'If you don't mind my saying Sir, it's a classified matter, for the Colonel's attention only.'

'Oh really Captain, I'm the I-O on this base. I should be briefed on any matter.'

The Sergeant looked uncomfortable. 'Um, I think I should be getting along now, Sir, I have things to attend to.'

'Yes of course Sergeant,' Fuller returned the Sergeant's salute. 'Um, Dan?' he said to the Second Lieutenant. 'I think you can clock off now, don't you?'

'Oh, yes, of course, Sir, thank you,' the Lieutenant took the hint and headed to the rest area. With very dark eyelashes lining his large blue eyes, he had somehow reminded Dolman of some cute furry toy from an advert. Dolman shook the image, concluding that he was probably tireder than he'd thought.

After he watched the Second Lieutenant leave, Fuller turned to Dolman and shook his head, 'Mister Enderby, keen as mustard, but… Anyway, okay, Captain. It'd be quite out of order for me to oblige you to disclose the purpose of your visit here. I know that you served with Martin, but I'm guessing this is more than a social call to talk about old times. Is it anything to do with tomorrow?'

Dolman, who by now stood with his arms crossed, frowned. 'Sorry, come again, Sir?'

'Ah, right. Well, suffice it to say, you may see a few of your black ops buddies around this place.'

'Something big going on?'

'Big, and damned inconvenient. Especially after a night like tonight.'

Dolman looked intrigued.

Fuller grinned. 'Captain, I thought I was the one doing the interrogating! When you get tired of fieldwork, do put in an application to intelligence and ask to work in this battalion, you'll go far!'

Dolman smiled. Perhaps Fuller wasn't as much of a 'cock' as he'd initially seemed to be.

'Anyway,' Fuller continued, 'you'll see what's going on tomorrow. If you haven't got a fresh uniform then I'd just keep out of the way, that's all,' Fuller tapped the side of his nose meaningfully, and walked off.

Dolman returned to the armoured vehicle to pick up the rest of his kit and then headed towards the bar.

29

In the bar, Jonathan and Marcus met up with the others. They sat around a small table with drinks and a bowl of salty bar snacks. They were not alone, for the place appeared to be the social hub of the base, for those who were not on duty. Like many other bases, it was an all-ranks bar. Since the thinning out of the British Army there simply weren't enough left for separate Messes, except for senior officers.

'How's your accommodation?' Jonathan asked. He glanced at them all but lingered on his wife. She looked down at her drink and ignored him.

'Good,' Stan replied positively.

'Well, good,' Jonathan said. 'Now, I really want to be away from here by eighteen-hundred hours tomorrow, maybe sooner. Does anyone have anything new to add?' he looked at them meaningfully.

'Nothing much,' Stan said, 'but, will the parade affect our timings?'

Jonathan affected to know all about it but winced. 'No, I should think not.'

'Only,' Stan replied, 'we've been roped in to help out. I've been asked by a Sergeant Major if I could be a duty N-C-O, standing in for some guy out on patrol right now.'

'Alright, I'll see what I can do to get you out of it,' Jonathan stated. 'Any more information on what it's all about?'

'Someone's visiting, but no one seems to know who,' Stan replied.

Jonathan watched nine rough, mostly bearded fellows walk in. They wore civilian clothing and looked alert and confident. He noticed that other soldiers were also aware of them but pretended that they weren't. The newcomers went to the bar, and the barman ignored any other patrons who had been waiting. No one complained.

Marcus coughed; he had seen them too and made sure Jonathan was aware. Jonathan also noticed a man with a grade two haircut in an American uniform jacket and black cargo pants walk up to the bar to ask for a refill. As he waited, a young officer with thick dark hair struck up a conversation with him.

'Well, I'm for an early night,' Jonathan stated, as he replaced his beret. 'It'll be a long day tomorrow, so I suggest you all get some rest.'

'Yes good idea,' agreed Marcus. They got up as one and made to leave.

On the way out, Jonathan saw and recognised Major Fuller, as he walked by. Fuller glanced at him without recognition at first but then appeared to give a confused frown, pausing half a second before shaking his head. He continued to the bar.

Once outside the team sucked in the cool night air with a palpable sense of relief.

'God, it was close in there!' Marcus stated ambiguously.

'Yes, just a bit,' Jonathan replied.

Waiting until they were clearer of the building, Marcus spoke more openly. 'That officer definitely clocked you, Jonathan. Do you know who he was?'

'Um, yeah,' Jonathan admitted. 'A Captain –now obviously Major– called Fuller. He's Trant's Intelligence officer.'

'Oh Jeez,' Marcus replied. 'If he gets his head together then we're toast.'

'He was headed to the bar,' Jonathan replied. 'Let's hope he ties one on and has a thick head tomorrow.'

'Yeah, and another thing,' Stan said. 'Did you see those pirates who walked into the bar? Pound to a penny they were black ops.'

'No shit,' Jonathan replied. 'But we know why they're here.'

'Absolutely,' Marcus said. 'And that funny looking Yank who was there, he looked familiar, but I just can't place him.'

'Okay, well, once you do…' Jonathan replied.

'Yeah,' Marcus replied. He looked at the others. 'Okay, you lot, just get back to your quarters, try not to get involved in too much more small talk, and get your heads down.'

'Sure Marcus, goodnight,' Stan said.

'Goodnight darling,' Jonathan said to his wife.

However, shivering and with arms crossed, Julie just ignored him, turned without a word and walked off across the parade ground to her block.

'Don't let the bed-bugs bite!' Stan called after her cheekily, but she didn't reply to him either.

30

The black-ops team congregated as one in the same corner of the bar, sitting on low chairs or bar stools. They stood out in their civilian clothing, and most of it was quite expensive and stylish. Many of them sported beards.

One exception was their team leader, now sitting opposite Dolman. His name was Captain Len Matlock. He was so 'old school' that his idea of style was a dark sports jacket and slightly flared grey trousers. It almost looked like casual office wear from the 1970s. His open-necked, white shirt offset his puffy and slightly shiny, tanned-leather face; this beneath a slightly receded helmet of dyed-black hair. His was a face which had seen one too many a warmer clime. With dark eyes but negligible eyebrows, he looked a tad startling.

Initially, Dolman had tried to ignore the group, but Matlock was ex-Airborne and had certainly remembered him. It would have been churlish to decline his offer to join them. However, now he was sat opposite him in facing easy chairs across a low table, he soon regretted it. Matlock was a short man, and as Dolman soon remembered, given to cyclic mood swings that went from outgoing and sociable one minute to personally vindictive the next. He had the ability to simultaneously bind a group with a certain animal magnetism and to exclude anyone he regarded as being errant in some way or other.

Second Lieutenant Enderby, with whom Dolman had previously been talking, placed his pint on the low table and sat down beside him. Enderby was clearly a bit too curious about these shady black ops men, perhaps wanting to bask in a bit of reflected glory. Matlock glared at the Lieutenant with sullen disapproval and flicked his head to indicate to him to leave. The young officer suddenly looked uncomfortable and embarrassed, and he glanced at Dolman with his big eyes. Dolman ignored him; he wasn't interested in standing up for a naïve young twit just now, and the Lieutenant got the message. He reddened, then picked up his drink and left without a word.

Matlock turned his attention back to Dolman. 'Paul Dolman, eh? You know, your name just keeps on cropping up, on the circuit. You're way too famous, or shall I say, infamous, now,' he scoffed.

'Occupational hazard,' Dolman retorted. 'We can't all stay in the shadows.'

'Oh, some of us can. But then, you always had a talent for making the headlines.'

Dolman sipped his beer. 'So, how is the assassination business going these days,' he asked. 'Closed down any cells yet, have you? Or have you just been taking out more intellectuals and environmental campaigners?'

Matlock's dark eyes flashed almost imperceivably, and then became more hooded, yet he hadn't been able to hide the look of disdain on his face. Several of his team sitting nearby had glanced back at the two of them, alert and aggressive. Matlock raised a small hand from the arm of his chair then lowered it, as if to get attack dogs to stand down.

Dolman realised that he had crossed a line in terms of security, and 'face'. These men prided themselves on being the most elite of elite soldiers, with a legend afforded to latter-day fighter pilots. Being labelled as little more than sneaky assassins of defenceless innocents who happened to hold different views didn't sit well with the image they'd liked to project.

Matlock regained his poise. 'Ah, Paul, you know there's such a thing as keeping that old cake-hole of yours shut. You'd never have made this outfit and you know it. You never had the right psychological profile. I respect what you've done, of course. But you're still way too green-Army.'

'Whatever, Len,' Dolman said, now bored of the one-upmanship at the first mention of psychological profiling. This group was too self-consciously perfect, with their spotless style-outfits and low-voiced, affected machismo. They'd strayed from being just soldiers or just men, into becoming demigods. By comparison, Dolman's unit was a 'broad church'; all he asked was that they were switched-on and effective in combat. He had little interest in them otherwise.

'So, anyway, what brings you to these parts, Paul?' Matlock asked, 'and without your little Sancho Panza driver? Funny, the hero of the populist Right, reduced to having illegals as sidekicks.' He sniggered.

Paul ignored Matlock's jibe. 'Ah, now, there is this little thing called opsec,' Dolman stated.

Again, Matlock's face didn't hide his peevishness.

'Well, if I were you, I'd go back to your boys, they're good at tilting at windmills, and if there's no one else to fight they'll start on themselves!' Matlock said spitefully. 'There's a group of them around here, holed up in block three. It's like a bloody monkey pen!' When he talked his thin lips curled and revealed an ugly yellowed row of lower front teeth, highlighted by black plaque at their edges.

'Come again?' Dolman asked.

'Airborne. Airbone assault troops. What the Yanks call Dopes on a Rope. I like that,' he chuckled, and repeated it, looking at the others. 'Dopes on a Rope!' His team chuckled dutifully.

'It's where most of us started out, Len,' Dolman reminded him.

'Indeed,' Matlock admitted, 'but if we're any good, well, we move on. Onwards, and upwards. Away from all the bullshit.'

'From what I see, the bullshit never goes away,' Dolman retorted. 'And I can see you believe all of yours.'

Matlock's superior smile became a sneer, and he leaned closer. 'Be careful, Paul. No one's loyalty can be taken for granted these days, however good they think they may be, or what they've given. One hint of doubt in the cause, and we're all over them like a tramp on chips. Forget their rank, service, medals; that all counts for shit. Our job is to protect the state, the order of things. We've already seen what happens when it all goes to rat-shit, haven't we?'

'Really? Taking out your own side now?' Dolman asked, truly amazed at what had just been admitted. 'What heroics that sounds like!'

Matlock sat back, unimpressed by Dolman's cynical retort. 'Grow up, Paul. It's not all cowboys and Indians. Hybrid warfare involves war on *every* aspect of the enemy. Their food, their homes, their loved ones, and whoever it is who decides to shelter them. And then, in their heads, their morale, their opinions, their self-esteem, and their hope…which hopefully they'll lose, making them give up, then curl up and die. Or kill themselves. Result!' He raised an open hand and smiled gleefully.

Dolman sneered. 'Don't you talk to me about hybrid warfare, you piece of shit. Good men are getting killed out there because minds have been poisoned, by one side or another. The green Army is taking the brunt of it, whilst you glory boys are dipping in and out, choosing your battles, with more resources supporting you than most squaddies will ever see in ten years of combat.'

'Ah, standing up for good old Tommy Atkins! Commendable, I must say. Well done! Those thick clods and their dull, unimaginative dolts of officers; they couldn't even hold the line against civvies, let alone the Russkis in Estonia, could they?'

Dolman got up. 'You and your type make me sick,' he said.

'That's right, Paul, flounce off, throw teddy out of the pram!' Matlock taunted.

In one move Dolman grabbed Matlock by the neck, hoisted him up, and slammed him against the wall, holding his fist back ready to punch him. Almost immediately he felt an arm around his neck and free arm and he was dragged down to the floor as Matlock dropped to the ground. Someone landed Dolman a sharp kick to his kidneys.

'No!' Matlock shouted hoarsely through gasps and chokes as he touched his throat. 'That's enough. Leave him.'

Dolman got up, rubbing his back and glaring at the gang of special forces operatives around him. Blood from a cut lip trailed down his chin.

Matlock surveyed him with contempt. 'Go on, piss off, Paul, if you know what's good for you. And you'd better start looking over your shoulder.'

Dolman walked out, amidst a sea of shocked and incredulous looks from the regular soldiers in the bar, including a perturbed Lieutenant Enderby. A minute later two Provost soldiers walked in but were waved away by Matlock.

31

Jonathan and Marcus jogged around the perimeter of the camp. They had purloined some sports gear hanging in a drying area in the changing rooms. Now and again they periodically passed a couple of other runners at different points; a tall, middle-aged and equine-looking officer, and later in the cycle a shorter but athletic young woman in tight running gear, with long blond hair tied back in a pony-tail.

The wind had blown away the rain-clouds, and had itself died down to just a light breeze, which now and then picked up and whistled through the fencing topped with razor wire. Being atop one of the highest hills in the area afforded the runners a three hundred-and-sixty degree view as they ran around the perimeter. There were lots of deep valleys hiding entire towns which stretched several miles along their floors, any light barely showing. Occasionally, light from a lone farmstead on another hill was visible, and in the far distance the shimmering lights of Port Talbot. Otherwise, there was little light pollution to obscure the pinpricks of light of the stars in the black canopy above. Somewhere down the valley, on an unseen farmstead, a dog barked.

It made Jonathan philosophical, and more relaxed; less concerned about immediate threats. As he looked over at the distant lights of Port Talbot, he was pensive. Once the female runner had passed by them again without even a flicker of acknowledgement. Marcus spoke in a subdued tone.

'We can talk again, Jonathan. Are you okay? Is something on your mind?'

'Not much, Marcus. But up here, I wonder why we're still fighting. I mean, looking down there, one could imagine things were almost back to normal. Certainly, the virus wreaked its havoc, affected almost every family in the land. In addition to that disease, war and famine also took their toll. Now, what's left out there is attempting to start again. But you know what? It's not how I expected it to be.'

'No?' Marcus asked. 'How did you expect it to be?'

'Oh, I don't know. I had some naïve idea that what was left would be somehow better. In the event, it's just turned out to be a microcosm of what we had before. And it's worse because people are more desperate. And the wrong people are still in control.'

Marcus glanced at him. 'The virus wasn't selective. It didn't just get rid of all the bad people, Jonathan. We know it did do for a lot of young ones, though. And much older ones, who had no means to survive the famine. We've been left demographically unbalanced, with a low birth rate. And, what with the anti-immigration rules of the current regime, this country will just die out, like one of those remote Scottish Isles. I'll tell you though, we've been painted as the rebels; unpatriotic members of the liberal-left or whatever. But I'm a patriot, Jonathan. Britain must survive. Others can just as well carry on our values, our language, even on top of their own cultures. Many have lived here for years and proved it. Yet the regime won't see it. They live in an imagined yesterday, one they never actually lived but see in black-and-white movies. But those times have gone, Jonathan.' Marcus panted slightly as he talked and jogged.

'Agreed. Yes, I share your vision, and it's the only thing that makes logical sense. This is why we must win. And if you look at the composition of the Americans, I can see cracks forming with our Right-wing and implicitly racist regime, led as it is pretty much exclusively by old white men, and...' Jonathan paused, as the horsey officer approached, lean musculature over long limbs, and a suitably long, lined face beneath grey hair. Jonathan continued. 'And yes, I've emailed her many times, but I'm sure she doesn't remember me and probably just considers me a nuisance.'

'Oh no, I'm sure she'd remember you,' Marcus played along. Once horse-face was out of earshot, Marcus changed the subject. 'I'm worried about Julie, Jonathan.'

'Yes, so am I. But what can I do? Thanks to Comrade Pavel, she now believes I'm a war criminal.'

'Are you really innocent? Because if so, then she'll understand in time. If not, then you really shouldn't be with as liberal-minded a young woman as she is. Sorry to sound so brutal.'

'I'm guilty by association. I'm guilty for not running from the military when I had a chance. I'm guilty of being drawn in by the age-old clarion call to defend against an aggressor. Being honest, the lines between morality and what it took to win became blurred. I knew exactly what was likely to happen when I got the call to go to the Baltics. But as I said, I didn't release that virus.'

'No, I can believe that. Now you need to convince her.'

'Right,' Jonathan said, stopping his running for a minute to draw in some of the cool night air. He looked at some distant lights and felt hopeless. 'And what if she doesn't believe me? Or doesn't want to? She's the best thing to happen to me since I lost my previous wife and child, Marcus. For her to fall out of love with me for that…Don't you understand, I was complicit in the deaths of my own family. Now I'm being judged by the one person left in the world who means the most to me.'

'Give her time, Jonathan. She's raw, outraged. Yes, and not a little disgusted. She didn't know how far into it you were, and you were in it up to your neck. You were a fool to try to keep it from her. But if she's really as liberal-minded as she makes out, she'll understand.'

'Liberal minded? Hasn't that become a by-word for rigid uncompromising outrage, and upset over anyone who offers an alternative view on anything?'

'What, the touchy post-Millennials and all? Maybe. Some of us are more realistic, though. Hopefully, she is.'

'Hopefully,' Jonathan replied ruefully.

'So, about tomorrow,' Marcus began, as pony-tailed-blond passed again. 'What are your thoughts?'

'We make contact with Trant. With any luck, he won't just have us arrested and flown out on a special rendition flight.'

'You're behind the times, Jonathan, they stopped that business years ago. The regime deals with what it deems to be traitors in its own way, it thinks the Americans are way too soft now. Still, we can't expect a fair trial if we're found out, from our countrymen.'

Jonathan stopped again. 'Damn it, why did I let Julie on this mission? She shouldn't be here.'

'Look, if you'd tried to manfully stop her you would likely have waved goodbye to your relationship back in Bristol, Jonathan. She was once a field operative, remember?'

'Yes, I suppose you're right.'

'There's no suppose about it. And, look, we have to be fresh for the morning. Let's get back and get our heads down.'

'Of course. Any plan-B stuff we can discuss?'

'Jonathan, we're in the middle of an Army base, at the top of a hill in South Wales, with few options other than getting out of that main gate with the same bluff and bluster that got us in here. We're not going to jump that fence, ram it, pole vault it, or hope for a herd of wild elephants to trample it down! There is no plan-B, mate. We're just going to have to successfully wing it, right? All of us.'

'Yeah, I suppose you're right.' Jonathan said. 'You know, this place, a garrison, a barracks, it's central to the whole military mind-set. It defines them, makes them different from other government services, most of which get to go home at the end of each working day. These people don't. And now they're cut off from their own countrymen, as if in a foreign land.'

'I know, it was the same when I was in the Air Force,' Marcus said. 'It sort of encourages group-think, which can be good in that it bonds the team; and bad when it stifles original thinking and makes them utterly predictable.'

'This is the second time I've been holed-up with these people since I left the service, and it seems very claustrophobic. I wonder how Julie's coping with it.'

'I just hope she doesn't give anything away,' Marcus replied. 'She knows the standard military rifle but that's about it. If she gets roped into that show parade tomorrow we've had it. I don't think she could throw a convincing salute, let alone perform complex rifle drill.'

'Yes, she's going to find it all a bit carry-on. Maybe we'll need to pull out sooner than expected.'

'Hmm, we've come this far…I'm loath to pull the mission now, Jonathan. You just need to get to see Trant.'

'Which may be harder than ever now. It'll mean getting past his admin team, and especially that Major Fuller.'

'And risking bumping into those black ops guys,' Marcus added.

'Yes, we're indeed in the realm of trolls and orcs,' Jonathan said. He thought for a second. 'Hang on. I think we're missing a trick here.'

'How's that?' Marcus asked, intrigued.

'That carry-on Sergeant who greeted us. Didn't he say Trant goes for an early morning constitutional at seven A-M?'

'He did. Assuming that it's not over the hills, or on a running machine over in the gym, then he could only be taking this route around the perimeter.'

'No, he's definitely one for minimal fuss and fresh air. I think we'd better be up early then,' Jonathan said.

'For sure,' Marcus said. 'Good call, Jonathan!'

32

The Airborne unit block was familiar territory for Dolman. Although they'd do what they had to, these men didn't tend to take what they regarded as 'bullshit' parade prep overly seriously. Whilst some had just had showers and wandered back to their rooms, several others were arriving back from the bar in inebriated states. Music blared from one of the rooms; an eclectic compilation ranging from a form of populist skinhead music to anti-establishment neo-punk, through to German techno music. It didn't seem to matter what, as long as it had a manically fast beat and was loud.

Dolman stopped the most sober-looking and fully dressed of them. 'Who's in charge here?'

'Captain Halshaw, boss,' he replied.

'Halshaw? Ex-C-S-M Halshaw?'

'Yeah, guess he might once have been that.'

'Whereabouts is he?'

'Just discussing tomorrow with Sergeant Booth, his office is just down the corridor,' the soldier said, pointing out the direction.

'Thank you,' Dolman replied. As he continued down the corridor he noticed another of his team from Estonia.

'Silcott?' Dolman asked. 'Good to see you made it!'

'Sir? Lieutenant Dolman?' the soldier, now a Corporal, replied. 'Good to see you. I heard about your unit.'

'Yes, it seems to have gained a bit of a reputation.'

'Is it here as well?' Silcott asked.

'No, I'm on my own,' Dolman replied. 'Anyone else left?'

'Sergeant-Major Halshaw, he's now a Captain, he's just in there with the Sarge now.'

'Yes, I'm just going to see him. Anyone else?'

'Josh Keegan, Ritchie Booth, Matt Clayton, they're around here somewhere. Josh is a Colour Sergeant now, did well but is bored with all the admin. Ritchie's a Sergeant. Matt only made Lance-jack though, got into one fist fight too many, but says he prefers to keep operational. To be honest that's about it though. Rest have moved on, or are pushing up the daisies.'

'Damn it. Well, tell the lads there's always a place in my outfit.'

'Will do, boss. Anyway, the Captain's just in there.'

The door was open and Dolman knocked on the doorframe just to be polite as he entered. Halshaw was discussing something with the Sergeant and looked around. He got up when he saw who it was.

'Paul Dolman! Good to see you,' he offered his large hand which Dolman shook. 'Please, take a seat.'

'Glad to see you finally took the commission,' Dolman said.

'Yes, well I'm just seeing my time out now,' Halshaw growled. 'Would have retired ages ago, but there's nothing much to retire *to* just now.'

'Discussing tomorrow?' Dolman enquired.

'No, this is a de-brief on our earlier assignment. Our turn on Q-R-F meant it was us who saw to that supply depot.'

'Hmm, I was down there with an American supply column just after it happened. We dealt with some of the stragglers who hadn't scooted fast enough.'

'Yeah, a right mess the place was. We left some of the Colonel's lot down there to clear up. Between you, me and the garden gatepost, we apparently don't want the Americans involved on this. Colonel wants to show we can keep control of our own patch without their help.'

'Right. How is he?'

'Oh, you know Martin Trant, leads from the front. But he's older, like all of us. Transferred to infantry for the promotion prospects, got his own Battalion, but I'm not sure it's done him any good. To be honest, Paul, he's come off the boil. You knew how he was, switched on, decisive. Well,' he looked at Ritchie, 'Ritchie, weren't you just saying the other day how he dithers over trivial stuff now?'

'Yeah, that's right,' the sergeant replied guardedly.

'Such as?' Dolman asked.

Halshaw half grinned. 'Such as, there's this hippy colony just down the valley, a safe-haven that the Americans are still supplying. We had to do a check on them, as it seems they're self-sustaining to the point of even selling surplus produce. Colonel Trant had stated he wanted to reduce reliance on American aid, and this was a perfect opportunity. But I was in the orders group when the I-O, Major Fuller that is, suggested the op. And I tell you, Colonel Trant is just there wibbling and dithering about it being winter soon, and how they'll starve if we cut off their supplies.'

'Huh, doesn't sound like him at all,' Dolman agreed.

'You seen him yet?' Halshaw asked.

'No, I was just in tonight.'

'To be honest, I think the old man's gone a bit soft,' Halshaw stated. 'That's not good if things are going to kick off again, like tonight.'

'Maybe,' Dolman said. 'I met the I-O, Major Fuller, earlier. He seems pretty switched-on. How do you rate him?'

'He's been with Trant quite a while, turned down a command appointment when his majority came through. Trant wanted to retain him. He's switched-on.'

'Hm, maybe he'll have seen the change too?' Dolman asked.

'Yeah, you can always tell when he disagrees with the Colonel, he always goes as red as a beetroot.'

'Interesting. Thanks, Captain. I'll leave you be now.'

33

Julie lay on her bed and pretended to look at her phone. She had placed her backpack into the cupboard by her bed but was wary of leaving it there unattended to take a shower, as she had no padlock to secure it. It was too early to sleep, and in any case, the room lights were still on and the other women around were still talking and busy preparing their uniforms for whatever was happening the following day. Unabashed, several seemed to wander about in their underwear. Julie listened to their conversation whilst making every attempt not to get involved.

'…anyway, I says to him, not bloody likely. He don't give up easily though,' said one, a brunette with a London accent.

'Aye, he was a right one!' said another, in a northern accent.

'Tell you what though,' the brunette continued, 'I've considered taking the offer. Throwing in the towel with this lark. I could bag myself someone with a brain, money and prospects, not like one of the no-hopers round here.'

'You're joking, right?' said another. 'It's a scam. You'd just be a baby-factory. Anyway, you ain't the mumsy type, know what I mean?'

'I don't care,' said the brunette. 'The talk is you'd be fixed up with someone big, someone with money and power and status, and a good home. Think of the life you'd have. Why, I bet you'd even have servants who wipe all them babies' arses for you!'

'Seriously, ducks,' the northerner, Jocelyn, said. 'Aven't you got more self-respect than that? I have. Here, I'm something. I'm my own person. And I've got all the status I want, with a rifle five-point-five-six. Anyway, t'ain't right, you pretending to be straight and all, know what I mean? I don't think you've even got over your thing about Hayley. I can't believe you've forgotten about her already?'

'Screw her! She was never going to risk her promotion prospects with anything funny,' the brunette replied, and smiled knowingly, 'even if she wanted to. Well, she was cute!'

The northern girl scoffed. 'In your dreams! Even if she was into any of that, which I doubt, she was well out of your league, know what I mean?'

'Ah shut-up!'

And on it went. Initially outraged at the subjects of the discussion, Julie was beginning to get bored with the banal sniping, and it affirmed some of her prejudices about women in the military. Also, she was beginning to feel just a little threatened. With occasional glances in her direction, the brunette seemed somewhat predatory. Someone else entered the room; a blond girl in running kit, hair tied up. She looked a bit friendlier.

'You got your stuff ready for tomorrow then, Sam?' the brunette asked, for some reason appearing to change the subject.

'Yep, ahead of the curve there, Shaz,' the blond female called Sam answered, without the slightest self-consciousness she undressed.

'How about you then?' the brunette, Sharon, asked Julie.

'Me? No, I won't be involved. I'm just passing by,' Julie answered, wishing she was already a hundred miles away.

'Well then, you'd better make yourself scarce, that's all I can say,' Sharon advised her. 'I thought you were here as part of the shadow force or something. You're not special forces or nothing like that, are you?'

'Oh don't be simple, Sharon, she wouldn't exactly tell you if she was that, now would she?' the Yorkshire girl reasoned.

'Alright, I was just asking, you never know. So she don't much look the type I'll say that,' Sharon replied. She turned back to Julie. 'So, what is your line, then?'

Julie thought quickly. 'Comms, it's hush-hush stuff, I'm not allowed to talk about it. Pretty dull, really.'

'Oh, okay. Tell you what, there's loads of black-ops looking types around here just now. One or two looks pretty fit if you know what I mean,' she grinned.

'Not my type,' Julie replied. She instantly regretted saying it as she caught Sharon's expression.

'No?' said the girl from Yorkshire. 'I saw you with your team in the bar earlier, that geeky looking Captain of yours had eyes for you, I can tell you. If he's more your type then you'd be in there, ducks. A Captain and all, you could do worse!'

'Yeah, maybe,' Julie conceded, getting up. 'Look, I need to get a padlock for my locker. Does anywhere here supply them?'

'The camp shop does them,' Sam, the blond woman, informed her. 'But is it really worth it for just one night here?'

'Well I could do with the walk, I think I need some air, it's stuffy in here.'

'I wouldn't go wandering, darling,' Sharon advised, 'it'll be lights-out soon.'

'I won't be long,' Julie replied.

'Ignore her,' Sam said. 'Just take the back entrance out, turn left, and make your way past the cook-house. You can't miss it. They'll be closing soon though.'

'Thanks,' Julie replied as she picked up her jacket and took her backpack from the cupboard. Out of the room, she followed the corridor through to an area in a quadrangle, lit by a dim white light. Outside was what appeared to be a smokers' area. She walked past it and saw a few of those still committed to slow-burn suicide puffing away. With the ban on cigarettes since the last virus outbreak, she thought it hypocritical how the security forces could still partake.

She followed the path just as Sam had instructed. It was quiet and deserted, and she could have imagined that the buildings that lined it were deserted, when in fact they surely held several hundred soldiers.

As she neared what looked like the cook-house, now completely dark, she saw another building that resembled a tiny corner shop sized store. She entered and saw a couple of severe-looking middle-aged ladies, one at the till, and another busily filling a shelf.

'We close in five,' the one on the till warned.

'Yes, I just want a padlock,' Julie replied in as friendly a manner as she could muster.

'Over there, far wall, second shelf down,' the assistant told her. Julie walked over to see a small selection of padlocks with long shanks, clearly a good fit for the cupboard doors back in the barrack block.

The shop bell rang again.

'Aw hallo, it's not in yet,' the assistant said to someone else.

'Oh, that's fine,' replied a well-spoken male voice. 'When do you think they will be?'

'Ooh, can't say, a day or two?'

'Fine,' the man said.

Julie couldn't pretend to look at padlocks and cleaning materials for much longer. She turned to see an officer with receding grey hair with hints of ginger in it, and a moustache. She noticed him glance at her, so picked up a padlock and took it to the till.

'Hello,' Major Fuller said. 'I think I saw you earlier, leaving the bar with your friends.'

'Hello,' Julie replied. 'Yes, just getting a padlock for my locker.'

'New in? I don't think I've seen you before.'

'Yes, just here for the night.'

'For the show tomorrow I expect?' he asked, picking up a packet of mints.

She didn't answer and addressed the till assistant. 'Can I take this one, please?'

'Certainly,' the assistant replied and swiped it.

She paid, and then glanced at him.

'Goodnight, Sir.'

'Yes, goodnight.'

She left the shop with as little haste as she could manage, leaving a frowning Major Fuller looking at her as she left.

'She seemed a bit of an uptight one, didn't she?' the till assistant said.

'You thought so too, eh? Interesting,' Fuller said, rubbing his chin.

'Mind you,' she continued, 'we've had a lot in today, all new faces, wanting this and that. I'll tell you, I'm running low on some of the basics, polish, dusters, and so on.'

'Yes, well I'll be glad when this standing-on-ceremony business is done. There's too much else going on just now. Goodnight,' he said before he turned to leave.

34

As Dolman walked to his own block in the officers' quarter, he was unexpectedly joined by Corporal Phil Gresham. 'Sir, mind if I have a word?'

'Not at all, Corporal,' Dolman replied.

'Well, me and my team have been talking –minus our new Second Looey- and, well, we got to thinking…that guy seems mighty strange.'

'Why do you say that?'

'Well, he's a bit of a screw-up, but he's green outta depot, so that's no surprise. But the goofball stuff, well that's just irritating if you know what I mean? But then down at that supply depot, he suddenly switches on, all the drills and skills. And he nails that guy in the warehouse, no problem!'

'Yes Corporal, I saw it, I was there too if you remember.' Dolman wished this voluble American would get to the point.

'I tell ya, Captain, it just don't add up. I mean, I seen guys like him, come dressed up with all the gear, real P-X commandoes, but this guy's none of that. Then he goes and does that!' He burped. 'Oh, excuse me, Sir.'

'One too many bottles of light, maybe?' Dolman asked.

'Oh no, Sir, I know my limit.'

'Well let's just say you had a good evening in the bar, now please get some water down your neck. I need you sober for that drive back tomorrow.'

'Sure thing, Sir.'

'Goodnight, Corporal.'

'Goodnight Sir,' Gresham saluted and stumbled off into the night.

Dolman shook his head and smiled, then sipped in the cool night air. The stars were out. He liked these moments of peace, alone, looking at whatever was around, be it the night sky or a few distant lights on the hills. He felt such times gave him energy, like a machine having its batteries re-charged.

He walked back to his block, hoping Gresham was doing the same; and that he hadn't just returned to the bar.

35

The next morning, they were running around the inside of the perimeter again. There was low cloud or fog, they couldn't decide which, and a light mizzle that quickly dampened their running clothes. Jonathan ached from the night before. Marcus coughed the cough of an ex-smoker. Neither of them had yet woken up fully. And there was, as yet, no sign of Trant. However, there was already some activity on the base, the occasional truck going in and out, and lights being turned on in the cook-house as they passed it. Generators were whirring, and little columns of steam issued from ground vents.

'He doesn't turn up now, we go to plan-B, the hard way,' Marcus said.

'No alternative,' Jonathan said tiredly and without enthusiasm. 'I didn't rate him as a fair-weather runner though.'

'No? What was he like?'

'Vehement. Confident. Dominant. And afraid. He saw his world falling apart. I don't think his garrison in Bristol would have held out another month. Luckily for him, the Americans arrived shortly after the Army evacuated from Bristol. But at one point, I was actually his last hope. And he sent me out with some hapless infantry officer with a bad case of P-T-S-D.'

'The guy you had to shoot?'

'Yes,' Jonathan replied grimly. 'He was about to order an airstrike down on us. I didn't have a lot of choice at the time.'

'That saved King and a lot of others.'

'Yes. But I still feel bad about it. I'd gotten to know the chap. However, they were all so fixated on my finding a cure. Getting things back to normal as fast as possible, so that they could regain control. Yet they were the ones who had mucked it all up in the first place.'

Marcus coughed again. 'Lord, I'm almost done! This really isn't pleasant, and I hardly slept.'

'I'm getting my second wind. Look, go on in if you like,' Jonathan replied.

'No,' Marcus said bravely. 'I'll do one more lap, and then it'll be a shower and breakfast, courtesy of H-M armed forces.'

'More like courtesy of Uncle Sam.'

'Hello…' Marcus said, looking into the mist. 'Is that our man?'

Jonathan turned to where Marcus was looking. It was at the extent of visibility, the figure of a lone runner in the mist, appearing briefly between buildings then disappearing. He would meet with them naturally if they each kept on the same course.

They lost sight of him for several seconds, but he then appeared around from behind a building close to the wire. As he ran towards them, Jonathan instantly recognised the same longish, lean features, and high cheekbones. His hair was greyer now. And his eyes weren't quite as bright. If anything, Colonel Trant looked as tired as they felt. There came a look of vague recognition in his eyes, turning to bewilderment as he slowed down.

'Professor? Colonel Barnes? How can it be?'

'Yes, it's me,' Jonathan replied.

'My God, I thought you'd…'

'Perished at Morton Down? No.'

'You've been missing, presumed dead for three years. Where have you been?'

'Away,' Jonathan replied tersely. 'Colonel, we need to talk. This isn't what it seems, I'm no longer with the Army. I'm with an organisation which has…a different view as to how the UK should be governed.'

'Well, if that's the case, however it is you got in here you should probably leave. We can't be seen to be talking. Keep running.'

As they set off together, Marcus continued the conversation. 'There isn't much time, Colonel. The present regime is on the wrong track. They are more of a danger to the unity of this country now than anything. They could even drive the American support away with their excesses, and their insistence on fighting their own people. We want to talk to the Americans before that happens. Sue for peace. And you can help us.'

'How?'

'Come with us.'

'Impossible. I can't leave my command,' Trant replied.

Marcus was unfazed. 'Well if not, vouch for us. Agree to a meeting with our leader. Then try to arrange the same with the American commander-in-chief. We know you're disenchanted with the current regime.'

Trant considered what they had said with a confused frown. 'Am I?'

'Here,' Marcus said handing Trant a card, 'this is how to contact us. Keep it safe. It employs proxy servers, but just the fact that it's hard to trace will put you under further suspicion.'

'I'm under suspicion already then?' he replied in a disbelieving tone.

'Oh yes!' Marcus said emphatically. 'Part of the reason we're here is to warn you, Colonel.'

'Impossible. I've not been in contact with yourselves or any other rebel group.'

'Believe what you like, Colonel. But we have our sources.'

'Yes, I can guess what they are. I'm sure it's probably no more than agitprop from the East, gentlemen. Look, I'm sorry, but you've wasted your time coming here. I suggest you get out of my base now.'

'Or what, Colonel?' Marcus asked. 'You'll turn us in? Four good men lost their lives just so that we could have this conversation.'

'Okay.' Trant stopped running and looked at the card. He tucked it into a pocket in his track pants. 'Seeing you here Professor tells me something about your group. You told me there was no cure for the virus, and I've come to think that you were right all along; it just had to run its course. You obviously survived Morton Down and went to ground with the resistance. And, being honest, I'm not happy with some things I've been seeing. But, I can't just desert my post, it goes against the grain. It'd make me a…a traitor to my own country!'

'Colonel,' Jonathan said, 'I think you've already been deemed as such. One of the strongest traits of the current regime is paranoia. They totally lack trust, even in loyal and decorated officers like yourself. They're always looking for traitors, and if they can't find them, then they invent them. You've appeared on their radar, don't ask me how. Something you said in an email, online, perhaps quite innocent even. But believe me when I say that your tenure here is coming to an end, probably fairly shortly. And when it does, we won't be able to help you.'

Trant looked earnestly at Marcus and Jonathan as he considered it. 'Alright then. If I get the slightest hint that something is wrong, I'll be in contact.'

'Colonel, be sure,' Marcus cautioned, 'that line is single-use only. You make your choice to join us, and you come alone. Any tricks and we'll be gone. And you'll have nowhere to go because your own people will be onto you. So it's your choice; us, or them.'

Trant suddenly looked even older, greyer, and more tired. 'Okay, let me think on it. I can't decide just now. It's all too much at once, do you understand?'

'It was the same for that officer you sent with me to Morton, Captain Barrett. His ability to think on his feet was shot to pieces.'

Trant looked at Jonathan and realised the irony.

'My medal, that's a sham. It cost a whole village. Men, women, children, babies…Damn it, Professor, these things catch up with one. I feel old.'

'I know how you feel, Colonel,' Jonathan replied wearily. 'We all have history.'

'Okay,' Trant said, as he spotted another jogger. 'You men had better make yourselves scarce. Get out of here, A-S-A-P. We've got visitors in today, try and make sure you're out of here before they arrive. Okay, go on. Best of luck.'

'You too, Colonel', Marcus said. He glanced at Jonathan, and they continued into the mist just as the runner appeared around the corner.

36

Marcus sent messages to the phones of Julie and Stan, telling them to prepare to leave. It instructed them to meet at their armoured vehicle at seven-thirty a.m. However, the recipients were in different states of undress and going through their morning ablutions in their respective wash houses and shower blocks. Each had done the only thing possible and left their mobile phones in their lockers.

To make matters worse, on Julie's return from her shower she checked her mobile phone in her locker only to find that she'd left it on and the battery was dead. When she attached it to the charger and turned it on the message was to be delayed for another half hour.

Stan was luckier with his phone once he returned from the shower block, and he hot-footed it out as soon as he opened the message.

When only three of them arrived at the armoured vehicle, they waited for another ten minutes before realising that they had a problem.

'When did you last see her?' Marcus asked Stan.

'Last night, I saw her to her block. Look, relax, Marcus, it's probably just a comms problem.'

'Don't tell me to relax!' Marcus snapped back. 'We all need to stay alert, get focused. We should have been driving out of here by now.'

'Maybe Stan and I should return to the block to find her?' Jonathan suggested.

'Fine. Keep me in the loop,' Marcus agreed, sorry to have lost his temper at Stan. He watched as they headed off.

*

Still unaware of the new orders, Julie headed separately to the canteen, missing Jonathan and Stan by minutes. As they made enquiries at Julie's block, she was already standing in queues and about to select her breakfast.

It was another quarter of an hour before Jonathan and Stan returned to Marcus, who was by now sitting in the back of the vehicle trying to look unobtrusive, face like thunder.

'I think she may have gone to the canteen,' Jonathan told him flatly as he climbed inside.

'Yeah, it figures.'

'There're no signs of tension or gossip amongst the others, things that might be expected if there'd been an incident.'

'Right,' Marcus said, unimpressed. 'Every needless extra minute here risks the entire team, the whole operation. If we're captured now they could quite probably get it out of us.'

'Yeah,' said Stan. 'But what do we do now?'

'Well, we can't exactly go in and haul her out,' Marcus stated. 'Let's bloody well go and have breakfast!'

37

Trant swiped his pass on the rotating glass security door and took the lift down to the first subterranean level. He walked down a well-lit corridor to his office. He was a little later than usual and found Major Fuller waiting outside for him.

'Martin, have you got a moment?'

'Certainly, Bernard. What's up?' Trant unlocked his door.

As usual, Fuller waited to speak until closing the door behind him. He then placed himself in an easy chair alongside Trant's small meeting table; his habitual spot when consulting with the Colonel. Trant meanwhile sat at his desk, unlocked a drawer, removed some paperwork then turned his computer on.

'Sorry Bernard, I'm a little behind with things. What is it?' Trant asked.

'Well, to be honest, I'm not entirely sure myself,' Fuller began.

'Look, if you don't mind getting to the point, today is looking to be busy and I'm going to have to be in at least three places at once. Can this wait, maybe?'

'I see, of course. Well, maybe it's nothing. It's just that I've just noticed a few new faces around here, and they don't seem to fit.'

'Quite, we've got that visit today, we're inundated with security and flunkies and such-like,' Trant replied flippantly.

'Well, assuming that the guards at main gate are doing their job, all should be fine.'

'Are you suspecting a security breach?' Trant asked lightly, trying hard to hide the fact that he knew full well that there'd already been one. 'That's certainly your responsibility. We don't want anything going wrong with the proceedings today.'

'My problem is that I have to be suspicious, it's part of my job. However, it's calibrating the sensitivity gauge to the optimum level. Maybe I've got it set at too fine a limit just now. However…well, Martin, some of the faces around here just don't seem to fit. As in, fit the bill.'

'Do you have anyone in particular in mind?' Trant asked as mildly as he could as he pretended to glance at his computer.

'Yes, yes I do. Last night there was a new team in, I initially took them to be Army Media or such-like. The officer, a Captain, seemed familiar, but I just couldn't place him. It was frustrating, as it's my job to put names to faces, but in this case, I simply couldn't. Then, last thing last night, I happened to meet the female soldier from their group in the camp shop. This girl was the most diffident character I've ever seen in uniform. I mean, shut-in, introverted, and with what can best be described as a hunted look.'

Trant thought for a moment. 'Well, Bernard, you know Media Ops types, they're not your standard green Army exactly, now are they?'

'Hmm, maybe. But this morning, I woke and it came to me whom that Captain resembled. Well, don't call me mad, but if I didn't know otherwise I'd have sworn it was that Professor chap we sent out from Bristol two years ago; Lieutenant-Colonel Jonathan Barnes.'

Trant scoffed. 'Now that does sound a bit far-fetched, Bernard! In the uniform of a Captain, you say?'

'Yes, for sure, a Captain.'

'All intelligence reports agree that he perished at Morton Down.'

'Although a body was never found, Martin,' Fuller retorted.

'The amount of ordnance the Americans used on that place meant that we only ever had a chance of identifying those underground. Most were up top,' Trant replied grimly. 'But, okay, saying Professor Barnes *did* survive…why on Earth would he have turned up here, in the uniform of a Captain?'

'Because he went over to the resistance,' Fuller said flatly.

'Okay, whoa! That's quite a jump, Bernard,' Trant replied, privately marvelling at his Intelligence Officer's powers of deduction.

'Well, yes, I admit it sounds a bit far-fetched,' Fuller conceded. 'But let's just consider the threat, if it is true. Surely better we err on the side of caution, eh?'

'Well, the simple thing is to find out who he is. If he signed in last night we pull up a photograph and you or I will soon tell.'

'Okay, I'll run a full check on the man. Let's go belt and braces; we'll find him and question him.'

'Fine, but we haven't got long. They're due in at nine-fifteen.'

'Damn it, why so early?' Fuller asked.

'They're due to meet with the director of that commercial biochemical research lab that thinks it has a vaccine developed, down in Cardiff.'

'I'm not surprised those commercial places got there faster than us, especially after Morton Down. Better late than never,' Fuller replied.

'Between you and me, Bernard, we had no choice but to tender it out and share what little we knew.'

'Makes sense. Whatever works, we'd all agree on that. By the way Martin, you have a visitor, an old friend by all accounts. He pulled in with the usual American supply convoy last night.'

'Oh, that's odd. Who?' Trant asked.

'Captain Paul Dolman,' Fuller replied.

'Paul Dolman? Goodness, why didn't you tell me earlier? Where is he?'

'I expect he'll be around shortly. You two served together in the Baltics, I know. But he is still a rather contentious figure. Ruthless and unorthodox, I expect you've heard about his latest exploits?'

'Yes, I have. We need more like him,' Trant lied.

'He's not unlike you were five years ago. Three, even. But not now. You've changed, Martin.'

'I'm not the man I was?'

'I'm not saying that. But you're older and wiser. You've been doing this too long. It's taken its toll. On active service abroad you could return to a home. Here your home *is* the active service, and there's no getting away from it.'

'We've all got older, Bernard,' Trant said tiredly. 'You think I should have reported down to Fairfield for that psychological evaluation?'

'I'm saying you can't put it off much longer. No one disobeys orders, you know that.'

'Damned American psycho-babble!'

'Everyone's taking it seriously, Martin; them, us. We just don't have the facilities to run them just yet, we're still struggling to recruit and re-build the entire Army. You have to see an American evaluation as being the same as ours, for the time being. In reality, they're years ahead of us in this stuff, always were. And now they've got it set up with artificial intelligence systems,' Fuller explained.

Trant looked at him, unimpressed. 'Bernard, you're getting all gee-whizz on me here again.'

Fuller looked back at his commanding officer. He could certainly be mulish at times, and on this point to his own detriment. 'Okay Martin, but I do urge you to give it serious consideration.'

'I will, Bernard,' Trant replied, staring at the map on his wall with uncharacteristic petulance. 'I'll give it consideration.'

There was a knock on the door.

'Come,' Trant instructed, voice characteristically deep.

The door opened, and a female soldier appeared. 'Sir, there's a Captain Dolman waiting to see you.'

'Fine, tell him I'll see him shortly,' Trant replied.

38

They had met up in the breakfast hall and cleared up the source of confusion with as little fuss as possible as they sat around a table eating breakfast.

Rather than sustain his anger, Marcus now looked rueful. 'Not good, but my fault, I should have pre-arranged a rendezvous. Anyway, once we've re-fuelled we're outta here, right? It's now…eight-twenty-eight, we can be on the road in ten.'

As Julie drained her mug of tea, she noticed that the mess hall had suddenly thinned out, as if to order.

'Lord, its hive mentality,' Marcus muttered under his breath.

'I think we'd better do the same, don't you?' Jonathan urged, dropping his spoon back into his muesli.

'Agreed,' Marcus said and put his knife and fork together. Big Stan mopped his plate with his toast and glanced around, as he stuffed it into his mouth and wolfed the lump down with a swig of tea. They all got up and took their trays to the racks in what was now a nearly-empty canteen.

39

Dolman walked into Trant's office. Trant stood up and walked around the table to greet him with a genial smile, and they shook hands.

'Paul, good to see you. How long have you been in?'

'I got in last night, with an American supply transport.'

'Right,' Trant replied. 'Well, glad you could make it. Do take a seat, please.'

Major Fuller got up. 'Colonel, if you'll excuse me, I must get going. I'm sure you and the Captain have some catching up to do.'

'Yes, of course,' Trant agreed.

Dolman turned sharply. 'No, do stay if you would, Major. This isn't, I'm afraid, a social call.' He then sat down, and the others followed suit.

'Not a social call?' Trant asked with a frown. 'So, I take it you're here on business. What's this about, Paul?'

Dolman looked down and mentally braced himself, then back at Trant. 'Colonel, I've come from Fairfield Airbase. Major-General Easton tasked me to collect you, and escort you back there for a psychological evaluation.'

Trant sat back and surveyed Dolman with a look of distaste.

'So, this is what it comes to, eh? The Americans send a flunky to do their dirty work. After all we went through together, Paul, I'm sorry it had to be you.'

'And believe me, I'm sorry too, Sir.'

Major Fuller spoke up. 'Martin, if I may say, the Captain is only doing his job-

'YES, I know damned well what he's doing, Major!' Trant thundered, slamming his fist on his desk. 'Damn it, whose country is this?'

Paul was unfazed. 'Colonel, you've done some good work, but I've been sent here to temporarily relieve you of your command, and escort you back to Fairfield.'

There was silence. Trant gazed at Dolman with disgust for a second, then put his hands together and dropped his head into his palms.

'How long have I got?' Trant asked.

'It's with immediate effect, Colonel. Please go and pack your belongings. I plan to get moving within the hour. It'll be on the American supply transport bound for Fairfield Airbase.'

Suddenly and inexplicably, Trant began laughing.

'What is it, Colonel?' Paul asked with chagrin, slightly bewildered.

'That's impossible,' Trant sat back and put his hands behind his head.

'What do you mean?'

'Because I am to host the Defence Secretary and Brigadier Jack Trelawney within the next forty minutes.'

Dolman looked around at Fuller, who nodded in confirmation. 'They are due to touch down on our main parade square at nine-fifteen A-M.'

'Why didn't you make me aware of this last night, Major?' Dolman asked Fuller with some irritation.

'Because I wasn't aware that you were planning to relieve my commanding officer at eight-thirty-five the next day, Captain!'

Dolman was silent for a second, frustrated. 'How long are they here for?'

'Ooh, it's a flying visit, literally.' Fuller answered again. 'You know, Captain, photo opportunities with the troops, propaganda bullshit, that sort of thing. They'll be gone by two I should think.'

'Alright, then you do your meet-and-greet thing,' Dolman told Trant. 'Then we're off, as soon as they're gone.'

Trant surveyed him with a dangerous smile that showed that the Trant of old was still very much alive and kicking. Dolman got up haughtily and walked out without saluting.

40

As they left the breakfast hall, the Battalion Sergeant-Major shouted at them. 'What the bleeding heck is this? Where are you lot going? Stop there! Stand to attention when you hear me speak!'

He saw Jonathan and Marcus's rank straps as they turned. 'Oh, sorry Sirs, I didn't see you. May I ask where you're headed?'

Jonathan, playing the senior officer, spoke. 'Yes, of course, Sarn't-Major. We're just leaving.'

'Sorry Sir, but the base is on lock-down for the next four hours, no one in or out. There'll be a party of V-I-P's landing very shortly. If I was you, I'd get in line with the others,' he said and surveyed their uniforms with disgust. 'Rear rank, if you don't mind Sir!'

Jonathan looked at Marcus, who looked vaguely perturbed, but nodded with the corners of his mouth pulled down. He might have shrugged if it were possible. 'Fine,' Jonathan said. 'Where exactly do you want us?'

41

They heard them coming in long before they saw them. They were formed up around the edges of the parade ground, an impressive number of troops. Three ground attack helicopters swooped in low and hovered overhead noses pointing outwards, forming an aerial perimeter guard, whilst the transport helicopter containing the passengers descended within. It landed, creating a mini vortex around it, whipping up the odd leaf that had been missed from the parade ground. The engine was turned off, and the rotor blades came to a slow stop. As they did so, the side door opened and a well-armed bodyguard appeared from the inside, followed by two officers and a man in a dark grey suit and tie. They bent low and walked towards Colonel Trant, Major Fuller, and the company commanders, all Majors, and their Adjutants, all Captains, lined up behind them.

Julie could barely contain herself when she saw the senior of the visiting officers was none other than Brigadier 'Mad' Jack Trelawney. Behind him was the Defence Secretary, Selwyn Barton-Smith, holding his orange comb-over down against the down-draught of the slowing helicopter blades. She let out a small squeal of horror, and Jonathan kicked her boot.

'Why am I standing at attention for *these* men?' she said out of the corner of her mouth. 'I hate you, I really do!'

'I'm sorry, but I think it's about to get worse,' Jonathan murmured.

The visiting party shook hands with Trant and his field officers. Trant showed them around other elements of his command, and then they walked towards Marcus's group. Whilst they stood two lines behind, they could clearly see the visiting party now as they ambled up, and could hear them talking.

'And this is part of my reconnaissance platoon, led by Captain Anderson,' Trant said, as the Captain in front saluted smartly.

'Two sections are out on the ground,' Trant added.

'Ah yes, reconnaissance,' the Defence Secretary said, affecting familiarity. 'The eyes and ears of the battalion, eh?'

'Indeed, Sir,' Captain Anderson agreed.

A media group soldier was taking photographs of the visiting party as they walked.

'So,' Brigadier Trelawney asked one soldier, 'I heard you've got this sector pretty well locked down. And, an all-British effort too; very well done!'

'Thank you, Sir.'

The Brigadier then made a vaguely racist comment about immigrants in Wales. 'Yes, even in these little mining towns,' he continued, 'I really can't see why an earth they'd want to come here, I'm told it gets quite bitter in winter. Mind you, I'm told that they do some good ales around here, so I suppose one can sort of understand it. I've heard that's one of the perks of having the place in order, you can visit the local pubs again!'

'Whenever we're not on duty, Sir, yes,' the soldier admitted cautiously.

'Jolly good show,' he said, 'and I take it the interlopers do damned good street food to soak it up afterwards. But you know I can only abide their music for precisely five seconds.' He chuckled and then turned to Trant. 'You know what, Colonel, I never would have believed it possible two years ago. It shows you how far we've come.' Trelawney looked at the soldier before him. 'Wonderful, well keep up the good work, eh?'

'Yes Sir,' the man replied.

The Defence Secretary walked past, nodding at the men with a rictus of a fixed grin. 'Do you enjoy your work here?' he asked one soldier just as a gust of wind again blew his orange comb-over off the top of his head, revealing his shiny pate. He rapidly brushed it back.

'Well, yes Sir,' the man answered, slightly nonplussed, restraining a snigger.

'Good. Are you getting enough supplies to get the job done, now?'

'Yes, though a lot of it is still American kit. But it's good quality, so we can't complain.'

'Yes, indeed they've helped us out considerably,' Barton-Smith replied.

Trant looked vaguely irked at that conversation, but then spotted Jonathan and Marcus, and he distracted the party in another direction, pointing to the headquarters building and officers' mess. As they headed off, Marcus, Jonathan and the others relaxed.

When the Sergeant-Major gave the order to dismiss, all but Julie turned to the right and marched off two paces, but no one appeared to notice.

They talked relatively freely amongst the others.

'What now, Lieutenant?' Jonathan asked Marcus.

'I don't know, Jonathan. We wait. Keep as low as possible. That Sergeant Major said four hours. I suggest we regroup at the armoured vehicle at one, once these characters have left.'

'We'll probably be waving them off, too,' Stan joked.

'Quite likely,' Marcus replied morosely.

42

After the meet-and-greet tour, the Defence Minister was treated to breakfast in the Officers' Mess. Colonel Trant had assembled most of his Company Commanders as well as his Adjutant, and Major Fuller. They sat round in an opulent room adorned with regimental silver, and paintings of campaigns going back to Waterloo, or portraits of historical senior officers.

Trant was pensive throughout but tried to mask it with erudite opinions in their conversation, in between listening to hollow plaudits from the Defence Minister and Brigadier Trelawney. The breakfast was extensive, with hot and cold selections, and vegetarian options. Soldiers in white jackets and gloves poured tea and coffee into cups from silver pots.

'What's your preference, Colonel, Earl Grey, or Darjeeling?' Brigadier Trelawney asked.

Trant answered with a smile. 'I do have to admit to having had my taste buds blown away by M-R-E curries! So builders' tea is quite sufficient. Anything more is wasted on me, I'm afraid to say!'

The others laughed. 'Oh dear, that is a shame!' Trelawney said.

'Colonel?' Barton-Smith addressed Trant, 'I hear that you believe that you can be self-sufficient up here? Surely, that's impossible?'

'Not at all,' Trant answered. 'It's being achieved throughout the valleys here. People have learned to make do with less. When the supply system failed, so did capitalism effectively. For a time it was trade and barter.'

'But we couldn't have grown *all* of our own food in time. The Americans made it possible. Most of us wouldn't be alive if they hadn't stepped in.'

'Quite so,' Trant agreed. 'But in a year or two, we won't be half so dependent. Once we resume trading links with Europe then things should become a lot better. Shipping all we need over the Atlantic is hugely expensive, and we'll be beholden to America economically for the next hundred years if it continues.'

There was an awkward silence at the table.

'It makes no sense,' Trant continued, unabashed. 'Most countries trade with their closest neighbours. Otherwise, you accrue all the costs of increased transportation, which has rocketed since the latest wars in the Middle East stopped the oil flows. America meanwhile is self-sufficient, which is why it stepped back from the Middle East, and Europe was too weak to intervene for its own benefit.'

'I'm sensing maybe you want to be back in Europe, Colonel?' Barton-Smith asked.

'Actually, no I don't. But just broker us more effective deals that we've had.'

'Ah!' Barton-Smith said as if it explained everything. 'Well, anyway, how wonderful, Brigadier, that you permit such an eclectic mix of officers in your command. It'd be so boring for everyone to think the same thing, after all.' Barton-Smith gave Trant a mirthless smile.

Brigadier Trelawney looked at Trant with exasperated ire.

*

Later, as they left the table after the usual platitudes, Brigadier Trelawney stopped Trant. 'Martin, a word, if I may.'

'Here?'

'No. Your office. I'll need your Adjutant, and Fuller along with you.'

43

They had split up out of necessity, so as not to draw attention to themselves as a group. Big Stan walked with Julie for a while and suggested they head to the armoured vehicle to do some maintenance.

'The hardest thing to do on an Army base,' he advised, 'is to always appear busy. But you have to become a professional slacker, or else you'll end up getting dicked for some shitty job way below your pay-grade.'

'Right,' she replied unsurely, as much over his use of expletives as to his message.

'It's a bit of an art, becoming a professional dodger, but once mastered, service life becomes a bearable and even enjoyable routine. You don't have to think too much, everything is laid-on for you. Food, accommodation, the lot. When times are bad it's an umbrella. I mean, look at this lot round here; sure, things got a bit touch-and-go a few years ago, but now they're the fattest people in the country. If I could disengage my brain from what's been going on, well I'd think about signing on again!'

This was almost lost on Julie, who could only give a polite smile.

When they returned the vehicle, Stan checked his pack, and then began some routine maintenance, starting with the tires. Julie pretended to look at things but realised that she knew next to nothing about vehicles.

'You could sit it out in the back?' Stan suggested politely.

'No. I'm too nervous. I actually feel better with the pretence out here. I'll see if I can find Jonathan and Marcus.'

'To be honest I'm not sure that'd look right. They're officers, you're a private soldier. Think of your role. You wouldn't be hanging around them without a reason.'

'No, I suppose not.'

'How're things going with you and your husband, if I may ask? Just tell me to shut up if I'm being nosy? Only, I sensed things weren't quite right between you two, after what that Russki said last night.'

'It'll take me a while to get used to what he was.'

'To be honest, most of us did stuff in the last few years that wasn't always nice, just to survive. None of us are the people we were before. Those who were too decent or passive are probably dead.'

'True,' she replied, reluctantly admitting that he probably had a point. 'Look, I'll see you in a bit.'

'Where do you think you'll go?'

'My block.'

'Okay, but just remember, look busy!' he said.

'Yep, will do,' she replied as she walked off.

She wandered back towards her block, hoping she'd see Jonathan and Marcus. She also hoped she'd not meet any of the dignitaries.

Various soldiers passed her, some kitted-up and clearly on duty, others perhaps not, but all looking purposeful. As she neared her block, someone spoke to her with a rough voice.

'Oi, you! Yes, you!'

She looked around to see two large soldiers who somehow reminded her of warthogs. They had armbands denoting that they were Provost, and carried batons. They seemed almost as wide as they were tall, and with their thick bull necks resembled all-in wrestlers.

'Pick that up,' one of them, a Corporal, said.

'Ur, what?' she answered, perplexed.

'On the ground there! That litter.'

'I didn't drop it?'

'I don't care! We keep this place clean, especially when we've got visitors.'

She looked at the paper tissue on the ground, probably just fallen from someone's pocket in passing. She walked over and picked it up, hoping it wasn't used.

'What unit are you from? You look like a sack of shit in that uniform you really do. Have you ever heard of an iron? Don't try telling me you're from some secret squirrel mob. Where's your papers?'

She reluctantly stuffed the tissue into one of her pockets then fumbled to find her papers.

'Er, Corporal, is there a problem?' came another voice, that of an older man.

'No mate, just checking this one's papers.'

'Oh really. Well, she's on an assignment for me, and I'm working for the Colonel. You'd better hurry up because the party wants to get off onto the next part of their tour soon.'

'Is that right?' the Provost Corporal asked Julie. She looked at the older man – another Corporal, who looked sincere and kindly- and nodded. 'Yes, that's right.'

'Fine, well piss off then, go on. Just remember to iron your bloody kit next time! I don't want to see you again.'

As the two warthogs waddled off, Julie looked around at the man next to her, short and lean, who was molded in an altogether different scale to the Provost soldiers. 'Just keep quiet and walk with me away,' he said quietly out of the corner of his mouth, keeping his eyes on the two camp enforcers.

She did as she was told and quietly walked with him.

'You don't want to get noticed by that lot, they'd have you in the guardhouse in one-one-two,' he stated. 'They're just bullies, wanna-be Policemen. Mind you, they're also a bunch of Billy-no-mates.'

She smiled, realising that it was the first time that she had done so in days. He continued. 'Unless you've anything in particular to do, you look like you could do with a strong coffee.'

She was indeed shaken and felt a bit light-headed. She glanced at him; he couldn't have been under sixty if it was a day. 'Okay then,' she agreed.

They walked towards the canteen, and he talked to her. 'Well, I could do with one myself. I've been walked off my feet all morning. I may have lied to get you out of trouble, but what I said about being an errand boy for the Colonel's entourage was absolutely true.'

'Oh, I see,' she replied.

'I'm Eric, by the way,'

'Julie, Corporal,' she replied respectfully.

'No, please, none of that Corporal stuff, just first name terms. I'm sick of this lark, to be honest.'

'Okay, Eric.'

'Yes, well I get all the best jobs. Didn't quite make it to Sergeant, you see; hated the idea of all that paperwork. Only took Corporal because Lance-Jack's the worst rank in the British Army. I'd be pulling my retirement by now if it wasn't for the emergency period. They didn't have many left and were desperate. It's nice to feel so valued, I can tell you.'

'I see, yes,' she replied again.

'Tell you something though; those dignitaries are a right pain in the behind. The Brigadier keeps on trying to remember each man's name like he's ruddy Monty. As far as he's concerned I'm freaking Burt! I mean, he could have at least called me something a *bit* like Eric; Ernie maybe. But he's miles off. I'm just going with Burt in his presence.'

She laughed again.

'And that Defence Minister, old what's-his-face, right obnoxious git I can tell you, superior bastard. But he has a habit of picking his nose when he thinks no one's looking. And he's smarmy, well they both are, all that hail-fellow-well-met stuff and pretending to know you. I don't know what fee-paying school the minister went to but I tell you the money were wasted, he's uncouth. I wouldn't vote for him, if there was a vote, which there isn't just now.'

'Really?' Julie was truly amazed that a member of H.M. Armed Forces could even think like this.

'Well, we were once a democracy, I'm old enough to remember how it was when the adults were in charge, men of dignity, or at least they made a damned good pretence at having it. Now I don't know what we are, and I wouldn't trust the bunch in charge any further than I could throw 'em. And it's not as if they're any good. I mean, we've all worked for bastards in our time, haven't we? You know, the types who don't tolerate fools gladly and all. But in the old days, they'd at least get it right, half the time. This lot are incompetent; they keep on making bad calls, and they plainly wouldn't be alive today if it wasn't for the Americans being here.'

Julie was dumbstruck.

'Do you know what the Defence Minister is doing right now?'

'No?' she answered, fascinated.

'He's out having fun, sitting in the cupola of an armoured vehicle, with media guys and their cameras. First thing he did before they left was to take a selfie with his helmet on. He'll no doubt be posting that one on social media later, maybe even as his profile picture.' Eric then mimicked a posh voice. 'Here's me, on active duty with our brave boys on the front line'. He scoffed. 'What you don't see is practically the whole battalion out there making sure the area is safe, plus all those black ops guys and a load of top cover up in the sky. All for one guy to have a joy ride.'

As they neared the canteen, Eric lowered his voice again. 'Anyway, keep it neutral in there,' he advised. 'Walls have ears.'

'Okay,' she replied.

As they walked into the canteen, she had almost forgotten where she was and was acting naturally. She realised that this was the best cover out.

Eric bought her a coffee, and they sat down in easy chairs around a low table full of military magazines. He picked one up, glanced at the cover, and showed her; it was of smiling troops in the snow, eating rations around an armoured personnel carrier.

'The Minister's off in one of them,' he said and chucked the magazine down dismissively with the others.

He sipped his coffee then sat back with a humorous glint in his eye. 'Anyway, did you hear the one about a horse who walked into a bar…?'

44

At least Brigadier Trelawney hadn't taken Trant's seat. When Trant had entered, however, Trelawney's face was grim, and he stood with his own ADC.

'Martin, I'll get straight to the point. I think you know what this is about. I'm relieving you of your command.'

'I see,' Trant replied, unconcerned.

Brigadier Trelawney was taken aback, he frowned and was quiet for a second, and surveyed Trant. He continued, undeterred. 'With immediate effect. I'm sorry Martin, it's not my decision; this has come from higher up. But after that display at breakfast, well, I'm less inclined to question it, I can tell you. I mean, what on earth possessed you to air views like that in front of Selwyn Barton-Smith, of all people?'

Trant took the rebuke with silence, assuming it to be rhetorical.

Trelawney glanced at the officers around him, few of whom made eye contact. 'Well, that aside, I can only say that I *am* sorry, you've been a loyal and effective officer over the years and a very good commander.'

'May I ask what you intend to do with me, Sir?'

'Well, that remains a decision for the ministry. But in the immediate future, you will travel back to headquarters.'

'Hm, that might be awkward, Sir,' Trant said.

'And why is that?'

'Because, Sir, I have effectively already been relieved.'

'What? By whom?'

'By Major General Wesley Easton. I am due to leave for Fairfield later today.'

'Well, I wasn't aware of this.'

'As I wasn't aware of your trip in by helicopter until this time yesterday. Which was, by the way, terribly ill-advised, if I may add?'

'No you bloody well can't *just add*!' Trelawney was furious. He turned, looked daggers at a too-amused Fuller, and walked out. His ADC glanced at Trant and Fuller and raised his eyebrows apologetically before following his commander out.

45

Julie received a text and excused herself to answer it. Eric had finished with another joke.

Julie laughed. 'Oh that's so bad it's actually good!'

Shortly after, Jonathan, Marcus, and Stan turned up. Julie didn't see them, but Eric got up, stood to attention and saluted. 'Sir!'

Jonathan and Marcus saluted.

'Stand easy, Corporal,' Jonathan told him.

Jonathan looked at his wife, wiping her eyes. 'I'm, um, glad to see you're having fun, but we're ready to go shortly.'

'Oh, okay,' she said, sounding a trifle disappointed.

'Yes, well, I hate to have to break up the party,' Jonathan added.

Eric looked at his watch. 'Oh my goodness, I've got to be somewhere. The guests are due to leave anytime soon.'

'Yes, we'll be going shortly after, too,' Jonathan said, hurrying Julie along. She got up and joined them, then turned to Eric.

'Well, goodbye. And thanks, for earlier.'

'Oh, think nothing of it,' Eric said.

'And for cheering me up,' she added.

'It was good to chat', he said. 'And remember…'

She completed it for him, giggling, 'be alert, your country needs lerts!'

Eric looked at the 'officers' sheepishly then excused himself, saluted, and walked off. The canteen was almost empty again.

'Who was *he*?' Marcus asked, more in amazement than suspiciousness.

'Oh, that was Eric, he's a nice old man,' Julie replied.

'You know he's still on the wrong side, just now?' Marcus reminded her. 'I think you've just gone soft.'

'No, no I haven't,' she protested.

'Tell me that next time you've got one in your sights and you fail to take the shot,' Marcus said.

'Oh that's horrible,' Julie said.

'That's war,' Stan replied flatly.

'Tell you what though,' Julie said, just remembering, 'he was helping the entourage with those scumbag V-I-P's earlier.'

'Really?' Marcus replied, now interested. 'Tell me more.'

Jonathan changed the subject. 'Well, I propose that we either try to hide in here, or we remain less conspicuous and join the others on the parade ground for the send-off.'

'You're right, Jonathan,' Marcus said, 'let's get outside.'

46

Trant sat alone in his office. He didn't need to see the Defence Secretary off; that was no longer his job. He considered his options, which were few, and was now thinking that Dolman was the lesser of two evils. Either way, his career was effectively over. He had resented Dolman's impertinence and been disappointed by being betrayed by someone he had regarded as a trusty Lieutenant, a right-hand man.

The business during the London riots hadn't shocked him; and in the same position, he had to admit he might have acted similarly. It was the start of the break down in law and order, something many had seen coming for years and precipitated by what Trant saw of a weakening of resolve to impress self-control from school age. Then there'd been the cuts in the police and military. However, when Dolman had faced rioters baying for police and Army blood, there were still sections of the government in denial. Had it been a few months later, no one would have given it a second glance. Paul Dolman had been accused by the press of lighting the spark. Most in the military thought that fuse had already been lit many years before. If anything, as far as Trant was concerned, it just gave the rebellious elements an excuse.

What had occurred since was that Britain had become a one-party state; essentially a right-wing dictatorship being propped up by America. He knew that Marcus and Jonathan had been right. Anything moderate had gone long ago, but now sanity was fast disappearing with it, and the regime was beginning to exhibit psychotic traits such as paranoia, and losing its grip on reality in favour of its *own* version of political correctness, stemming from anti-left polemic. The mindless rhetoric and propaganda being churned out by the government had been concerning to Trant, who liked as much as possible to act on solid facts. He had never tolerated fools gladly, nor had he much truck with tall stories, and it made no difference whether it came from feckless or intimidated subordinates or superiors who were towing the party line. He had learned long ago that to lose grip on reality was to court failure and defeat.

Now he had been officially relieved of his command, and Brigadier Trelawney was care-taking until his replacement could be found, or promoted from one of the companies. It wouldn't be Fuller. But, after a short time of speculation, he realised that he didn't really care any longer. For a second he felt so black that he considered ending it all then and there but scolded himself for the thought. Instead of pulling a pistol from his drawer, he pulled out the card from his pocket that Marcus had given him earlier. He considered it for a minute, but then put it into a breast pocket of his combat jacket. He saw it as insurance for another time. For now, he would return with Dolman and see where fate led him.

There was a knock on his door. 'Come,' he said.

It was Major Fuller. 'Martin, have you got a moment?'

'As long as you like, Bernard,' Trant replied. 'Sit down. Have a drink won't you?'

'No, thank you.'

Trant look a bottle out of his desk drawer and poured himself a generous amount of whiskey into a mug. He then sat back in his chair, and uncharacteristically put his feet up on his desk.

'What can I do for you?' he asked Fuller.

'Well, it's more about what I might be able to do for you, Martin. I shouldn't be here, but sod it.'

'Come on Bernard, get to the point,' Trant said with slight impatience before taking a swig of whiskey.

'Martin, the safe-haven. What about her?'

Trant was silent and surveyed his intelligence officer fondly. He shook his head. 'I don't know, Bernard.'

'It might have been your liaisons with her that have done this. She's mellowed you, made you more liberal-minded. And, damn it, Martin, you couldn't keep that sort of thing secret forever.'

'Well, I certainly couldn't keep it going under your nose for long, you wily old fox!'

'No, maybe not,' Fuller smiled.

'So?' Trant asked. 'So what? It's surely my business, not theirs.'

'Of course, Martin, but you commanded this whole area. I warned you ages ago that it potentially compromised your position.'

'Well, that's over now.'

'Okay,' Fuller replied skeptically.

'Does anyone else know?'

'No. And no one will.'

'Thank you.'

'Martin, it has to end now. You're one hundred and eighty degrees different from what's down there, and you know it.'

'It's my business, Bernard. And now, it doesn't matter.'

'Look, I'm going to fight your corner. But if they're right and that AI turned something up, then there's no doubt in my mind as to why, where it's coming from.'

'No, you're wrong.'

'Maybe. But you *have* changed, Martin.'

'We've all changed. We're all older.'

'Maybe. But you can't let it end like this. Everything you've fought for, believed in, achieved.'

'Bernard, thank you. Thanks for offering to stand with me; I appreciate your loyalty and your friendship. But leave it. Save your career. I'm through.'

'Martin-

'No, really Bernard, you've done enough.'

'Alright. Well, if you need anything else…'

'Thank you.'

Bernard showed himself out of the office.

47

They stood on the parade ground again and waited whilst the Defence Secretary shook hands with Brigadier Trelawney and other officers. He was followed into the helicopter by a mean-looking and beefy bodyguard in sunglasses and a dark-grey suit.

Soon the rotor blades of the helicopter rapidly picked up speed. Marcus and his team had found a place beside Eric, again in the rear rank of three lines of soldiers.

Very soon the helicopter was lifting off between the phalanx of attack helicopters, and they ascended rapidly and changed direction. It was when were at about three hundred feet that there was the sound of distant thunder. Then they noticed a stream of white smoke snaking its way rapidly up, making a bee-line for the transport helicopter. Before anyone had time to say anything, it had exploded into a ball of fire and black smoke, and the wreckage fell into a wooded valley beneath.

'Oh, bloody hell!' they heard Brigadier Trelawney shout, as the senior officers viewed the few bits of lighter and still burning debris floating down, smoke now drifting lazily off in the wind.

'Well,' Eric murmured. 'It couldn't have happened to a nicer guy!'

Stan choked back a laugh, Marcus was less successful and bowed his head to hide it, and Julie tried not to giggle by biting her lip. Marcus was clearly overjoyed as Jonathan looked around at him with a cautious smile.

'Hopefully they saluted the wreckage as it went down,' Eric quipped.

An alarm siren was set off, and the parade dispersed unceremoniously without an order being given, but amid plenty of panicked shouts to man positions, and for certain platoons to stand-to. A quick reaction force was already jumping into armoured vehicles and moving off. The helicopter gunships roared around and a few seconds later opened fire into patches of forest nearby, the presumed site of the missile launcher.

'Come on,' Marcus said quietly, 'this is our chance.'

'Okay chaps,' Jonathan continued with the pretence, 'we need to be off.'

'Well, best of luck,' Eric said, really to Julie. 'It's getting a bit cheeky out there again. Kinetic, as they say.'

'Indeed, Corporal,' Jonathan said.

'Um, one thing Corporal,' Marcus asked. 'I've not seen the garrison commander around for a while. Wasn't he to have seen his guests off?'

'What, you mean Colonel Trant? Haven't you heard? Brigadier what-his-face over there just went and relieved him of his command! He's to return to H-Q forthwith, apparently.'

'He wasn't in that helicopter?' Marcus asked. Although he hadn't seen him get in, he wanted to be sure.

'Oh no, lucky for him, but he should have been,' Eric said. 'No,' he gestured for Marcus and Jonathan to get closer, and then managed a conspiratorial stage whisper over the hubbub. 'Gen up, I heard he's being transported back to Fairfield Airbase this afternoon, and would you believe it, in the back of an American supply wagon. I mean, how demeaning is that, for a man of his rank? What a come-down!'

'That's appalling,' Jonathan said.

'How the mighty fall, sometimes literally,' Eric said, and couldn't help himself from grinning.

'Now steady on, Corporal,' Jonathan cautioned, getting back into his role.

'Oh, sorry Sir,' Eric reddened, thinking he'd stepped out of line with a superior.

'That's okay,' Jonathan replied patronisingly. 'Well, we have to be on our way. Farewell.' Eric saluted as they left. Julie paused and squeezed his arm. He was still a bit nonplussed by his dressing down by Jonathan, but smiled.

'Bye,' she said. 'You take care too.' She left him standing there, looking a bit helpless.

A few minutes later Stan had started the engine of the armoured vehicle, and they were in their seats and fastening their safety harnesses. The armoured vehicle began to roll forward, but before Stan could pull out a platoon of tracked armoured personnel carriers sped by. He then saw his chance and moved the armoured vehicle straight out behind them, and sped up fast to catch up and join the column.

As they neared the gate Marcus shouted to Stan. 'Don't even slow down! They won't be interested in checking passes just now'. They sped through the open barrier behind the others. After a few seconds they were out and onto open-road, albeit trailing behind a small convoy of armoured vehicles.

'My God, can it be that easy?' Marcus asked incredulously.

'I don't believe it,' Stan said.

The relief was palpable; they were out of the lion's den.

Marcus regained his focus. 'Okay, Stan, I want you to take a left turn into the forest, next track you see. We absolutely can't stay with this convoy.'

'Then what?' Jonathan asked from his place in the front passenger seat.

'We wait,' Marcus replied. 'Come nightfall, we rendezvous with Akam and the Russians.'

'Really? The Russians again? You arranged this?' Jonathan asked.

'Oh yes. And that little coup back there, all down to a bit of cheap technology,' he held up his mobile phone.

As Stan stopped the vehicle in a forest clearing, Marcus then addressed all of them. 'Well, team, whatever happens next, well done. Our objective was achieved, we got out undetected, and we managed to take advantage of a situation and inflict a grievous blow to the regime.' He sat back, took his beret off, and drew his fingers through his thick dark hair. 'However,' he continued, 'we're not out of the woods yet, literally. We need to pick up Akam and that Russian commando team before the Army does. We're going to have to stick to our cover, stay in uniform, and bluff it out if there's any trouble.'

Despite their initial relief, they all stopped smiling, sat back, and quietened down, as they mentally braced themselves for more trouble.

Marcus started texting again.

48

It was late afternoon by the time Trant was escorted to the motor transport hangar by Dolman. He had just one rucksack of his personal belongings.

Brigadier Trelawney was already ensconced in his office, the name on the door having been changed already. One of Trant's company commanders had shunned him completely. However, a Captain just off duty from the operations room had had the temerity to stop him and shake his hand as he crossed the parade ground. A few of his men, who seemed to have figured out what was going on, did the same.

The fact that more hadn't was down to the fact that most of his battalion was now out scouring the hills for the enemy missile team which had destroyed the Defence Secretary's helicopter. But it was also down to the fact that his departure hadn't been formally announced. As far as Brigadier Trelawney was concerned, the less the men of the garrison were told, the better. Trant felt as if the floor might as well have opened and he had fallen into a pool of hungry sharks. The shock of it, he realised, was still offsetting the anger and resentment that he was bound to end up feeling.

He looked at the three large eight-wheeled American vehicles before him. A couple of American soldiers wearing helmets were doing last-minute checks around them. Standing by the back door of the lead vehicle was Major Fuller. As Trant approached, he realised that his Intelligence Officer was holding a bottle of whiskey.

Fuller was putting a brave face on it. 'Well, with more notice we might also have got you a leaving card,' he joked. 'But instead, we managed to cadge this from behind the bar. Don't drink it all at once, old man!'

Trant gladly accepted it. 'Thanks, Bernard. And, thanks for your support over the years.'

'I'm sorry to be losing you,' Fuller stated thickly.

'Just keep your head down, and you'll do fine.'

'Maybe. Mad Jack's already marking his patch, making his presence felt. I don't think I'll be sticking around here, whatever.'

'Well, see. Anyway, a last SITREP from you if I may, Bernard. What's the situation out there?'

'The Battalion is out there, scouring the hills. A route opening force has gone ahead, we're sending an escort with you down to the M-4, and there're top cover assets available too.'

'Good. And what about the missile team, have they been neutralised?'

'Er, no. To be honest, it's been handled shambolically,' Fuller said, glancing at a stony-faced Dolman. 'The new commander has nothing close to your doctrine of counter-insurgency.'

Trant looked around at the impassive faces of the American crew; and Dolman's; humourless and impatient.

'Ah well,' Trant said, 'point the Brigadier to a few of my journal articles. It takes a while to pick up.' He held his hand out to Fuller and he shook it. 'Anyway, another time Bernard.'

'Yes, all the very best, Martin. I hope it works out well for you.'

Trant got into the lead AFV, followed by Dolman, who pulled the door closed behind him. Trant glanced at Specialist Martinez as she strapped herself into her seat and looked at her consoles.

'Hi,' a large-boned but skinny hand moved into view and Trant clasped it in confusion.

'I'm Second Lieutenant Will Courtney, 32nd Brigade Support and Sustainment Battalion. I'm in command of this convoy,' he said self-importantly.

'Lieutenant-Colonel Trant. Nice to meet you, Lieutenant.'

'And you, Sir,' Courtney replied. 'I've heard a lot about you.'

'Good things only, I hope?' They both grinned for a second, as if in mutual recognition of how trite their conversation was. The engines revved up.

49

Julie sat in the back of the armoured vehicle with a blanket over her, shivering.

'You okay?' Jonathan asked. She nodded dismally in reply.

'Yes, I know,' Jonathan said, 'I've had enough of this game of soldiers too. I've just spoken to Marcus though. Akam contacted him, and it seems the Russians are onto something.'

'Well I just wish they'd hurry up about it,' she replied, her teeth chattering briefly.

It began to rain again, and Jonathan pulled the back door closed. 'It's my turn on guard soon, I can't leave it all to Stan.'

'I'll do my turn,' she replied, blowing on her fingers.

'No, don't you worry, Marcus has said for you to stay warm in here,' Jonathan replied. 'In any case, I want you here in case we need to make a fast get-away.'

For once she didn't argue.

'Are we friends again?' Jonathan ventured.

She looked at him and reluctantly smiled. 'I suppose so.'

'I'm no war criminal,' he said.

'I hope not, I really bloody well hope not,' she replied.

50

As they traversed the second bend in the downhill switchbacks, the heavens opened up with a cloudburst of rain. 'Steady Mike,' Corporal Gresham cautioned as Specialist Kowalski braked harder. The windscreen wipers worked hard against the deluge. Thereafter it all happened fast.

The first that they knew that something was wrong was when they heard their own .50 calibre gun open up from the top of the vehicle. Up above, a drenched Specialist Plaskett looked bewildered as the AI Advanced Targeting control on his gun automatically traversed his turret slightly left and began firing at some unseen targets in trees by the roadside, detected with their heat-seeking image sensors. The overly-calm female voice of the AI system informed him that it had detected the source of incoming fire, including the launch site of an RPG anti-tank missile (which had, unbeknownst to him, just missed their front wheel). Their .50 calibre gun had just neutralised the threat.

'Oh shit!' Kowalski exclaimed a second later, as the lead vehicle in front, a small British armoured vehicle, appeared to skid out of control in front of them and hit the grey safety barrier, before exploding.

Kowalski braked hard to avoid hitting the inferno and wreckage, but was now effectively driving blind.

'No, drive through it!' Corporal Gresham screamed.

In the back, people looked alarmed, but none more so than Colonel Trant, who was now staring down the barrel of a pistol aimed at him by Lieutenant Courtney. There was an enormous jolt and then vehicle lurched to the right. Courtney began to fire wildly, bullets ricocheting around the inside of the crew compartment. Martinez screamed as she was hit by a spent round just as Ned Plaskett's body dropped down limply from the cupola in a shower of water and blood, his neck gushing from an open wound. There followed another massive jolt and screeching sound. The lights began to flicker and anyone not strapped into their seat was thrown around as the vehicle began to lurch over and roll.

Their vehicle had been knocked off course by the burning escort vehicle in front, and had then hit the crash barrier. It was subsequently hit from behind by the unstoppable momentum of its two skidding companions. Their lead vehicle then tore through the crash barrier and proceeded to tumble down the hill, followed by its two companions, all in a small avalanche of loose grey shale.

51

The Russian special purpose detachment knew that it had just minutes. Whilst they had hoped to retrieve Trant from near the road IED, they had also anticipated that his AFV might end up down below.

Indeed, the armoured personnel carrier now lay on its side, a single back wheel still spinning slowly. Someone had opened one of the top hatches and weakly crawled halfway out. Up above Pavel and Nickolai waited in cover whilst Pyotr and Fyodor went down with the team of local insurgents they'd met up with to retrieve Trant. Pavel watched their progress closely through binoculars.

'Hurry up, but be careful with him,' Pyotr said.

'I am!' Fyodor shouted back, as he roughly tugged out the man in the hatch and then casually slit his throat.

'God, I hope that wasn't the Colonel…' Pavel said, still surveying the action with his binoculars from above.

'We have two or three minutes max,' Nickolai reminded him.

'I know, I know,' the Russian officer replied impatiently as he continued to look down the slope. 'I just hope he's still alive.'

'Shall I go and help?' Akam asked uncertainly.

'Nyet,' Pavel replied. 'Fyodor and Pyotr strong enough. Those gunships will be on us any minute.'

Around them, forming a loose defensive cordon, were members of a local resistance group. Several of them stood around the Russian commandos down by the crashed vehicles, more interested in seeing what was inside for the taking than in scanning for the Army.

With just a pistol in one hand, Pyotr had pushed past Fyodor to crawl into the top cover hatch of the command vehicle, and found himself in a scene of carnage. The inside of the vehicle was illuminated only by one remaining emergency light, and a computer monitor that flashed as its software attempted to re-boot. The walls were spattered with blood, and several of the occupants lay slumped amongst any equipment that may have been loose before the crash. The computer controller was still strapped into her seat, unconscious and slumped on her side.

Pyotr quickly identified Colonel Trant and called to Fyodor.

'Quickly, in here. He's still alive. Help me out with him.' He took off Trant's helmet and threw it away. Trant was barely conscious and groaning. Pyotr stuck him on the head with the handle of his pistol then holstered it.

The two Russians manhandled him out of the hatch. Then big Fyodor, 'the Bear', lifted him onto his back and, with Pyotr's help from behind, proceeded to scramble up and along the slope to the nearest section of the switch-back of the downhill road.

Pyotr turned to look back down at the resistance men. 'Take what you like now.'

The local militia was already all over the vehicle, and only one bothered to acknowledge him, waving him off with an impatient grimace on his face. Several were already inside the AFV, pulling Dolman and Courtney out, and any weapons. One was vainly trying to dislodge the main armament from the body of the vehicle.

'Hey, there's a girlie still in there, quite exotic if, you like that sort of thing,' one exclaimed.

'Now don't none of you be getting any ideas, it's just equipment we want,' their leader growled. He was a large man with a grey beard and wore a brown jacket and a black flat cap. He looked on as his men plundered what booty there was. 'Remove their combat jackets,' he continued, 'they're also useful, and their boots. Check for any ammo. And their wallets, for cash and passes.'

Pyotr glanced back at them and shook his head before carrying on to catch-up with Fyodor. They soon reached the road to be met by Pavel and Nickolai, who had a make-shift stretcher. Between them, they moved rapidly back up the slope and into the trees. A few seconds later they heard vehicles approaching, and helicopters overhead. There was a sudden burst of automatic fire from one of the helicopters as it engaged the resistance team that had lingered too long down near the vehicle.

52

In just his T-shirt and trousers, Dolman stumbled bare-footed from the scene of the crash, down the hill. There was no one around, and he just carried on, stumbling over several times. The ground kept on meeting his head. With a huge effort he righted himself and continued down the slope. He was unaccountably thirsty and knew that there may be water down there. However, that was the only thing that he knew. He didn't know where he was. He no longer knew that he was a soldier. He no longer even knew *who* he was.

The edges of his vision were tinged in mauve, and little white and coloured flashes kept appearing. He continued, fell, and rolled. A couple of minutes later, he resumed consciousness and dragged himself onwards, crawling. He crawled over some rocks and down a bank, and just inside a tree line he eventually found the stream that he was seeking and thirstily palmed water into his mouth.

He lay back for a minute and heard the helicopters and vehicles again. He was sure that they were after him. He was certain that he had heard some men speaking in Russian. He didn't know why that was bad, but he pulled himself up and continued, determined to find cover. He decided to stay on level ground, and walked onwards, following the path of the stream under a road. He heard more gunfire. It'd make operational sense to remain under the road bridge for a while, but he knew he'd have to continue in case his pursuers had dogs.

He stumbled on until he found that he was looking down into a basin containing a small lake or reservoir. Nearby was an eclectic collection of make-shift shelters, tents and tarpaulins, and a fenced-off garden where rows of vegetables grew. People were walking around, including women and children, even dogs. As the clouds began to clear and sunlight shone down on the scene, it looked like a Shangri-La. It made no sense to him. Maybe this was his path to Heaven. He collapsed and rolled down the slope, unconscious.

53

By the time Akam and the Russian team had caught up with Marcus's team, they were hot and sweaty from the effort of carrying Trant on his stretcher. It had stopped raining and the clouds had blown away, and now a setting sun was about to dip below the horizon. Higher up they would retain the light a little longer than down in the valleys, but the last orange rays projected little light into the pine trees that hid them and their armoured vehicle. In there, as in the valleys, it was already twilight, and birds sang mournful evening songs.

The Russians laid Trant down by the armoured vehicle as Stan, on guard, went to fetch Marcus from the back. He was speechless.

'Here you go!' Pavel grinned triumphantly. 'Your Colonel.'

Jonathan emerged from the back of the vehicle. 'How…? Just what the…?'

'Well done!' Marcus told Pavel, shaking his hand vigorously. 'All of you.'

Julie stepped out of the back of the vehicle, arms crossed and shivering from the chill of the late October evening.

'We go now, yes?' Pavel asked.

'Yes, we go now,' Marcus replied with a smile.

Jonathan raised the palm of his hand. 'Hang on, just a minute, please. You mean to say, Marcus, that your plan to release Trant relied upon this bunch of ruthless killers, who are masters in ambush and assassination techniques and little more?'

'I had no choice, Jonathan,' Marcus protested, 'We were hardly in a position to stop a convoy now, were we?' He turned to Pavel. 'How did you do it?'

'Huh, we lay an ambush,' Pavel replied defensively with a frown, shooting a hostile glance at Jonathan.

'And, they just stopped?' Jonathan asked.

'Eventually, yes,' Pavel answered, too honestly. 'Somewhere down a slope.'

'It was unfortunate,' Akam explained. 'The American driver seemed to panic.'

Jonathan rolled his eyes and held his hands up in exasperation. Marcus glanced at Jonathan with a sheepish grin.

Pavel continued. 'No matter, we got your bloody Colonel! Now let's move, eh?'

'He's lucky to be alive,' Jonathan said. 'How many others died?'

'So, why should you care?' Pavel asked aggressively.

Marcus changed the subject. 'Come on, let's get away from this place. There's still a lot of movement out there, one more armoured vehicle won't be noticed.'

Pavel glared again at Jonathan before he ordered his team to get Trant into the back of the vehicle.

54

After listening to incoming radio traffic in the operations room of the garrison, Brigadier 'Mad Jack' Trelawney demanded an intelligence briefing with Major Fuller later that evening. Trelawney was incandescent with rage and banged his fist on the table.

'Damn it all, just what the blazes is going on in this sector, Major? I thought you had it all locked down! You know, there'll be hell to pay. This is your career effectively over. And maybe mine too.'

Major Fuller flushed red but remained relatively calm. 'With respect, Sir, I counted Colonel Trant as a personal friend. As to the visit, we gave the government plenty of warning. We strongly urged against transporting the Defence Secretary in that manner, due to solid intelligence regarding the recent threat of Russian made anti-aircraft missiles having been supplied amongst insurgent groups, which is surely a game-changer for us. All communications have been recorded, and can be cited in our defence.'

'DAMN your bloody defence, Bernard! We've lost a member of the cabinet and a battalion commander, in one afternoon! Plus, a valued and high-profile anti-insurgency commander, Captain Dolman. That alone would be a political coup for them. If they put either of those two up for ransom, well Lord knows what the PM will do, have my guts for garters I should imagine! I want to know what is happening out there, and you will tell me if it's the last thing you do!'

'Sir, I can assure you that everything possible is being done. We have patrols out, helicopters, drones, and satellite tracking. My signals units are all over the electronic and radio transmissions emanating from this area, and so is Cheltenham.'

'And?' Trelawney asked, eyebrows raised and cheeks red.

'And there's been very little out of the ordinary. We know that resistance groups have learned to co-ordinate off-grid and use communications sparingly. Where used it's always cryptic. Yes, we've picked up mobile signals, and we're still analysing them. They'll probably be telling a girl called Megan down in the valley to look at the latest cat video on social media, and it'll be code to take out a helicopter or AFV.'

In disgust, Trelawney turned to a Captain. 'What's the situation at the crash site?'

The Captain tried not to flinch or appear over-deferent and kept his tone very steady. 'Still two dead, two missing Sir. They caught some insurgents, just local boys it seems. Lots were killed by drone and helicopter fire. It appears that the ambush was well-planned, I-E-D which took out our P-P-V escort. Looks like the American driver made a bad call in avoiding the wreckage, went through the crash barrier, and took his whole convoy with him. He survived the crash but they slit his throat and looted the rest. We have the survivors back here, they're being treated in the infirmary.'

'It's pure scum who did this. If we can't get anything out of the prisoners we took then I want them all disposed of.'

'Um, hold on, Sir,' Major Fuller cautioned. 'Don't you think they might prove strategically useful, given the current state of affairs with our American partners?'

'Come again, Major?' the Brigadier asked irately, arrogantly affecting not to understand him.

'I mean when they find out that one of their men was slaughtered out of hand, rather than be taken prisoner?'

'Hmm, I really think that could go either way, Major, don't you? The American public are sick of this engagement, and if the administration in Washington should change next month then we could see them leaving well before we're ready to take back control.'

'That's a distinct possibility in the long term. No, I was thinking it might harden the resolve of local commanders.'

'To what end?'

'To pushing harder on all fronts; and, to re-taking more of our major urban centres. A surge before the election could prove most beneficial to the incumbent in Washington.'

'Maybe, if he had a chance of gaining the finance, but we know without control of Congress and the Senate he's a lame-duck President now. The Democrats will never agree to the funding of a surge here. They'll have the majority of their boys' home after a couple more Christmases, with perhaps a few left in training teams; and we'll be back to square one. Probably being forced to broker deals with the insurgents, and watch our way of life go down the drain again.'

'One last push, and we'll have more bargaining power,' Fuller suggested.

55

Dolman slept fitfully and dreamt of hastily dug trenches in snowfields at night being illuminated by explosions, briefly exposing the dead.

The next morning, as he slowly opened his eyes he thought he might have been erroneously been admitted to Heaven from the battlefield. He was looking into the face of a woman with long blond hair and a silky white dress, who was wiping his forehead with a damp cloth. All around her was white. To cap it all, strange and slightly random music was emanating from a flute.

The white-clad woman's words didn't detract any from the delusion. 'Peter, go and get Michael. He's waking up.'

'Yes, okay,' came a boy's voice excitedly. Dolman saw a boy of perhaps eleven or twelve put a flute down onto a trestle table and run out, followed by a small brown dog, some sort of Dachshund cross.

As his eyes began to focus, the white surroundings become more distinct and rather off-white. It was clear that he was inside some sort of small marquee, sides occasionally billowing in the soft breeze. With his left hand, he felt the familiar metal tube frame of a military camp bed.

'Where am I?' he asked.

'You're with the colony of Michael Meekin's New Age Pioneers. This is also a safe-haven.'

'Safe-haven?'

'Yes,' she replied as if she didn't need to explain. 'You've taken a nasty knock to your head, it seems.'

'Have I? Which country am I in? Is this England?' He started to sit up.

'No, it's South Wales. Now please, lie back, relax.'

Dolman frowned and looked slightly perturbed as he attempted to remember why he would be here. Or even who he was.

He heard some commotion and laughter. The boy returned with the dog, followed by a young woman holding a tray of food, laughing and joking with the young man who had followed her in. The girl, perhaps in her late twenties, had wavy brown hair and was diminutive, and slightly cherubic. As she placed the tray down onto the trestle table by Dolman's bed, she glanced at him. Their eyes locked for a moment too long. Dolman tried to ignore her as he regained his composure but glanced at her again as she left. He caught a hostile look from the young man who was with her before he turned to follow her out.

'Pretty young thing, isn't she?' a slightly effete male voice said. Dolman looked past the willowy blond woman who had been treating him, to see a rotund man in a three-quarter-length white robe with ornate gold trim around the edges, over a black jumper. 'But don't get any ideas. She's spoken for, I'm afraid.'

Dolman heard a baby crying somewhere in what he now understood to be an encampment. He had a memory of seeing the basin with the reservoir, and the tents and small dwellings nearby.

The large fellow continued in rueful pronouncement. 'Emily's chosen her fate, along with a few of our band, and will be leaving us shortly, foolish girl. Using her natural attractions to win comfort and security, and maybe who could blame her? She's done well, too; promised to some civil service official. Sleazy as hell, but what do I know? She's broken the hearts of plenty a young man around here, I can tell you, but to be honest they're all dependent no-hopers.'

Dolman shook his head, he was none the wiser.

'The scheme?' he asked, assuming Dolman would know. 'The Replenishment Scheme? Re-population? Oh my, where have you been these last few years?'

'I wish I knew,' Dolman replied in all earnestness.

'Hmm, it's that bump on the head I should imagine,' the tubby man said with mock sympathy. 'I'm Michael, by the way,' he held out a small, limp hand for Dolman to shake. 'Michael Meekins. I run this colony for my sins. I won't ask who you are, because it seems …you don't actually know yourself!' He scoffed.

Whilst Dolman looked down at his own hands, Michael surreptitiously surveyed Dolman, his athletic frame and good musculature beneath his torn T-shirt, and frowned. 'Hmm, methinks you're a soldier. Yes…a soldier would fit. But, from which Army?'

Dolman looked up. 'I don't know. I can't claim to be that,' he tried to sound certain, but recent memory of his nightmare made him suspect that Michael's assumption might be correct.

'Oh, yes, I think you are. And I think that once you remember, you might be dangerous. If you happen to be on the wrong side, depending on who comes looking for you, you could be very dangerous, for us. Claire here found you, I warned her to leave you where you'd fallen, but she was insistent. These haven't been good times for the soft-hearted.' He glanced at the blond woman, who looked anxious. 'She may as well have brought back a ticking time bomb,' he said acerbically.

Dolman was silent.

'You see, we're a peaceful band of beautiful and spiritually enlightened people, mostly keeping ourselves to ourselves. We came together from all over Britain to this small valley for safety. We were all scared and very hungry, on our last legs. The Americans came in, provided us with security from the roaming bands, and food. Well, we grow a lot of our own now. We've come a long way, and I'll tell you now, we don't want any trouble.'

'I assure you, I shall be of no trouble to you.'

Michael smiled ironically. 'That might not be in your hands, soldier boy. I sense bad karma on its way. We've been hearing what's been going on out there. Has the Colonel lost control?'

'Colonel?' Dolman replied.

'Colonel Trant. Our good Lord Protector.'

For a second there was a flash of recognition.

Michael looked intently at Dolman. 'Hmm, seems you know him, yes? Maybe we might risk ascending to his lofty fortress and depositing you back, and that might just be the end of it. Yes, when you're on your feet, I think that's what we'll do.'

Michael looked down and found Peter's little dog, sniffing around his feet. He gave it a sharp nudge with the toe of his sandal. The dog gave a small squeal and looked up in surprise, then moved away towards her owner.

'Get that flea-bitten thing out of here, boy!' Michael told the boy.

'She's doing no harm, leader,' Peter protested.

'This is a hospital, can't you see? Be off with you, unless you wish to donate her to the dinner menu tonight?'

'No!'

'Then go!' Michael said.

Emily was back with a hot drink for Dolman. 'Come on Peter,' she said mildly. 'Take him away from here.'

'Okay, Molly knows when she's not wanted,' Peter said ruefully.

'Oh, that's pathetic, she knows she's loved,' Emily called after Peter before she put the drink down.

Michael nodded at her to leave, and then looked around at Dolman. 'The only reason that the animals here survive is that most of us are vegetarians. But in the emergency I certainly developed a taste for dog. Hmm, far superior to rat, don't you think?' he licked his lips at the memory.

'I wouldn't know,' Dolman replied, realising that he was the first fellow he'd seen with such large jowls in a long time.

'Ah, no, but then you soldiers never had to descend to such things, did you? You never suffered any of the privations. You had all of the food, after all.' He gave Dolman a resentful glance before turning to leave.

56

'Sir?' the young signals Lieutenant asked.

'Yes, what is it?' Brigadier Trelawney asked irritably.

'Sorry to interrupt, but we've had a message from US TACSAT control. A vehicle, one of ours, was spotted leaving our area of operations at eighteen-fifty-five yesterday, headed North-east. It stopped at a deserted location overnight but is now entering the outskirts of Bristol. They've asked if it's authorised.'

Trelawney looked at Fuller. 'I think you'd better make some enquiries, Major, don't you?'

'Definitely, Sir. Sounds like it could be heading *into* Bristol.'

'Have we got any vehicle checkpoints in the area?'

'Oh, plenty. We can certainly put out a general alert if we've got time.'

Trelawney considered the possibilities. 'Hmm, Bristol, eh? One of the biggest thorns in our side. I'd *love* to have a go at that multicultural hotchpotch myself. Say those *are* our hostiles heading back to their hive…?'

Fuller looked at his commander dubiously. 'And, if so…'

'And if *they* had murdered the American, in cold blood…,' Trelawney continued.

Fuller didn't like the way this was going. 'Yes?'

Trelawney ushered him aside and talked quietly. 'Stand down all vehicle checkpoints on that road. Let them through the cordon.'

'Being honest, Sir, they could probably get through on foot if they needed, and are probably likely to.'

Trelawney flicked a hand at him impatiently. 'Whatever, I don't care. I want them back there, and want Uncle Sam to know it! And I want the PM to know it, too. And if they demand ransoms for Trant and Dolman then all the better. We can then put a damned good case to the cabinet and Washington for going in there to get them. Also, not least of all, we can hold them criminally responsible for the death of Barton-Smith. If I'm leading the show then we might yet be able to recover something from this shambles and keep our careers and pensions intact. Are you with me?'

Fuller swallowed. It was not for nothing that Brigadier Trelawney had earned the dubious accolade of 'Mad Jack', one which he had proudly embraced.

57

Claire had helped Dolman get up. 'You might be going back, soon,' she said. 'But I'd like you to see our gardens, and how our people live.'

'Okay,' Dolman said uncertainly.

'If you like, you can help us sell some of the produce, down in the local estates,' she said, handing him some sandals.

'Really, I'm not a good salesman.'

'Well, it's up to you. A few of us shall be going. Emily too.' She glanced knowingly at Dolman, and she met his eyes in unspoken recognition.

She continued. 'I don't know who you are, and it could be that Michael is right. But that girl is numb, doesn't know what she wants. She's taken to drinking too much, I don't know where she gets it from; she's got friendly with some of the locals I think. You seem a decent man. I could tell she liked you from the moment she saw you. The man she's going to sounds like a...,' it was clear that she was too decent to say something too disparaging. 'Well, let's just say he sounds like a very dull cog in the system. And she feels nothing for him, I know that instinctively. I'd hate to see her become some baby factory for such a man, stuck in a loveless union.'

'I'm a decent man? I think you honour me with an accolade that I suspect I really don't deserve,' Dolman stated. 'And, if indeed I am a soldier, then I'm almost certainly not as nice a fellow as you seem to think.'

'It doesn't matter to me. We are all working through our karma, living out the results of our actions, learning from them, and changing; always changing. Redemption is always possible.'

'I'm not sure it is for me, Claire!' Dolman grinned.

Claire didn't smile. 'Well, anyway. Come with us. The weather is truly wonderful today.'

And indeed it was, for the last week in October. Whilst the early morning had been cool, as the day wore on it had warmed up considerably. Once outside the marquee, Dolman squinted into the glare of the sunlight, which also reflected dazzlingly from the surface of the reservoir a little way away. A soft breeze played on his face, carrying with it a fresh aroma of flowers.

'Jasmine, lavender, and dahlias are still growing in our gardens,' Claire said. 'The growing season is nearly at an end, though, for almost all of our crops, save for the winter vegetables.'

They wandered through the encampment. In addition to the tents and marquees, several semi-permanent shelters had been erected with disparate materials. Dogs ran around and children played, and a few men and women walked about, mostly carrying things to and from the garden, or washing and hanging clothes. Some worked on repairs to shelters damaged by the recent wind-storms.

Claire took him past some pens of goats, rabbits and chicken coops, to the gardens. They were surrounded by low chicken wire and other assorted bits of fencing, and she opened a small gate. As they walked down a path between rows of plants, mostly root vegetables, and then frames growing beans, Dolman saw people watering from cans, weeding, and harvesting. They arrived at a small group, which included Emily. She was on her knees, digging out potatoes.

Claire went up to another, a lady with plaited, hennaed-dyed red hair, and nose and ear studs. 'Rachael, are we ready to go down to the estate?'

'Yeah, Steven has today's stuff ready in the packs. I'll be with you in a sec, and so will Emily.'

Emily looked up at Dolman and seemed glad to drop her trowel. She eased herself up and took her gardening gloves off, and made an attempt to wipe the mud off her jeans.

Rachael continued. 'We've only got a couple of the younger lads with us today to carry the potatoes and parsnips, but Peter said he'd help.'

Claire beamed. 'Well, we've got this fine fellow here to help us as well.'

'Oh, good, well let's go then!' Rachael said enthusiastically.

They walked over to a bench and table stacked with packs. Dolman dutifully hauled on a backpack containing sacks of potatoes, carrots, and parsnips. He suddenly flashed back to moving fast towards a treeline from a helicopter insertion into a field towards a forest, ensuring his assault rifle was made ready. He was beginning to remember. However, as he began to piece his history together, he was aware that there might be swathes that he'd be missing.

They walked out of the gardens at the other end and down a now-unused grassy farm track. Emily and the younger ones began to pick blackberries growing on the hedges on one side, eating some and saving some. A late-season wasp buzzed around lazily.

Emily approached Dolman and held out her hand, which was stained with the juice and contained five blackberries. 'Do you want some?'

'Yes, thank you,' he replied and took them gratefully.

She smiled and turned to find some more.

'Come on, we can get more on the way back,' Claire urged. 'Maybe enough for pies tonight!'

'Mmm, yum!' Peter replied. 'Come on, Molly,' he told his dog as she ran around their feet, eating the odd bit of fruit which had dropped. 'Can I have fruit pudding at Christmas?' he asked Emily.

'Yes, I'm sure. We've already stored the fruit,' Emily replied.

'And what presents have you got me?' he asked excitedly.

'Ah, well, you'll have to wait, won't you,' Claire replied.

They continued down the valley until they neared one of the housing estates, and wandered in through an entrance beside a block of garages, to emerge into a close. A few children played in the road, and an old man was on a step ladder cutting his hedge. Someone in the distance was sawing something.

The sun shone through one of the small trees, most of its orange-yellow leaves having been stripped by the recent wind-storms. Despite the warmth of the late morning, it cast a shadow reminiscent of winter on one of the end walls of the houses.

'It reminds me of a place where I grew up, many miles away,' Emily told Dolman wistfully. 'Sometimes, when I'm here, it seems as if things were back to normal.'

'They may well be, someday,' he replied.

'I hope so,' she said.

'What did you do before this?' he asked.

'Oh, I left school, went to work in an office,' she said.

'Not University?' he asked.

'No, I'm a working-class girl,' she replied. 'Mum and Dad couldn't afford that.'

'I'm surprised,' he replied.

She looked at him askance, but said nothing, and walked away.

A door opened and a middle-aged woman waved at them, smiling.

'They see us coming each day,' Claire told Dolman. 'We rarely have to even knock on the doors.'

At their seventh house, Claire and Dolman approached another lady. 'What you got for us today, Claire? Any tomatoes?' the woman asked.

'No, sorry, they're all done; lots of vegetables though. Potatoes, carrots, parsnips.'

'Oh, go on then,' the woman replied. 'We still don't see much fresh in the stores.'

As they were making the transaction, there was a scream from Peter, and the woman put her hand to her mouth. 'Oh, my!'

Claire and Dolman turned to see Peter's dog, Molly, hanging from the garden gate-post by her lead, surrounded by three teenage boys who were now laughing cruelly. Peter himself was on his back on the ground, pinned down with one of the boy's boots on his chest. He flailed uselessly. 'No! Leave her alone! Mister, help her!'

The dog was being strangled to death by her collar, eyes bulging, unable to even squeal. Dolman launched forward and lifted her off.

'Hey, mister, you don't want to get involved,' said the tallest boy, who had a top-knot of curly blond hair and narrow eyes.

'Piss off,' Dolman said, 'all of you. Let him go.'

In a move the larger boy lunged at Dolman with a knife, aimed at his groin. Dolman moved slightly but not enough, and it pierced his inside thigh. Dolman ignored the wound and grabbed the boy by his arms and neck, disarming him, turning him around and lifting him from the ground, surprised at how light he was. He held him by the neck in a lock. The boy went puce red in the face and let out a muffled cry. 'Get him offa me! Let me go!' As the other two boys ran away, Dolman began to crush his windpipe.

'Please, let him go!' Claire shouted urgently.

Dolman turned the teenager ninety degrees so that he was horizontal, then dropped him straight down onto the pavement. He attempted to get up but remained on his front, clasping his throat and rasping. Dolman restrained himself from kicking him in the ribs for good measure. Eventually, the boy got his wind back and used the fence to lift himself. Dolman dropped his knife down a drain.

The boy staggered off, turning to shout in a rasping voice. 'You're dead, d'ya hear? You're a dead man walking.'

Claire looked at Dolman in shock.

Peter ran up and hugged him. 'Thanks, mister, you saved Molly!' He then discovered that Dolman was bleeding. 'Mister, you're hurt!'

'It's nothing,' Dolman said, looking down the street for more trouble.

'Come on,' said Claire, 'we'd better get you back. You'll need that wound dressed.' She turned to the woman at the door. 'Gwyneth, please can you look after the pack. Take as much as you want; pay us when you can.'

Gwyneth, still shocked, looked at Claire. 'Yes, of course. Damn, those boys are little devils, they run riot on this estate; think they own the place and all. To think, the flu took so many good ones, but left them.'

Claire looked at Dolman. 'Come on, we're going back. Peter? Get the others. Oh, now, where's Emily? She's always slipping off.'

58

It was surprisingly easy to get through the cordon. Marcus had considered ditching their armoured vehicle and returning on foot, but with its AI-controlled .50 calibre Gatling gun with its rotating barrels with firepower of 1,300 rounds per minute, he was loath to do so. It was a valuable asset, which Nickolai had re-programmed, and they'd not fired a single shot with it.

Back at the garage in Wales, the head mechanic had told Marcus that they'd added large amounts of extra ammunition, in case they'd needed to get themselves out of any scraps. Marcus decided to try and get the vehicle through the last checkpoint either peacefully, or by brute force. Once on the other side, he knew he could count on the UK Resistance firepower to cover them. He asked Akam to radio ahead and get the fire teams in place in case such fire support was necessary. However, in the event, they were just waved on through the final checkpoint. It didn't even require a cursory glance at their passes. Marcus and Jonathan had fully expected that they would need to dismount.

'That was too easy,' Jonathan said, squatting behind Marcus' passenger seat, as he removed his beret.

'Yes, it was, wasn't it?' Marcus agreed as he did the same. 'I'd anticipated their I-STAR assets being all over us once we broke out of their area of operations. But this was indeed far easier than it should have been. Ideas?'

'They let us get through their cordon,' Jonathan stated simply.

'Hmm, it seems that way. But why?'

Despite his fatigue, Jonathan thought it through fast. 'We've got a senior officer of theirs, with the probability that we'll hold him to ransom. He, however, has just been relieved of his command and is an embarrassment to them, thus expendable. It can mean only one thing. It's an excuse for their coming in to extract him, and maybe for an attack in force.'

'I think you might be right, Jonathan,' Marcus said. 'I was thinking along the same lines but hoping I was wrong.'

'Um, Marcus?' Akam interrupted. 'The Colonel has just come-to'.

Trant, lying on the floor of the vehicle in a sleeping bag atop a roll-mat, propped himself up stiffly. He rubbed the back of his neck and glanced at the faces around him, before recognising Jonathan.

'Hmm, I thought as much,' he said with a tired grin.

'Hello, Colonel. Welcome to the UK Resistance Party,' Jonathan replied.

'And, these guys?' he looked at Jonathan and tilted his head towards the Russians.

'An asset,' Jonathan replied.

'Right,' Trant replied, dubious.

'Don't worry,' Jonathan said, 'we're in Bristol. There'll be a de-brief, and then you'll be made as comfortable as possible.'

'Am I a prisoner?' Trant asked.

'No more than I am,' Jonathan replied. 'It's up to you, to consider what we discussed. It seems that you'd been relieved of your command. I'd suggest that your career with the current regime is finished. I think you need to think things over.'

'Yes, I think I do,' Trant replied, and lay back down, covering his eyes with his arm.

59

It was late afternoon, and as Dolman lay on his bed he knew that his time in the colony was nearly done. He'd likely be gone before suppertime and was sorry to be missing those pies made from the fruit that the youngsters had collected, which, along with some fine vegetable stew, he could already smell cooking.

Emily had disappeared whilst they'd been doing the door-to-door selling, and on the way back she seemed to have avoided him. He marvelled at the shallowness of such women and thought bitterly that he was better off failing early. Failing early? An image of Lieutenant Courtney's sheepish smile appeared, from the time the power-pack on one of the vehicles had failed as they'd left Fairfield airbase. Then, his last memory of him crept in. Why the hell had he aimed a pistol at Trant? The crash, the rolling…

Things were indeed slowly creeping back into his consciousness, and like a person with a hangover in the cold light of day, events from the night before were returning to sting a bit. He began to believe that Michael's assessment of him was probably more accurate than Claire's.

Emily walked in, holding another hot drink. She wore a white mini dress.

'How's your leg now?' she asked, with a tinge of honest concern and sympathy.

'I'll live,' Dolman replied, as he touched his bandaged leg.

'I think you saved Peter's dog. Those kids on the estate have been a problem for some time now. They're nasty little bullies. Sometimes they've just taken the food from us.'

'I think that I may have just made the situation far worse for you all,' Dolman stated.

'That one you took on has had it coming to him for a long while. No father figure around to do it. I'm sorry they did that to you.' She looked at him a moment too long, and their eyes locked.

'You could come with me,' he said simply.

'I can't. I'm committed to someone else.'

'Do you love him?'

'No. It didn't seem important.'

'Hmm. Who is he?'

'He's some sort of civil servant,' she replied, looking down.

'Rich?'

'Not particularly, but massively so compared to these folk. He can provide a home, security. I could have a family with him, a life.'

'That's nothing that I couldn't provide. I'm an Army Captain, I know that now. In this world, few people argue with me. We are first in the queue when it comes to a choice of partner. You can forget that dull civil servant of yours, he'll be no bother.'

She looked at him and sat down beside him on the bed.

He continued. 'I can tell you honestly, I'm very choosy. But you've had an effect on me, and it's not just that bang on my head talking. It's not too late, for either of us. If I'm not wrong I think we both feel the same. And if there's anything that I've learned in the last few years, it's that one should follow one's instincts, especially if it also makes logical sense. Especially when life is as short as it has been.'

He took Emily by the shoulders and kissed her. She pulled away from him and stood up, looking a little shocked. 'My, you're a fast worker!'

Michael walked in with Claire, followed by two of the heftier men in the group. Behind them was Emily's young male follower, who had a silly grin on his face when he saw her.

Michael looked in astonishment at what she wore. 'My dear,' Michael said, 'what on earth do you think you look like?'

'What?' she asked insouciantly.

'What, she asks! What you're wearing! It's totally anachronistic, as well as being quite demeaning to your sex.'

'It's the latest style from down there in the valley. I bought it from a girl on the estate.' She half-turned to show them what a good fit it was.

Michael remained unmoved. 'I assure you, it's more nineteen-sixties Carnaby street than Welsh hillside settlement. And it's not in keeping with our values. Have you been drinking again? Go on, go away, and put on something more appropriate, please.'

Emly laughed. 'Okay, whatever,' she replied. Unabashed, she glanced at Dolman with vague exasperation, turned, and walked out.

Dolman watched her young friend look at her as she left before he glanced at him triumphantly. From the look of the young man's eyes, Dolman thought that he looked more stoned. Michael turned on him. 'And you, Patrick, you should know better than to encourage her. She's a bad influence on you all. The sooner she's gone from here the better. I'll have words with you later.'

Patrick looked vaguely chastised, brushed his fringe of long dark hair away from his eyes, and then followed hastily after Emily.

'Kids!' Michael said disparagingly. 'Some of them have missed out on a large chunk of their growing up. They're a bit feral and immature I'm afraid.'

Dolman tried to hide his amusement. 'Yes, I suppose so. That Emily's bright, though.'

'Oh yes, she's that, alright, and can carry her weight in potatoes down to the market. But she's no good really. That Patrick was once a good boy; they all were until she arrived,' Michael said ruefully. 'She leads them astray, in the most underhanded way out. Well, you saw that display.'

'I don't think I'll un-see it!' Dolman replied, as seriously as he could manage.

'She's been sneaking out with several of them, going to the local pubs, getting back at goodness knows what time. There's still a curfew in these parts, and now with battles being fought around the valley again, I fear for their safety. Well, *you'd* know all about that, of course.'

'Yes, perhaps,' Dolman replied.

'So, are you ready to go, then?' Michael asked.

'Yeah, I suppose so,' Dolman answered, more resentfully than he intended. He felt cheated of something, and it was more than a pleasant smelling dinner.

Michael seemed amused and looked at him probingly. 'Hmm, you don't sound so keen now. Maybe you've seen how life can be, on the other side. You know, once all the wars have dried up and become meaningless, you can't get much better than this. Other men I'd invite to stay, but as I said, you'd be a liability for us. We don't accept soldiers. And frankly, I'm glad to have shot of you. Especially now I know who you are, even if you still don't.'

Dolman looked at Michael, whose face now showed a mixture of sorrow and revulsion. He looked at Claire, who seemed sad and evasive, unable to look at him. Instead, she looked down at her clasped hands.

'Captain Paul Dolman,' Michael stated, 'the war criminal. It seems you've been missing in action for nearly twenty-four hours. I'd hate to keep you from your grim work any longer.'

Dolman had already suspected as much and oddly felt as if he had betrayed their trust. 'How did you find out?'

'I sent a runner to Colonel Trant's garrison. They'll be down to collect you in a while.'

Emily walked back in again, with a look of surprise. 'Is that true? You're Captain Dolman?' She had been listening outside the tent.

Dolman looked at her and felt terrible. 'That's who your leader says I am.'

'Did you really do what they said you did?'

Michael answered for him. 'Yes. He only started this whole mess off, opening fire on civilians in London when the riots started.'

Dolman looked at Emily, but she just stared at him. He couldn't read her.

'Because we were outnumbered and felt threatened,' Dolman stated flatly. 'Not too dissimilar to today, those boys on the estate earlier; but these thugs were armed.'

Claire spoke up. 'But you were soldiers, you had guns.'

'It's not just soldiers who kill,' Dolman retorted. 'The Army was almost wiped out by civilians just a few years ago.'

'Yes, well, that's as maybe,' Michael said, wishing to halt the conversation, as it didn't appear to be having it's intended effect on Emily. 'Now you get along, Emily.'

After she had silently left, Michael looked at Dolman. 'Oh dear! You know, it's quite touching to see, almost sweet. I'm not sure it'd have made any difference if I'd told her that you'd been lining women and children up against a wall and machine-gunning them! For some reason, she appears to have fallen for you. Such a pity you have to go, you'd have made such a lovely couple. You can now go back to your trade in death, and she to fulfill her sad, tawdry little destiny, apparently with some dull, bloodless little government bureaucrat. Karma is indeed an odd thing, isn't it? It regularly bites us on the arse.'

60

As Michael and Claire walked to the refectory, Rachael approached them. 'Michael, are those men the soldiers coming to take the Captain?'

Michael squinted at the small ragged group running down the side of the hill by the reservoir, holding an assortment of weapons. 'Oh my…they're not Army, they're locals! Damn, I told them to keep away!'

'They probably just want more food,' Rachael stated.

'Maybe, but the Army will be here any minute now! I don't want this place to become a shooting gallery. And if they discover the Captain they'll execute him for sure. Come on, we have to get rid of them!' He waddled towards the visitors. Claire, arms crossed against the early evening chill, looked at Rachael with concern and they followed on.

'Good evening, Mickey!' the lead insurgent said to Michael in an over-familiar and disparaging tone. However, when he closed in on Michael his expression changed to fearful. He looked hunted. 'Now look here, Michael, you got to help us, see? Things have taken a turn for the worse. Man, we're running for our lives! The Army's all over this area.'

'Why? What did you do?'

'Not us, Michael, the Russians! It was the Russians, see?'

'Did what, Hugh?'

'The Defence Minister, he's dead! And an Army convoy, destroyed. And now they want us all dead! They're after our scalps, Michael. The Russians, well they went and buggered off, didn't they? Disappeared like ice cream in hell, they did, and left us as bait. Twenty-five of us, down to just five…they're not taking prisoners, man! Please, if you have the heart you say you do, give us sanctuary!'

'I cannot! You men have made your own karma. It's up to you to accept the consequences. You must not involve my people in it.'

'Please, man, hide us!' Hugh begged, close to tears. It was clear he was exhausted and at his wits-end. 'Else I'll think, well, you're just pious, but lack any real guts. You know, not like the saints and all. Please!'

Michael turned to Claire and Rachael. They looked doubtful and wary. He looked back at Hugh.

'Okay, but you lie low. And be sure to be gone by nightfall.'

'Oh Michael, that's no good, they have drones, dogs, helicopters, infra-red…why it's even worse at night!'

'Then sunrise!'

Hugh's face momentarily creased up into a grimace as he let out a single sob, tears filling his eyes. He clasped Michael by the shoulders and hugged him. 'Oh, thank you, man! Thank you.'

Michael gently pushed him away. 'Now, get rid of those weapons and equipment, and find something different to wear.'

'Will do,' Hugh said, as he patted Michael on the shoulder.

61

Ten minutes later, as Dolman was preparing to leave under the watchful glare of Michael, young Peter ran up, breathless and upset. 'Michael? Molly's gone. I think she ran off. Or did you really put her in the hot-pot?'

Michael chortled soundly. 'That's right, boy!'

'No!'

As his jibe failed, Michael stopped grinning, largely at the thought that the child actually doubted his spiritual purity. 'Oh, don't be so damned stupid! She's probably just gone off after rabbits or sheep again. If she isn't shot then I'm sure she'll be back in time for her supper too.'

Peter was aghast at the thought. 'Shot? By the farmers? Or the soldiers?'

'Oh, hasn't she always come back before?' Michael replied, rolling his eyes.

'Mister?' the boy turned excitably to Dolman, 'can you help me find her?'

'I'm sorry, but I've got to leave,' Dolman said gently.

'Already? But you just got here. I don't want you to leave!'

'I'm sorry, but I have to,' Dolman told him.

Michael looked sternly at the boy. 'Now go and ask someone else to help you.'

'Aw…Okay then,' Peter replied, downcast. He looked at Dolman. 'Bye, Mister.'

'See you round,' Dolman replied. 'Hope you find your dog.'

Peter ran off.

As they began to walk through the camp, they heard the helicopters from a distance. Dolman looked up and recognised them.

'Oh my, here are your friends,' Michael stated without enthusiasm.

They landed in the bowl near the reservoir, and several sections of troops disembarked from them. They fanned-out, and rapidly made their way towards the haven. A Sergeant approached them, speaking into a personal role radio transmitter. It was Sergeant Steve Rodriguez. 'Roger that, positive identification, I have eyes on him.'

He looked at Dolman and smiled. 'Hey, Captain! I thought we'd be the ones to find you. I tagged on to this outfit when I'd heard you'd gone missing. Brit Intel thought you'd been taken hostage and transported up to Bristol.'

Dolman raised his eyebrows and smiled. 'No, apparently not. This lot are only armed with carrots and turnips, no threat to anyone,'

Rodriguez grinned again and looked down at Dolman's sandals. 'Hey, dig the sandals! You know, you suit the hippy look, Sir!' He glanced around and put on a look of mock-solemnity as a staid-looking Lieutenant with a thick neck and built like an All-Stars football player approached.

'All good, Sergeant?' the Lieutenant asked humourlessly.

'Yes Sir,' Rodriguez replied respectfully.

The Lieutenant saluted Dolman. 'Are you Captain Dolman?'

'Yes,' Dolman replied.

'Sir, we're to take you back to your nearest base. Are you wounded?'

'Yes, I sustained a head injury and a laceration to my leg.'

'Are you able to walk?'

'Yes, just about.'

Dolman glanced back at Michael and Claire, and just nodded a farewell at them. He was just sorry that young Emily didn't want to say farewell, it seemed that she had taken against him; if indeed she was ever really for him.

62

Dolman sat in the helicopter with Rodriguez, and they were the first to take off. It took no more than five minutes before they were landing within the grounds of the garrison. As Dolman was helped off, they had no idea as to what was occurring back at the colony as the rear-guard was disembarking.

Back there, whilst the last of the cordon of American troops returned to their helicopters, a ground attack helicopter swooped in low over the area to cover them. Another began a similar run, and as it approached the haven the tell-tale sign of a smoke trail of an anti-aircraft missile being launched towards it became evident to its pilot. In a sudden effort to avoid it, he made a wild manoeuvre, whilst his helicopter automatically jettisoned some diversionary flares. The pilot then rapidly gained height.

Upon hearing what sounded like a crack of thunder from nearby, Michael ran out from the refectory with a napkin still tucked into the top of his gown. 'What was that? Oh no, no! Please don't let it be what I think it is. HUGH!'

Hugh ran towards him. 'Michael, I'm sorry, another team joined us. They didn't understand why the soldiers were here.'

Michael panted, and looked fearful and outraged. 'Hugh, I want you gone! I want you all gone from here, straight away.'

'But don't you see man, they thought they was defending you? They're heroes!'

63

Since getting into position, Captain Matlock had been surveying the camp through binoculars. To his immense chagrin, his unit had been diverted from the head-hunting role that they'd been engaged in earlier and assigned to cover the 355th Airborne in its extraction of Dolman. That was despite his team having killed at least ten insurgents in gunfights, or after capture. It was nowhere near enough for him, given the enormity of what had recently taken place. Were it up to him he'd now be taking reprisals on locals, as he would have done before arrival of American forces.

He had seethed when he saw Dolman emerging from a tent in sandals, being escorted onto a helicopter. He privately hoped someone would take his helicopter down. He rued how, when he had such wishes, they so often seem to be fulfilled too late; and without the desired consequences. It didn't, however, stop him from feeling just a little bit god-like.

Whilst he hadn't been in position to see the first insurgent team enter the camp, he had seen two other armed men wander in but had thought better than to communicate the information to the Americans. He wanted to wait to see what might transpire. And whilst it hadn't unfortunately ended in Dolman's demise, it gave him a suitable excuse to vent some spleen on a group he despised as being an oddball religious cult, full of liberal-left fakes and charlatans.

He received a call from one of the British Army ground attack helicopters. *'Frenzy five-zero, Troll three-zero. Am visual with armed pax. Lasing the launch site, this is the grid, 9856356921.'*

'Roger that, awaiting authorisation to engage,' Matlock replied. He called headquarters, and informed them of the new developments to the situation he'd been observing, and asked for permission to engage. Ten minutes later, permission was given, as the last of the cordon troops had been airlifted out. Matlock spoke to the man he had placed next to him, his Forward Air Controller.

'Bill, get on TACSAT, dial-up fast air. Get a seventy-seven in there.'

'Yes boss,' the soldier replied flatly without emotion, then spoke into his transmitter. 'Zombie eight-one, Frenzy five-zero, do you copy, over?'

'Frenzy five-zero, Zombie eight-one, roger that. Sitrep?'

'Zombie eight-one, Frenzy five-zero, we have eyes on enemy pax, engaging extraction force with manpad. This is the grid, 98565692. Recommend mark seven-seven-three. Friendlies now clear.'

'Roger, 98565692. Stand by.'

A few seconds later, the pilot spoke again. *'Affirm target. Tipping in. Call for clearance.'*

As the ground attack fighter began its attack run it made a screeching sound, followed by a low, thunderous roar which rapidly increased in intensity as it closed in on the target.

'Clear hot,' the air controller said.

'*In hot,*' the American pilot replied.

Matlock had asked for a 750 pound air-dropped incendiary full of fuel gel, supposedly banned. He watched as it engulfed the 'safe haven' in fire, and a huge black pall of smoke arose.

'Fine,' Matlock grinned. 'Tell the gunships to deploy flechette on the second run.'

'Troll three-zero, Frenzy five-zero. Use flechette on second run,' his air controller said to the helicopter pilot.

The pilot replied. '*Roger. Second attack run to use flechette. Stand by.*'

This second run was made by the helicopter that had almost been hit by the Russian missile, and used 70mm folding-fin rockets filled with eighty tungsten darts, another hitherto banned type of ordnance which had been hastily resurrected and put back into production after the Baltic War. The helicopter commenced its attack run, and the rockets streaked away from under the stubby wings. Hundreds of tungsten darts were launched into the burning area to finish off what was left. Captain Matlock had found from experience that the combination of the incendiary bomb and flechette to be very effective in fighting the insurgency in the Welsh hills, leaving very little alive. He attributed the low casualty rate in his unit to their frequent use. However, in this situation, it was over-kill.

He looked at the sunset and smiled to himself. Today had turned out to be a better day than he thought. Then his Forward Air Controller received another message from the helicopter gunship pilot who had just made the second attack run.

'Frenzy five-zero, Troll three-zero. Have lost my wing man, they are refusing to engage in the third attack run.'

'Bloody hell!' Matlock exclaimed, grabbing the headset. 'Troll three-zero, they're cowards! Tell them they'll be on a charge. They're finished, do you hear?'

He shoved the headset back to his air controller and looked around at his team. 'We can't afford to have such crises of confidence. Two years ago, our light almost went out forever, overrun by the forces of socialist anarchy. Down there were naïve liberal-left traitors, harbouring murderous anarchist scum. They may have seemed 'nice', but be sure, they would turn us back to a new dark age. One look at how basically they lived surely confirms that.'

He looked searchingly at each man, looking for traces of doubt or dissention. He needed Positive Mental Attitude in his unit and nothing less. Several of them looked morose and doubtful, and one man glanced down. Matlock determined that he'd have him RTU'd (Returned to Unit) as an example to the others. Then, alarmingly he switched mood, to that of the laughing cavalier. 'Right lads, we all live to fight another day. Back for tea and medals!'

Most of them gave a dutiful chuckle or smile before getting their kit together. Matlock kept his eyes on the dissenter a second longer than was necessary. The man knew that he'd be packing his kit and shipping-out that evening. Matlock was glad, he was the one he least wanted in his unit anyway, as he knew him to be a bit of a joker.

64

It was Halloween. In the infirmary, Dolman awoke in a cold sweat from another uncharacteristic nightmare that was in keeping with the date. However, he was still unaware of the fate of the haven.

By his bed was a fresh uniform that had been left out for him. He had lost enough blood from the knife wound to his inner thigh to have been placed on an intravenous drip for a while. He pulled it out and sat himself up and on the side of the bed. Across the ward, he noticed another now-familiar face; that of Lieutenant Courtney. He was resting, with his forearm over his eyes to shield them from the morning sunlight.

Dolman walked over towards him and noticed that he had a bandage around his head, and another on his left arm. He shook him violently.

'Ugh..yeah? Whaddya want?' Courtney woke and looked at Dolman with bleary eyes for a second or two before recognising him. 'Huh, Captain. Well, how about that, you made it back! Why we'd thought you'd been taken hostage too?' He noticed the bandage on Dolman's thigh, and the blood trailing down his forearm from the drip and smiled. 'Gee, we'd sure make a great couple of ghouls for trick-or-treat, wouldn't we?'

'You surely tricked us. Who are you? Why did you try to kill my Colonel?'

Courtney looked around the ward in mock consternation. 'Whoa! Cap'n, hold on there! Reckon you may have taken a nasty bang to the head an' all, too. Why, you just can't go round saying things like that, accusing people and all-

'Dammit, you piece of shit! Don't give me that flannel!' Dolman shouted, grabbing Courtney by the collar of his night-gown.

'Captain! Please!' one of the nurses had finally noticed. 'Return to your bed, Sir!'

Dolman turned to the nurse. 'This man tried to kill Colonel Trant. I want him arrested and put under armed guard.'

Two male orderlies appeared either side of him.

'Now please, Sir,' the nurse talked to him soothingly, 'like the Lieutenant here, you've taken a nasty knock to the head. Please, return to your bed. We need to run some more tests on you later.'

Dolman looked around at Courtney, who was deadpan.

'You can see me perfectly well, can't you? You can, can't you?' Dolman said. 'Where're your glasses, you bastard?'

Courtney smiled in his self-effacing manner and reached inside his cabinet. 'Ah, thought there was something wrong with the picture, thanks Cap'n!'

Dolman sneered and walked back to his bed.

65

With Jonathan and Marcus beside him, and an armed guard standing by the door, Colonel Trant sat down before King in his office.

'Colonel Trant, I'm sorry you've been treated like this.'

Trant remained silent.

'Anyway, after all this time on opposite sides, it's good to make your acquaintance,' King said as he extended a hand, which Trant refused.

'No? Oh well, as you will.' King kept his equanimity, but Jonathan glanced at Marcus, who looked alarmed at Trant's surliness. King had taken the death of his nephew, Riordan, relatively well. But his patience might be tried if Trant turned out to be too uncooperative.

'I'm King,' he continued, 'Commander of the Bristol Brigade of the UK Resistance Party.'

'Yes, I know who you are,' Trant replied wearily. 'What can I do for you?'

'Oh, much, but it's what we can do for you which is of more importance, at least in your case, Colonel.'

'And what may that be?' Trant replied, unimpressed.

'Offer a new life, a fresh start. And a new command. I take it you'd lost the faith in your old regime, and they in turn with you?'

Again, Trant didn't reply.

'Oh, come now Colonel, just admit it. Technology is ahead of us all. Apparently, it now knows what we're going to do before we do. Sure, it doesn't always get it right. But in your case, something came up on their radar; and, in turn, *our* radar, thanks to a nifty bit of hacking.'

'Well it seems you know more than me,' Trant replied. 'Look, it's one thing to have doubts. It's another thing to become a traitor to one's own country.'

'To be honest, Colonel, it's your country that has betrayed you. All your service, all your loyalty, it all amounted to nothing in their paranoid eyes. One blip in a hokey bit of computer software and it's you who is labelled as a possible traitor, career over. Tell me it isn't true? Tell me that you *weren't* in the back of that American armoured personnel carrier, having been relieved of your command? Even if their A-I was off-whack, that's still your career over and done with.'

Trant surveyed King pensively.

'All that you gave them,' King continued, 'all your loyalty, was ignored. They preferred to believe their iffy computer system and listen to their own paranoia.'

Trant considered what King had said. 'I want no part of this. I'll not fight my own side.'

'And you don't have to, Colonel,' King assured him.

Trant frowned in confusion. 'Then what do you want of me? How can I be of any use to you, other than as a hostage?'

'I'll tell you how. You can help us negotiate peace with the Americans. Talk on our behalf.'

'What can I possibly do to change things? In the scheme of things I'm only a lowly battalion commander.'

'Ah, that's as maybe. But you're a national hero and until recently a successful senior commander. Now, your government doesn't want the Americans here much longer, and equally, they don't want to stay themselves. These overseas gigs cost them billions of dollars, and already there's disquiet in Washington on both sides of the house, what with another recession on the way. From whatever internment you were about to be subject to by your regime, you'd have been silenced, maybe terminally. And yes, we have evidence that it happens, and I'm not just talking about certain-death postings to the battlegrounds in the north. But from here, Colonel, you have a voice.'

'I'm sorry, but from here they'll think I speak under duress.'

'Maybe,' King admitted. 'But you've points to make. And then, you'll be free you leave, if you so wish.'

Again, Trant considered what King said. 'Those cases of officers who were – how did you put it – 'terminated'…?'

'Oh, it's true indeed. We've been intercepting messages, communiqués. These men just disappear. Notes are sent to their families to say that they were killed in action, or had "accidents".'

Trant looked around at Jonathan and Marcus, who nodded their heads in confirmation of what King had said.

'Well, I'd had my suspicions, but could never be sure.'

'Indeed Colonel,' King said, 'it was a good thing that it was the Americans who got to you, and not your lot. They don't want the stain of such allegations tainting their operations in the U-K; they're already looking down the barrel of Democrat investigations into the running of this campaign. Now, had it been one of your black ops lot that got to you first, then it might have been a different story.'

It was too much for Trant to take in at once.

'Colonel,' King said sympathetically, 'you look all-in. I'm not expecting any answers straight away. Go away and sleep on it. But, just one thing, don't take too long about coming to a decision, now. We're expecting your lot to try for an extraction anytime soon. And that will almost certainly be black-ops.'

Trant looked at King and swallowed.

66

Dolman had again left his bed, this time on the pretext of needing the bathroom; but he had taken the new uniform with him. Twenty minutes later he was eating breakfast in the Officers Mess.

He was noticed by Brigadier Trelawney, who was sitting by Major Fuller and Second Lieutenant Enderby. Trelawney looked at him knowingly, but affected ignorance. 'Ah, Paul! How are you? You're out already, I see?'

'Yes Sir,' Dolman smiled.

'Well, good to see you have a healthy appetite,' he smiled. He looked at Dolman with concern. 'You know we lost Trant?'

'Yes Sir, I had heard.'

'Yes, bad business, bad business. We thought they'd taken you as well, but it seems they were targeting him specifically. Fuller here thinks it was the Russians.'

'Russians?' Dolman looked at Fuller and then the Brigadier, surprised. 'But, what could they want with Colonel Trant? Is there any evidence for this?'

Trelawney looked at Fuller, who continued. 'The ordnance that brought down the Defence Secretary has been positively identified as being of Russian manufacture. A manpad-type ground-to-air missile. We picked up canisters near the launch site. Then, the prisoners we've interrogated say that they were led by what probably fits the description of a small Special Purpose Detachment, commanded by a bi-lingual officer.

The local insurgents we captured talked freely, mainly because they felt that they had been betrayed, and sacrificed as diversionary bait by the Russians to aid their escape from the area with Colonel Trant.'

'And,' Trelawney interrupted, 'we believe they made for Bristol.'

'Strange choice of destination,' Dolman remarked.

'Quite, and no bad thing indeed,' Trelawney stated with a smile. 'We've got the place surrounded. No one can get in or out. They're caught like rats in a barrel. And, we're just awaiting permission from the PM to mount an operation to go in and flush those rats out. Hopefully, we'll retrieve the Colonel alive in the process.'

'Of course,' replied Dolman.

Trelawney's eyes had taken on a vaguely manic glare. 'Well, Paul, are you up for it? I could use someone with your experience in counter-insurgency operations on my flank.'

Paul considered it. 'My unit is still engaged up in the north.'

'Yes, and I'm afraid we can't redeploy them just now. But I've suggested to Captain Halshaw that you take command of one of his platoons. How about it?'

'Fine, Sir,' Dolman replied steadily.

'Good man! We've armour, airborne assault troops, and American support. It'll be just like old times, Paul!'

'Yes indeed, Sir. When do we leave?'

Fuller answered. 'Once we've been given the all-clear, operations will commence at O-four-hundred hours tomorrow. We'll mobilise today so that we're in-theatre this evening, in time for the PM's go-ahead.'

Trelawney grimaced. 'We want maximum surprise; shock and awe. They won't know what hit 'em!'

'Yes Sir,' Dolman replied.

'Anyway, are you sure that you're fully recovered? You went a bit pale there for a second.'

'Yes, Sir, fine.'

'And they treated you well in that haven, eh? Good organic home-grown food and all, I should think.'

'Oh yes, the food was fine. Nice people, a little naïve perhaps…' Dolman mused.

Fuller looked awkward, and young Enderby stopped smiling and looked down with distaste at some burnt bacon rind on his plate. It was Trelawney who said it, trying to make as light of it as possible. 'Yes, well, damned shame about them.'

'I'm sorry, Sir?' Dolman asked, with a feeling of rising agitation.

'The colony,' Trelawney continued. 'Damned shame. Seems they'd been harbouring terrorists. Attacked the force that extracted you yesterday evening; they almost downed another helicopter. Our special forces J-TAG team had to call in an airstrike. Camp got hit by an air-dropped incendiary. There'll be an investigation of course, and between us, I'm not one bit happy. It was totally unnecessary.'

Dolman almost gagged and got up. 'Excuse me, Sir, I don't feel well.' He placed his napkin onto the table and hurried out.

67

Trant was lying on his bed when he heard the knock on the door. 'Yes?' he answered.

'Colonel, it's me, Jonathan, I'm with Brigade Commander Samuels. I need to have a word.'

Trant sat up. 'Alright, come in.'

Jonathan entered with Marcus but remained silent. They both looked genuinely somber.

'What can I do for you, professor?' Trant asked. 'If you're hoping to report back to King that I've changed my mind then you've got another thing coming. You said I wasn't a prisoner, yet there's an armed guard outside my door.'

'It's for your protection,' Marcus lied.

'Hmm, whatever. Well, this is a wasted visit I can assure you. You'd have been better off sending room service up with some breakfast.'

'Colonel,' Marcus began. 'We have some bad news for you.'

'What about?' Trant asked.

'Yesterday evening, we received intelligence from a local group in the area. The safe-haven below your base was destroyed by an airstrike,' Marcus said. He paused to let the news sink in.

Trant sat down on his bed, totally winded.

'Is this true?' he asked.

'Yes,' Jonathan said. 'The whole haven. Every man, woman, and child.'

'No survivors?'

'None.'

'Can this be confirmed?'

'Yes.'

Trant tried to collect his thoughts.

'Colonel,' Marcus said, 'we also know that you had someone there whom you cared for.'

Trant looked at him.

Marcus continued. 'It was an open secret in the area.'

Trant sat back down. 'You seem to know a lot. How do I know you're not just making this all up?'

'Well Colonel, if it convinces you that you're on the wrong side-

'Damn you!' Trant shouted. 'We all choose our sides, we all think we're right, and I'll tell you what, no side is perfect.'

'Correct, Colonel,' Marcus agreed. 'But some are less perfect than others.'

Trant looked at him. 'This could still be a cynical ruse.'

'I wish that it were,' Marcus said. 'You can come to our ops room if you like, look at Russian satellite images, and the local photos taken by our people in the area.'

Trant looked suddenly distraught.

68

'You sure this is a good idea, Captain?' Sergeant Rodriguez cautioned with a wince. 'It 'ain't gonna be a pretty site.'

Dolman stared sullenly out at the view through the windscreen of the four-by-four. 'I need to know.'

Rodriguez glanced at him, but let it be and said nothing more. He reasoned that the Captain had been affected by the crash, and had also formed some sort of bond with the people in the encampment. Both of these things were somewhat out of character, but could be as a result of the knock to the head and maybe therefore transient. In no time they'd cleared the switch-backs where the ambush had occurred, and Rodriguez turned left into a single lane. He pulled up to a gate, and after opening it they proceeded along a farm track, and then through a field leading to what remained of the camp. They pulled up near the charred area and got out.

Amongst debris, some blackened and bloated bodies could be seen, although maybe not as many as might be expected. A few charred poles and bits of fencing still stood, and bizarrely one live goat, it's tether broken but standing as if stunned, waiting for someone to see to it.

Dolman led, and strode over to where the hospital tent had been. He stood and surveyed the area before him, the former safe haven; the former Shangri La.

'Damn those who did this,' he said, without looking at the choking Rodriguez, who held a handkerchief to his mouth.

'Why'd they do it, Captain? All those people? I just don't get it. I mean, sure, they nabbed one of those Russki missile launchers, but they could've just sent one of the teams in.'

'I don't know. But I think I know who.'

'Who, Captain?'

'One of our teams, black-ops.'

'Jeez, they're bad hombres, Captain. Protected by the brass. No investigation will touch 'em, they're above the law.'

'I know. So these people won't have any justice.'

'I don't think it'll make any difference to them now, Sir.'

Dolman glared at his Sergeant for the flippant comment.

'Sorry, Captain, just telling it as it is.'

Dolman walked on, scanning the ground.

'Captain, come on, they ain't nothing here but death.'

'I want to know,' Dolman replied.

'Know what, Captain?'

'If they got her too.'

Rodriguez looked confused for a second, then realised. 'Oh, sure. You had someone down here too?'

Dolman looked at him for an explanation. 'Well,' Rodriguez continued, 'talk back at the base was that their Colonel was hot on some dame down here. Got together with her whenever he could. I thought you was talking about her for a minute there.'

'No,' Dolman replied. 'Someone else. But that's sad, if Colonel Trant has also lost someone.'

Dolman wandered further on, glancing down at the bodies clinically, and Rodriguez followed dutifully. After a while, Rodriguez spoke to him imploringly. 'Come on, Captain, even if she was here you wouldn't stand a chance of identifying her. Please?' He touched his arm.

Dolman turned. Whilst not registering that he was crying, tears streamed down his dusty face. With reluctance, he gave up on his futile search and walked back to the patrol vehicle with Rodriguez.

69

They sat in the canteen with Trant. He was ignoring his coffee and staring into space with lacklustre, bloodshot eyes. Marcus took out a flask and poured some whiskey into his mug. Trant looked down at it without recognition.

'There's nothing left in this world,' he said. 'Not for me.'

'Colonel,' Marcus said, 'you've suffered a great loss. But life will go on. It did after the virus. And for you, there's the chance of a new life, new beginnings.'

'I'm old and tired. Too old to start again.'

'No, no you're not,' Marcus said. 'And what's more, you more than anyone here has a chance to affect the future, bring real change and stability back to this country, more than you could ever have done, sitting up there in your garrison. You can change the course of events. Bring people to the negotiating table. What did that to the haven, that wasn't right. The men that did that aren't on the side of the angels and you know it.'

Trant looked at him and Jonathan. 'You want me to make that broadcast, for King?'

'No, for all of us. Help get this country back on track, end the bloodshed. End further airstrikes.'

'Alright,' Trant replied.

'Alright?' Marcus asked.

'I'll do it.'

70

The pre-op orders group meeting ('O-group') conducted by Brigadier Trelawney had surprised Dolman. Whilst Trelawney was going to take the bulk of Trant's battalion into Bristol using conventional tactics, the Brigadier had also been granted temporary command over a company from the US 355th Airborne based at Fairfield Airbase. These would be part of his spearhead and would have ground attack helicopters, jets, and drones as potential fire support. The target was where Intelligence had pinpointed the resistance headquarters to be; a fifteen-storey office block called Wraxall Towers. Whilst the plan was ostensibly a shoot-and-scoot operation to lift Colonel Trant, it seemed to Dolman that Trelawney really intended to use the operation as a *raison d'etre* to take the city centre and thus eliminate the resistance there. The fact that Trelawney also proposed to spearhead the operation with a platoon of British main battle tanks seemed to suggest this.

What had particularly irked Dolman, as they sat listening to Trelawney and watching him expound his plan on a large screen above, was that Dolman's platoon of special forces support troops was to be used as the support group to Captain Matlock's black-ops team in taking Wraxall Towers. In reality that meant they'd be sent in first as the more expendable assault team, as they were deemed to be less valuable assets than highly trained black ops troopers. He glanced at Matlock, who was listening intently to the Brigadier, a cruel set to his face punctuated with his lifeless dark eyes and thin eyebrows.

Dolman was just about giving a reasonable act of giving a damn, when in fact he simply wasn't interested anymore. He had often wondered how post-traumatic could render a man virtually useless in the military, and now he was beginning to understand. Everything he had once found interesting or exciting about his job now seemed flat. The only thing that excited him in the slightest was the thought of pulling out his sidearm and shooting bits off of Matlock. He had to work hard at controlling that compulsion. The main thing that stopped him was that he wasn't one-hundred percent certain that Matlock had been the one involved; nor that he had ultimately given the order to destroy that haven.

A little later, as Dolman had briefed his team, he found to his surprise and initial chagrin that he was one man up. It was with one of Matlock's men. His name was Julian Ashcroft, and Dolman knew him from the distant past, from a course in urban warfare. Ashcroft was quite a character, normally one of the more extroverted members of any team. Short and athletic, he was also a base jumper and keen cross country skier in his spare time. Irritatingly for Dolman, he showed no sign of being in the least bit ashamed or subdued at having been kicked out and 'returned to unit', as he walked up the corridor towards their meeting room. He greeted several with a familiar grin and high-fives and rubbed his face indicating the beard he had recently shaved off.

'That's better', he said. 'It was just one more form of bullshit,' he said to Corporal Silcott. 'It's great to be back in the green Army – no, really, fuckin-A!'

He approached Dolman. 'Sir, reporting for duty.' He saluted and handed him his transfer papers. Dolman scanned them briefly.

'I'd heard we'd been assigned one of Captain Matlock's men, Corporal. I'm under strength in section commanders just now and appreciate you're bringing a lot of skills to the table. You can join my H-Q section, and we could use your J-TAG skills. So, just how did you foul-up over there in E-squadron?'

'I think the boss sussed I wasn't fully one-hundred-per cent up for war crimes,' Ashcroft replied flatly.

'And, I take it you saw one recently?' Dolman asked, trying to sound disinterested.

'Er, yeah,' Ashcroft looked round as people passed, clearly still very security-conscious.

'Was it the safe-haven down by the reservoir?' Dolman prompted.

Julian Ashcroft glanced back at him with a haunted look, one that was enough to tell Dolman that his assumption was correct. Now he knew for sure that it was indeed Matlock's unit that had committed the crime.

'Okay,' Dolman said, 'sit in on our O-group, I want everyone to be switched on. If you have anything to say, don't keep it to yourself. Then go and draw any extra kit you need. Many of us have American weapons now so you can keep your A-R. Just make sure you're ammoed up, we're going in hot.'

71

The studio was formerly used by British Broadcasting Bristol, and the offices had hardly changed since they had vacated the building. Julie sat in an office chair and prepared Trant, who sat opposite, for the interview. Jonathan stood nearby, with Marcus.

'So this isn't a live broadcast?' he asked again.

'No,' Julie replied, 'it's a recording. Once the timing is right, it will be uploaded and will go out on internet and terrestrial channels, and on Russian Television. They might be able to hijack a satellite signal and upload it, they've got the ability. The Chinese cracked the encryption on the encoder systems months ago with their quantum computers.'

'Damn it all, I feel like a traitor,' Trant said.

'Think positive,' she said. 'Remember what Marcus told you. You're reaching out to millions, but importantly to the American administration.'

'If I had a gun to my head, it'd look better,' Trant quipped.

'But it wouldn't be convincing,' Julie replied earnestly. 'Are you sure you're ready to do this?' She looked directly at him, then glanced at Marcus and Jonathan, wondering what to do if Trant actually said no.

He nodded. 'Yes, I'm ready.'

72

The next morning, it was clear that the weather wasn't going to co-operate with the plan, and if they were to retain some element of surprise they'd have to go in despite it, with more limited air cover and transport. In any case, 'Operation Samhain', as it had been designated, was about to commence.

The force was in-theatre by four a.m. despite further strong winds and rain. Troops inside armoured personnel carriers were glad of the cover from the elements, whilst any outside who had to ready the vehicles and equipment quickly became drenched. A few wore waterproof clothing but knew that they'd have to dispense with these at H-hour. Vehicle antennae bent and swished in the rain-heavy gusts, which ripped anything off vehicle superstructures which wasn't lashed down. Occasionally something would clatter along the ground, possibly part of the contents of a half-empty box of supplies that hadn't been properly secured earlier.

Undeterred by the weather, Brigadier Trelawney was unequivocal about wanting to lead from as near to the front as possible and sat inside a six-wheeled armoured command vehicle which contained several screens showing the target area, for what he was still referring to as a strike operation. Major Fuller was with him, plus a small staff of junior officers and staff. The vehicle would trail in the third echelon behind the spearhead units.

'Two minutes to the off,' Fuller said.

'Fine,' Trelawney replied. 'This is it, Bernard. If something good is to come of the Defence Secretary's death, then it's this.'

Fuller was a little perplexed. 'Getting Trant back?'

'No. Re-taking Bristol from the insurgents! Oh for God's sake, get with the program, Bernard.'

Fuller looked chastised but also skeptical. 'Sir, we need five times the number to secure a city this size.'

'Nonsense! With the fire-power and tech we have, all we'll need to do is to hold the ground. Once we're a call-sign in distress the Americans will be obliged to snd in the cavalry our rescue.'

Fuller was beyond words, and glanced at Trelawney's ADC, Captain Manning; but the craven officer remained poker-faced. Only the signals officer, Lieutenant Beresford, betrayed a look of doubt. Despite the seemingly carefully planned extraction operation that Trelawney had described to his company commanders, the true nature of the operation that he envisaged was, to Fuller, astoundingly unhinged. Trelawney was clearly making his modest force into a tripwire, a sacrificial goat to oblige the Americans to launch a far larger operation.

As Trelawney gave the order and the command vehicle began to move, Major Fuller sat there feeling suddenly trapped with a lunatic in a tin box on wheels, about to embark on a suicide mission.

73

Recently awoken in the early hours, King received the news from his Staff Captain, as he walked along the corridor towards his command bunker. 'Sir, they're definitely on the move and now entering city limits.'

Once they were inside the command centre, King waited a minute as he surveyed his monitors and CCTV screens.

'What do our recce units estimate the size of the force to be?' he asked his Intelligence Officer.

'Of re-enforced battalion strength. We're looking at roughly a thousand men, many A-F-V's, and we've counted four main battle tanks.'

'Any Americans?'

'Some infantry, we think an airborne company.'

'I'd laugh if it was the 355th again,' King smiled. 'Is everything ready in place?'

'Yes.'

'And what's the weather forecast like?'

'Abysmal,' the Intelligence officer replied with a smile.

'It's a probe or a feint,' King stated. 'But they're really after Trant. Expect some boys in black to come flying in.'

'Shall I arrange evacuation procedures?' the Staff Captain asked.

'No, not just yet,' King answered. 'This is still winnable. The threat will come if they're reinforced by the Americans, and also if they use heavy ordnance. I'll not turn this city into Stalingrad. Once that happens, we'll bug out, but only then. Get all units to stand-to.'

74

Dolman was amazed that the helicopters had actually made it into the air, and then that they remained airborne, as they were buffeted by the gusts of wind and driving rain. The teams were surely earning their airborne pay in this. The one concession was that they'd be harder to hear and see, and what was making them unsteady would equally make them harder to see and hit.

They flew in danger-low, seeing the lights of the perimeter just feet beneath them, and looking over to see columns of vehicles and troops already moving into the city. It was still dark, and vaguely perturbing to know that the pilots were flying by radar and infra-red, as there were few lights on in the city before them.

He looked around to see his immediate team. Corporal Ashcroft sat beside Lance-Corporal Matt Clayton, now his section second-in-command. Dolman had told Rodriguez that he was good to continue his temporary attachment as a section commander back in a regular platoon of the American 355th Airborne, just for the duration of the operation.

The three helicopters that contained Dolman's platoon were to take the roof of the fifteen-storey building. Captain Halstead's platoon was landing on the ground, by a car park and play area, to secure the ground floor and lower storeys.

As they closed in on what intelligence had pinpointed as the possible command centre of the operation, Wraxall Towers, all hell let loose. From another tall building, a missile from a Russian-made launcher streaked up and destroyed one assault helicopter. Debris fell two hundred feet to the street below. At the same time, Dolman's helicopter began taking heavy machine-gun fire as it hovered over the roof. The pilot began to panic and descended too fast. He tried to pull up but realised that the forward motion would either take them into a small rooftop service building or take the rotors off if he turned sideways. 'Brace!' was all he had time to scream as he attempted in vain to pull the joystick back and avoid the building. The helicopter ploughed into the wooden structure and then turned in its side, precariously close to the edge.

Although the pilot and co-pilot were unconscious or dead, Dolman and the other men inside were still strapped in and just shaken and dazed, and began to release their seat belts. They had sustained minor injuries and nothing more. As the second helicopter landed, a supporting helicopter gunship raked the roof area where the firing had come from. Dolman and his team used this as their opportunity to pull themselves free of their wrecked vehicle. His and the troops from the one other surviving helicopter led by Colour Sergeant Keegan co-ordinated, and then made for the roof exit to begin securing the lower floors. Dolman confirmed to Matlock's team that the roof was secure. At the same time, Captain Halstead had radioed in to say that his teams had been caught in a cross-fire and sustained heavy casualties on the ground, with two of his helicopters destroyed as they'd landed, but that he and ten others who weren't wounded were now in the lobby and going to fight their way up.

'Negative, stay where you are,' Dolman advised. 'Call in casevac'.

'By my reckoning, we've lost one section with the destroyed chopper, and another two below,' Sergeant Keegan stated, 'and our ability to extract.'

'We've already lost too much to take and hold this building,' Dolman stated.

'Do we radio my old team to tell them?' Ashcroft interrupted.

'Do we fuck!' Dolman said. 'They can join us in hell.' He smiled, and so did Ashcroft.

'Okay, there's only one way down,' he said to his Colour Sergeant. Dolman turned to the exit as he heard Matlock's helicopters approach, followed by the others.

Momentarily, Ashcroft squinted up into the rain, and as he saw the black shapes of Matlock's team helicopters close in he turned to Matt Clayton. 'Come on, fuck black ops; let's follow the boss!'

75

With the noise indicating that the operation had commenced, Jonathan and Julie were the last to put on their combat belts and ready their weapons. She looked at him.

'I've been assigned to the south-western sector with Stan,' she told him.

Jonathan was unequivocal. 'Julie, I want you out. You need to get away from here.'

'No, darling. I'm fighting.'

'This will get nasty. It's more than just an operation to extract Trant. I'm told they're attacking in force.'

'I thought they were only after Trant?' she replied.

'Maybe, but we can't let them get him, he's too important.'

'So, I need to be part of the defence.'

Jonathan knew that it was pointless to argue with her; and also knew that he had less sway with her since the mission. He took her and hugged her. 'Just take care, won't you?'

'I will. And you, too.'

76

The signs of action at the city centre were barely noticed by the advancing forces, although the radio traffic was being received by various signals and intelligence units. Trelawney had ordered his vehicle to temporarily stop as he digested the contradictory reports relayed from his communications officer, Lieutenant Beresford, about the special force attack onto the suspected resistance headquarters. It was too late to call it off, but it looked like the support group had taken heavy casualties, and that American helicopters would have to be called in to extract the teams.

'If that was a recce, you'd have called them in by now,' Fuller stated.

'Quite, but it's too late for them now. It's up to the commanders on the ground to reach them.'

'I don't think any of those men have perspective anymore.'

'Really, Bernard, you're way too pessimistic. Those are the crème de la crème, the best we have.' He turned to their driver and shouted. 'Okay, move on!'

None of the other officers in the command vehicle dared exchange glances.

77

The wind was dying down a little, and as they moved towards the centre, swarms armoured drones flew silently above them or ahead. The street was abnormally quiet. It was as if no one was about, and no lights were on. Even after the sound of distant explosions and gunfire was heard, there was no sign of life.

'Hey Sarge, this just ain't normal,' a Private First Class said to Rodriguez. 'I mean, there's a city full of people here, but it's just like a ghost town.'

Rodriguez glanced at him. 'I know, but it's early. Keep moving, keep wired, and stay in the shadows. This is classic insurgent tactics. The only mistake they're making is keeping it too quiet.'

The buildings began to loom over them. Rodriguez's squad went to a holding position as he checked his location.

His Platoon Commander, Lieutenant Forrest, approached. 'Sergeant, why are you stopped? I need you to keep pace with the A-F-V's, they can't hug the sides like you can.'

'Yes Sir,' Rodriguez said. He looked around at his squad. 'Okay boys, let's keep moving!'

78

The men and women of the UK Resistance who hadn't already been in combat waited patiently in their pre-arranged positions.

Meanwhile, underground and in one of a complex of rooms connected by a storm drain, part of which comprised his command bunker, King watched the enemy progress on a series of monitors.

'Wraxall Towers has been taken,' one of King's Staff Captains said.

'Good,' King smiled. 'Black ops?'

'Looked like it from the uniforms and equipment. We took out three helicopters as they landed, but estimate there's about thirty of them in the building still.'

'Fine,' King replied. 'That's just fine.'

A communications operator approached them. 'Commander King, Commandant Samuels reports a platoon of tanks is heading towards his position. Also, that the troops are ready covering the barricades, and that he thinks they've been spotted by the attack helicopters.'

'Good. All going to plan, then,' Brigade Commander King smiled at his Staff Captain.

'Seems so, Sir, just as you planned,' the Staff Captain replied.

79

As they took each floor of the building, they encountered no resistance. Dolman and his team raced through old offices but found little evidence anywhere of the Resistance, and none of its command structure. By the third floor he realised that they were unlikely to find much.

'There's something wrong here,' Dolman turned to Colour Sergeant Keegan as they got to the first floor. 'It's as if we were expected, well ahead of time.'

Corporal Ashcroft ran up the stairs from below, leading three from the team that had taken the ground floor. 'Boss, Captain Halshaw is in the lobby, badly wounded. His team was caught in a cross-fire on landing. There's no sign of any insurgents now, let alone Colonel Trant.'

'Damn!' Dolman replied. 'I think this is a set-up.'

'Well, well, well, fancy this? It is another green Army cock-up or what?' It was Matlock, walking up behind Dolman, followed by a group of his black-clad troopers in assault vests and wearing helmets with drop-down microphones.

'Keep out of my hair, Matlock. You, and your bearded wonders,' Dolman replied with disdain.

'*Major* Matlock, now. Sir, to you! I'm a squadron commander now.'

'Whatever, we need to get the fuck out of here, now.'

'Ooh, whatever's the matter? This is one secured position as far as I'm concerned. We hold the highest ground in the city. Now, get your men into position so that we can cover the incoming cavalry. We can search for Colonel Trant later.'

Dolman ignored him and turned to Keegan. 'Colour Sarn't, get your men downstairs and out of this building, now.'

'Belay that order, Sergeant!' Matlock shouted. He pointed his assault rifle at Dolman. 'You, you're finished here, Captain. Put down your weapon!'

Dolman looked at him. 'No Major, you're finished. You committed a war crime back in Wales, there're witnesses, and I've filed a report to that effect.'

'Witnesses?' Matlock scoffed. 'What, this joker Ashcroft here?'

'And the crew of a ground attack helicopter.'

'Careful, Captain, these are dangerous times for traitors. Accidents happen.' Matlock turned and nodded to his team and they raised their weapons.

Keegan, Ashcroft, and the other assault group team around raised their weapons at the black ops troopers. Instantaneously both groups opened fire. One black ops trooper emptied a clip of ammunition into a one of Dolman's team, before having his brains blown out by his oppo. As others fired simultaneously, many fell, dead or wouned. Colour Sergeant Keegan fell to the ground, dead. Dolman had raised his weapon at a distracted Matlock and fired, hitting him across the chest and arm. Matlock's body armour saved him, but he dropped to the floor.

Outnumbered, three remaining black ops troops dropped their weapons at the sight of their commander writhing on the ground and reluctantly raised their arms.

'Argh, you're finished Dolman! Your career's over, do you hear?' Matlock screamed. 'This is it, the end! You realise this is all on headcam? This is a court-martial for sure, and they'll throw away the key this time!'

'Yeah, whatever,' Dolman said as he kicked Matlock in the guts, before reaching down to remove his pistol and pick up his assault rifle. His men removed the ammunition and side-arms from the remaining black ops soldiers. They emptied their sub-machine guns and assault rifles of rounds and made them safe.

Dolman looked at the dead Sergeant Keegan, lying back on the ground with glassy eyes half-open. He reached down to close them. 'Farewell, old warrior,' he murmured.

He got up and looked at the bodies of other dead and wounded men, before turning to Corporal Ashcroft. 'Corporal, get you and your men out of here.'

He turned to who he assumed was Matlock's second in command. 'I have reason to think we've walked into a trap here, this building is probably rigged. We'll leave your hardware in the lobby.'

The black-ops soldier, a Sergeant, betrayed his indignation with a flash of momentary concern at Dolman's pronouncement.

'Don't listen to him,' Matlock shouted weakly as he continued to bleed. 'He's a traitor and a coward. He'll hang for this.'

Dolman ignored Matlock, at looked the black ops soldier. 'Give us five, then you can do what you want. And, you'd better see to that piece of shit before he bleeds out.' Dolman turned to Ashcroft. 'Okay Corporal, let's go!'

The assault troopers slowly withdrew from the area and made for the exits. They filed down the stairs, followed by Dolman, who covered behind in case the black ops team decided to follow.

In the lobby, Dolman saw Captain Halshaw as he was stretchered-out.

'How are you, you old war-horse?' Dolman asked.

'Been better. What's the hurry?'

Halshaw's question wasn't answered by Dolman, but a series of deep, sonorous, distant-sounding explosions, followed shortly by a thunderous rumbling. They looked up at the ceiling.

'Go!' shouted Dolman. 'Get the fuck out of here!'

80

'Sir, it's going!' one of Marcus' team shouted.

'Yes, I can see, well done.'

'It was the engineering team who deserve the credit, Commandant,' the man replied. 'They managed to get all the demolition charges in place in time.'

'Right,' Marcus replied, as the building began to fall in on itself. They'd let a stretcher team through but no one else, aware as they were that it was a black ops team which had landed on the roof half an hour earlier.

'Caught, like rats in a barrel!' Marcus said, allowing himself some gloating. As the team commander of this particular operation, he knew that he'd achieved his objective. However, he also observed that it would have been impossible to net such a high-value target as a black ops team without his inside man.

81

Rodriguez's squad and the rest of the platoon went to ground when they saw the barricades at the end of the street, and the tell-tale signs of firing.

'Sergeant,' Lieutenant Forrest said to him, 'stay firm. We're just getting authorisation to put in a low-collateral bomb in there, or for the tanks to use main armament.'

'Jeez, Sir, this is still a civilian zone!' Rodriguez protested.

'Not my call, Sergeant,' the Lieutenant replied, 'at least they're not using the swarm drones.'

'Sir, that's not effective fire coming from those barricades,' Rodriguez persisted. 'If you just let me and a few of my men go forward I'm sure we can neutralise it.'

'Negative, Sergeant, I want you to....' the Lieutenant hesitated. 'Oh, hang on,' he said as he listened in on his personal role radio receiver. 'Well, it seems a U-A-V drone is going to do the job instead, followed by ground attack helicopters to rake the area with twenty-mill.' He glanced around at those of Rodriguez's squad in view. 'Okay men, you know the routine; stay firm, keep low.'

'Sir, we don't have eyes on the enemy,' Rodriguez protested. 'If we could withdraw and take another street-

'Sergeant, that's a negative. This is a clear ambush situation, and I'd assume any egress is covered.'

They waited, and very soon through the wind and rain they heard the sound of an approaching missile whoosh in. It struck the barricade, the explosion launching part of vehicles and other debris into the air, landing on the ground nearby. It was followed up by ground attack helicopters on a strafing run, which raked the remainder of the barrier with twenty millimetre rounds.

A few minutes later, Lieutenant Forrest received notification that they could move forward again. 'Okay, we've got the threat reduced. Hey Feldmayer, get your boys moving! You too, Rodriguez.'

Rodriguez and his troopers moved tactically forward towards the remains of the barricades. He ordered several into position, covering nearby doors and windows, and set up a machine gun position with an arc of fire up the street ahead. There was, however, no further incoming fire.

Rodriguez inspected the remains of the barricade, built-up on some old car hulks, as Lieutenant Forrest approached, followed by another man with a radio set and binoculars.

'Sergeant, I want you to make faster headway up this street, why aren't you moving?'

'I wanted to inspect these barricades, sir.'

'Sure, but you can collect souvenirs later, Sergeant.'

'No, it's nothing like that, Sir. Just take a look round. There're no bodies. We were being shot at just a minute ago.'

'I don't know Sergeant, maybe they scooted,' the Lieutenant replied impatiently.

The Corporal beside Lieutenant Forrest, who was an air controller, had been following the conversion. He contributed in a rich southern drawl. 'Naw, Lootenant, ah was up there, brought those birds in, an' I didn't see no-one skedaddle.'

Lieutenant Forrest was silent.

'Lieutenant,' Rodriguez continued, 'all that seems to be around here is lots of them bins,' he said, pointing to black and green plastic bins strewn up the street. 'And take a look at this one.' He walked up to one that was still standing and had just lost its lid. It was peppered with shrapnel and fast was leaking water. 'That's warm water in there.'

'Why what the hell…?' Lieutenant Forrest asked.

The Air Controller answered. 'Ah reckon they's been messing with the I-R sensors on our helicopters and I-STAR. They filled those bins full of hot water and wheeled em here to give out a heat signature the same as live bodies.'

'For what reason, Corporal?' Forrest asked.

'To draw our fire, get us to waste ammo. Reckon it'll take the choppers a forty minute round-trip back to Weston to replen, at least. They's playing us for time, Lieutenant.'

'No,' Rodriguez disagreed, 'it took them time to build all this. Sir, I think this is a trap.'

'Um, what seems to be the hold-up here?' It was a British accent, an octave above the Americans' voices, sounding well-educated and well-heeled. The Americans turned to see an approaching tank officer in green overalls, with goggles atop a black beret.

'Sir,' Lieutenant Forrest began, unsure as to what rank the officer was. 'We have reason to believe that this is part of a trap.'

'Nonsense! This position's clearly just been neutralised,' the tank officer stated dismissively. 'I want to secure the city centre before sunrise. Now come on, we haven't got all day!'

As he watched the British officer trot back towards his tank, Lieutenant Forrest muttered, 'Goddam stupid son-of-a-bitch Limey! Go kill yourself for all I care.' He turned to Rodriguez's team. 'Okay men, get moving, the armour's coming through and I want you to keep pace with it.'

As Rodriguez ran to re-join his section, which had picked itself up and began to move in file up each side of the street, Lieutenant Forrest and his J-TAG Corporal stood aside from the breach in the barricade to let the four British tanks thunder by, engines screaming, followed by four armoured personnel carriers that trailed some ways behind, as if more warily.

They continued to watch in dumbfounded astonishment as the two lead tanks surged forward down the street as if in a race, losing Rodriguez's infantry protection as they vainly attempted to sprint to keep up. Even the armoured personnel carriers passed them.

Suddenly, both tanks disappeared as the ground beneath them gave way, and despite the rain, dust and smoke rose from the massive hole in the street, as well as a plume of water from a burst water main.

'Jeez, tank trap!' Lieutenant Forrest shouted as the two trailing tanks screeched to a halt, one overshooting and slowly lurching over into the hole. It tried to reverse but only succeeded in pulling more rubble down into the hole, before sinking further. In panic, its crew began to abandon it. That's when the shooting resumed.

All of the escaping tank crew were gunned down, and three of Rodriguez's men were hit as they attempted to take cover. The rest of his section dived to the ground. An anti-tank projectile hit one of the armoured personnel carriers and it quickly began to burn. Another began to reverse and hit the remains of the barricade. As more anti-tank rounds found their targets men began to disembark from the other two, but many were caught in a cross-fire from the surrounding buildings.

'Cover them!' Rodriguez shouted.

His men aimed at muzzle flashes in windows above.

A car drove down the street.

'Aim for the windows!' Rodriguez commanded.

'What for, Sarge, it's an autonomous! Just keep out of its way!'

Soldiers darted for cover as the autonomous vehicle, which had effectively been converted into an intelligent robotic bomb, sped past, and a little way behind found the commander of the Third Platoon in consultation with the Company Commander and some members of his headquarters staff. It decided that they were important enough targets to expend itself over.

There was more firing, this time from street level. Enemy fighters were appearing behind them, and from areas already cleared.

'We're pinned!' one of them shouted.

'No we're not,' Rodriguez replied. 'Just select targets, put down effective fire! Just make sure you've got something to shoot at, right?'

'We're just getting shot at from all sides and taking casualties. Where the fuck are they coming from?'

'Wherever,' Rodriguez shouted, 'we've got to get the threat reduced. Only then we can get casevac in.' He turned to another of his men. 'Cody, get a round from your forty-nine-mike into that shop-front. The rest of you, scan for targets! Call 'em out as you see 'em. Lopez, come with me, I've got you covered!'

Suddenly out of nowhere, three drones landed near clumps of troops, with shaped charges, and before most had had time to notice them, they exploded.

'Fucking explosive drones!' Rodriguez shouted. 'Watch the skies, target them before they land! I'll call E-C-M to find what band they're on and neutralise them.'

After Rodriguez had made his call to the Electronic Countermeasures Team, he was joined by Lieutenant Forrest. 'Okay Sergeant, we're going to have to hold here and await re-enforcements. Seems they've got this whole street and effectively taken out three Brit M-B-T's. We've got casualties out there, including

Captain Krantz, our I-O. He's in a burning A-F-V. I want you to take your squad and work round to try to extract him. Watch your ammo, make sure you've got something to shoot at, right?'

'Yes Sir,' Rodriguez shouted. He turned to his squad. 'Okay team, with me.' He sprinted forward, keeping low and hugging the side of the building.

'Okay, down here. Al? Ches? Cover those windows up there. I've gotta get to the boys in that wagon!' At that, Rodriguez sprinted out to join the team behind the burning armoured personnel carrier.

He stopped at one dazed soldier without his helmet, blood running down his face. 'You seen Captain Krantz?'

'Yeah,' replied the wounded soldier, and pointed at the armoured personnel carrier. 'He's in there, dead.'

'Dead, you sure? You sure?'

'As sure as I can be, Sergeant, he looked a real mess. There're three left in there. Jeez, Sergeant, it's on fire!'

'I want to check,' Rodriguez replied.

'You're nuts, they got that rear doors covered, no one else is getting in or out!'

Without hesitation, Rodriguez threw down a smoke grenade and moved behind the vehicle. He jumped in the back, as bullets ricocheted off the door. Once inside, the smoke made him cough, and he could barely see. Blind from the smoke he frantically pulled bodies aside. One, a Private First Class, was still alive. The last was Captain Krantz, the Intelligence Officer.

'Hey, there's still two alive in here, including the Captain. Help me get him out.'

With reluctant trepidation, two men appeared at the back, one took the Private and dragged him around the side, as Rodriguez and the second man took the Captain. The second man fell, hit in the leg, and Rodriguez dragged the Captain to safety, before going out a second time to pull his helper back.

'Okay, patch them up,' he ordered a medic, as more troops and armoured personnel carriers moved past, and another platoon of troops began to fight their way into the buildings.

Twenty minutes later, the fighting in the street had died down.

Lieutenant Forrest approached Rodriguez. 'It looks like they were using the sewers or something to outflank us. Seems like the UK Resistance outfit is more into shoot-and-scoot.'

'Yeah, it seems so, Sir.'

'Sergeant, that was a damn-fool act you did just there. So damn-fool, I'm going to recommend you for a medal.'

'Thanks Lieutenant, but I was just doing my job,' Rodriguez replied. He realised his hands were shaking.

'Look like you saved a Captain's life. With the weight of fire on the back of that wagon, that's worth something. Okay, anyway, we've gotta keep going, those of us fit enough to do so anyhow. Get your squad together, we're going to follow that last Brit tank to the city centre.'

82

Marcus now nursed a leg wound from shrapnel, as he'd been last out of a room in the process of being cleared by US Paratroopers. As he hobbled on a makeshift crutch with the help of a comrade down to the tunnels, he passed the cavern that they had created beneath the road, strengthened just enough for light motor vehicles, but not for a seventy-five-ton main battle tank; and not one going at full speed. Not even its hydro-pneumatic suspension would have saved the crews from injury in that drop. Seeing the three vehicles, one perched on top of another, with the burst water main spurting over the vehicles and bodies of slaughtered crewmen, adding blood to the pools of water in the now-open subterranean cavity, he felt that they were on the edge of victory.

However, twenty minutes later he was back with King and Jonathan Barnes in the control room of his bunker, and his assessment wasn't so optimistic.

'Three tanks, eh?' King smiled. 'To be sure, I never truly expected them to fall for that.'

'Oh, they did, all twenty feet,' Marcus replied with a grimace.

'Great! You realise that's taken out half of the remaining U-K armoured capability left in this benighted land. However, gentlemen, with the material and firepower that the U-S can throw against us, we need to be realistic. We were never going to win this. And with that in mind, I've ordered our remaining units to evacuate.'

'Remaining units?' Jonathan asked with surprise and some consternation.

'Yes. The evacuation of our main logistical, command, and intelligence structures has already occurred. They've scattered into the countryside and will regroup at a time and location known only to myself and a few top commanders. When we're ready the signal will go out.'

'Why didn't you tell me?' Jonathan asked, irked.

'Need to know, sorry,' King replied.

'But my wife is still out there somewhere.'

'She and the others are effectively a rear-guard.'

'But she believes she's still defending the city.'

King looked at Jonathan. 'I'm sorry, Jonathan, I'm playing a bigger game here. We're playing for time. It's lucky she completed that interview with Trant at the old studios, once he eventually decided to co-operate. I tell you, if he hadn't, I think I might have shot him myself. Anyway, long story short, we uploaded it twenty minutes ago.'

'And where is he now?'

'He's on his way here, from where he was being held at the old artillery barracks that's across the road from the studios. Ironically it was his old headquarters when the Army was still in control in Bristol.'

'And Julie?' Jonathan asked with increasing irritation.

'She and her unit are as far from the action as possible, covering the suspension bridge.'

'Damn you, King! That's my wife you're talking about.'

'Jonathan!' Marcus cautioned.

King waved down Marcus' concerns. 'That's okay, Commandant. Professor, I understand your concerns, but I assigned her and Stan to the quietest sector, mainly in return for their part in the intrepid capture of the Colonel. They have a good chance of making it out into the countryside from there, at any rate as good as any of us. The main action is happening up there,' he pointed upwards to the street above, 'and it's brutal. If the enemy feel too thwarted, however, they'll be tempted to use artillery and airpower, and I'm not inflicting that on the people of this city. We've taken out three tanks and a Black Ops team in an empty building. We've done very well this morning, but it's time to get out whilst we're ahead.'

As King turned to talk to his Staff Captain, Jonathan's rage was only just assuaged. He looked around at King's staff as they shut down computer systems, drilled through hard disks, and collected portable storage devices. Only the AV monitors showing the fighting at street level were still operating.

Marcus took Jonathan aside. 'I'm sorry it's gone this way,' he told him quietly. 'But with any luck, Julie will make it out into the countryside with Stan. You know he's one of the best in the business, he'll look after her.'

A noise in the corridor made Jonathan look at the door, in time to see Pavel enter, followed by Fyodor, Nikolai, and Pyotr. They flanked Trant, who looked alert.

'Commander?' Pavel said, 'here is the Colonel. We escort him back to you safely.'

'Thank you, gents,' King replied. 'Now I suggest you find your way out of here, I wouldn't want you caught up in this.'

Pavel smiled mirthlessly. 'No, commander, I can see how it would not do well for your propaganda!'

King ignored the jibe and turned to a desk with an opened map of Bristol, which had a clear plastic overlay marking the waste-water and storm-water relief drains beneath the streets. 'Take the storm relief interceptor, south. It'll lead you out to the River Avon, just north of the suspension bridge...here.' He pointed. 'It'll emerge out into the river valley at Portway and the A4. Cross that, head down to the river and you'll find a number of dinghies. Take one West and it'll get you out to the Avonmouth docks and mouth of the Severn. Where you go from there is up to you,' he said, scratching his chin. 'But whilst the docks may present you with plenty of tempting targets, maybe refrain from any more acts of sabotage, at least until we're well clear?'

'Certainly, Commander King,' Pavel said. 'We wait until you pass us.'

'Good.' King hesitated for a second but then went to shake Pavel's hand. 'Look, thank you for your help.'

'No trouble. Don't worry, we go now. No point to dying here.' Pavel turned and indicated to his team to go.

As the four Russians left, King breathed a sigh of relief.

Jonathan glanced at him. 'If once you have paid the Dane-geld, you never get rid of the Dane,' with a wry smile he quoted Kipling.

Marcus momentarily raised his eyebrows at the cheek but smiled when King did. Even Martin Trant grinned at the irony.

'They have their uses,' King replied. 'Whatever,' he said to change the subject as he turned to Trant. 'Well, Colonel, it's so good to see you. Thank you for your co-operation. However, you did leave it rather last minute to co-operate. As you've probably been hearing, your friends are coming to get you. We, however, are not hanging around to meet and greet them. We don't go in for any of that fighting to the last round nonsense, not like you lot. Oh no, we far prefers to live to fight another day. Now, it's up to you as to what you decide to do, but whatever it is, please be quick about it!'

'I could come with you?' Trant asked.

'Yes.'

There was suddenly an explosion above them, making the lights flicker and plaster fall from the ceiling.

'Feck, what in hell's name was that?' King shouted above the diminishing rumble.

Pavel and Nickolai rushed back into the command centre, both blackened from smoke and coughing, followed some seconds later by a facially injured Pyotr supporting a limping and very bloody Fyodor.

'It too late, they on us!' Pavel shouted.

'Commander!' the Staff Captain shouted. 'We've a breach of the tunnel complex! They're using charges to gain entrance from above.'

'Jesus, Mary, and Joseph!' King exclaimed. 'Pick up any weapon, we'll have to fight our way out of here.'

'No!' Marcus replied, looking around at the still-live monitors. 'You go. I'm going up there.'

'Are you mad?' King asked.

'Probably,' Marcus said. 'But I think I've seen a way to buy you some time.' He turned to the Russians. 'Maybe you can help me?'

'We go nowhere up there, it is crazy,' Pavel replied.

'Pavel,' Fyodor said weakly. 'I go nowhere. Shoot me or leave me with him, I die soldier.'

Pavel didn't think twice about it, and said something in Russian to Fyodor, before turning to King. 'Commander, you need to leave. I come with you to fight our way out, but Fyodor and Pyotr will stay to fight with the Commandant.'

'Alright. Are you sure, Marcus?' King asked.

'Yeah, with my bad leg I'll just hold you up. Now go!'

'Thanks, we owe you one,' King replied, holding Marcus by the shoulders and embracing him. 'God go with you.' He turned to Trant. 'Colonel? You can take your chances with us, but you're what they're after. You're probably better off staying here.'

'Thank you, that might buy you some time also. I wish I could help you further.'

'You have, Colonel, you have,' King said, shaking his hand. 'Thank you for all the help you have given. It might change things.'

'Okay, now GO!' Trant urged.

They needed no second bidding. Trant watched King, Jonathan, Pavel, Nickolai, and the remaining five bunker staff leave. There was another explosion above and the lights flickered.

Marcus looked at Fyodor, now slumped in a chair, eyes closed. 'He's in a bad way.'

'He make it,' Pyotr said. 'I look after him.'

Colonel Trant looked at him. 'Ready, Tovarich?'

Clearly in pain, Fyodor 'the bear' opened his eyes and nodded his head in assent, dark curly hair matted with blood. 'Da, we go.'

Trant looked at Pyotr. 'I'll help to get him up to the street.'

'It's your funeral, Colonel,' Marcus replied.

Trant helped Pyotr get Fyodor up, and in addition to his own assault rifle, Marcus picked up the Russian's and followed them, hobbling out of the office with his makeshift crutch. Trant and Pyotr supported the wounded Russian as they ascended the old, damp steps from the drain tunnel to a ledge, thence awkwardly hauling him up via some rusty rungs to a manhole cover, and the street above.

83

There had only been one place to go once those following Captain Halshaw's stretcher had been gunned down outside the lobby. Once the power had gone all that operated were the emergency lights that led them through the reception fire door and down some steps to the basement and car park. Following up fast, Dolman had leaped over the banister and landed, rolled, and then headed for the emergency exit. He followed his remaining team just as debris began to smash down on the pavement outside. At the bottom of the steps was another fire door out to the car-park, and they sprinted across the empty parking lot to a ramp as they heard a thunderous roar. They could see dust already beginning to travel down the ramp.

'Respirators!' Dolman shouted, and he went down onto one knee by a stand of old bicycles as he pulled on his own. He looked around at the silhouettes of the men around him and indicated to them to remain where they were. They were no longer directly beneath the building and so stood a good chance of making it out, but they needed to avoid the falling debris above and let the dust settle. 'Once we're up there we need to extract fast from this area,' he shouted.

A few minutes later they were back up at street level and moving tactically in pairs, covering each other off. They made as much distance from the building as possible before Dolman indicated with hand signals for them to stop.

Corporal Ashcroft approached.

'Sitrep, Corporal,' Dolman asked.

'It's what you see. Counting you and me, we're down to six guys, boss. And we're low on ammo, only five to six clips each, including what was useable from my old team.'

'No one else made it out?'

'Seems not,' Ashcroft replied. 'It was dark, noisy, only those of us who saw that emergency exit stood a chance.'

'Yeah, I was there too. Okay, I'd hoped for more,' Dolman said grimly.

They were joined by Lance-Corporal Matt Clayton. 'Alright boss? We made it out at least.'

Dolman was visibly cheered by the sight of Clayton. 'Any of the rest of the old crowd make it?'

'You mean any of us with the Estonia ribbon? Soz, boss, just you and me now. Kev Silcott bought it following Captain Halshaw out. Don't reckon either of them made it.'

Dolman was quiet for a second.

'Boss? What's the plan?' Clayton asked.

Dolman glanced at him, suddenly unsure.

'Boss?' Corporal Ashcroft asked.

Dolman shook himself out of it as the sound of armoured vehicles and firing got closer. 'We rendezvous with the cavalry.'

It was an obvious decision, one any of them could easily have made. Dolman realised that the loss of so many of his team, on top of the horrors of the destruction of the haven, had somehow put him into a state of indecision. For the first time in his life, he was beginning to doubt his ability to be decisive.

84

Sergeant Rodriguez's squad had made it to a street leading off from the 'Bearpit', which was a large roundabout and junction of most of the main roads into Bristol; and also effectively the city centre. It was also close to their objective, Wraxall Towers. Rodriguez watched with some relief as British infantry and armoured personnel carriers moved past. Officially, the combined operation was supposed to have been some sort of 'leap-frogging' or 'relay race' between the 'hares' and the 'hounds', which he'd heard Lieutenant Forrest dismiss under his breath as 'a load of Goddam stupid Limey sporting terms, some bullshit way to plan a battle.'

In the event, their company of the 355th had been consistently acting as the spearhead; and with the associated losses of having been so. Now it was the turn of the British to "pick up the baton". Rodriguez was irked at the losses suffered by his unit. This was after all supposed to be a British operation.

An armoured command vehicle stopped, and two officers got out. The Americans recognised the British commander, Brigadier Trelawney, and his Intelligence Officer, a Major.

Lieutenant Forrest walked up to them. 'Sir, please be aware that we have only just cleared this street, and there could still be snipers or I-E-D's in the vicinity.'

'Fine Lieutenant, we'll take our chances,' Trelawney replied haughtily. 'Is there anyone more senior in the area?'

'Er, no Sir,' Forrest replied. 'Our O-C Major Kinkaid was killed recently, and our I-O has been put on a casevac out.'

'I think that makes you one of the most senior officers on the ground in your company,' Trelawney said. 'Well, anyway, we've made damned good headway, and no small thanks to your unit.' Having just heard about the collapse of Wraxall Towers together with his entire special assault team, and the loss of most of his tanks, Trelawney was attempting to sound as upbeat as possible.

'Yes, Sir,' Forrest replied lethargically. He was getting tired. 'We must be near the condo, aren't we?'

'Yes, well, there's been an incident, and a change of plan,' Trelawney admitted.

Forrest looked at the Brigadier dumbly, waiting for him to continue, but all Trelawney did was glance at his Intelligence Officer. *Jeez, these Brits could be evasive!*

'Sir, can you be more clear?' Lieutenant Forrest pushed. The officer before him may have held a one-star rank, but he'd lost Forrest's unit too many men for him to want to adhere to any polite protocol.

'Yes, well, it seems that Wraxall Towers was booby-trapped, wired. We lost our entire assault team.'

Despite his weariness, Lieutenant Forrest was visibly shocked. This whole operation was fast becoming one big Limey shit-show, and he quelled a sudden urge to just extract what was left of his company straight away. If the British force hadn't already 'leap-frogged' ahead, he would seriously have considered at least going firm where they were, and not moving another inch forward.

'So, Lieutenant,' Brigadier Trelawney continued, 'it's now a clearing-up exercise. I want you to support the Mechanised Company that's just passed, and then consolidate the immediate area.'

'Is there any news of your missing officer, Sir? The Colonel?' Forrest asked.

'No, none I'm afraid. If he was in that building when it collapsed then he's almost certainly dead.'

Lieutenant Forrest released his helmet strap and rubbed his chin. 'Sir, if you don't mind my saying, my hunch is that they got him out and that the condo was a set-up all along.'

Trelawney's attempted to hide his surprise and appear as if he'd already considered this. 'You're possibly right, Lieutenant. However, we can't deal in supposition at this stage. I'm going to do my damndest to find my officer, but at the very least we've scored a major victory against the resistance this morning, and all before breakfast! And remember, no small amount of that credit goes to your unit, Lieutenant. Carry on.'

Trelawney and Fuller returned the American's salute, but Trelawney was visibly annoyed as he turned back to the wagon. Fuller nodded his appreciation, but as he turned to follow the Brigadier back into the command vehicle he swallowed nervously.

85

Marcus, Trant, and the two Russian commandos had made it to the armoured vehicle, which had been Marcus's original objective back down in the control room after seeing it on the monitor. Trant pulled open the rear door and, once in, helped to haul the Russian soldier up into the back of the vehicle, with the help of his comrade. Fyodor groaned in pain and looked close to unconsciousness. As Pyotr propped him up in a seat, giving him some water from a half-empty canteen, before heading to the driving seat. Trant wondered if Fyodor would be of any use to them whatsoever.

However, from a jacket pocket Fyodor took out his medical kit, tore it open and emptied it out onto the seat next to him. He picked up an epinephrine pen, slammed it into his thigh and sat back. He looked at Trant defiantly before closing his eyes.

Marcus had busied himself switching on the vehicle weapons system but had trouble activating the main armament, the multiple-barrelled .50 cal Gatling above them.

Behind him, he was surprised to hear Fyodor speak. 'No worry. Nickolai, he over-ride system. Pick up control box on console, press switch.' Only just able to lift his large head from his chest, Fyodor nonetheless seemed to have revived a bit, and spoke better English than any of them would have hitherto believed he could.

Marcus did as Fyodor had instructed, and picked up a make-shift plastic box patched into the circuitry beneath the console. He pressed on a switch and the console of LEDs and the screen above him suddenly lit up. 'Security clearance granted, armament activated', a computerised female voice announced. 'Switch to manual or automated mode for target selection.'

Trant glanced from Fyodor to Marcus for a second with the glee of a ten-year-old boy on Christmas morning. For the first time in too long he had a new toy to play with, and a purpose. He watched as Marcus opened the hatch above him.

Marcus looked down at him. 'Colonel, just what the hell are you still doing here?'

Trant was momentarily surprised that his erstwhile captor should ask such a question.

'Um, is there anything more I can do to help?'

Marcus continued and shook his head. 'Don't be stupid, you just get out of here, Colonel. This isn't your battle. Those are your men approaching.'

Trant's disappointment at being assigned to the side-lines was assuaged by Marcus' unassailable logic, as Pyotr tested the engine.

'This is a one-way ride, Colonel,' Marcus continued. 'Get away from here. You've helped us more than enough. Now we're just buying Commander King some time.'

'Not on your own,' Trant replied. 'I've got a score to settle.'

'As I said, it's your funeral, Colonel,' Marcus replied.

86

Trelawney was swift in his judgement as he called through to his bodyguard, who sat beside the driver. 'Corporal Sutton? Will you make your way back here, please, and place Major Fuller under house arrest?'

Between the Corporal's affected nonchalance, and Fuller's prior realisation that he could be held directly responsible for sending the special force assault team to their doom due to clearly faulty intelligence, the only person who looked at all surprised was the signals officer, Lieutenant Beresford. Fuller expected nothing less than the stony-faced silence from Trelawney's sycophantic ADC, Captain Manning.

As Corporal Sutton walked through to the rear of the vehicle he removed his pistol from its holster and stood before Fuller with the barrel aimed at his belly.

'There won't be any need for that, Corporal, the Major won't be going anywhere,' Trelawney instructed. 'Just remove his sidearm, and keep watch over him, please.'

'Yes Sir,' Sutton replied and proceeded to removed Fuller's pistol from its holster.

'Sit down, Fuller,' Trelawney instructed.

'Am I to know what this is all about?' Fuller asked.

'Let's not play games, Major. It's clear that the faulty intelligence you supplied resulted in the loss of our entire special assault team.'

'And so you take the supposition of some hick American platoon commander at face value as evidence?' Fuller asked with rising irritation.

For a second Trelawney was taken aback at the challenge, but then smiled. 'Not entirely, Major. We've had our suspicions about you for some time, and have been monitoring all of your dispatches. And, at the very least, you are responsible for gross incompetence. I don't care just now whether I'm right or wrong. I am, however, relieving you of your duties and putting you under arrest forthwith. When this is over you will be detained, pending further investigations.'

Fuller looked beaten.

'Okay driver, get a move on,' Trelawney ordered. 'I want to get to the remains of Wraxall Towers A-S-A-P.'

87

Once the Engineers had blown through to the storm drain tunnels at street level, assault troops surged down with flashlights and lasers attached to their automatic rifles. Anyone who moved in front of them was liable to be shot out of hand.

As King and the others moved quickly down the tunnels away from the area, small rear-guard defence teams had moved into position to cover their retreat. Within minutes there was a subterranean running battle going on, as well as the one going on at street-level. King and his team surprised one section of assault engineers who had made it down to their level, and there was a brief and bloody skirmish. King himself had used his assault rifle to deadly effect. But thereafter it was a chase, with the Army in hot pursuit of King's headquarters team.

As other UK Resistance fighters before them were caught in deadly cross-fires, the Army assault teams began to feel confident and picked up their pace.

Further down the tunnel, King inexplicably halted. Jonathan looked at him. 'What's the matter?'

'I'm waiting for the last of my rear-guard,' King explained.

'Do you think we really have time for this? The enemy will be hot on their heels.'

'Quite, which is why they need our cover,' King said.

'But they'll be over us with the numbers we have,' Jonathan protested. In the half-light, he could see a sneer of disapproval on King's face, before he clicked his fingers. His Staff Captain approached with a detonator box.

'We learned a thing or two about fighting underground at Morton Down!' King grinned at Jonathan, as the noise of approaching soldiers got closer; a cacophony of shouting, shooting, and slapping of boots in shallow water. Within a minute or two, his rear-guard troops appeared. They filed past, damp, dirty, and exhausted. The last one passed him and said breathlessly, 'only hostiles behind!'

King kneeled. 'Cover your ears and open your mouths', he instructed. They heard the soldiers before they saw their approaching outlines. Very soon they could see some detail. The soldiers stopped for a second in confusion when they saw the UK Resistance HQ element in the distance, standing beside a kneeling King. Jonathan fancied he saw the look of realisation on several of their faces, and one raised his assault rifle, the torch beam flashing and a laser crossing his vision. King pressed the actuator.

There was an almighty explosion suddenly lighting up the tunnel. They took cover as the blast wave passed them, followed by billowing dust. Part of the tunnel roof further down was falling into the water.

King got up and chucked the actuator away. 'Come on, that'll only delay them.'

88

Second Lieutenant Enderby's platoon was now on point as the spearhead unit, a role he felt privileged to have been assigned; his only concern being that he didn't muck it up. Being the newest commissioned officer this was exactly the reason he had been assigned such a role, as most of his more experienced colleagues would have been more cautious, and more scared. This was exactly what Brigadier Trelawney didn't desire; he needed to keep speed and momentum going. He had privately hoped for more from the American 355th Airborne, rated as a 'can-do' unit. As soon as he'd learned that they'd been held up by bins full of hot water and a few snipers, he'd lost his temper, and angrily ordered his troops to surge forward.

Enderby had gone at full pace forward, much to the chagrin of his Platoon Sergeant, Sergeant O'Brien, a grizzled older war-horse who'd survived too many contacts to be impressed by the naïve recklessness of a young officer who was barely out of school. However, whilst O'Brien considered Enderby to be a bit of an inexperienced and over-educated twit, he knew that he was an essentially decent one; and if he survived long enough could probably one day make a damned good officer. O'Brien just had to keep him alive long enough for that to happen. At the present moment in time young Mister Enderby was behaving like a bit of a 'dick'; which was also risking the entire platoon.

As Enderby rushed forward like a Subaltern on the Western Front, O'Brien swore to himself and followed up with his multiple, each section moving tactically with its own fire support team to cover. Now and then Enderby had had the sense to call in fire support from a helicopter or ensure that the sniper section had them covered as they advanced down another street. However, as he rushed forward, it was clear that the young officer now sensed victory in the air, and had taken the Brigadier's demand for expediency seriously. Occasionally an assault rifle would open up from a window above, spraying the street around the boy's feet and he would just continue to run forward shooting from the hip, as O'Brien or his men returned more effective fire. O'Brien was just about keeping pace with his reckless platoon commander.

They turned the corner into a narrower street, one that seemed quieter and relatively empty, save for some of the debris from the collapsed Wraxall Towers which had made it out from an adjacent street, and also a parked-up armoured vehicle. It was two hundred meters in front of them, parked with two nearside wheels on the pavement by an office block, covered in dust and light bits of rubble. With its main armament pointing forlornly at the ground it looked abandoned or knocked-out.

As Enderby walked casually towards the vehicle O'Brien caught up with him, and a section ran down the opposite side of the street to cover them.

'Looks like this one's clear,' Enderby said to O'Brien with disappointment. 'One of our units got here first.' He turned to his satellite phone operator, as their personal-role-radios were somehow having trouble. 'Grant, tell the O-C that we're near to the objective but that-

All of a sudden the vehicle seemed to come alive, it's gun traversing very rapidly towards Enderby's covering section, which was about to flank it. The Gatling gun opened up with a rate of fire of 1,300 rounds a minute, shredding the entire section before they had a chance to react. O'Brien tackled Enderby to the ground as the weapon turned automatically and took the head off of Private Grant, thereafter shredding two more men behind who hadn't taken cover fast enough. As the vehicle engine gunned to life it began to move forward, rapidly accelerating, and Enderby's men scattered. O'Brien pulled his shocked officer out of the path of the tires. The vehicle drove sickeningly over the bodies of two of his dead men, and Enderby's face was spattered with blood and brains.

89

Marcus knew that with all the assets that the enemy could deploy, their survival time might be numbered in minutes only, but their mobility would help. They were not a static position that could be outflanked or easily targeted from the air, and at the present moment in time, they still had an element of surprise. As any soldiers lucky enough to be missed by the Gatling gun jumped aside, Marcus knew it was more shock and awe. As their armoured vehicle drove into a more open street, he realised they were more prone to aerial attack.

'Keep away from open spaces!' Trant advised from the rear. 'Take that side street.'

Pyotr manoeuvred the armoured vehicle roughly to the left. They scraped the edge of a building as they turned, straight into the path of another infantry platoon advancing to engage the new threat. The men barely had time to look perturbed, let alone raise their weapons before the Gatling engaged them, and in seconds Pyotr was crushing more shredded bodies.

90

Once word got out that there was a rogue AFV taking out his infantry, Trelawney knew that he had to muster his forces fast to counter the threat. It sounded to him like an effort at last-ditch defence, possibly as a distraction to allow an enemy withdrawal. He also knew how such a bold move with that sort of asset could turn the tide of battle, and just how sparse his lead infantry elements now actually were. Whilst a relatively small city, Bristol had sucked his force up like a sponge. If the enemy was to gain the initiative now, his gambit to take it would be finished.

He listened to his signaller as more reports were collated from observation posts and snipers on the ground, and also from any helicopter, satellite, and other ISTAR (Intelligence, Surveillance, Target Acquisition, and Reconnaissance) assets above.

'Okay, tell all infantry platoons in the vicinity to go to ground and get into hard-cover. Deploy any anti-tank assets and other heavy weapons available. The ground attack helicopters are low on fuel and returning to base again, we've done with the drones, so tell the U-S tactical wing above to be ready, tell them their own 355th Airborne is taking casualties.'

'Sir, are they?' the signaller asked.

'Well, if the thing carries on in that direction they bloody well will be soon!' Trelawney thundered. 'But equally, I don't want their jets putting in heavy ordnance down onto our streets from five miles away. It has to be eyes-on. Ask our J-TAG controller to say we need a low attack run with armour-piercing thirty-millimetre. That should be sufficient.'

Trelawney was being prescriptive because he didn't want to be held accountable for any more damage to Bristol real-estate, in the inevitable enquiries that would be held later. As it stood, he could legitimately state that the insurgents had so far caused most of the destruction, and he wanted to keep it that way.

91

Using the catacombs and storm drains beneath the streets as cover, Akam's unit had surprised the enemy on countless occasions. They had moved fast from tunnel to tunnel before the enemy had surged in their sector. As the opposing forces had wised-up to the threat beneath them and began dropping charges into the vaults and tunnels, and cleared them with flame-throwers, Akam's team moved up to street level, and finally got holed-up in a shop. Eventually, they ran out of ammunition, and as the government forces moved in, Akam knew they had no choice but to surrender.

They contrived a white flag from a bit of rag on the end of a curtain pole and pushed it through a smashed window. Minutes later they were walking through the door with their hands raised above or behind their heads, with British infantry soldiers twitchily holding their weapons at the ready.

92

Dolman and his surviving men turned into another narrow side street and saw a variety of prisoners lined up and being searched by a section of eight soldiers. The section commander was interrogating one, a well-built, moustachioed man of Middle Eastern origin, and getting nowhere. She nodded to one of her men, and he duly cracked the prisoner's knee with a rifle-butt. The prisoner gave out a brief howl of pain and crumpled to the ground, and she moved on to the next one, obviously hoping to elicit more information from him, having made an example of how brutal she was prepared to be.

As they got closer, Dolman realised from the flashes on their arms that they were Field Intelligence. Two, including the section commander, were female. Even in his short time at Trant's Welsh hilltop base, he'd noticed the other woman, a notable fitness fanatic given to running circuits around the base. But he barely gave her a second glance, as his eyes were drawn to the shorter section commander, and it was at that moment that he began to doubt his own sanity.

'Looks like we're home and dry, boss,' Ashcroft said to him cheerfully, 'back on our side of the lines.'

Dolman didn't hear him. His heart jumped when he actually saw her face; beneath the helmet and ballistic visor, sparkly blue eyes, and a slightly freckled complexion. It surely had to be someone who looked very similar to her. It was, after all, hard to tell; this was not necessarily an uncommon face to find amongst female military personnel.

'Boss?' Matt asked impatiently, 'yes, it's a *girl*.'

Matt Clayton found his sarcasm rewarded by two sets of glares, one from Dolman, and one from the female section commander herself. It was then that she noticed Dolman. It was unmistakably her.

'Emily?'

She hesitated for a second and answered neutrally. 'No, Sir. Corporal Hayley Eldridge, eighty-first military intelligence company.'

'But I saw you, down at the safe-haven by the reservoir. You were a civilian.'

'I'm not sure who you saw, but you're mistaken, Sir,' she answered, trying to keep her voice level, but betraying a hint of defensiveness as she avoided his gaze.

Dolman glanced at the other female, whose face told him all he needed to know. He looked back at 'Emily'. 'Oh, you're good, you're damned good. You had me fooled,' he said. 'Corporal, I want a private word with you,'

'If it's about my methods, I had my orders-

'Over here,' he told her.

She looked at him with some irritation and turned to one of her men. 'Take over for a minute, Steve.' Then she followed Dolman to a doorway.

Once they were out of earshot from the rest, he began. 'So, what's the sketch? I'm security cleared up to your level. Tell me. You were Emily, in that camp, weren't you?'

Hitherto avoiding eye contact, she finally looked up at him. 'If I was who you think, what difference does it make?'

'For the last day or so I've assumed you to have been dead, killed in the inferno brought down on that place by one of our black ops teams. How did you extract?'

'Well, it wouldn't be breaking opsec to say that there was an American heli-borne unit in the area at the time.'

'To hell with opsec! How did you know to get out before that bomb hit?'

She hesitated for a second, considering what to tell him. 'I got out just after before you left, Peter had lost his dog, asked me to help him find it. It took ages to locate the animal; it had gone as far as that farm track where the blackberries were growing. I was then messaged to extract straight away, the American 355th would send in another helicopter. As we were making our way back up the track I saw a terrible black cloud of smoke over in the direction of the haven, and then the attack helicopters go in. Michael had been harbouring some insurgents and they'd engaged the Americans. I avoided letting Peter return to the camp to see that horror. He's very confused, but he's alive.'

'Whereabouts?'

'He's back at the base, with the Padre's family for now. I made sure he kept that dog, it had effectively saved our lives.'

'So, who sent the message, Major Fuller?'

'No, one of my team, he'd been scanning the radio traffic.'

'Did any of you know what would happen to the camp?' he asked.

'No,' she replied, her eyes suddenly distant and sad. 'Until the air attack, I just assumed that my cover had been compromised.'

'Well, that's something, after what I've just seen you're capable of.'

'It's easy to be nice in heaven! Those prisoners are rebels and traitors, and we need information fast. I lost friends in that camp. They were no threat to anyone.' Her eyes filled with tears.

'Yes, I know,' Dolman replied.

'You know, that rebel scum who got in amongst them were using them as a human shield?' she told him, wiping her eyes.

'I'd heard,' he said. 'Is that what *this* is all about?'

'No, it's not about revenge.'

'Oh, and the bloodless bureaucrat you're supposedly marrying?'

'Part of my cover story, my excuse to leave as my mission was nearing its end,' she answered. 'Look, Sir, I suggest you find the rest of your unit. And this isn't, as one of your men suggested, safely behind the lines. There isn't a front line in this sector, it hasn't been fully cleared yet. Once we've interrogated those prisoners we need to rendezvous with the headquarters echelon.'

Just then Corporal Ashcroft ran up.

'Boss, sorry to disturb but the net's gone crazy. It looks like they're mounting some kind of counter-attack with at least one armoured vehicle. It's got a Gatling mount, and it's dropping our lot like flies. Apparently, it's circling back, probably in this direction.'

'Alright, but we can do fuck-all about it without anti-tank,' Dolman stated irritably.

'Not an issue, boss,' Ashcroft replied. 'One of our Toms picked up a discarded LAW on the way here.'

Dolman considered the options for a second or two longer than he once might have done.

Knowing about his prior head injury and temporary amnesia, Hayley realised that he was probably still not fit enough to make a quick and decisive decision. She took the initiative.

'Okay,' she said, 'I suggest we set up an ambush. The ruins of the demolished building back there would be a good place to set up that anti-tank. My section will cover.'

Julian Ashcroft looked surprised but impressed and rubbed the back of his neck as he tried to restrain a smile. 'Boss?'

'Yes, good call, Corporal,' Dolman conceded to Hayley.

Her eyes betrayed a flicker of amused triumph before she turned to join her section and issue orders for two of her team to cover the prisoners, whilst the others were to follow her to the ambush site.

Dolman was intrigued by how bossy she could sound, and also the look of respect and even admiration in the eyes of her section. It wasn't that he was normally sexist with regards to women he had served with, more that he was having trouble reconciling this image with that of the mini-dress wearing young civilian in the haven. Now he had to get used to the idea that she was in fact some sort of deep-cover intelligence operative from Trant's garrison, now leading a section in the middle of a battle.

93

Marcus' instinct was not to go further towards trouble, but to double back to their original position. As they traversed yet another street as they continued to circle back, they surprised the crew of an incapacitated armoured vehicle and lit them up. As their rounds went in they ricocheted off of the vehicle with sparks, and the crew and repair team were knocked to the ground.

They stopped temporarily whilst Marcus figured out the best route back to their original position.

'Keep being unpredictable,' Trant advised. 'You've caught them off guard with the element of surprise, but it won't be long before they mobilise some major assets.'

'Thanks, Colonel, I long ago learnt to avoid being predictable, but this was always going to be a short term contract. We're centre stage just now though. I just hope we've bought Commander King enough time.'

'Yes, a lot more.'

'And what are you still doing here?' Marcus asked with a spirited smile.

'Watching karma play out. I'm half hoping they'll bring in the same air assets that took out the safe-haven, and my Claire.'

'Ah, I see, it *is* revenge you want. Well, if they do, the bomb that gets us will be launched miles away. We'd probably not even see the aircraft, even if it was daylight.'

'Maybe,' Trant said.

'Colonel, if you want revenge, you won't find it here. Find the man that ordered that airstrike.'

Trant looked down pensively. 'Yes, perhaps you're right.'

'Damn right I am! And you've got to be alive to do it. This isn't your time. Now get out, whilst the going's good.'

'No, not yet.'

'Whatever. Anyway, we've got to get moving again.'

'Yeah, go for it,' Trant replied.

'Okay, Pyotr, go!' Marcus shouted as he climbed back up to the gun position. They started to move again.

As they headed on and towards the rubble of Wraxall Towers, Marcus realised that he was seeing less and less of the enemy. He switched the gun back to auto mode, turning the control over to the AI program, which would likely see threats with its motion sensors and infrared imagery better and react faster than he could.

Suddenly they were being engaged from the rubble, and he and the Gatling automatically turned rapidly to the left to engage at close range. He saw infantrymen nearby getting blasted apart, as chips of debris from the ricochets hit the armour plating of the gun shield. The gun's AI had targeted the greatest immediate threat, an anti-tank launcher, then the rest of the ambush according to their armament and even physiques, as far as they could be seen.

Instinct made him look forward even before he heard Pyotr's desperate shout. As the Gatling continued to target the rubble, a lone figure had run into the road in front and was now firing at him. He barely had time to register it as female, but the surprise made him delay a fraction of a second too long as rounds hit his shoulder and neck. He instantly crumpled down into the crew compartment.

94

Hayley dived out of the way of the oncoming vehicle as Dolman's section now targeted Pyotr's bullet-proof windshield. Hitherto, breaking away from a last-minute consultation with him, she'd ignored Dolman's sudden shout of concern, as she'd stepped out in front of the vehicle and raised her assault rifle. It was a close call as the armoured body of the twenty-three-ton vehicle itself just missed her. However, it was its very proximity that had saved her from the Gatling gun, which was unable to depress any lower as it raked the building beside her pointlessly, shattering office and shop-front windows as Dolman's remaining men dived to the floor inside.

She knew that she'd had no effect whatsoever on the vehicle, but didn't realise the serious wounds that she'd inflicted on Marcus. It was sheer desperation that had made her attempt to take the vehicle on, once she realised to her horror that the AI automated fire control system of the vehicles Gatling gun was destroying her entire section. Unheard over the noise of battle and helicopters overhead, it had surprised them as they were getting into position. Whilst irrational, her only purpose at that time had been to try to take out the gunner, oblivious to the fact that the vehicle was rushing towards her; its path more dangerously erratic and unpredictable due to small chunks of rubble and debris from the recently collapsed building.

'What in hell's name was that all about?' Dolman shouted at her. He'd felt sure that he'd been about to lose her again.

Without answering or even glancing back in his direction, she got up, cursorily dusting herself down, and with tear-filled eyes ran towards the blood-spattered rubble that contained the now dead or wounded remnants of most of her section. Many were already far gone, one or two not much more than virtually unrecognizable bundles of cloth. One had dragged himself to another and was administering vital first aid treatment. She ran over to help him, and as she got closer noticed her friend Samantha lying over rubble, helmet off, her long blond hair having tumbled out. Her already glassy eyes were open, staring up to the sky as if in search of the dawn she'd never see. Hayley wondered if she could resuscitate her until she noticed the size of the hole in her chest, and that she was missing part of her left arm.

Dizzily she turned and knelt beside the other two, the wounded man desperately trying to save his comrade. As she watched dark blood ooze from the open mouth of the man on the ground, she realised it was probably too late from him.

'Jason, he's gone. You can't help him,' she said quietly, and when she saw his bloodied leg she shakily pulled out one of her field dressings. 'Come on, you've done enough, let me see to you. We'll get you on a casevac out A-S-A-P.'

Dolman arrived with three of his men. 'We'll get him moved into cover. I want you out of here too, Corporal. We're still in the middle of a battle here.'

Hayley looked up at him with hatred. 'Damn them! They'll pay for this.'

'Yes, they will,' Dolman looked around at the dead of her unit and felt her pain. He looked at the young assault team trooper who had picked up the anti-tank weapon earlier. Having identified him as the greatest threat, the vehicle had targeted him first.

'We've all lost many comrades and friends today,' Dolman added.

After Hayley had finished applying the bandage to what was the only survivor of her section, she sat back exhausted. She could only watch as he was lifted away to safety by two of Dolman's men.

Dolman helped her up and walked her towards a doorway across the street.

'That was a foolish move you made there, but it just might get you a medal. At the very least, you made that gunner drop back into the vehicle. I think you may have hit him.'

She seemed to ignore him as if she was in her own world. Suddenly the sound of shooting began to get closer again, and with it, the engine of a reversing vehicle; the rogue AFV.

Dolman looked at her and she shook herself loose from him, stepped back, and pulled a full clip of ammo from her ammunition pouch. She changed magazines and made her rifle ready.

'I'm going after that thing!' she said.

'You're staying right here, Corporal,' he told her.

She looked back at him but he wasn't sure she was seeing him. 'Please don't try to stop me, Sir.'

As she ran off down the street, Dolman felt helpless. He'd seen that look in men, often before they'd gotten themselves or others killed. But occasionally, they also ended up with an enemy position taken, and maybe a citation.

He turned back into the doorway and shouted hoarsely at his men. 'I need support, now! One man to stay with the casualty, the rest follow me. We're going to try and take out that fucking vehicle again.'

95

Pyotr had counted the hits on the glass and knew it was specified to take up to twenty direct rounds from average calibre military weapons. He put his foot down and sped by the threat as fast as possible.

Very soon they had turned the corner into the next street and were taking more fire.

'How Marcus?' he shouted at Trant in his broken English.

'Bad. I'm patching him up as best I can,' Trant shouted back as he swayed with the motion of the vehicle. He looked around, and with some surprise saw Fyodor about to get up into the gun position with an assault rifle. 'The Bear' smiled at Trant, and explained. 'Can't let Mamushka there decide all targets!' Once up in position above he began firing with his assault rifle.

After emerging out into a road junction near the 'Bearpit' roundabout, Pyotr hit the brakes. 'Fuck! Tank!' he shouted, at the sight of a large main battle tank amongst a load of troops and parked-up armoured vehicles. The barrel the tanks long gun was inadvertently pointed in their direction. 'Okay, that way no good. I go back.' He crunched gears desperately before he began to reverse back up the street they'd just stormed down, straight back into a shop front, raining bits of wood, plaster, and glass down onto the roof of the vehicle and over Fyodor.

'Pyotr! Ty mudak! Idiot!' Fyodor swore at his comrade as he ducked back into the crew compartment and removed pieces of glass and plaster from his curly black hair.

Pyotr moved the vehicle forward, pulling out the remaining window frame with it as a four-wheeled armoured vehicle sped towards them, 12.5mm gun blazing. The Gatling traversed and aimed for the windscreen. The vehicle careened into a parked truck and ended up driving headlong into a flight of steps, but by then Fyodor was already back in position and engaging any infantry on foot who had been foolish enough to follow the path of the hapless vehicle. In another second they were reversing fast up the street.

Down below in the crew compartment Marcus was in a bad way, as Trant finished applying the bandage to his neck. He choked blood at Trant.

'Get…lost,' he whispered hoarsely, with a pleading look in his eyes.

Trant looked around at the two Russians, and then looked at Marcus and nodded. 'Okay Marcus, it is time to go. Farewell, my friend.'

'Let's all get out of here,' Trant called to the Russians. They appeared to ignore him, as the Gatling gun again began to automatically fire. Something rocked the vehicle, and it lurched down slightly. Trant deduced that a tire had just been taken out. 'Pyotr, Fyodor, it's over, let's go!'

'You go, coward!' Fyodor shouted down to him. 'Fight another day, Colonel!'

Ignoring Fyodor's taunt, Trant realised that he probably had seconds to get clear of the vehicle. He made for the rear door. Once he was out he attempted to slam it shut and secure it as best he could, but found himself under fire.

He noticed dark shapes moving at the end of the street, and as bullets ricocheted off of the back of the vehicle he felt the sting of a ricochet hit his thigh. He darted into a shop doorway. Kicking open the door, he ran through an old toy and model shop, and through to a stores room. As he opened the back door to a courtyard behind he realised that he'd been hit more deeply than he'd initially thought by the ricocheted round, and was bleeding. He began to feel weak and leaned against the door frame. He heard the sound of distant thunder high up and knew that he needed to make much more distance from that vehicle yet.

96

Hayley looked down the street and saw one person leave the vehicle. As she ran she fired at him wildly from the hip before he disappeared into a doorway. She saw more of her side running down on the other side of the street, and dart into doors and behind flights of steps, just before the Gatling opened up on them again.

By now she was close enough to again be out of sight of the gun. She got to the rear door of the vehicle and removed a grenade. She pulled the pin as she grabbed the rear door lever. It opened just enough for her to lob the grenade in, and it exploded with a crump just as she reached the doorway.

Protected from the main part of the blast in the driving compartment, Pyotr was nonetheless stunned and covered in lacerations. His hearing had gone. He dragged himself slowly, from his seat to see what the damage was in the rear, but only succeeded in collapsing on Marcus' lifeless, shredded body. He looked up to see Fyodor's legs, one bleeding profusely and the other partially shredded to the bone.

The AI on the Gatling gun was damaged, and the female voice was repeating itself. 'Alert, system malfunction, please refer to diagnostics… Alert, system malfunction, please refer to diagnostics…re-booting…'

98

Dolman and four of his men were following close behind before they spotted Hayley by the vehicle, as they heard the thunder of the jets above. He made brief eye contact with her, and she smiled briefly at him before stepping into the shop doorway to pursue Trant.

Dolman turned to his team. 'She's done it, but they've called in fast air all the same. You need to get the hell out of here, now!'

'What about you, Boss?' Corporal Ashcroft asked.

'I'm going after her,' he replied.

'Like fuck you are,' someone to his right said, and a rifle butt hit his cheek. He was knocked to the ground, unconscious. Two of them picked him up and dragged him away.

99

Trant realised someone had caught up with him before he even looked around. He had weakly hauled himself up against the door frame.

'You, stop! STOP!' It was a female voice.

He turned to face her, arms slightly up, as much in supplication as surrender.

'Colonel Trant!' she said with surprise, lowering the rifle from her shoulder slightly. 'We've been looking for you. Why were you in that vehicle, Sir? Were you a hostage?'

He looked at her. 'We need to leave, now.'

'No!' Hayley raised her rifle again and aimed at Trant's head. 'I've just lost five of my section to that vehicle. Tell me, were you a hostage, or did they turn you?'

'Corporal Eldridge…Hayley, you're a good soldier, but you're missing the big picture. They killed Claire and all of the others. Instead of serving society… we've turned into the storm-troopers of a police state. We are complicit in the killing of innocent men, women, and children.'

'No, it was an accident! They were being used by the enemy as a human shield.'

Trant remained calm. 'When we began to accept collateral damage we began to lose the moral high ground; and we tend to also lose the wars, by the way.

There was no need to incinerate that whole camp for just a few insurgents, Hayley, and you know it.'

'I don't. Our society, our way of life-

'Not worth becoming that for!' Trant interrupted. 'We've dropped the ball, and lost our reason for existing if we murder the very people we're supposed to protect.'

100

Pyotr hauled himself up and looked out the front windscreen, just about making out the approaching troops. The Gatling gun began to re-activate. 'Targets being engaged,' the AI voice told him.

Again, he saw the soldiers in the open getting hit or diving for cover, and others begin to run. However, several hadn't been and were still running for cover. It was clear that the targeting system was no longer functioning one hundred percent correctly.

The vehicle bucked as another missile hit the side of the vehicle and Pyotr was again knocked off his feet. When he got up the turret was traversing wildly, and began firing uncontrollably. Fyodor had revived and was laughing manically before dropping back down into the crew compartment.

'Medved! Tovarich!' Pyotr shouted to him.

'I die in fucking England!' It was a weak but spirited reply. 'Fucking rain…' he added, laughing weakly before time stopped for him.

The Gatling continued to fire and engaged an air target, hitting the wing of the fighter jet that it had correctly identified as being an imminent threat as it executed its attack run. Before he had time to fire, the pilot's left wingtip and was cut off, and his aileron and tail-plane were simultaneously damaged, and neither he nor his computer could make the correct adjustments to compensate for such catastrophic disruption to the airframe in the time available. Without even having time to rue the fact that the ground attack fighter he flew in was no adequate replacement for the almost indestructible A10 Warthog of old, he delivered the rest of his explosive payload in person, albeit slightly off-target; taking out the row of buildings next to the rogue armoured vehicle. They were the buildings into which Hayley had followed Trant.

101

As the sound of approaching thunder increased it morphed to a high pitched shriek, and Trant realised they only had seconds left to bargain. 'Hayley, lower your rifle,' he urged.

The wind blew hard and something clattered in the yard. She faltered for a second, and he moved and pushed the barrel upwards. She fired, rounds hitting the wall and ceiling. He grabbed her combat jacket arm and pulled her out of the back door into the yard.

'Colonel, get off me!' she protested lamely, realising she was no match for his strength and vice-like grip.

'Don't be stupid!' he replied, 'Trelawney has called in fast air to take out that armoured vehicle, and if we're not careful *we'll* become collateral damage!'

He dragged her out and kicked open a back gate, pushing her into an alleyway, just as the jet hit the building. As soon as he heard the imminent danger he dived on top of her as he felt the ground shake. The shock wave of the explosion blasted over them, and they were covered in masonry, glass, and burning debris.

102

After the blast wave had bucked the vehicle almost over onto its side, it landed back down hard onto its starboard-side wheels, rocking hard on its suspension and knocking Pyotr into an empty seat. Rubble then rained down on top of the vehicle, and bits fell through the open top cover hatch. Pyotr covered his head instinctively but then realised that the blast-protected vehicle had done its job and had saved him. He weakly hauled himself up again and turned back to look down at the open eyes and lifeless face of his comrade, Fyodor.

'My friend, we have come a long way, but this is the end of the journey for you,' Pyotr said.

He looked out of the front windscreen and saw the Main Battle Tank traverse the street corner.

An alarm buzzer sounded. 'Emergency, lase detection from heavy ordnance, take evasive action! Emergency, lase detection from heavy ordnance, take evasive action! …' the AI voice warned repeatedly.

'And, I think it is the end for me now, too,' he added.

The main battle tank fired a single 120mm round into the armoured vehicle. In the ensuing explosion, the gun mounting was blown clean off and into the air as the vehicle erupted into a ball of flame and twisted metal.

103

She pushed Trant off her but discovered that he was unconscious, his head bleeding from a light wound. Choking from the acrid smoke and smell of aviation fuel, she got up and dragged him away from the burning debris. Once in a safer area, she laid him flat on the ground, opening his combat jacket and shirt collar, and then wiping his head wound with a steri-wipe. He groaned and slowly began to revive.

'Stay still, Sir, we'll get you on a casevac.'

Slowly and painfully, Trant pushed himself up, to sit with his back against a building wall. Hayley took out her water-bottle and gave him water.

He looked at her. 'I'm not going back, Hayley. Not whilst that regime's in charge.'

'Is it because of Claire?'

'Yes. They took someone I loved from me. I just didn't know how to progress things. Claire and I had a lot in common but we were essentially from different worlds. She couldn't have become a Colonel's wife, and I was too pig-headed and intransigent to resign my commission in time. But we had discussed sharing a life, away from all of this.'

'In the colony?' Hayley asked.

'No. No, that'd never have worked. I was going to retire, live simply with her, somewhere quiet. Dammit, I did my bit for my country!'

'So, what now Sir?'

'You leave me here, re-join your unit. All I ask is that you give me an hour's head-start.'

'I don't think I can do that, Sir,' she stated, yet with a note of uncertainty.

'Hayley, your personal-weapon lies somewhere back in that rubble. I may be wounded, but I think we know which way it'd go if it came to a show-down.'

She considered it. 'What would I tell them?'

'In truth, if you want to avoid recriminations and an enquiry? Tell them nothing. Walk away now, and your career path will continue uninterrupted. But be careful. The regime won't let you go. And any dissention will be picked up fast. Also, be prepared for when the Americans pull out. Things could change yet again.'

'Hmm,' she replied, 'I think you must be a bit dazed from that knock to the head you sustained, Sir! You're the second officer I've seen in that state in as many days. One turned up from the vehicle you were ambushed in.'

'Paul Dolman?'

'Why, yes. You know him?'

'He became my second in command in Estonia. He's a good officer, but like you, he hasn't seen the light yet. You two would make a good pair,' he smiled ironically.

'I wouldn't be so sure about that, I don't go for presumptuous bastards. And he's clearly lost his edge since that accident.'

Trant frowned. 'Well, whatever, we can't stay talking here all day. The sun's beginning to rise, and I need to get away.'

She looked uncertain again, so he pulled himself up.

'Farewell, Hayley. And…be careful.'

He turned, and she watched him limp down the street, and then he disappeared down a side alley. She looked around, uncertain of what to do next before she heard the sound of armoured vehicles slowly moving up the street behind her.

104

They had emerged out of the darkness of the tunnel to early morning twilight, through a pumping station. Gingerly they crossed the A4 road, and quickly scrambled down the bank of the River Avon.

'We need to wait, I can't leave her!' Jonathan said.

'Jonathan,' King said, 'there's no time. You don't know where she is.'

'Up there, at the bridge you said.'

'Ay, I did.'

'I need to go and find her. She could be wounded, or captured.'

'Or dead,' King stated flatly. 'But if wounded or captured, they'll take care of her. There's no point them getting both of you. This place will be crawling with them soon. Are you with us?'

Jonathan was pensive. 'Alright,' he said reluctantly. 'Let's go.'

They made for one of the dinghies, hidden beneath foliage by the river below.

105

Half an hour later, the rain had stopped and the wind had died down to sporadic gusts. As daylight began to filter through, the day emerged as steely grey and dull.

On the outskirts of the city, at the Clifton Suspension Bridge, Julie sat in the shadows inside a ruined building overlooking the bridge. She looked through a sniper scope at the rear-echelon troops holding the bridge. Some were in tactical positions, kneeling or lying prone whilst looking through their rifle scopes. However, the ones that she found particularly irritating sat in an open-top four-by-four with a .50 cal machine gun mounted on the back. These men seemed so sanguine that they had removed their helmets and instead wore their berets. They were smoking, chatting, and were even drinking mugs of tea or coffee.

What really annoyed her was how smug they looked. Once or twice it was clear that they were cracking jokes and laughing, whilst her friends were fighting for their lives back in the city centre. Even with their bulky waterproof jackets and camouflage face paint, it was clear these men were heavily set, like members of a Rugby club, with the arrogant confidence of the sort you might find presenting programmes on fast cars. The leader, probably a Sergeant, was middle-aged and looked the brightest. He was almost affable looking. Although she was determined to prove Marcus wrong after softening over Eric in Wales, she knew it couldn't be him first. She moved the cross-hairs of her scope to the driver's forehead, and then up to the pudgy head of the gunner, presently standing with his arm resting over the .50 cal, whilst taking a drag out of the last of his cigarette.

As soon as the firing began at ground level, she took the shot. As the vehicle started up and went into reverse, she lowered the scope by a fraction and took out the driver. The passenger looked around in horror as his driver slumped down in his seat. He tried to grab the wheel as the four-by-four reversed into the side of the bridge, crushing one soldier and knocking another over the side, for a long drop to the river below. The passenger was jolted back, his arms comically thrown up into the air a second before his body was pushed forward again. She moved her cross hairs onto him but hesitated. A second later he had thrown himself out of the vehicle and was on the ground, out of sight. The UK Resistance attacking team surged forward. She directed her attention towards more immediate threats and found one of the guards returning fire from behind a barricade and another behind a bridge pillar. A minute later it was done, and the surviving defenders were retreating to the other side of the bridge. She was privately glad to see through her sights that the vehicle passenger was scurrying away with them.

She sat back down in the dusty corner of the room, re-loaded, and mused on what had just occurred. She could still kill, but she could also still be merciful. She was glad. Whilst it meant that she was still combat-effective, it also meant that there was still some humanity left in her.

In her personal-role radio earpiece, she heard a squad leader. '*Delta-zero-one, this is delta-zero-two. All good, bridge secure. Over.*'

'Fine, we'll be down. Out,' Stan replied, then spoke to his fire support team nearby, which consisted of Julie and another young female fighter called Rona.

'Okay, that's us done, Stan said. 'No prisoners to deal with.'

Rona frowned. 'Why did we need prisoners? I'd have just shot them anyway,' she stated. Stan looked appalled and rolled his eyes at Julie.

Julie answered Rona as patiently as she could. 'Well, at this stage in the game they might have provided us with vital intelligence as to the size and objective of this attack. Also, it means that we stand a better chance if things go badly for us.'

'And believe me,' Stan cut in, 'thing can go wrong on the turn on a sixpence. With the Americans here the regime needs to be seen to be behaving lawfully now, even with irregulars like us.'

Rona seemed unconvinced, but she wasn't going to argue further. 'Okay, if you say so,' she replied reluctantly.

'Hold on a sec, I'm just receiving a message on the brigade net,' Stan said, holding his hand up to indicate silence. Julie glanced at Stan with concern, as he listed to his personal-role radio. It was then that Stan received the news that the city had been taken. He looked at her. 'Julie, the city's fallen. It's over. We need to get away from here, now.'

Stan spoke into his microphone to the assault at the bridge. 'Delta-two this is delta zero, the city has fallen. It's over. Save yourselves.'

Julie thought quickly and looked outside. 'It's too light, we'll never make it any distance, and they still hold the other end of the bridge' she said. She got up from the dusty floor. 'Follow me.'

'Eh? Where to exactly?' Stan asked.

'Quickly! We can't escape, but we can hide.'

Once downstairs, Julie led them towards the bridge. 'Stay low,' she urged, 'it's vital they don't spot us'. She led them down a ladder beside the abutments on which the bridge rested. Rona was slow in climbing down.

'Get a move on!' Stan quietly hissed at her.

On a platform below, Julie found a metal door and smashed the padlock open with her rifle. She opened it and after it had creaked open she peered into the darkness. She took out her torch and lit up a gloomy cavern. 'Okay, we need to get in there, now!'

'Shit, seriously?' Stan asked.

'Yes, sorry,' Julie replied with an uncertain smile.

Once inside, they lit a fire for light and warmth and sat around it with their collars pulled up, shivering.

'What's the plan?' Rona asked.

Julie reached into her jacket pocket and pulled out a pack of biscuits. 'We stay here until nightfall. Then we can make a run for it.'

Rona groaned. 'Really?' She directed her flashlight up to the ceiling above, full of thin, yellow-white hanging stalactites. 'This is shit.'

'Okay, Rona,' Stan said to her, 'you'd rather go up there and risk surrendering to them, would you? And hope they don't have the same attitude towards prisoners that you do?'

Rona said nothing.

'Well,' Stan continued, 'we'd better make ourselves as comfortable as possible. If you've got any food on you, I suggest you eke it out. We're going to be in here for a while.'

106

In the operations room back at Fairfield, General Wes Easton surveyed the large screens showing satellite, drone, vehicle, and helmet-cam footage of the on-going assault in Bristol. Beside him were various operations officers and staff, as well as his ADC, Melanie Cartwright.

Major Schreiber approached him. 'Excuse me, Sir, can I have a word?'

'Eh? Not now, Chuck, not now.'

'Um, this is urgent intel, Sir.'

'Goddammit! What is it?'

'If you don't mind, can we use a meeting room?'

'This had better be good, Chuck,' Easton said irritably. 'The Brits have lost three M-B-T's and over a hundred men killed or wounded, we've lost half our airborne company and most of its officers, and now one of our CAS assets, which took out a block of shops when it went down. Bristol's a fucking mess!' He looked at Captain Cartwright. 'Get me if the situation changes any, Mel.'

'Sir,' she replied.

As they walked to the meeting room, General Easton demanded instant answers.

'So what's this all about, Chuck?'

Schreiber didn't mind answering in a circumspect manner, just to placate the General. 'He finally talked, Sir.'

'Who? The prisoner from the farm?'

'Yes Sir.'

'So? So what? Can't you see we're in the middle of a major battle?'

'For sure, Sir, and one we need to shut down.'

'What in the hell's name are you talking about, Chuck?'

They entered the meeting room, lights activating automatically, and Major Schreiber closed the door.

'So,' he said, 'we got the prisoner to talk. In the end, we used drugs. It appears he's from the Bristol faction of the UK Resistance Party. It's called the First Brigade and was the one that took out Morton Down. We knew they'd retreated up to Bristol, and remained embedded and hard to dislodge.'

'That's why it's proved such a tough nut to crack,' Easton stated.

'Yes Sir. But what's interesting is who it's commanded by. The prisoner stated unequivocally it was none other than King.'

'Brigade Commander Sean Kerrigan! But I thought he'd hot-footed it back to Ireland?'

'So did we, Sir. It seems he didn't get that far.'

General Easton considered the problem for a second or two and then stared at his intelligence officer. 'Goddammit Schreiber, this will be poison on Capitol Hill. If we've nailed Kerrigan by accident it'll be more than my career that's over. There'll be Senate inquiries and all sorts of fallout. And you can also bet on a Democrat victory next month.'

'One more thing,' Schreiber said. 'That mission to Wales was led by a leader called Marcus, Marcus Samuels. He's a second cousin once removed of the Israeli Foreign Minister. He's also been positively identified by the turncoat, and is in the thick of the action in Bristol.'

'Dammit Chuck, this could all have been avoided if our insurance policy had worked and taken Trant out. So how is our intrepid snake-eater doing?'

'He's still recovering at the Wales garrison, Sir, along with the rest of the surviving members of the logistics team.'

'Good. Get them out as soon as the dust has settled. And let's pull the plug on 'Mad Jack' and his crazy attempt to take an entire city with a battalion. I feel duped by the bastard, Chuck. It's cost us some good men today.'

107

They were in the foyer of a disused fitness centre. Clayton, Ashcroft, two others who were standing guard and one wounded man were all that was left of both Dolman's platoon and Hayley's section.

'He's reviving,' Matt Clayton said.

'Good,' Julian Ashcroft replied. 'I'll leave it to you to explain why you nutted him. And to let him know the bad news regarding that girl he'd lost the plot over.'

One of Hayley's section approached them. He was an older man who, on having removed his helmet and equipment, looked as if he'd given up. 'Excuse me? Did you say something had happened to Corporal Eldridge?'

'Yeah mate,' Clayton answered him without much sympathy, 'I think she copped it in that airstrike.'

'Oh,' was all the soldier replied, and went to sit down dejectedly next to his wounded comrade.

'Well he's not playing anymore,' Clayton murmured.

'None of them are,' Ashcroft replied.

'So, what do you reckon our chances will be, once our lot catch up with us?' Clayton asked.

'Not good, mate. With that black ops headcam footage, we're screwed. My old boss was liked by the top brass. This guy's got previous. We're probably looking at a few years in Colchester prison.'

Dolman slowly opened his eyes, rubbed his head, and attempted to get up. 'No, take it easy, boss,' Ashcroft advised, and then looked at Clayton. 'Over to you, mate.'

'Thanks.'

'Whatever,' Ashcroft said under his breath, 'keep it short, we need to leave this lot where they are and make ourselves scarce.'

108

Trelawney received the communication with astonishment, and then rage. 'What the blue blazes…? They want us to withdraw?'

'Yes Sir, that's come direct from Major-General Wesley Easton himself', Lieutenant Beresford replied.

'I give a damn who it's from, Lieutenant! Tell him we've taken the city and that it's now under the control of British forces.'

As Lieutenant Beresford instructed his signaller to send Trelawney's reply, the Brigadier turned to his ADC, Captain Manning. 'So, what do you make of that?'

'I'm sure I don't know, Sir,' Manning replied. 'It's perplexing, to say the least.'

'No it's not,' Fuller spoke up.

'If I'd wanted your opinion, Major, I'd have asked for it,' Trelawney told him haughtily.

Fuller brazenly continued. 'What we're seeing is probably down to politics. The American resolve is faltering, both here and back home. If they pull out, which they could well do given a change of administration next month, we might all eventually be looking to our laurels.'

'Alright Major, you've made your point,' Trelawney said. 'But I won't brook any more of this defeatist talk, do you hear?'

Fuller noticed Manning glance uncertainly at Lieutenant Beresford and realised that he'd probably said enough.

There was a metallic knocking against the back door. Captain Manning checked the situational display unit for the view outside before opening the back door. He saw an infantry officer, the commander of the guard unit outside, uniform dusty, face obscured with camouflage cream and dirt. 'Sir, there's a Corporal from Field Intelligence just entered the cordon. She's asked if she could see Major Fuller.'

'Tell her that Major Fuller is presently indisposed, and to make her report to Lieutenant Baker.'

'Yes Sir.'

As Captain Manning closed the door and relayed the message to Trelawney, Fuller spoke up once more. 'That could be vital intelligence we're delaying, Sir.'

'Quite,' replied Trelawney. 'I think it's about time we had you escorted away from here forthwith, and Lieutenant Baker here in your place.'

'Fine,' Fuller replied. 'Baker's a competent officer.'

'Corporal Sutton, see to it that this man is escorted away from here. Manning, organise a guard detail if you will.'

'Yes Sir,' Sutton replied to Trelawney, then to Fuller, 'Excuse me, Sir, would you please come with me?'

As Fuller exited the vehicle with Corporal Sutton, Lieutenant Beresford approached Trelawney. 'Sir, we've received a message from Major-General Easton, we can hold fast but there will be no further assistance from U-S assets, nor direct support from any U-S units. They say this was misleadingly presented as a raid and are demanding an explanation as to why it's turned out differently. They strongly suggest that we withdraw.'

'Damn it all!' Trelawney thundered.

The wincing Beresford delivered the last part of the message. '…an in addition, they wish to extract the 355th Airborne from the theatre of operations, with immediate effect.'

'Blast!' Trelawney exclaimed, but for the first time, he looked downcast, and sat down in Fuller's recently vacated seat, quiet and pensive.

'Sir?' Beresford asked. 'What are the orders?'

Trelawney looked up at him as he was joined by Captain Manning. 'It's over. We cannot possibly hold this city without American assistance. I haven't got enough bloody troops, for a start.' He looked at his ADC, Captain Manning. 'Quite frankly, Tristan, Fuller was probably right, damn him! Let's hope this is not a precursor for things to come.'

Trelawney got up and swept the fringe of hair back from his forehead. 'Well, we've achieved some objectives, but at too high a cost. Alright, Beresford, order a general withdrawal; timed for after we've had the casevac and reclamation teams in. Destroy anything we can't move, and for goodness sake, leave no ordnance for them!'

He turned to Captain Manning. 'And Lord knows what happened to Trant, probably somewhere at the bottom of what's left of Wraxall Towers for all I care.'

'What's the official line, Sir?' Manning asked.

'Hm, post him as missing, presumed dead. Captain Dolman and Major Matlock too, whilst you're at it.'

109

They had made it as far at Clevedon, well away from Bristol or the Avonmouth docks. The safe-house was a former military operating base which had been vacated in a hurry. It was a large, grey, Gothic Victorian house on a street near the top of a hill. It had a forlorn-looking, broken-down four-by-four in a basement garage.

It was already late afternoon on what was the first of November, and whilst the early morning storm had given way to bright sunshine by midday, the sun had now set and the last rays were disappearing.

As the others made their final preparations to leave, King looked out of the first-floor window and down the street. 'What a fine evening after all the bad weather. It should make for a calmer crossing, at any rate.' He turned to Jonathan. 'You know you're still welcome to come with us, Jonathan. The boat leaves in half an hour. It's a regular night time fishing boat. Without attracting too much attention, we expect to be in County Wexford by mid-morning. Will you reconsider and come with us?'

'No, no thanks,' Jonathan replied. 'I need to go back, try to find Julie.'

'I fully understand, Jonathan,' King replied. 'However, I'd wait a day or two if I were you, let the dust settle. Pavel has heard that they're still clearing up all of their knocked-out stuff. You know, we made quite a dent, stung them badly. Maybe we could even have stayed.'

'Would you go back?' Jonathan asked.

'No, we played out our hand there. And, it was a strategic victory. The Americans clearly weren't willing to throw anything more in. The regime forces are weakened. Now, we can direct the next phase from across the water. Other outfits will keep them busy, but we're playing the long game, disengaging for now. We don't want want to let the Americans see us as a hostile force any longer.'

Having initially doubted King's strategy, Jonathan looked at him with a hint of respect. 'Yes, I think perhaps you're right. I would like to help you more, once I've found Julie.'

King shook his hand. 'I was hoping you'd say that, Jonathan! There's probably a position going for Commandant. I doubt Marcus made it out alive. Pavel heard no more from his two team members who stayed back with Marcus.'

'I'm sorry to hear that,' Jonathan replied. 'And thanks, but Marcus was a tough act to follow.'

'Marcus, bless him, but he always took more risks than he needed to. And he stayed operational when his role really wasn't. I'm hoping you'll be a bit less so yourself, I'm starting to run short of good field commanders. So, do you accept?'

'Well if that's the case, then yes, I'll be glad to. Just…no more commando missions, eh?' Jonathan replied.

King smiled. 'If it came to it, I'd be by your side next time.'

'Let's hope it doesn't,' Jonathan replied.

'Ay. Anyhow, this isn't goodbye,' King said, as he picked up his pack and nodded to the others to leave. He shook hands with Jonathan once more. 'Just take care of yourself now, and I hope you find your lady. You know how to find me.'

'Yeah, I do,' Jonathan said.

Epilogue

South Wales, a month later.

He'd put his screen lock on and walked to join the others in the bar. It was already festooned with Christmas decorations. He sat down by a low, wall-side table. Sharon, opposite, looked at him. 'We thought you'd never make it over, you're a right workaholic you are!'

'Yeah,' Malcolm smiled shyly, and coughed a little. 'I think I may be.'

After cleaning his glasses, he glanced furtively over at the bar, whilst Sharon took a swig of her drink, and Jocelyn talked to Aaron and Chris. Their section commander, Hayley Eldridge, was still talking to the 'poison dwarf', as he was known about the base. Even as an Intelligence Analyst with high-level clearance, it made Malcolm feel a bit unsettled. Still, on the plus side, he liked seeing her in civilian clothing again. This was the first time they'd been given passes to leave the base for a long time, following the mess of the last few weeks.

As the others continued to chat inanely, he noticed that the television screen was on; presently a news and current affairs programme. Whilst not managing to hear the commentary, from the on-screen charts he could see it was a more in-depth analysis of the results of the US election, and the recent landslide to the Democrats. This had caused consternation the previous month, when, a little after bonfire night, the results had appeared on the main news channels. At the time, Lieutenant Enderby had proclaimed dramatically that it would also be the end of the British government, and with it any law and order.

Not surprisingly he'd received several hostile glances from superior officers. However, Malcolm knew that the gauche young officer probably wasn't far wide of the mark, even if he'd been coming out with some rather pessimistic, negative comments since the combat in Bristol.

Indeed, the new President was a centre-left, black female who was already known to be unsympathetic towards the present British government and had pledged to withdraw troops; starting with a halt on frontline operations, with immediate effect. To follow up on her election pledges, one of which was to widen social provisions in her own country after the devastation that the virus had caused, would require a big shift in budget priorities. Furthermore, she had advocated UN intervention in the UK, with the European Army taking its fair share of the burden. Whether that would ever be agreed on remained to be seen, but overall the change in administration would almost certainly hasten the total withdrawal of American forces, or at least lead to the scaling-down of their foot-print in the UK.

With the security clearance he'd had, Malcolm had been able to access some classified reports as to the probable impact of such an event, and if anything it made him more certain that he'd chosen the right side. The stages that would be played out were clear from history, but the end result would be inevitable, ending in defeat (although they wouldn't call it that), and then negotiations with the insurgent factions, 'for the sake of peace and stability'. It'd essentially be ignominy for the government, although some might manage to make political capital out of it; some always did. But it'd be the soldiers who would bear the brunt of the trouble, have to hold the line until that agreement was reached.

The incoming President had also pointed to divisions within the British chain of command, mentioning the interview with a certain Lieutenant-Colonel Trant that had hit news channels and been all over social media. Trant had criticised the Government's conduct of operations within its own country and pointed to needless loss of life in both the battle for Bristol and the destruction of the local safe-haven, which he said was, in fact, a war crime that would need investigation by the International Criminal Court at the Hague. Colonel Trant had been branded a traitor by the British establishment, he had been stripped of his rank and his awards, and his name wasn't permitted to be mentioned on the base at any time.

To Malcolm, he was of course a hero, although an unexpected one, and perhaps also an unwitting one. Malcolm once had him taped as the typical old-school establishment type, and it was only the intelligence he'd received from his Russian handler which had told him otherwise. In turn, he fed back what he knew, in particular information pertaining to Hayley's mission at the haven.

That mission had been organised by Trant himself, but only at the behest of Major Fuller, once he had gotten wind of Trant's affair with Claire. Trant had met Claire during a banal series of committee meetings with the haven's group council, concerning such things as the distribution of food, clothing, tools and other supplies. Fuller insisted that Claire was checked out, for if her views and affiliations had been too extreme they could easily compromise the Colonel. Reluctantly, Trant had agreed to the surveillance.

Although Malcolm knew that the haven was mostly composed of peaceful types, he had made it his business to keep good tabs on Hayley, as she was essentially off-base. Had her cover been blown, she could easily have been kidnapped and executed by insurgent forces. In the event, as soon as he saw the radio traffic just before the airstrike on the camp, he short-cut procedure and went straight to Major Fuller to get his permission to pull the op and extract her. He had personally sent the procedural message to her just in time; and felt that he had personally saved her life.

Malcolm's one mate, 'CJ', was talking to their new platoon commander, a hearty young Lieutenant named Jackson, whom they'd nicknamed 'Superhero', for his physique and his exaggerated manner of speaking, always with impossible enthusiasm and positivity. Malcolm smarted over this; he knew that he been Christened as simply 'Before', as the antitheses and foil to Jackson's 'After' physique and character.

Hayley arrived back at their table with more drinks. 'Oh, hi Malcolm,' she said, 'I didn't know if you'd actually make it or not. Would you like one too?'

He felt himself redden. 'Aw, look, you don't have to. It's about time I bought a round isn't it?'

'Don't be silly, you can get the next one in when we're down in the valley. It'll be more expensive there!' she said with a cheeky smile.

'Okay, yeah, go on then. Make mine an alcohol-free lager.'

'Sure,' Hayley replied, unimpressed, but without sarcasm.

He knew that the others joked behind his back, but he didn't care; he wasn't a drinker. He knew that she was a hard drinker; and to him, it was her one fault. However, he wished that he could be a bit more like her and the others; the warriors and hard-drinking brigands that she seemed so attracted to. He'd recently started to work out, however, thinking that a bit more muscle mass might do it. One day she might see him as something other than just the geeky, boring intelligence analyst.

As she returned to the bar, he made the mistake of following her backside with his eyes. He glanced around to see Sharon's eyes boring into him as she sipped her pint. But, more concerning by far, he noticed that 'the poison dwarf' had also clocked him, and maybe for an entirely different reason. After a second he glanced back again, but Major Matlock affected to ignore him and had struck up a conversation with another officer.

Malcolm suddenly felt a cold sweat on his forehead. There was now bound to be more focus on his department, especially following the recent release of Major Fuller, with all charges dropped. Whilst he was glad for Fuller, he knew it would only be a matter of time before they closed in on him. They'd soon trace the source of the faulty intelligence regarding Wraxall Towers, and other stuff he'd fed to them. Also, the intelligence that he'd leaked back to UK Resistance, via his Russian contact.

With rising anxiety, he realised that he needed to leave and that it had to be now! He didn't need to pack, and he had the memory card stashed; that and his wallet was all he needed. Luckily he was already out of uniform.

After they'd finished their drinks, they'd left to Lieutenant Jackson telling them to 'have a really marvellous time down there, team,' in an exaggerated macho accent.

Malcolm stood outside in the cold with Hayley and the others, waiting for one or two tardier members of the section to catch up, before they'd make their way down to the town in the valley. It was ironic; he'd wanted to leave for so long, yet now it was so difficult. He would miss her. And he worried about her. She was too feisty by far, took too many risks. Maybe that was part of the attraction. He'd heard about what she'd done in the Bristol operation, whilst he'd been safely 'in the rear with the gear'. Drones had captured her taking out the armoured vehicle, and she was up for some sort of medal.

Initially, he'd been very glad to have remained out of it and had no idea that it was her section that had gone into the field. As the operation progressed it had horrified him to think that he might have been indirectly been responsible for her possible death. That would have been a bitter irony, and for sure, not many of her section had made it back. People he knew well had died.

He realised he'd now have no chance of proving himself in her eyes. She'd soon just see him as some lowlife traitor. But, in the battles to come, she'd probably die needlessly for a game of political chess that she knew little about. He wished he could convince her of that, make her see sense; but he also knew that it'd be totally futile. But, more, it wasn't in her karma. She wouldn't be who she was if she actually turned and followed him. Unlike him, she wasn't complex, nor conflicted. The world to her was relatively simple, un-analysed, black-or-white. It made her decisive. But it also meant that he had to leave her to her probable fate. The thought that he probably couldn't ultimately save her made him sad. Yet he reasoned that it could never have worked out; they were essentially too different.

It had begun to sleet lightly. Tantalizingly, she looked great. With only a light denim jacket and jeans, and an inadequate if stylish silk scarf around her neck, she dug her hands deep into her pockets and stamped her boots to try to get her feet warm. 'Oh, where's Sharon? She's always holding us up.' She turned to him. 'Look, Malcolm, could you go back and see where she got to?'

He looked down at her dumbly for a second, with a heap of conflicting emotions going on inside; and wondered how she could make a simple request seem so enticing. Maybe it was just in his head. She was just charismatic. Without further deliberation, he turned and headed back towards the club.

'Hope you find a telephone box on the way, or you'll never manage it!' one wag in his section called after him, and several of the women giggled at the reference to his imaginary superhero alter-ego. He didn't glance back to view the levity at his expense and hoped Hayley wasn't one of those laughing. He didn't need to see that.

Still smarting at the jibe, he entered the club and walked along the corridor towards the bar entrance. It was then that he suddenly felt trapped. He silently swore to himself about damned butch lesbians, before chiding himself for betraying his liberal values. Then he reasoned that Sharon might be in the lavatories and that he was completely the wrong person to have been assigned to find her. Why hadn't Hayley sent Jocelyn or Melissa? For a second he suspected a set-up and hesitated in opening the double doors to enter the bar. However, as he noticed her exit the ladies from the corridor entrance, he realised that his initial deduction about Sharon's whereabouts had indeed been correct.

'They're all waiting outside,' he told her resentfully.

'Alright, don't give me one of your passive-aggressive hissy-fits,' she retorted sarcastically. 'I can't stop a call of nature, can I?'

He didn't answer. He'd never been any good with come-backs. However, just now he didn't much care; his heart was thudding as hard as if he'd just sprinted in a two hundred meter race. Ultimately he knew that he was playing a bigger game, and at any moment expected to see Matlock and a few of his thugs round the corner, together with some Military Police from the Special Investigation Branch.

Once they were outside, however, Hayley smiled at them. It was an open, genuine smile, and it was in that moment he knew that he'd be alright. He breathed the freezing air deep into his lungs.

'Well done, Malcolm,' she said to him, then noticed how stressed he looked. 'Are you alright?'

'Yeah, thanks,' he said to her, glancing at the others in the section who were waiting.

'Got his knickers well in a twist,' Sharon told her. 'And I was just paying a visit and all.'

'Oh, sorry,' Hayley said to him, 'silly me, I should've sent one of the girls in.'

'Yeah, ducks, should have sent me,' Jocelyn said pointlessly

'Anyway,' Hayley said, 'let's get going, it's freezing!'

They signed out at the guardhouse and then got into their transport, a four-by-four. Malcolm sat in the back with six others, on one of the back seats, and looked out of the rear window. As he watched the base recede, he was also glad he didn't have to listen to the jokes that the driver was telling Hayley and Jocelyn in the front. He saw the vehicle tires now make a trail through the light dusting of freshly fallen snow, illuminated by the last lights of the camp, and then just by the red tail lights of the vehicle. They went through the last of the gates and thence down the lane, towards the town in the valley below, with its pubs and its one small nightclub.

There, later on, he would slip away unnoticed and disappear, never to return.

Acknowledgements

Many thanks to my wife Steph for her help, support, and tolerance. Also to J.S. and L.M. for their inspiration.

Printed in Poland
by Amazon Fulfillment
Poland Sp. z o.o., Wrocław